Praise for the novels of Maya Banks

"Heated investigative romantic suspense . . . Intense, transfixing."
—*Midwest Book Review*

"Definitely a recommended read . . . Filled with friendship, passion, and most of all, a love that grows beyond just being friends."
—*Fallen Angel Reviews*

"Grabbed me from page one and refused to let go until I read the last word . . . When a book still affects me hours after reading it, I can't help but Joyfully Recommend it!"
—*Joyfully Reviewed*

"I guarantee I will reread this book many times over, and will derive as much pleasure as I did in the first reading each and every subsequent time."
—*Novelspot*

"An excellent read that I simply did not put down . . . A fantastic adventure . . . Covers all the emotional range."
—*The Road to Romance*

"Searingly sexy and highly believable."
—*RT Book Reviews*

"A must-read author . . . her [stories] are always full of emotional situations, lovable characters and kick-butt story lines."
—*Romance Junkies*

rush

maya banks

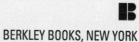

BERKLEY BOOKS, NEW YORK

THE BERKLEY PUBLISHING GROUP
Published by the Penguin Group
Penguin Group (USA) Inc.
375 Hudson Street, New York, New York 10014, USA

Penguin Group (Canada), 90 Eglinton Avenue East, Suite 700, Toronto, Ontario M4P 2Y3, Canada
(a division of Pearson Penguin Canada Inc.) • Penguin Books Ltd., 80 Strand, London WC2R 0RL,
England • Penguin Ireland, 25 St. Stephen's Green, Dublin 2, Ireland (a division of Penguin
Books Ltd.) • Penguin Group (Australia), 707 Collins Street, Melbourne, Victoria 3008, Australia
(a division of Pearson Australia Group Pty. Ltd.) • Penguin Books India Pvt. Ltd., 11 Community
Centre, Panchsheel Park, New Delhi—110 017, India • Penguin Group (NZ), 67 Apollo Drive,
Rosedale, Auckland 0632, New Zealand (a division of Pearson New Zealand Ltd.) • Penguin Books
(South Africa) (Pty.) Ltd., Rosebank Office Park, 181 Jan Smuts Avenue, Parktown North 2193,
South Africa • Penguin China, B7 Jiaming Center, 27 East Third Ring Road North,
Chaoyang District, Beijing 100020, China

Penguin Books Ltd., Registered Offices: 80 Strand, London WC2R 0RL, England

This book is an original publication of The Berkley Publishing Group.

This is a work of fiction. Names, characters, places, and incidents either are the product of the author's
imagination or are used fictitiously, and any resemblance to actual persons, living or dead, business
establishments, events, or locales is entirely coincidental. The publisher does not have any control over
and does not assume any responsibility for author or third-party websites or their content.

RUSH

PUBLISHING HISTORY
Berkley trade paperback edition / February 2013

Berkley trade paperback edition ISBN: 978-0-425-26704-2

An application to register this book for cataloging has been submitted to the Library of Congress.

PRINTED IN THE UNITED STATES OF AMERICA

10 9 8 7

For my family, who was patient with me
while we were on vacation
and Mom had a new idea that wouldn't leave her alone.
And to Kim, for listening when I told her
there was something I had to do asap and for making it happen.
To Lillie, for hanging with me every step of the way.
And finally, to Cindy, who went to bat for me in a huge way.

prologue

"Mia, the doorman just buzzed to say a car is here for you," Caroline called from the other room.

Mia's breath hiccupped, and she reached for the contract that was lying beside where she sat on the edge of the bed. It was slightly rumpled and was showing signs of wear for all the times she'd read over it.

She'd memorized every word of it, and it played over and over in her mind. Along with it, images fired by her imagination. Of her and Gabe together. Him controlling and possessing her. *Owning* her.

Shoving it into her purse, she stood and hurried to her dresser to look in the mirror one last time. She showed signs of little sleep. There were dark smudges under her eyes that makeup couldn't disguise. Her color was off as well. Even her hair had refused to respond and had a rumpled look to it.

There was little to do now except go.

Taking a deep breath, she left her bedroom and walked through the living room toward the door.

"Mia, wait!" Caroline said as she ran to where Mia held the door open.

Caroline hugged her tightly and then stood back, her hand going to push Mia's hair behind her ear.

"Good luck, okay? You've not been yourself this entire weekend. If it's stressing you out this much, don't do it."

Mia smiled. "Thanks, Caro. Love you."

Caroline made an exaggerated smacking sound with her lips as Mia turned and left.

When she left the building, the doorman opened the car door for her and ushered her inside. Mia leaned back against the comfortable leather seat and closed her eyes as the car pulled away, heading from her apartment on the Upper West Side to Midtown, where the HCM building was located.

Her brother, Jace, had called her the day before, and she felt terribly guilty about keeping this from him. He'd apologized for missing her at the grand opening and told her that if he'd known she was coming he would have made certain he was there.

The two had talked for half an hour. Jace had asked how things were with her and then told her he was going to be in California with Ash for the next several days. They'd made a date to spend an evening together when he returned and then she'd rung off, melancholy descending, because she and Jace were close. She'd never hesitated to share anything with him. He'd always been there, willing to listen and offer comfort even through her girly teenage-angst years. She couldn't ask for a better big brother, and now she was keeping secrets—huge secrets—from him.

She barely tuned in to the drive, the typical stop and go of traffic, until the car stopped some time later.

"We've arrived, Miss Crestwell."

Her eyes flew open and squinted against the wash of the bright autumn sun. They were indeed just outside the HCM building. The driver had already gotten out to go around and open her door for her. She rubbed her hands over her face in an attempt to revive her dulled senses and then she stepped out, a cool breeze ruffling her hair.

Once again she found herself walking into the building and riding the elevator up to the forty-second floor. There was some serious déjà vu going on. Same butterflies. Same sweaty palms. Same attack of nerves. Only there was more panic involved because this time she knew what he wanted. Knew exactly what she'd be getting into if she agreed to this.

When she entered the reception area, Eleanor looked up and smiled and then said, "Mr. Hamilton says you're to go straight back."

"Thank you, Eleanor," Mia murmured as she headed past Eleanor's desk.

Gabe's door was open when she arrived. She hesitated just outside and stared in to where he stood, hands in his pockets, staring out the large window overlooking the Manhattan skyline.

He was gorgeous. Beautiful to look at. Even relaxed there was so much raw power emanating from him. She was suddenly struck by why she was so drawn to him—or at least one of the many reasons. She felt safe with him. Just being near him gave her a measure of comfort. She felt secure and . . . protected.

In essence, the relationship he'd proposed would provide her with all of those things. Safety. Security. Comfort. Protection. He'd guaranteed all of those things. All she had to do was agree to cede ultimate power to him.

Any reluctance evaporated, leaving her lighter and almost euphoric. There was no way she was walking into this agreement scared to death. It was no way to begin a new relationship. She would be confident and she'd embrace the things that Gabe had promised her. And in return, she'd give her all to him and be confident that he would cherish the gift of her submission.

Gabe turned, seeing her standing in the doorway. She was astonished to see relief in his eyes. Had he been afraid she wouldn't come?

He strode toward her and then pulled her inside his office, shutting the door firmly behind her. Before she could say a word, he hauled her into his arms and crushed his mouth to hers.

She moaned softly as his hands ran possessively up her arms to clasp her shoulders and then upward again, to her throat, and finally to cradle her face. He kissed her as though he were starved for her. Like he'd been held away from her and had finally broken free. It was the kind of kiss that lived only in her fantasies. No one had ever made her feel so . . . *consumed*.

It wasn't just a show of dominance. It was a plea for capitulation. He wanted her. He was showing her just how much. If there had been any doubt as to whether he truly desired her or whether he was simply bored and looking for a new challenge, she was convinced now.

One hand moved from her face and his arm curled around her, anchoring her tightly against him, his arm a steel band across her back.

She could feel his hardness against her belly. He was rigidly erect and straining against the expensive slacks he wore. His breath exploded over her as he broke contact with her lips and they both gasped for air.

His eyes glittered as he stared down at her. "I didn't think you'd come."

chapter one

Gabe Hamilton was going to burn in hell and he didn't give a damn. From the moment Mia Creslwell walked into the ballroom of the Bentley Hotel where HCM Global Resorts and Hotels was holding its grand opening, he hadn't taken his gaze from her.

She was forbidden fruit. His best friend's little sister. Only she wasn't so little anymore, and he had definitely taken notice. She'd become some kind of twisted preoccupation for him. He'd fought it but found himself unable to resist her powerful lure.

He wasn't fighting it any longer.

The fact that she was here, tonight, and Jace was nowhere around, only confirmed to Gabe that the time was right and it was time to make his move.

He sipped at the glass of wine he held and listened politely to the group he was conversing with. Or rather that he was *mingling* with since he rarely engaged in anything more than polite pleasantries as he made his rounds through the crowd.

He hadn't known she was going to be here. Jace hadn't said a word. Had Jace even known? Gabe thought it was likely he hadn't because, not five minutes earlier, Jace and Ash had slipped away, a tall, leggy brunette between them as they headed to one of the luxurious suites on the top floor.

Jace wouldn't have bailed—even for a woman—if he'd known Mia would be here. But it was just as well Jace wasn't here. It made things a lot easier.

Gabe watched as Mia's gaze swept the room, her brow furrowed in concentration as if she searched for someone. A server stopped and offered her wine, and she took one of the elegant, long-stemmed glasses but she didn't put it to her mouth.

She was outfitted in a killer dress that hugged her in all the right places, complete with fuck-me shoes and an upswept hairstyle that practically pleaded for a man's hand to tug it down. Dark tendrils floated softly down her neck, drawing attention to the slender column that begged for a man's lips. He was damn tempted to stride across the room and wrap his coat around her so that no one else would see what he considered his. Jesus, and if that didn't make this even more insane. She wasn't his anything. But that too was going to change.

The off-the-shoulder cocktail dress drew attention to her breasts, and he damn sure didn't want anyone else looking. And men *were* looking. Already she'd drawn the attention of others. They stared—like he did—their gazes predatory.

She wore a delicate chain with a diamond solitaire around her neck, and diamond studs adorned both ears. Both had been a gift from him a year earlier. For Christmas. It gave him satisfaction to see her wearing the things he'd bought for her tonight. For him, it was one more step in the inevitable direction of her being his.

She didn't know it yet, but he'd waited long enough. He'd endured enough time feeling like the worst sort of criminal for lusting after his best friend's baby sister. When she'd turned twenty, it had marked a huge difference in the way he viewed her, but he'd been thirty-four and he knew she was still far too young for what he expected from her. And so he'd waited.

She was an obsession, and it made him uncomfortable to admit, but she was a drug in his veins he had no desire to cure himself of. Now that she was twenty-four, the age difference didn't seem so insurmountable. Or so he told himself. Jace would still go ballistic—after all, Mia would *always* be his baby sister—but Gabe was willing to take the risk to finally taste forbidden fruit.

Oh yes, he had plans for Mia. He had but to put them into action.

Mia took a cautious sip of her wine—a glass she'd only taken so she didn't feel quite so out of place in a sea of beautiful, rich people—and she looked anxiously around for Jace. He said he'd be here, and she'd decided to surprise him by popping in for the grand opening of HCM's newest hotel.

Located in Union Square, it was modern and lush, obviously catering to an upscale clientele. But then Jace—and his two best friends—lived and breathed in that world. They'd worked damn hard to get there, but they'd achieved success beyond most people's imagination, and they'd done it by the time they reached their thirties.

At thirty-eight, they were touted as some of the most successful hoteliers in the world. But they were still just her brother and his best friends. Well, except Gabe, but perhaps it was time to get over her embarrassing teenage fantasies where he was concerned. At sixteen, it was understandable. At twenty-four, it just made her desperate and deluded.

Ash and Gabe had been born into wealth. She and Jace had not, and she still wasn't entirely comfortable in the circles her brother moved in. But she was inordinately proud of Jace for making such a success of himself, especially since he'd been saddled with a younger sibling after the unexpected deaths of their parents.

Gabe was close to his parents, or at least he had been when they'd been married. In a shocking move, his father had divorced Gabe's mother right after their thirty-ninth anniversary. Ash . . . his was an interesting situation at best. That was the most diplomatic word for it. He didn't get along with his family—any of them. He'd gone his own way young, spurning the family business—and money—and perhaps his success was all the more infuriating to his family because he'd done it without them.

Mia knew that Ash never spent any time with them. He spent most of his time with Jace and Gabe, but in particular Jace. Jace had made it clear to Mia that Ash's family were, in his words, assholes, and she'd left it at that, not that she'd ever have occasion to meet them. They pretended that HCM didn't exist.

She wanted to turn and flee when two men approached her, smiling like they were about to score for the night. But she hadn't found Jace yet, and she wasn't going to leave so quickly when she'd spent a ridiculous amount of time getting ready. Just in case she happened to see Gabe, which was pathetic enough, but there it was.

She smiled and braced herself, determined not to embarrass her brother by acting like a twit on his big night.

And then, to her complete surprise, Gabe appeared, wading through the crowd, a scowl marring his face. He stepped in front of the two approaching men and took her arm, effectively herding her away before the men got to her.

"Hello to you too, Gabe," she said shakily.

There was something about the man that just made her stupid. She couldn't talk, couldn't think, couldn't form a single coherent thought. He probably thought it a miracle that she actually completed her degree and graduated with honors. Even if he and Jace thought it was a perfectly useless degree. Jace had wanted her to pursue a business degree. He wanted to bring her into the "family" business. But she wasn't sure yet *what* she wanted to do. Which was another source of exasperation to Jace.

That made her feel guilty. Because she had the luxury of taking time to make decisions. Jace had always provided generously for her. An apartment, whatever she needed, even though after graduating she'd made the effort not to rely on him for support.

The people she'd graduated with had already moved into jobs. They were making careers. She was still working in a pastry shop part-time and dragging her feet as to what she wanted to do with the rest of her life.

And that hesitation likely had a lot to do with her deluded fantasies regarding the man hauling her away by the arm. She *had* to get over this fixation with him and move on. She couldn't spend her whole life with the ridiculous notion that he was going to one day notice her and decide he had to have her.

She greedily drank in the sight of him, like an addict getting their next high—like she'd gone far too long without that fix. He was a man whose presence filled any room he occupied. He wore his black hair cut short, styled with minimal product. Just enough to give it an expensive, sophisticated look.

He had the look of the sinful bad boy all the women went wild for. He had a total "don't give a fuck" attitude, and what Gabe wanted, Gabe always got. His confidence and arrogance were two things that drew her to him—had always drawn her to him. She was helpless to fight her attraction to him. God knew she'd tried for years, but her obsession showed *no* signs of waning.

"Mia," he said in a low voice. "I didn't realize you were coming. Jace didn't say anything."

"He doesn't know," she said with a smile. "I decided to surprise him. Where is he, by the way?"

Brief discomfort entered Gabe's eyes. "He was called away. I'm not sure if he'll be back."

Her smile slipped. "Oh." She glanced down self-consciously. "I guess I wasted a perfectly good dress on the occasion."

His gaze slid lazily over her, making her feel as though he stripped her with no effort. "It's a nice dress."

"I should probably go then. Not much point in my being here if Jace isn't."

"You can stay with me," he said bluntly.

Her eyes widened. Gabe had never really gone out of his way to spend any time with her. In fact, it seemed like he tried to avoid her. It was enough to give her a complex. Oh, he was nice to her. He sent her gifts on special occasions. Checked in on her to make sure she had what she needed—not that Jace would have ever neglected to do the same. But he'd certainly never made it a point to spend more than a few moments in her presence.

"Would you like to dance?" he asked.

She stared at him in bewilderment, wondering where the real Gabe Hamilton was hiding. Gabe didn't dance. Oh, he *could* dance, it was just that he rarely did.

The dance floor was filled with other couples, some older, some Gabe's age. She didn't see a single person her own age, but then most of the attendees were of that uberwealthy, ultrabeautiful class that most twenty-four-year-olds hadn't yet entered.

"Uh, sure," she said. Why not? She was here. She'd spent two hours getting ready. Why let a perfectly good dress and awesome shoes go to waste?

He put his hand to her back, and it was like being branded. She barely suppressed a shiver as he guided her toward the area reserved for dancing. Dancing with him was a bad idea in so many ways. How was she supposed to get over her infatuation if she kept putting herself in close proximity to him? But there was no way she was passing up an opportunity to be in his arms. Even if it was only for a few minutes. A few glorious, amazing minutes.

The sultry tones of a saxophone mixed with the tinkle of a piano and the low throb of a bass. The music invaded her veins as she slid into Gabe's arms. It was heady and intoxicating, and it made her feel as though she were in the middle of a really vivid dream.

His hand slid over her back, coming to rest on the portion bared by the low-cut dress. The material skimmed just above her buttocks, a seductive tease she'd had to talk herself into wearing. Now she was *really* glad she had.

"It's a good damn thing Jace *isn't* here," Gabe said.

She cocked her head and stared up at him in question. "Why do you say that?"

"Because he'd have a heart attack if he saw you in this dress. Not that there's enough of it to call it a dress."

She smiled, her dimple deepening in her cheek. "Since Jace isn't here, he can't very well say anything, now can he?"

"No, but I damn sure can," he said bluntly.

Her smile turned down into a frown. "I don't need two big brothers, Gabe. I assure you one's enough."

His gaze narrowed and his lips thinned. "I have no desire to be your goddamn big brother."

She gave him a look of hurt. If spending any time with her was such a chore, then why had he approached her? Why hadn't he done what he'd been doing all this time and just ignore her?

She stepped back, the warm buzz of being so close to him, of having his arms around her, his hands on her body, slowly dissipating. She shouldn't have come. It had been stupid and lame. All she had to do was call Jace. Let him know her plans and he could have told her he wouldn't be here. Then she wouldn't be standing in the middle of the dance floor embarrassed by Gabe's rejection.

His eyes narrowed as he took in her reaction and then he sighed, abruptly turned and nearly dragged her from the dance floor in the direction of the terrace. The doors were open, allowing the chilly night air inside, and he stepped out, pulling her protectively into the crook of his arm.

And so she was back in his arms. Enveloped in his heat. She could smell him, and damn he smelled so good.

He didn't stop until he was well away from the door and into the shadows cast by the overhang. The lights of the city twinkled and dazzled the sky, and distant sounds of traffic disrupted the quiet.

For a long moment he simply stared at her, and she wondered what it was she'd done that offended him so much.

His scent taunted her. A touch of spice without being overpowering. The cologne he wore was a good match. It complemented his natural scent while giving that tantalizing hint of male, rugged, wood, outdoors and . . . sophistication.

"What the hell," he muttered. It was a sound of resignation, as if he were giving in to some unknown force.

Before she could respond, he hauled her forward so that she landed against his hard chest. Her mouth flew open in surprise, and a small sigh escaped. Her lips were close to his. Tantalizingly close. She could feel his breath, see the muscle twitch at his temple. His jaw was tight and bulging as if he was holding himself back. And then he seemed to lose the battle.

His mouth crashed down over hers, hard, heated, *demanding*. And oh God, but she loved it. His tongue pushed inward, hot and sensual, gliding over hers as he licked playfully at the roof of her mouth and swirled around her tongue in a delicate dance. He didn't simply kiss her. He devoured her. He possessed her with just a kiss. In that span of time, she was owned completely by Gabe Hamilton. Any other man she'd ever kissed faded into obscurity.

She sighed, allowing herself to completely melt into his embrace. She became boneless, seeking more. More. More of him. His heat, his touch, that sinful mouth. It was everything she could have possibly dreamed and more. Her fantasies, her imagination . . . they had nothing on the real thing.

His teeth grazed over her lips and nipped at the fullness. It had just enough sting to tell her who was in charge. And then he gentled his movements, following it up with a sensual lap of his tongue, and then soft kisses over the bow of her mouth.

"God help me but I've wanted to do that for the longest time," he said in a raspy voice.

She was stunned. Her legs wobbled and shook, and she prayed she wouldn't go down, a victim of the heels she'd worn. Nothing could have prepared her for what had just happened. Gabe Hamilton had kissed her. Not just kissed her, but he'd dragged her onto the terrace and ravaged her.

Her lips still tingled from his sensual assault. She was wrecked. Utterly wrecked. It was like having a total buzz, the highest of highs. She hadn't had *that* much to drink so she knew damn well she wasn't reacting to the alcohol. It was him. Pure and simple. He was lethal to her senses.

"Stop looking at me like that or it's going to get you into some serious trouble," he growled.

If it were the delicious kind she suspected, she wouldn't mind getting into trouble with him at *all*.

"How am I looking at you?" she asked huskily.

"Like you want me to peel that flimsy excuse for a dress from your body and fuck you right here on the terrace."

She swallowed. Hard. It was probably better not to say anything at all. She wasn't at all sure what had just happened here. Her senses were reeling, and she couldn't quite come to terms with the fact that Gabe Hamilton had just kissed her and then talked about fucking her on the terrace of his hotel.

He moved in close again, until his heat swallowed and consumed her. Her pulse beat erratically at her neck, and her breathing was ragged and tight.

"Come see me tomorrow, Mia. At my office. Ten sharp."

"W-why?" she stammered out.

His expression was hard, and his eyes glittered with a fierce light she couldn't interpret.

"Because I said so."

Her eyes widened, and then he reached out to take her hand, pulling her back toward the entrance to the ballroom. He never paused, and kept walking until they reached the lobby. She struggled to keep up with his determined stride as her heels tapped across the polished marble floor.

Her mind was a flurry of upheaval. "Gabe, where are we going?"

He walked outside and motioned to his doorman, who rushed over the moment he saw Gabe standing there. A few seconds later, a sleek, black car pulled to the front and Gabe ushered her inside.

He stood, bent over so that he could see inside the back of the car as his hand grasped the door.

"You're going home and getting out of that fucking dress," he said. "Then tomorrow you're going to come into my office at ten." He started to close the door but then leaned over to stare at her once more. "And Mia? You better damn well be there."

chapter two

"So let me get this straight. You bailed on going to the club with me and the girls so you could go to some stuffy grand opening of your brother's hotel, and while you were there, Gabe Hamilton dragged you onto the terrace, kissed you and then sent you home with explicit instructions to be in his office at ten this morning."

Mia slouched on the couch across from her roommate and best friend, Caroline, and rubbed her eyes in an effort to get rid of the fog hanging over her. She hadn't slept at all the night before. How could she? Gabe had tilted her entire universe and now ten o'clock was bearing down on her and she had no idea what she was supposed to do.

"Pretty much, yeah," Mia replied.

Caroline made an exaggerated face and then fanned herself with one hand. "And here I thought you couldn't possibly have as good a time as we did. But I sure as hell wasn't kissed by a gorgeous billionaire."

"But why?" Mia asked, frustration making her voice edgy. It was a question she'd asked herself repeatedly during her sleepless vigil. *Why* had he kissed her? Why did he want to see her now when he'd seemed to spend so much time avoiding her?

It hadn't been a request, but then Gabe Hamilton never *asked* for anything. He gave orders and he expected results. And she didn't know what it said about her that she found that particular trait delicious. It made her all warm and shivery inside.

Caroline rolled her eyes. "He wants you, chica. And why wouldn't he? You're young and hot, and I bet you've starred in his fantasies a time or two over the years."

Mia wrinkled her nose. "You make it sound so icky."

"Oh for God's sake. It's not like you haven't lusted over him since you were a teenager. And it's not like he ever acted on those urges. You're twenty-four now, not sixteen. Big difference."

"I just wish I knew what he wanted," Mia said, worry evident in her tone.

"If you have to wonder that after he threatened to fuck you on the terrace then there's no hope for you," Caroline said in exasperation.

She made a show of checking her watch and then leveled a pointed stare in Mia's direction.

"Girlfriend, you've got less than an hour to get ready before you have to leave. I suggest you get off the couch and go make yourself look fabulous."

"I don't even know what I'm going to wear," Mia muttered.

Caroline smiled. "I do. Come on. You've got a man to dazzle."

Dazzle? Mia wanted to laugh. If anyone was dazzled, it was her. She was so befuddled by the events of the night before that she was going to be a walking disaster if and when she actually made it into Gabe's office.

Gabe fingered the contract he'd taken out and stared at the front page, silent as he contemplated the exact path he wanted to take with Mia. It was new for him to spend any time pondering how he handled his approach. He only did things one way. Straightforward. He treated his personal relationships as he did his business. There was no room for emotion, even in a relationship. He'd got caught with his pants down once—completely blindsided if he was going to be brutally honest with himself—and he'd sworn it would never happen again.

There was nothing like being made a complete fool of by a woman he'd trusted implicitly to ensure he didn't travel that path again.

It wasn't as if he'd sworn off women—he liked them too much. Loved the feel of a submissive woman under his hands and tutelage. But his approach had changed. The way he dealt with them had changed. He hadn't had a choice.

But Mia . . .

He couldn't pretend she wasn't different from any other woman he'd had. She was. She wasn't just another female face that he might view with affection, but keep his distance from any messy entanglements. The women he chose to be with knew the score. They knew what was expected of them and what they could expect in return.

Mia was Jace's baby sister. Beyond that, she'd been a girl he'd watched grow up. Hell, he'd attended her high school graduation. He'd scowled at her prom date when the little prick had come to pick her up. He'd enjoyed watching the jerk's balls shrivel up when he, Jace and Ash had told him in no uncertain terms what would happen if he disrespected Mia in any way.

He'd seen her when she'd visited Jace at holidays and when she was out of school. He'd even gone to her college graduation.

That had been a hell unto itself, because Mia had blossomed into a stunning young woman. She no longer had the look of a much younger, innocent girl. He didn't even want to think of how many lovers she'd had. It would just piss him off. He wasn't concerned with them anyway, because they were in her past and that's where they were going to stay.

Mia didn't know it yet, but she was going to be his. He just hadn't quite settled in his mind how bluntly to put his approach. She was . . . different. Younger, yes, but she was quieter, more naïve maybe. Or perhaps that was merely his perception. Who really knew what she did away from Jace's eagle eye?

No matter how he decided to approach her, it had to be done with finesse, and in such a way that he didn't completely overwhelm her and scare her off before he ever got in the door. Because there was no way in hell he was backing down or taking no for an answer when he'd finally decided to make his move.

And then there was the whole bloody issue of Jace. That was one factor Gabe hadn't figured out, but there was no sense in addressing it now before he even reeled Mia in. Jace would simply have to be dealt with later.

A noise at his door had him glaring up in annoyance. His instructions to the receptionist for HCM had been explicit. He wasn't to be disturbed. By anyone. And it wasn't time for Mia to have arrived. He had over an hour yet.

Jace and Ash sauntered through the door and Gabe's irritation only grew. What the hell were they doing in the offices today? They were both supposed to be on a plane to California to meet with a contractor to go over plans for a new resort.

All three men traveled extensively, often splitting the duties of overseeing foreign and domestic projects. And they had several in various stages of work at the moment, including a hotel about to break ground in California, one still in the early planning stages in Paris and a potential site in the Caribbean for a luxury resort. Lately, however, Gabe had been stuck in the city overseeing the finishing touches of the Bentley, their newest luxury hotel in Union Square. He was the closer. He was too anal to trust even his best friends with that task.

Jace and Ash were the middlemen, as Gabe referred to them. Though they both had equal partnership in the corporation, Gabe initiated projects, bid them out, got every detail down to his ultimate satisfaction. Then Jace and Ash came in to oversee, get construction off the ground and make sure things went smoothly. Then Gabe came back in to put the polish on.

It was an arrangement that suited the three of them well. And they all dealt with the day-to-day operations and management of the hotels and resorts.

The three had been friends since college. Looking back, he wasn't even certain what had brought them together other than alcohol and frat parties and plenty of girl chasing. They'd just clicked and hit it off.

Things had gotten difficult for Jace when his parents had been killed in a car accident and he'd had to assume responsibility for a much younger sister, but Gabe and Ash had banded around him, offering their support, and they hadn't left him to make it on his own.

Later, it had been Jace and Ash banding around him during his very messy and public divorce.

Perhaps, in a way, Mia was very much responsible for the strong bond between the three. Ironic, since she could well mean the end of it if Gabe didn't handle this just right.

"What's got your shorts in a knot this morning?" Ash drawled as he slouched into one of the chairs in front of Gabe's desk.

Jace settled in the other, quieter and slightly less irreverent than Ash.

Yeah, Jace and Ash were the only two people he considered friends in the true sense of the word. He trusted them—the only people he trusted—and they had his loyalty, which was something he didn't blindly offer to anyone.

Jace was the quiet brooder of the two, while Ash was the charming playboy who attracted women like flies. Gabe was convinced it was the combination of the two that made women a little crazy. They certainly had no shortage of women lining up to have a threesome with them.

Ash was always on the front line. Flirty, outgoing, he made women breathless and fluttery. Gabe had witnessed Ash's charm and how it affected women firsthand. Jace merely stood back and observed with those dark eyes and that silent demeanor. Women found him a challenge, and maybe they considered Ash an easy enough conquest, but they went after Jace with single-minded determination only to discover that he was unreachable.

All three men had their kinks and were unapologetic about it—another of their discoveries during their college days. They'd made enough money and reached a level of success beyond their wildest imaginations that they had no issue finding willing participants for sex, or even a longer relationship, as long as the women always knew the score.

It was an unspoken agreement among the three of them that they played hard but lived free. Especially after the debacle of Gabe's marriage.

Just as Gabe and Ash had rallied around Jace when he'd stepped in to raise Mia, Ash and Jace had been an unbending source of support for Gabe when Lisa had divorced him. And they'd been his staunchest defenders when Lisa had made baseless accusations that forever tarnished Gabe's reputation both personally and professionally. To this day, Gabe still didn't understand what had made Lisa snap. But he'd always be grateful to Jace and Ash for their unconditional support during some of the worst months of his life.

Had he been the best husband? Maybe not, but he'd damn well given Lisa everything he thought she'd wanted and desired. Their sexual kinks were consensual. He'd never forced her to do anything she didn't damn well want, and it still made him seethe to remember all she'd accused him of.

He'd been crucified in the media and in divorce court. And

Lisa had walked away, the seeming victim of a manipulative, abusive bastard.

Never again had he entered a relationship without full disclosure and legal documents signed by all parties. It may be viewed as extreme—or even ridiculous—by some, but he had too much to lose to ever risk having another Lisa go after him.

"I thought you two were supposed to be on a plane to California," Gabe said impatiently.

Jace's eyes narrowed. "We're leaving in half an hour. Our pilot called and there was a mechanical issue with the jet. Earliest we can take off is eleven when he can get a replacement fueled and flight plans filed."

Gabe did a mental calculation. They should be gone well before Mia arrived. He just had to hope she wasn't the superpunctual type who arrived early for everything. As fastidious as he was about time and hating people who weren't punctual, this was one time he'd be forgiving of tardiness.

Under his desk, his fingers curled into fists and then relaxed as he flexed them back and forth. Mia had been all that had occupied his mind ever since she'd walked into the ballroom the night before. Now that he'd allowed himself to think of her as more than his best friend's baby sister, he was consumed with an edginess that defied explanation.

He could only describe what he felt as . . . eagerness. Anticipation. Adrenaline pumped through his veins. She had shaken his carefully ordered world and tilted it on end. He could hardly wait to have her under his hand, his direction. His blood heated just thinking about it.

Christ, he had a hard-on just thinking about her, and he was sitting in front of his two best friends. Awkward didn't even begin to cover it. He just hoped like hell they stayed where they were and didn't take notice.

And then because he knew if he didn't mention it, Jace would only raise more questions about why Gabe hadn't mentioned it to him, he looked at Jace and said, "You missed Mia at the grand opening celebration last night."

Jace straightened in his chair, a frown marring his face. "She was there?"

Gabe nodded. "She wanted to surprise you. She arrived shortly after you disappeared with the brunette."

Jace let out a curse and blew out his breath in disgust. "Damn it. I had no idea she was planning to come. I wished she would've let me know. I would have made damn sure I was there. What happened? Did you talk to her? Did she stay long?"

"I took care of her," Gabe said casually. "Told her you were called away. Danced one dance with her and then sent her home in a car. You would have had a heart attack at what she was wearing anyway."

One corner of Ash's mouth twitched upward. "Our little Mia is growing up."

Jace scowled at him. "Shut the hell up, man." Then he looked back at Gabe. "Thanks for looking out for her. Not the scene I would have wanted her at, especially if you're right about what she was wearing. Bunch of old farts all looking to step out on their wives, and Mia would have looked like the Holy Grail. I'll be damned if she ends up another notch on their bedposts."

Gabe should have felt guilty. But then he already knew he was consigned to hell for all he planned to do to Mia and for *what* he had planned for her. She sure as hell wouldn't be just another notch on his bedpost, so he could put aside any discomfort caused by Jace's heated retort.

Gabe's intercom buzzed and then, "Mr. Hamilton, a Miss Houston is here for Mr. Crestwell and Mr. McIntyre."

Gabe's eyebrow rose. "Taking the brunette to California with you?"

Ash grinned. "Hell yeah. It'll make the flight time a lot shorter with her along."

Gabe shook his head. "Send her in, Eleanor."

A moment later, the gorgeous brunette Gabe had seen Jace and Ash with the night before walked into his office. Her high heels tapped on the marble floor, then went silent when she stepped onto the carpet.

Ash held out his arm and the woman slid comfortably onto his lap, angling her legs in Jace's direction. Jace laid his hand over one calf and slid it possessively up to her knee, never once glancing in her direction. It was as though he were simply reminding her that at least for the present, she was his.

Gabe couldn't help but make comparisons between the woman on Ash's lap and Mia, which was stupid, given that this woman was far out of Mia's league. She was older, more experienced, and she damn well knew the score with Jace and Ash. Mia had no idea what Gabe had in mind for her, and he'd be lucky if she didn't run screaming from his office.

In the past, Gabe wouldn't have minded the scene in front of him. It wasn't unusual for Jace and Ash to have a woman in the offices. But today he was anxious for them to leave. He didn't want Mia to suffer any more discomfort than she had to and he damn well didn't want Jace privy to what Gabe had in mind for his little sister.

He made a show of checking his watch and then glanced back at Ash, who had a possessive arm around the curvy woman. Hell, they hadn't even bothered to introduce her, which was sign enough that they didn't plan for her to be around long.

"Car picking you up here?" Gabe asked.

"Are we keeping you from something?" Jace inquired.

Gabe leaned back in his chair, forcing a bored look to his face. "Just have a lot of e-mails and messages to catch up on. I didn't get a damn thing done yesterday with all the last-minute details of the reception to take care of."

Ash snorted. "You sound like you're trying to make a point that Jace and I were conspicuously absent and you were forced to take care of things all on your own, but we all know what a control freak you are. There was little point in Jace or me trying to step in because you have to have things just so or your universe is tilted."

"Anal bastard," Jace said in agreement.

The brunette giggled, the sound annoying Gabe. So she may be older than Mia, and more experienced, but he couldn't ever recall Mia giggling like some silly teenager.

"Get the hell out of my office," Gabe said with a scowl. "Unlike you two, I have work to do. Get your asses to California and get the contractor lined up. We need to be damn sure we break ground on time. We don't want a bunch of pissed-off investors when I spent the last months schmoozing and stroking them to get where we want."

"Have I ever failed?" Ash asked mockingly.

Gabe waved his hand, making a dismissive motion. No, Ash hadn't ever failed. Gabe had no worries on that issue. The three of them made a solid team. Their strengths and weaknesses complemented one another very well.

HCM wasn't just a business. It was a corporation forged in friendship and fierce loyalty. The very things Gabe was about to test, all because he was obsessed with Jace's little sister. Jesus, but if that wasn't fucked up.

Thankfully, Jace rose, his hand sliding from the woman's leg. He reached to pull her up from Ash's lap, and she settled comfortably between him and Ash as they moved toward Gabe's office door.

Jace paused and then turned, a frown on his face. "I'll try to call Mia on my way out but can you check with her while I'm gone? Make sure everything's okay and she doesn't need anything? I hate that I missed her last night."

Gabe gave a short nod, controlling his features carefully. "I'll take care of it."

"Thanks, man. We'll see you on the other side."

"Keep me posted on how things are going," Gabe said.

Ash grinned. "Control freak."

Gabe flipped up his middle finger and Jace and Ash exited, their latest conquest sandwiched between them. Gabe leaned back in his chair, checked his watch, relief edging him. He still had half an hour before Mia was due to arrive. Jace and Ash should be well away by then.

chapter three

Mia got out of the cab on Fifth Avenue, a short walk to the building that housed the HCM offices, and sighed at the positively gorgeous weather. The wind ruffled her hair, hinting at the chill that was inevitable. The days were getting cooler as fall wound down to winter.

Gabe lived a short distance away at 400 Fifth Avenue, a sleek, modern residential development, while Jace lived on the Upper West Side closer to Mia—she was convinced she was why Jace had never moved closer to his office. And Ash lived at 1 Morton Square, which overlooked the Hudson River.

Mia hurried into the high-rise Midtown building that housed HCM and hastily dug out her security pass to get by the turnstile leading to the elevators. Jace had given her the pass when he'd given her a tour of the HCM suite of offices a few years earlier, but she hadn't had to use it very often since she was usually with Jace when she visited. For all she knew the damn thing might no longer work, and then she'd have to register with security. With that much time, she may well chicken out and just leave.

Thankfully she had no problems.

She checked her watch when she got on the crowded elevator and then shifted toward the back as even more people pushed in. It was five minutes to ten, and she hated being late. Not that she was—at least not yet—but she was one of those people who was always early. Being late made her twitchy, and coming in this close to the wire made her anxious.

Not that she had any reason for why she was so bent on obeying Gabe's command. It wasn't like he'd have her head if she were late. But still . . . There'd been something in his voice that had made her wary of antagonizing him. And if she were honest, she was eager to know why he'd summoned her so imperiously.

Caroline had rushed her through the shower and then dressed Mia as though she were a child with no clue what to wear. After choosing jeans that hugged every curve, she picked out a cami top and an oversized, cut-off T-shirt that bared one shoulder. It was short in the waist and bared the tiniest portion of her midriff, particularly when she moved just right.

Caroline had fluffed and dried Mia's long hair and curled some of the layers so the result was a messier wild look. She swore that hair like Mia's drove men wild. Mia wasn't sure she wanted to drive Gabe to anything. Sure, he'd starred in more than one of her teenage—and adult—fantasies, but now that he'd gotten up close and personal, she sensed an immense power that radiated from him.

It had intimidated her and made her think twice about whether she'd ever be able to handle a man like him.

Mia had applied minimal makeup; not that she didn't wear it, but somehow overdoing herself for this mysterious meeting with Gabe seemed . . . desperate. Like waving a neon sign stating her infatuation and intentions. What if this meeting was something completely mundane? Wouldn't she feel like a huge moron going in dressed for seduction only to discover he wanted just to see how she was doing? Who the hell ever knew what he was thinking anyway? Gabe wasn't someone who broadcast his thoughts or feelings to the world.

At exactly one minute to ten, she escaped the elevator and hurried into the reception sitting area of HCM. Eleanor, the receptionist, smiled and greeted Mia as she approached. Mia didn't have time to ponder whether she was crazy for agreeing to this meeting or even to collect and calm herself before diving into the fire. She had one minute to get into Gabe's office.

"I'm supposed to see Gabe at ten," Mia said breathlessly.

"I'll let him know you're here," Eleanor said as she picked up the phone.

Mia turned away, unsure of whether he would come get her or if she would go back. Whenever she came to see Jace, she always just walked in. There was no waiting as if she had an appointment.

"You can go back," Eleanor called.

Mia quickly turned and then nodded, taking a deep breath and heading down the hallway, past Jace's office to the end where Gabe's spacious corner office was situated. She paused at the doorway and stared down at her polished toes that peeked from the sexy heels Caroline had suggested she wear.

She suddenly felt like the world's biggest idiot. Whatever had come over Gabe at last night's party was probably hugely misinterpreted by her. And she'd come dressed to kill.

She was just about to turn around and go back to the elevator as fast as those heels would take her when the door swung open and Gabe Hamilton stood there staring intently at her.

"I was wondering if you changed your mind," he said.

She flushed guiltily, hoping like hell he couldn't read her thoughts. Her guilt was probably plain to read on her face.

"I'm here," she said bravely, notching up her chin to stare back at him.

He took a step back and swept his arm past him. "Come in."

She sucked in her breath and entered the lion's den.

She'd seen Gabe's office once before, years ago when Jace had taken her on a tour of the floor HCM occupied, but she'd been excited and it had all been a blur. Now she studied the interior of Gabe's office with keen interest.

It screamed classy and expensive. Rich mahogany wood, polished marble floor that was partially covered with an elegant oriental rug. The furniture was dark leather with an antique, old-world look. Paintings adorned three walls while the last wall was all built-in bookcases filled with an eclectic mixture of works.

Gabe loved to read. Jace and Ash teased Gabe about being a bookworm, but it was a passion that Mia shared with Gabe. While Gabe had given her the necklace and earrings she'd worn to the party the night before, that same Christmas, she'd given him a signed first edition of a Cormac McCarthy novel.

"You look nervous," Gabe said, breaking into her thoughts. "I won't bite, Mia. Not yet anyway."

Her eyebrows lifted and he motioned for her to have a seat in front of his desk. He pulled the chair out and put his hand to her back as he guided her into place. She shivered at the heat of his touch, and he let his hand linger a moment even after she'd taken her seat.

He let his fingers slide up her shoulder before he finally walked back around his desk to take his seat across from her. For a long moment he stared at her until heat crawled up her neck and to her cheeks. He didn't simply look at her. He made her feel devoured by his gaze.

"You wanted to see me," she said in a low voice.

The corner of his mouth crooked upward. "I want to do more than see you, Mia. If I had only wanted to *see* you, I would have spent more time with you last night."

Her breath stuttered raggedly over her lips and then for a brief time she simply forgot to breathe. She licked her lips and ran her tongue over her bottom lip in agitation.

"For God's sake, Mia."

Her eyes widened. "What?"

His nostrils flared and his hands curled into fists on top of his desk. "I want you to come to work for me."

Of all the things she thought he might say, that hadn't been one of them. She stared in astonishment at him as she tried to process the fact that he'd just offered her a job. Good God, she'd been well on her way to making a giant ass of herself. Her cheeks tightened in humiliation.

"I have a job," she said. "You know that."

He made a dismissive gesture with his hand and a sound of impatience erupted from his throat.

"It's not a job worthy of your capabilities and education and you know it."

"It's not like I intend this job to be forever," she defended. "They've been good to me and they're shorthanded, so I promised I'd stay on until they can hire someone else."

He gave her a look of impatience. "How long have they been telling you that, Mia?"

She flushed and dropped her gaze briefly.

"You're cut out for more than being a cashier in a pastry shop. Jace didn't spend all that money and you didn't spend all that time in college to pass out donuts."

"I never intended it to be long-term!"

"I'm glad to hear that. So give your notice and come to work for me."

He leaned back, staring intently at her as he awaited her response.

"What exactly is the job you're offering me?"

"You'd be my personal assistant."

Just the way he said the words sent a shiver down her spine. The emphasis on *personal* couldn't possibly be mistaken.

"You don't have a personal assistant," she accused. "You never have. You *hate* them."

"It's true you'd be my first in a long while. I trust that you'd prove a very capable employee."

It was her turn to study him. Her eyes narrowed as she took in his intense, brooding expression.

"Why?" she asked bluntly. "What is it you want, Gabe? And while you're at it, explain last night. Because I'm at a complete loss."

His smile was slow and deliciously arrogant. "So my kitten has claws."

His kitten? She didn't miss the significance of that little word.

"Don't toy with me. Something else is going on here. Why do you want me to come to work for you?"

His upper lip worked up and down and his nostrils flared as he stared across the desk at her.

"Because I want you, Mia."

Silence fell, cloaking the room, suffocating except for the loud pulse in her ears.

"I d-don't understand."

He smiled then, a predatory smile that slid over her like the smoothest silk. "Oh, I think you do."

Her stomach flipped and butterflies swarmed her chest and tickled her throat. This wasn't happening. It had to be a dream.

"What you suggest isn't possible," she said. "If I work for you . . . we can't . . ."

"Can't we?" he asked mockingly. He leaned farther back into his chair, indolent and confident as he turned to the side to stretch his long legs. "The purpose of your working for me is so you'd be at my side at all times. And I'd have you when I want and how I want."

Heat infused her entire body. She fidgeted in her chair, her hands twisting together.

"This is overwhelming," she confessed. It was lame. Completely lame as a comeback, but what else was she supposed to say? She was utterly speechless.

Her heart was about to beat out of her chest. She knew there was more to this than his words. There was a wealth of meaning in those dark eyes. She felt hunted. *Stalked*.

"Come here, Mia."

The firm but gentle command washed through the haze of confusion. Her eyes widened as her gaze found his, and she realized he was waiting for her to come to him.

She rose, her legs shaky, and she rubbed her hands down her jeans in an attempt to steady herself. And then she took that first step and walked around the edge of his desk to where he was still seated in his executive chair.

He reached for her hand and once he had his fingers twined with hers, he tugged her down onto his lap. She landed awkwardly but he sat farther up and shifted so she was nestled against his chest and tucked into his side. With his free hand, he delved his fingers into her hair, twisting the strands around his knuckles while he held on to her hand with his other.

"The relationship I'm proposing is not a traditional one," he said. "I'll not have you walking blindly into it without knowing exactly where you stand and what you can expect from it."

"Big of you," she said dryly.

He gave her hair a slight tug. "Little minx." His eyes became half-lidded as he stared into her eyes. He disentangled his hand from hers and lifted his fingers to her lips where he traced the outline of her mouth with the tip of his index finger. "I want you, Mia. And I'll warn you now. I'm *very* used to getting my way."

"So you want me to work for you and you want . . . me. Physically, I mean."

"Oh yes," he murmured. "Definitely."

"And this relationship you propose. What exactly do you mean by nontraditional?"

He hesitated for the briefest moment. "I'll own you," he said bluntly. "Body, soul. You'll belong to me."

Whoa. That sounded so . . . heavy. She couldn't even wrap her brain around it. Her mouth went dry and she tried to lick her lips but stopped when she remembered his reaction when she'd done it moments earlier.

"I'll guide you through this," he said in a more gentle tone. "I'm not going to throw you to the wolves. I'll be patient as you learn your way through the kind of relationship I expect."

"I don't even know what to say right now," she blurted out.

His hand slid over her jaw and to her cheek. They were on eye level, their mouths just a few breaths apart.

"I think this is where you tell me where I stand with you," Gabe prompted. "Do you want me as badly as I want you?"

Oh God, was this really happening? Did she dare to say the words out loud? It was like standing on the ledge of a skyscraper and peering over the edge. Wind in your face, knowing one misstep and you plummet.

His mouth moved closer, past her mouth, skimming over her jawline, his lips just brushing her skin. He nipped at her earlobe, eliciting a full-body shiver that sent chill bumps racing across her flesh.

"Tell me what I want to know," he commanded in a husky voice that whispered over the shell of her ear.

"Y-yes," she croaked.

"Yes what?"

"Yes, I want you."

The admission escaped with a sigh, reluctantly tugged from her lips. She couldn't even look him in the eye.

"Mia, look at me."

There was something about the calm authority in his voice that registered with her. Made her hyperaware of his presence, of him as a man. And it made her want him all the more.

She turned her gaze on him, saw the blaze in his eyes. He caught her hair again, tugging slightly as he toyed with the tresses.

"I have a contract," he said. "It outlines every nuance of our proposed relationship. I want you to read over it very carefully this weekend and then I want your decision on Monday."

She rapidly blinked, so startled that she didn't immediately find words. When she did, her tongue felt large and unwieldy.

"A contract? You want us to have a *contract*?"

"You needn't sound so horrified," he said in a level voice. "It's for your protection. And mine."

She shook her head in confusion. "I don't even understand."

"My tastes are extreme, Mia. Read the contract and, as I said, read it very carefully. And then consider whether you can commit to the kind of relationship I demand."

"You're serious."

His brows drew together and his lips tightened. Then he leaned over, putting his arm tighter around her waist to prevent her from toppling out of his lap. He reached into his desk drawer and pulled out a thick document that was paper clipped together. Then he dropped it on her lap.

"Take the weekend. Read over it. Make sure you understand it. I'd like your answer Monday morning. If there are things you need clarification on, we can discuss them then."

"So that's it then," she said, still bewildered by it all. "I go home, read your contract and then we meet on Monday to finalize the terms of our relationship?"

His lips tightened again but he nodded. "In a nutshell, yes, though you make it sound far more sterile than it is."

"I'm not sure it gets any more sterile," she said. "You make it sound like a negotiation, like it's one of your hotel or resort deals."

"There is no negotiation," he said softly. "Remember that, Mia.

You read the contract. You either sign or don't sign. But if you do, you'll adhere to those terms."

She smoothed her hand over the typed document and then lifted it from her lap. She sucked in a deep breath and then slid from Gabe's lap. She had to put her free hand on the top of his desk to steady herself as she made her way back around to the front. If only her legs would cooperate.

"How did you get here?" Gabe asked.

"I took a cab," she said faintly.

He picked up his phone. "I'll have my driver bring you back to your apartment and I'll arrange your ride here Monday morning."

"You're so sure of yourself," she murmured. "Of me."

He slid the receiver away from his mouth as he fixed his gaze on her. "The only thing I'm sure of is that I've waited entirely too damn long to have you."

chapter four

Instead of having the driver take her back to her apartment where she knew Caroline would be waiting to pounce on her, Mia had him drop her off at West 81st Street, just two blocks from where she worked on West 83rd Street. There was a small park that wasn't often overcrowded at this hour of the morning. Mostly strollers and nannies, young preschool children playing.

The contract was stuffed into her bag and she clutched it tighter against her side as she made her way to an empty bench the farthest distance from the playground where she could be afforded some measure of privacy.

She was supposed to be at work at noon, but somehow she knew she was going to need time to process what she was about to read. Gabe's autocratic demand that she quit and come to work for him echoed in her mind.

No, she'd never planned to make her job at the pastry shop permanent, but she liked the couple who owned it. They'd been good to her. It was a place she'd often frequented, and she'd struck up a rapport with the older couple. And no, it wasn't a job worthy of all the money Jace had put into her education. It had been an impulse to ask if the shop owners needed extra help. It bought her time to figure out her next step, and it made her feel good that she wasn't completely dependent on Jace for her support. He'd done enough for her over the years. She didn't want him worrying over her any longer.

As she settled onto the bench, she glanced around her to make sure no one was close enough to see what she was reading, and then she pulled the contract from her bag and nervously peeled the cover page up so she could begin to read the contents.

Her eyes widened as she read further. She turned the pages automatically as she battled between disbelief and an odd curiosity.

He hadn't lied when he said that he would own her. That she would effectively belong to him. If she signed this contract and entered into a relationship with him, she was ceding all power to him.

There were exacting requirements that she make herself available to him at all times. She was to travel with him, be at his disposal. Her work hours were what he made them, and her time belonged exclusively to him within those work hours.

Good God, there were even precise requirements when it came to sex.

Her cheeks blazed with heat and she hastily glanced up, afraid that someone would see her and know exactly what she was reading. And she wanted to make damn sure no one was close enough to see what was typed on those pages.

If she signed, she agreed to cede power to him not only in the bedroom, but in all aspects of their relationship as well. Decisions were to be made by him. She was his to command.

Perhaps most disturbing was that as detailed as the contract was, the actual description of what she may be required to do was vague because, in essence, everything was covered by the fact that she was to give him whatever he wanted, whenever and however he wanted it.

In return, he guaranteed that all her needs would be met, physically and financially. There was nothing at all about emotional needs. That wasn't Gabe's style. She knew enough about him to know he'd hopped off the trust train when it came to women. They'd have sex. And they'd have a quasi relationship as defined by the contract, but intimacy wouldn't come into play. Nor would emotions.

He reserved the right to cancel the contract at any time and could if she broke any of the terms that she agreed to. It was very cold, like an employment agreement that gave cause for termination. And she supposed it was very much a double job offer. One as his personal assistant and one as his mistress. Plaything. Possession.

The job as his PA was just a mask for having unfettered access to her. He wanted her at his beck and call in the office and on any business trips he took. But he took it a step further, because her time away from the office was his as well.

She frowned as she reached the last page. It was all very well and good to have her read the contract and arrive back on Monday with a decision, but the contract told her nothing other than the fact she gave up all her rights and he took over every aspect of her life. There were no specifics! What did it all mean? What did he expect from her?

Was he going to tie her to his desk and fuck her at thirty-minute intervals? Did he expect her to give him a blowjob while he was on a conference call? The only reference she'd discovered was a clause under the point referring to sex where it stated that such acts could and would involve bondage, restraint and pain play at his discretion.

She couldn't even wrap her brain around all that could entail.

She wasn't an idiot when it came to sex. She wasn't a virgin, and she'd had steady boyfriends. But they were decidedly vanilla relationships, and she was fine with that. It had never occurred to her to break out the kink.

It all just sounded very porny to her, and it was made sillier by the fact that there was an actual contract where she signed away the rights to her own body.

The longer she sat here and read over it, the more worked up she got.

She skimmed through another paragraph extolling the importance of her knowing precisely what she was getting into and that by signing the contract she agreed not to misrepresent her relationship with Gabe to any outside source, including various media outlets.

Holy hell. Media? What was she going to do, get on *Good Morning America* and tell the world that she'd been Gabe Hamilton's plaything?

When she got to the next paragraph, her eyes widened further.

A full physical report would be furnished to her by Gabe's personal physician, and she would be expected to undergo a similar physical so that both parties would be ensured of a clean bill of health and to be free of diseases. And furthermore, she would be expected to take birth control, and condoms would only be provided in the event of interaction with another person who was not Gabe.

She plopped the contract down on her lap as her mouth fell open. What the hell did that mean? Was she expected to entertain anyone of his choosing?

Her head spun with the implications.

She'd certainly been right to question whether she was capable of taking on a man like Gabe. He was so far out of her league that it wasn't even funny. She'd never even heard of half the stuff detailed in this agreement.

His comment came back to mind of when he'd said he'd be patient and guide her through his expectations. She wanted to laugh. Hell, she was going to need a full-on tour guide for this trip. Google was going to get a workout later, because she was going to have to look up most of the stuff detailed here.

Her hands trembled as she picked the contract up again and read the last page. This was insane. But more insane was the fact she hadn't already torn it up and let Gabe know exactly what he could do with it.

Was she actually contemplating agreeing to it?

Her emotions were a mixture of *holy fuck* and *oh my God*. Part of her wanted to find out just how debauched Gabe was. Judging by this contract, he leaned pretty far away from anything resembling conventional.

She vaguely remembered the fallout of his divorce from Lisa, but that had been several years before, and she'd been young. She knew it hadn't been pretty and that it had affected his relationships with women ever since, but had they had this kind of relationship? Had he been burned by it? Normal people wouldn't go to these kinds of lengths to cover every nuance of a relationship.

Now she wondered about all the other women Gabe had been with. Not that she'd ever been introduced to any of them, but she'd heard Jace and Ash talk. If he had a contract ready at the drop of a hat, that told her it was likely one that he furnished to all his women.

That left a sour taste in her mouth. No, she didn't expect that she'd be any different than anyone who came before her, but it was nice to think that she was special or at least original. Not lumped in with every other female he'd slept with.

But then she'd rather he be blunt with her and not mislead her. At least she knew precisely where she stood with him. And he had been clear that he wanted her to go in with her eyes wide open. Well hell, after reading this, her eyes were going to be permanently wide.

She checked her watch and realized she had time to get to the pastry shop if she started walking now. She folded the contract and shoved it back into her bag, and headed in the direction of La Patisserie.

She dug out her phone as she went, and not surprisingly, there were half a dozen messages from her best friend already. All wanting to know how it went with Gabe and threats that if she didn't spill soon, Caroline was going to kill her.

What the heck was she supposed to say? Somehow, typing *Gabe wants me to be his personal plaything* didn't sound right, even if it would probably make Caroline swoon.

And oh God, if Jace found out . . .

She sucked in her breath. Jace was a huge problem. He would lose his mind if he ever found out about any of this. Surely Gabe had considered that. Hadn't he?

There was no way she could ever let her brother know about this. It would ruin his friendship with Gabe and would likely ruin their business as well. Not to mention he would never understand, and it would put a huge wedge between her and Jace.

She was contemplating it. She must be if she was factoring in all the potential obstacles, right? Had she lost her mind?

She should *so* be running as fast as she could in the other direction, and yet . . .

She made it with ten minutes to spare and opened the door to La Patisserie. The bell jangled, a familiar sound as the door shut behind her, and she smiled a greeting at Greg and Louisa, the owners of the shop.

"Hello, Mia!" Louisa called out from behind the counter.

Mia offered a wave and quickly ducked into the back to get her apron and hat. It was a ridiculous French beret, and she always felt silly wearing it, but Greg and Louisa insisted on all the employees wearing them.

When she made her way back to the front, Louisa waved her over.

"I've got the counter today. Greg will be in the back baking. We have a huge order to fill by tonight, so can you man the tables?"

"Sure," Mia said.

There were only five tables in the tiny café. It was mostly a takeout spot for coffee, croissants and delicious confections, but a few of their regulars liked to take their coffee and food inside on their lunch break. There were an additional four tables on the sidewalk, but they were self-serve and she didn't have to wait those tables.

"Have you eaten?" Louisa asked.

Mia smiled. Louisa was always concerned that Mia didn't eat enough or that she skipped meals, and as a result she was forever trying to force food on Mia.

"I ate this morning. I'll grab a bite before I leave."

"Okay, be sure and try Greg's new sandwich. He'll want your opinion. He's testing it out on a few customers today to get feedback. He wants to add it to our menu."

Mia nodded and then headed toward a table where a couple had just sat down.

For the next hour, Mia worked the lunch rush and was too busy to give the matter with Gabe her full attention. It definitely still occupied a huge part of her brain. She was less attentive than usual, and she messed up two orders, something she rarely did.

Louisa sent concerned looks her way, but Mia stayed busy, not wanting the older woman to worry, or worse, to ask her if anything was wrong.

At two, the lunch rush started winding down, and the shop started to empty of the steady stream of customers. Mia was just about to take a break, grab a drink and sit down for a minute, when she looked up and saw Gabe walk through the door.

She stumbled in midstride and nearly went sprawling on the floor. Gabe lunged forward and caught her before she could fall. His hands remained firmly wrapped around her arms even after she'd steadied herself. Her cheeks flamed with embarrassment, and she hastily glanced around to see if anyone had witnessed her clumsiness.

"Are you all right?" Gabe asked in a low voice.

"I'm fine," she managed to get out. "What are you doing here?"

His mouth quirked into that half smile, and he regarded her with that lazy gaze. "I came to see you. Why else would I be here?"

"Because they have good coffee?"

He started toward the table in the far corner, his hand still curled around her elbow.

"Gabe, I have to work," she whispered fiercely.

"You can take my order," he said as he took his seat.

She huffed in exasperation. "You don't eat here and you know it. I can't ever imagine you eating in a place like this."

He lifted an eyebrow. "Are you calling me a snob?"

"I'm merely making an observation."

He picked up the menu and studied it for a moment before lowering it again. "Coffee and a croissant."

She shook her head and walked around the back of the counter to get the croissant and pour a cup of coffee. Thank God Louisa had gone in the back with Greg and hadn't witnessed her falling all over herself. She had no desire to answer questions about who Gabe was.

She had to wait for her hands to stop shaking before she picked up the cup of coffee. She carried it and the saucer with the croissant to Gabe and placed them both in front of him. When she would have retreated, his hand shot out to grab hers.

"Take a moment and sit down, Mia. No one's in the shop."

"I can't just sit down. I'm at work, Gabe."

"Are you not allowed a break ever?"

She wasn't about to tell him that she had been just about to do that very thing when he'd walked in. Hell, she wouldn't put it past him to have waited until the shop emptied when he knew she wouldn't be occupied to come in.

With a resigned sigh, she sat in the chair across from him and leveled a stare in his direction.

"Why are you here, Gabe? You said I had until Monday."

"I wanted to see what my competition was," he said bluntly.

He glanced around the shop and then back at her, a questioning look in his eyes.

"Is this really what you want, Mia? Where you want to be?"

She glanced over her shoulder, making sure Greg and Louisa were still nowhere in sight. Then she glanced back at Gabe, her knees shaking under the table.

"There's a lot in that . . . contract." She could barely get the word out. She lowered her gaze because she couldn't meet his stare any longer. "A lot to consider."

When she chanced a peek at him, there was a look of absolute satisfaction in his eyes.

"So you've already read over it then."

"I skimmed it," she lied, trying to sound casual and at least a little sophisticated. As if she entertained such offers all the time. "I intend to go over it more thoroughly tonight."

"Good. I want you to be certain."

He reached across the table and slid his fingers over her wrist. Her pulse leapt and reacted to the simple touch, and chill bumps raced up her arm.

"Quit your job, Mia," he said in a quiet voice that didn't carry beyond the table. "You know this isn't where you need to be. I can give you far greater opportunities."

"For you or for me?" she challenged.

He smiled again and it was so damn seductive that she nearly melted on the spot.

"It will be a mutually beneficial arrangement."

"I can't just leave them shorthanded. It wouldn't be right, Gabe."

"I'll ensure they get a temporary employee until they fill your position. There are plenty of people who need jobs, Mia. The Millers don't *want* to let you go. They aren't looking because they're perfectly happy for you to stay on for as long as they can keep you."

Mia hesitated and then nervously pushed back her hair with one hand. "I'll consider it."

Gabe smiled again, his eyes glowing with warmth. Before she could react, he pulled her forward, tilting her chin up with his finger. His mouth melted over hers, hot and breathless. She didn't move, didn't pull away. She went soft against him, leaning further into his embrace as he deepened the kiss.

His tongue brushed over hers, teasing lightly before retreating. He licked over her bottom lip and then tugged gently, sucking it between his teeth.

"Think about it, Mia," he whispered. "I'll be waiting for your decision."

And then he pulled away and walked out of the shop to his waiting car.

Mia stood staring at the street long after he'd pulled away. Her lips tingled from his kiss and she put her fingers over her mouth. She could still smell him, still felt the imprint of his body against hers.

She was startled from her stupor when the bell above the door jangled and a customer walked in. Louisa came from the back and rang the customer up while Mia removed Gabe's half-full coffee cup and the uneaten croissant from his table.

It was nearly time for her to leave for the day. She only worked a few hours, usually during the lunch rush, and sometimes on Saturday and Sunday mornings if they really needed her.

She walked slowly to the back to remove her apron and the beret, her mind in turmoil. Greg was baking and Louisa hustled back to rejoin him. Mia stood in the doorway for a long moment before Greg looked up and saw her.

"Is something wrong, Mia?" he asked.

She took a deep breath and slowly expelled it. "There's something I need to tell you and Louisa."

chapter five

"Holy shit, you quit?" Caroline asked.

Mia slowly nodded and then turned her attention back to the near-boiling water on the stove. She salted it and then added the spaghetti.

"Come on, you have to tell me more. What prompted this decision? I was beginning to think you were going to make a career as a pastry chef or something."

"You sound like Gabe," Mia muttered.

Caroline's eyes narrowed. "Is he why you quit? Spill, girlfriend. You're still holding out on me about today's meeting, and it's driving me crazy!"

Mia hesitated and then clamped her lips shut. She couldn't tell Caroline about the contract. Or anything with regard to her meeting with Gabe. If she was going to agree to this—and apparently she was giving it serious consideration—she didn't want the details of her private life—with Gabe—to be known. Even by her best friend.

But she had to tell her something. So she went with the lesser of the two evils.

"He offered me a job," Mia said.

Caroline's eyes widened. "Wait. He kissed you. He threatened to fuck you on the terrace. All because he wants you to work for him?"

Yeah, it sounded pretty lame to Mia too, but she wasn't saying a word about that damn contract.

"Well, there could be more, but for now, he wants me to be his personal assistant. He thinks I'm wasting my talents working at La Patisserie."

Caroline poured them both a glass of wine and slid Mia's glass across the bar to her. Mia stirred the spaghetti sauce and gave the noodles a quick poke.

"Well, I agree with him there. You didn't go to grad school to pour people coffee and offer them a croissant," Caroline said dryly. "But personal assistant? I think he gives a whole new definition to the word *personal*."

Mia remained silent, not rising to that particular bait.

"So you must have decided to do it if you quit, right?"

Mia sighed. "I haven't decided anything for certain yet. I have until Monday to make my decision."

Caroline shrugged. "It's a no-brainer if you ask me. He's rich, he's gorgeous and he wants you. What's not to love about that setup?"

"You're incorrigible," Mia said in exasperation. "Money isn't everything, you know."

"Said by someone who is indulged by her older brother, who also happens to have more money than God."

Mia couldn't deny that Jace was every bit as wealthy as Gabe, or that he did a lot for her. He'd purchased this apartment for her—though he didn't like that more often than not she walked the twenty blocks to work. She didn't need a roommate, but Caroline needed a place to stay and Mia liked the company. But she tried not to rely *solely* on Jace. She wasn't extravagant. In fact, she had learned to be quite frugal with her meager earnings.

"I think I'm more curious than anything," Mia admitted. "He's always fascinated me. I've had a thing for him for as long as I can remember."

"Curiosity is a valid reason for hooking up with a guy," Caroline said. "How will you know if you're compatible unless you take the leap?"

Taking the leap felt appropriate. Only it wasn't just a short hop. It was a full plunge off a cliff. She itched to take out that damn contract again so she could go over it one more time, but she couldn't do it in front of Caroline, which meant she'd have to wait until later to review it.

She forked out a noodle and bit off the end. "It's ready. Grab a plate and I'll drain the spaghetti."

"I'll get more wine," Caroline offered. "You're such an awesome cook, Mia. I wish I had your skills. Guys love that shit."

Mia laughed. "Like you have any problem in the guy department."

And it was true. Caroline was gorgeous. Only a little taller than Mia, she was way curvier with a lushness to her figure that attracted men like flies. She had beautiful burnt-auburn hair that had varying shades of red and gold under sunlight. Add rich brown eyes that twinkled with warmth and the result was a beautiful woman with a sunny personality that endeared her to everyone she met.

"The problem is finding the *right* guy," Caroline said wistfully.

Mia cringed, regretful of her careless words. No, Caroline didn't have any problems in the guy department as far as attracting them. But the last man she'd attracted had been bad news.

She held up her wineglass in an effort to smooth over her faux pas and said, "I'll drink to that."

• • •

Gabe's office phone rang, but he let it ring and continued typing the memo he was working on. It was after hours. No one should be calling his office.

The room went silent, and then just a few seconds later, his cell phone rang. A quick glance at the incoming contact and he briefly contemplated letting it go to voice mail. With a sigh, he picked up his phone to hit Receive. He couldn't ignore his mother even if he already knew why she was calling.

"Hello," he said.

"Gabe. There you are. I thought you might still be at the office. You work such long hours these days. Aren't you ever going to take a vacation?"

He had to admit the idea had merit. Even more appealing was the idea of taking Mia with him. Several days away from the world in order to initiate her into his world? Definitely something to consider.

"Hello, Mom. How are you?"

It was a question he'd learned better than to ask, and yet he always did. The problem with asking his mother how she was doing was that she never took the polite way out and said *fine* like most people did, regardless of whether they were really fine or not.

"I can't believe what he's doing," she said in clear agitation. "He's making a fool of himself and of me."

Gabe sighed. After nearly forty years of marriage, his father had moved out, served his mother with divorce papers and seemed determined to run through as many newer, younger models as quickly as possible. His mother wasn't taking it well, as could be expected. And unfortunately, Gabe was her sounding board.

He loved his father, but he was being a huge dick. Gabe didn't understand it. How could you be with someone for that many years and then wake up one morning and decide to walk away?

He wasn't certain that he would have gotten to the point of asking Lisa for a divorce. She'd been the one to leave him. It may not have been the right thing to do, remain in a relationship where it was obvious there was no love or true affection any longer, but he would have spared her the pain and humiliation of a divorce. She, however, didn't feel the same about sparing him. And he didn't hold the divorce against her. Maybe he should have done something before allowing it to get to the point it had. But he hadn't realized that Lisa was so desperately unhappy. What he held against her was the way she went about divorcing him.

"It's disgraceful, Gabe. Did you see the papers this morning? He had a woman on each arm! Now what would he do with two women?"

No way Gabe was answering *that* question. He shuddered even imagining his father . . . No, he wasn't even going there.

"Mom, stop reading the society pages," Gabe said patiently. "You know it's just going to upset you."

"He's doing it on purpose to punish me," she railed.

"Why would he punish you? What could you have possibly done to him?"

"He's showing me that while I'm sitting at home grieving over the death of my marriage, he's out having the time of his life. He's telling me with more than words that he's moved on and that I no longer have any place in his heart."

"I'm sorry, Mom," Gabe said gently. "I know this hurts you. I wish you would get out and do something. You have friends. You have plenty of pet causes that you donate to and volunteer your time. You're still young and gorgeous. Any man would be fortunate to catch your eye."

"I'm not ready to move on," she said stiffly. "It would be disrespectful to pick up with a man so soon after the divorce. Just because your father is acting like a classless jerk doesn't mean that I won't act with a little decorum."

"You need to worry less about what everyone else thinks and focus on what makes you happy," Gabe said bluntly.

There was a long silence and then his mother sighed. He hated her being so unhappy. It hurt him to see her in such pain. He tried to stay out of his parents' affairs, but lately it had been next to impossible. His mom called him every other day to bitch about what his dad was doing, while his dad was busy trying to shove his latest girlfriend down Gabe's throat. The problem was that he was with a different woman every time Gabe saw him, and his father was too focused on trying to bridge a gap in their relationship caused by the very thing he was trying to force on Gabe. Acceptance. He wanted Gabe's forgiveness and acceptance. And while Gabe could forgive his father—he could hardly hold his decisions against him, it was his life and his happiness—he couldn't accept another woman in the role his mother had performed for most of Gabe's life.

"I'm sorry, Gabe," his mom said quietly. "I know you must hate it when I call. All I do is complain about your father. I shouldn't do that. Whatever he's done, he's still your father and I know he loves you."

"Let's have dinner over the weekend," Gabe said in an attempt to lift her spirits. "I'll take you to Tribeca Grill."

"I'm sure you're busy."

"I'm never too busy for you," he said. "I'll always make time to have dinner with my mother. Now what do you say?"

He could almost hear the smile in her voice.

"I'd like that. It's been a while since I've been out."

"Good. I'll drive out and pick you up."

"Oh, you don't have to do that!" she exclaimed. "I can take a car into the city."

"I said I'll come get you," he persisted. "We can talk on the drive back. I'll have my driver take you home after we eat."

"I'm looking forward to it," she said, genuine excitement in her voice.

It had been a good while since he'd heard her be excited about anything. In that moment he was glad he'd made the effort to get her out of her self-imposed exile. She needed to get out and face the world and discover that it hadn't ended just because her marriage was over. He'd given her time to grieve and to hide away in the house his father had moved out of. But enough was enough. Hell, maybe he could even talk her into selling the house in Westchester and moving into the city. There was little point in her keeping it now. It held too many painful memories for her. She needed a fresh start.

He knew all about fresh starts. After his divorce, he'd gone through a period much like his mother had where he'd just wanted to be left alone. He understood it, but he also knew the sooner she got out and started living, the sooner she'd be able to move on.

"I love you, Son," she said, her voice thick with emotion.

"I love you too, Mom. See you Saturday night, okay?"

He ended the call and then stared at the photo that still adorned his desk. His parents on their thirty-ninth anniversary. They'd looked so happy. It was all a lie. Two weeks after that picture was taken, his father had moved out and immediately moved in with another woman.

Gabe shook his head. More and more he was beginning to realize that no marriage was safe. Divorce could happen to anyone. There was certainly the argument to be had for not setting yourself up for the emotional upheaval of a breakup. And definitely one to be had for protecting yourself from taking a huge financial hit. Divorces were a hell of a lot more expensive than marriage.

He was perfectly content with the way he managed relationships now. No financial or emotional risk involved. No bruised egos. No hurt feelings. No betrayal.

He glanced down at his phone and pulled up the photo he'd taken of Mia just a few weeks earlier. She hadn't even known he'd taken the picture. She'd never seen him, never known he was there.

She'd walked out of a shop on Madison Avenue just a ways in front of where he was standing, and he'd been transfixed by the image she presented. Standing on the sidewalk, hair blowing in the breeze as she hailed a cab.

He'd been nearly paralyzed by lust. Not that he hadn't already known, but in that moment, he'd realized that he *had* to have her. There was something about her that he found irresistible. His fascination with her had reached the point of obsession. He was taking a photo of her without her knowledge just so he could pull it up and see her as he'd seen her on that day.

Young, vibrant. So very beautiful. And her *smile*. When she smiled, she lit up the world around her. He failed to see how anyone could look beyond her when she was present.

She was . . . captivating.

He didn't quite know what made her so special. Perhaps it was nothing more than the forbidden nature of their relationship. She was his best friend's little sister. She was fourteen years younger than he was. She was a woman he should leave alone.

But what he should do and what he was going to do were two different things.

He wanted Mia, and he'd do whatever it took to possess her.

chapter six

Mia stood in the doorway of Gabe's office staring at him.

So he wasn't as sure of her as he'd initially appeared. Relief still simmered in those dark blue eyes.

She opened her mouth to tell him she hadn't given him her decision, but it wasn't a good idea to tease him. He seemed so on edge, and the last thing she wanted was to start things by pissing him off.

"I'm here," she said huskily.

He reached down and took her hand and then pulled her toward the sitting area on the opposite end of the room from his desk.

"Would you like something to drink?" he asked.

She shook her head. "I'm fine. Too nervous to drink anything."

He motioned her down on the small leather couch and then sat next to her, pulling her hands up and into his lap.

"I don't want you to be nervous or afraid of me, Mia. That's not my intention at all. I gave you a very detailed outline of what our relationship will be to allay any fears or confusion. I merely want you to know precisely what our agreement will entail. But I never intended for you to be frightened or intimidated."

She stared back at him, determined to be confident and straightforward. "I trust you, Gabe. I always have. It's the reason I've decided to accept your proposal."

Something primal entered his eyes. It made her feel extremely vulnerable, but the sensation was sinfully delicious, eliciting a shiver.

"But I have a few conditions of my own," she said cautiously.

One eyebrow lifted and amusement twisted his lips. "Do you now?"

If she wasn't firm and didn't stand her ground, she never stood a chance in this relationship. Regardless of whether she was turning over power to him, she wasn't going to be some spineless twit who chose to cower rather than to speak her mind.

"There was a clause that . . . bothered . . . me."

"And that was?"

She tried to control her blush because even saying it aloud made her extremely self-conscious.

"The one about birth control and condoms."

He frowned. "Are you unable to take birth control? It's not a problem, Mia. I would never force you to take something you can't for health reasons. While my preference isn't to wear condoms, I would do so if it meant protecting you when other means aren't available to us."

She shook her head. "Let me finish. There was a part that said condoms would only be used by . . . others. I don't understand what that means. But if it means what I think it does, then I want to reserve the right to refuse. Being given to someone else on a whim freaks me out. It scares me," she corrected.

Gabe's expression softened and he reached out to touch her face, sliding his hand down to her jaw. "Mia, listen to me. The contract is a little misleading in that it states I'm given all power and complete and utter control over you. To a point that's accurate. But I can assure you that I'm never going to do something that I feel you are absolutely uncomfortable with. My job is to be in tune with your wants, needs and desires. I'm not worth much as a man if I can't do that for the woman in my care. The ultimate power rests with you. Because you control my actions. I want to please you. It's very important to me that I please you. I want you to be satisfied. I want you to be so spoiled, pampered and cherished that you don't want to be anywhere but with me all the time."

She swallowed, barely stifling the sigh of relief that threatened to burst free.

"Were there other concerns?" he asked.

She nodded.

He let his hand fall from her face. "Let's hear them."

"There's not a safe word," she blurted. "I know enough about these kinds of . . . relationships . . . to know that most people use a safe word. But there's nothing about it in the contract."

"I wonder what you're imagining I'll do to you," he murmured.

"There were words like *bondage* and *pain*," she pointed out. "It's a reasonable fear."

"Yes, it is," he conceded. "But there is no mention of a safe word because for me, it's as simple as you saying *no*."

Her brow furrowed. "The contract was pretty clear that I don't have that ability. That if I sign, I give up any right to tell you *no*."

He sighed. "I'm not some monster bent on abusing you, Mia. You're right in that I don't like the word *no* very much. But my hope is that you won't be using it often. I'd rather reserve that word for rare occasions when you are truly frightened or uncomfortable. I don't want it popping out of your mouth just because you're uncertain and the idea strikes you wrong before you even give it a chance. But if you truly find yourself in a situation that you do not want to be in, *no* is sufficient for me to stop. I may not like it, but I won't ignore that word. Ever. You have my word on that. We'll discuss what made you uncomfortable and we'll either address it and soothe your fears, or we'll move on and leave it behind."

"So just don't cry wolf," she said.

"Exactly."

She was starting to lighten, some of the worry evaporating. There was a tinge of excitement that tugged at her as she contemplated being so close to something she'd desired ever since she'd been a teenager on the cusp of womanhood.

"Is there anything more?" he asked, staring expectantly at her.

She nodded and then drew in a deep breath. He may or may not take her next condition well. But it was something she refused to budge on.

"There's an entire paragraph devoted to the issue of my fidelity. However, there's nothing about you being faithful to me."

Amusement glimmered in his eyes. "That's important to you."

"Hell yes," she said with more force than she intended. "If that contract says I'm yours, then by God it's going to say you belong to me."

He threw back his head and laughed. "All right. I have no issue with adding that clause. Now, are we done?"

Slowly she shook her head. "There's one other thing. And it's pretty huge. The most important part of any agreement we strike."

He leaned back a bit, his brows coming together as he studied her. "It sounds like a potential deal breaker for you."

She nodded. "It is."

"I'm listening."

"If we do this thing . . . Jace can never know. The truth, I mean."

She hastened to add on because she didn't like the look on Gabe's face, "It's not what you think. I'm not ashamed of you or anything. But if Jace knew everything, he'd never accept it. You have to have given this thought, Gabe. You can't have made this kind of proposal without thinking of what it could do not only to your friendship but your business relationship. Jace would never understand. To him I'm still his baby sister, someone he's hugely overprotective of. Hell, he still runs a background check on anyone I date."

"I would hope so," Gabe growled.

"Can you imagine his reaction if he were to find out about us in the kind of relationship you're proposing?"

"I had no intention of him knowing the private details of our affair," Gabe said in a calm voice. "All he needs to know is that you're working for me. I am discreet if nothing else. I have no desire for my private life to be blasted all over the media as it was when Lisa and I divorced. People can speculate all they want, but I refuse to give them irrefutable knowledge."

"Jace won't take speculation well," she murmured. "And I don't want to lie to him."

"You'll only lie by omission. And if we're discreet, the only speculation will be whether we're having an affair. Jace understands gossip. He'll know you're working for me, and that will fuel rumors. As long as we don't give him reason to suspect differently, he'll only be angry that rumors circulate at all and he'll be very quick to put out those fires."

"I understand. It's just that if I'm supposed to spend all my time with you, that won't work. I have my own apartment. I have friends . . ."

She trailed off, realizing she was already on the defensive before they'd even embarked on their affair. She hated that word. She wished Gabe hadn't used it. It sounded so . . . sordid. Like he was married and she was his mistress on the side. As if she were his dirty secret, and she supposed in a twisted way that it was just the opposite. He was *her* dirty little secret.

"You have a choice to make, Mia," he said, a harder edge to his voice. "I'm not forcing you to agree to this. But if you do, I expect compliance. We'll work around the obstacles. I'm not saying you won't have time for your other interests. Just that my interests will come first."

His arrogance should *so* get her back up. It should annoy the hell out of her, but she found it so sexy and so irresistible that it sent butterflies winging through her belly.

"You don't expect me to move in . . . ?"

"No. I understand you must maintain the appearance of having your own apartment if Jace isn't to know that we're lovers. But you will spend a lot of time with me at the place of my choosing. Caroline can cover you with Jace, surely."

Her eyes narrowed. "How do you know about Caroline?"

He smiled then, his eyes gleaming with that predatory light. "There isn't much I don't know about you, Mia."

She bit the inside of her cheek in consternation. She hadn't ever imagined that Gabe had paid her much attention at all. Yes, he gave her gifts for special occasions. He'd attended both her graduations. But she hadn't imagined that he knew any of the personal details of her life. Why would he bother? She was just the little sister of his best friend. A passing acquaintance and someone he saw in conjunction with Jace.

She was beginning to realize that Gabe had had a much keener interest in her, dating back longer than she could have imagined. She didn't know whether to be alarmed or triumphant over that fact.

"So what is your answer?" he prompted. "Do we have an agreement? Have I allayed your fears or do you have other concerns to bring up?"

She could sense the impatience in his voice. He looked just as he did when wrapping up an important business deal. Hard. Unyielding. And uncompromising. Only he *had* compromised. He'd made concessions she hadn't truly thought he'd make, and that comforted her. It made her feel like the balance of power wasn't quite so out of her favor.

There was no doubt there would be a distinct inequality and that the power swung more heavily to his side, but she wasn't without choices. The fact that he'd shown he wasn't completely inflexible gave her the confidence to forge ahead.

"We have an agreement," she said in a quiet tone.

She reached into her bag and pulled out the contract that already bore her signature. She handed it to him, hating the awkwardness wrought by the fact that her sex life had become a business negotiation.

"I wasn't sure what to do about the changes. I mean, the things I wanted changed and also the part about Jace. I thought it was better to make sure everything was in writing so I struck through the clauses and reworded and initialed."

He looked a little taken aback and then he laughed, a deep, throaty sound that vibrated over her, sending pleasure up her spine.

"So were you prepared to walk if you didn't like my answers?" he asked.

She glanced up, caught his gaze and held it, and then she nodded.

He smiled as he took the contract. "Good. In business, the biggest power you have is the willingness to walk away from a deal. You're not the mouse Jace thinks you are. I think you're going to do very well as my assistant."

He rose and then extended his hand down to help her to her feet. She slid her hand into his, savoring the warmth and strength of his hold. Just having his hands on her now that the dynamic of their relationship had changed filled her with anticipation. No longer would his touches be casual. Each would have deeper meaning. She was his. His possession. She belonged to him.

"Come to my desk and I'll initial your changes and sign it. I'll have my lawyer finalize it and send you a copy."

Her nose wrinkled and he halted halfway to his desk. He simply lifted an eyebrow in question, and she sighed.

"It just sounds so . . . I don't even have the word. I know I'm being silly. I've never entered a relationship where a lawyer was involved beforehand. It sounds so . . . cold."

Gabe touched her cheek, just a simple gesture of reassurance. "I do this to protect myself as well as you. But Mia? I can guarantee you one thing. Our relationship will never be cold. It will be a lot of things, but cold isn't one of them."

His hand fell away, leaving her to contemplate the heat in his stare and the sensuality of his touch. And the quiet vow in his voice. No, she didn't imagine their relationship would be at all cold. Hot. Torrid. Breathless. Consuming. All of those words she could well imagine. But definitely not cold.

He went to his desk and hastily scribbled his initials, and then affixed his signature beside hers on the last page. Then he turned, pushing the contract farther across his desk.

"There's a lot that needs to be done. I'll set up an appointment for you with my personal physician to have the necessary physical done as well as set up your method of birth control if you aren't already on it. You'll be supplied a copy of my last medical checkup as well as a copy of all my blood tests. But first you'll need to visit my human resources director to set the terms of your employment, and of course your benefits and salary."

"Okay," she croaked out, suddenly overwhelmed by just how fast her life was changing. Was she prepared for this?

"It's going to be all right, Mia," he said in a low voice. "Trust me to take care of you."

Peace settled over her. Exhilaration took hold. Like riding a roller coaster and topping that peak only to plunge over, wind in your face, heart beating a mile a minute.

"I do trust you, Gabe. I wouldn't be here if I didn't."

And maybe that hadn't been entirely true before now. She'd be lying if she hadn't had some small fear that she was biting off way more than she could chew. But being here, hearing what he had to say and feeling the intensity and the sincerity of his words . . . She *did* trust him, and she had to, because she'd be the biggest fool on earth for ever agreeing to this kind of arrangement unless she implicitly trusted the man she'd just signed her life over to.

She just hoped she didn't live to regret her decision.

chapter seven

The rest of the day was a complete blur for Mia. She spent an hour in human resources filling out paperwork and going over benefits and salary. The amount of money offered as Gabe's personal assistant made her eyes go wide. She hadn't imagined he'd pay her much of anything considering they both knew it was a cover for their relationship. She wasn't even sure how much actual work would be accomplished, but maybe he'd surprise her.

But it gave her peace of mind that she wasn't completely dependent on him—or Jace—to provide anything for her. She already had in mind that she needed to save as much as possible for the day when Gabe no longer wanted her. She wasn't fanciful—or stupid—enough to believe that their relationship would be any more long-term than his others.

While she didn't know the exact details of his prior relationships, she'd heard Jace and Ash talk enough to know that one year was Gabe's max when it came to women, and more often than not, six months was normal.

The one thing she was glad of was that Gabe had made her see that she needed to do more than work at La Patisserie. Her education was going to waste because she was too softhearted to quit working for Greg and Louisa. And maybe there was a part of her that was afraid to brave the business world.

What better way to become initiated than to work for Gabe? If nothing else, it would give her experience and look good on her resume. It would ease the way to her finding another job after he broke things off with her. Whatever job that would be . . .

She reminded herself often that her relationship with Gabe wouldn't be long-term. She did so in order to numb herself to the inevitable. So she could accept it when the time came.

She wasn't a teenager anymore, even if Gabe inspired very teenage-like reactions. It was time to grow the hell up and be an adult in an adult relationship.

After her stint in human resources, she was whisked into a car and taken to a clinic several blocks away, where she was given rush VIP treatment. No waiting. No paperwork for that matter, which she found odd. She peed in a cup, had blood drawn and then answered a host of questions from the doctor, including her preferred method of birth control and whether she needed him to take care of the matter.

While everyone around her had moved with the times and used alternatives to taking a pill every single day, Mia hadn't had much luck with some methods, and she feared others. And so she faithfully took her pill.

By the time she was finished with the doctor's visit, she was weary and emotionally drained from the stress of the day. Oddly enough, Gabe hadn't ordered her in to work the next day. Instead he'd instructed her to take the day off and rest, almost as if he'd known how fried she'd be after the eventful day.

Grateful to have at least one day to ponder the arrangement she'd agreed to, she rode home in the car Gabe had assigned to her. The driver had been given instructions to pick her up for work the day after next. The driver left her his card with instructions that if she needed transportation at any time, she was to call him. And he hadn't spoken a word to her since the somewhat curt introduction and his shoving his card at her.

Already it felt as though Gabe was taking over her life. Sliding into every nook and crevice. He already occupied her thoughts. Soon he would possess her body.

A light shiver worked over her skin as she rode the elevator up to her apartment. She checked her watch, hoping Caroline wouldn't be home. Mia needed some time to think. She needed quiet, a moment to soak in all that had occurred today. And ponder just how much her life was going to change.

It excited her and scared her to death in equal parts.

When she let herself into her apartment, her chest squeezed with dismay to see not only Caroline but three of their other friends, Chessy, Trish and Gina, slouched in the living room. They bolted upright when they saw Mia, and there was a chorus of congratulations and whistles.

Mia stared at them in bewilderment. Caroline rose with a smile and walked over to Mia to put an arm around her shoulders.

"I filled them in on your new 'job opportunity' with the sex god that is Gabe Hamilton."

"For God's sake, Caro," Mia muttered.

And then she was surrounded by her girlfriends, and it was impossible to maintain any sort of irritation in their presence. They pelted her with questions, and it was so tempting for Mia to confide in them. To tell them just what she'd agreed to. But she wouldn't risk it. Not even with her best friends.

"So is the man stacked? You know, does he have a big peen or what?" Chessy drawled.

"Do you think he pulled it out during the job interview?" Mia asked incredulously.

The others dissolved into laughter, and a round of crude jokes went up as they all speculated on Gabe whipping out his dick.

"I bet he knows what to do with it," Trish said wistfully. "Unlike my last boyfriend. Maybe Gabe could give him some pointers."

Gina snorted. "For all we know Gabe sucks in the sack. Or maybe he's even gay. You know all the gorgeous to-die-for guys are always the ones who are unavailable. Though given a chance, I'd definitely see if I could turn him."

Mia groaned. "He's not gay."

"And you know this how?" Chessy asked with a raised brow.

"He's Jace's best friend," Mia said in exasperation. "I've practically grown up around him. He was married and he's had no shortage of women in his life."

Gina shrugged. "Maybe he just hasn't found the right man yet."

"I could be his right woman," Trish volunteered. "And I'd damn sure sign up to be his personal assistant. You're such a lucky bitch, Mia."

"I'd be happy to take on Jace," Chessy said. "I'd work overtime for that man."

Mia covered her ears and groaned even louder. "Stop. You're scarring me. I don't want images of you and Jace. He's my brother! That's gross, Chessy. Just gross!"

"I think we should go out and celebrate," Caroline announced.

Mia shot her a startled glance. Chessy and the others wore interested looks as they waited for more.

"We should go clubbing," Caroline said. "If Mia's going to be tied to a nine-to-five job, her late nights with us are over. At least during the week. I know the bouncer at Vibe, and he's promised me he'd get me and my girls in if I come by."

"Damn, I have to be to work early," Trish said, her lips turned downward in a frown.

"Oh, live a little," Chessy urged. "It's not like you can't do your job in your sleep. Besides, you can catch up on your rest after work tomorrow. Tonight we'll go have some fun. It's been way too long since we got to hang together."

Trish looked indecisive, and then she finally nodded. "Okay, I'm in."

"Mia?" Caroline asked.

All eyes turned to Mia, looking at her in anticipation. The truth was, Mia wanted to sequester herself and have time alone to process the day. Gabe. Everything. But she loved her friends, and in her gut she knew her time would likely be limited with them from now on, at least until it was over between her and Gabe.

"I'm in," Mia said with a smile. "I need to go change, though. I have office clothes on. If we're going out, I don't want to look like a secretary."

"Rock on," Chessy crowed.

"Wait a minute. I'm not dressed for the club either!" Trish exclaimed. "I need to run home if we're doing this."

"Yeah, me too," Gina agreed.

Caroline held her hands up. "Okay, here's the deal. We do a hurry-up on the prep and we meet outside the club in an hour and a half. Deal?"

The others were already scrambling off the couch and heading for Mia's front door. They waved and called back good-byes, and then they were gone.

Mia started to get up to go into her bedroom to change when Caroline stopped her.

"Everything okay with you, Mia? You seem . . . quiet. Or at least different."

Mia smiled. "I'm fine, Caro. A little tired. It's been a strange day."

"Would you rather not go?" Caroline asked anxiously. "I can call and cancel with the girls."

Mia shook her head. "No, let's do it. I may not be able to do it again anytime soon. At least until I know how things are going to work out with Gabe. I have no idea what my schedule is going to be like. He'll expect me to work when he does."

Mia started again for her bedroom and when she reached the door, Caroline called out to her once more.

"Are you sure this is what you want? To work for Gabe, I mean?"

Mia met Caroline's gaze, some of her earlier trepidation easing from her chest. "Yeah, this is what I want."

Gabe was what she wanted. The job was just a means to have him. And if it gave her experience outside of working in a cafe, it would just be an added benefit.

As she hurried to arrange her hair and reapply her makeup, her cell phone went off, signaling a text message. She dug it out of her purse, which she'd dropped on the floor in front of the sink, and saw an unfamiliar number with a local area code.

REST TOMORROW, BUT BE AT MY APARTMENT AT
7:00 P.M. DON'T BE LATE.
—GABE

She sucked in her breath, her hand shaking as she held the phone so she could still see the message.

And so it had begun.

chapter eight

The car was scheduled to pick Mia up at six thirty, and heeding Gabe's directive not to be late, she made certain she was waiting when it arrived. She could feel a yawn lurking and pressed her lips together to stifle it. She and the girls had been out late the night before, but that was no excuse when she'd had the entire day to rest and get over her hangover. Only she hadn't been able to sleep for fretting over her impending trip to Gabe's apartment.

It was ridiculous, and she hoped at some point she'd get over her nervousness every time she had to be in his presence. She was supposed to have sex with the man for God's sake, and she couldn't even think about seeing him without having a meltdown. So much for any attempt at sophistication. One would think she was some blushing virgin who'd never so much as seen a man naked. Although she was pretty damn certain she'd never seen a man like Gabe naked. At least not in person.

The men she'd been with were . . . boys, for lack of a better term. Young men as unskilled as she was for the most part. Her last fling—she refused to call it a one-night stand since they'd actually dated more than once—had been her only superior sexual experience, and she was convinced it was because David had been older than her usual dates. And more experienced.

He was responsible for her swearing off guys her own age, and validation for her fixation with Gabe. David had been great in bed. It was just too bad he wasn't so great in other areas.

Somehow she just knew that Gabe was going to be off the chart, and that after being with Gabe, David would pale in comparison, which was saying a lot since up to now, David was the standout in the men—okay, *boys*—that she'd been with.

The driver dumped her in front of Gabe's apartment at precisely five minutes to seven. Okay, so he didn't dump her, but the man never spoke. He just appeared, drove, and then disappeared again, only to reappear later when it was time for her to go home. It was a little unnerving. Almost like he'd been ordered never to speak in her presence.

There was an actual security guard at the entrance to the apartment building, not that this was just any apartment building. It was one of those cushy setups that was like living in a hotel, only with an entire apartment instead of a room or a suite.

After she presented her ID, the guard called up to Gabe's apartment to inquire as to whether she was allowed up. Hopefully she wouldn't have to go through this every time Gabe summoned her to his apartment.

A moment later, she was escorted to the elevator, and the guard inserted the key card for Gabe's floor—the penthouse, of course. Then he gave her a courteous nod and backed away from the elevator.

The doors opened on the fiftieth floor and into the foyer of Gabe's apartment, and he stood, waiting, his gaze focused on her as she stepped off. The doors slid closed behind her, and she and Gabe were alone.

She devoured the sight of him. Rarely had she seen him in jeans, and they fit him like a dream. Faded and worn, as if they were a favorite pair he couldn't bear to part with. He was wearing a Yankees T-shirt that molded to his muscled chest and was snug around his bulging upper arms.

The man worked out. There was no other explanation for how a guy who spent so much time in an office could look so damn good and be so stacked.

She suddenly felt overdressed. She'd put on a simple navy blue dress that clipped the tops of her knees and bared the lower expanse of her legs. The heels she'd chosen gave her much-needed height to put her on a more even level with Gabe, but even then she felt small standing in front of him.

He was larger-than-life, filling the room, even in the faded jeans and T-shirt. His presence was indomitable. The way he looked at her made her feel branded.

His lazy gaze drifted over her, warming her skin as if he'd actually touched her. When he reached her eyes, he smiled and then simply held out his hand.

She closed the remaining distance between them and slipped her palm over his. He circled her fingers and squeezed before pulling her into a breathless kiss. He sipped at her lips and then grazed them with his teeth, nipping with just enough force so they tingled. Then he licked over the seam of her mouth, coaxing until she opened again and allowed him entrance.

"I arranged dinner for us. I hope you're hungry," he said in a husky voice.

"Starving," she admitted.

He frowned. "Did you not eat today?"

"I had some orange juice. Didn't really feel like eating."

She didn't mention the fact that she was hungover, had little sleep, and that the thought of food until now had made her want to hurl.

He guided her toward the elegant dining room table that stood in front of a huge picture window overlooking Manhattan. There was a dazzling array of lights from the surrounding buildings that were silhouetted against the sky at dusk.

"You're not still nervous, are you?" he asked as he seated her.

She laughed. "I'm in uncharted waters, Gabe. You have to know that."

He surprised her by pressing a kiss to the crown of her head, and then he moved away. A moment later, he returned carrying two plates. He set a delicious-smelling steak in front of her. It was so tantalizing that her stomach instantly growled.

He frowned again. "No more skipping meals, Mia."

She nodded and then waited as he returned to the kitchen again. This time he came back bearing a bottle of wine. He sat across from her and then filled both their glasses.

"I wasn't sure of your likes and dislikes when it comes to food. We'll certainly have time to go over that and I'll learn your preferences. But I figured I couldn't go wrong with a filet."

"No, not at all," she said. "A good steak cures most anything."

"I couldn't agree more."

She dug into her meal, watching Gabe from underneath her eyelashes. There were a million questions buzzing around in her head, but she didn't want to inundate him. As he had said, they had plenty of time to learn one another. Most people waited a little further into that learning curve before jumping into a sexual relationship, but she supposed Gabe was well used to doing things his own way, and damn convention. Besides, it wasn't as though they were complete strangers. Gabe had been a fixture—albeit a distant one—in her life for years.

The silence stretched between them. She could feel his gaze on her, knew he watched her much as she watched him. Almost like two wary opponents studying one another before engaging in battle. Only Gabe didn't look as uncertain and awkward as she felt. He looked confident. Like a predator closing in on his prey.

Butterflies took wing in her belly, and lower, until she squeezed her thighs together in an effort to assuage the ache.

"You aren't eating," Gabe pointed out.

She stared down at her plate, realizing she'd paused, fork still in hand, her steak only half eaten. She set it down and then calmly fixed her gaze on Gabe.

"This is nerve-wracking, Gabe. This is all new to me. I've never been in a situation like this. I'm unsure of how to act. What to say. What not to say. Or whether to say anything at all! You sit across from me staring at me like I'm dessert, and I have no idea if this is a simple dinner. A get-comfortable session. Help me out here because I'm floundering."

A half smile curved his lips upward. Amusement flared in his eyes. "Mia, darling, you *are* dessert."

Her breath stuttered over clumsy lips as she read the hunger in his eyes that had nothing to do with the steak in front of him.

"Eat," he said in a quiet voice that brooked no argument. It was a command. One he didn't intend for her to ignore. "I'm not going to jump you at the table. Anticipation makes the final reward all the more sweet."

She retrieved her fork and knife and cut into the steak, but she had no idea of the taste. She ate mechanically, a tingle of awareness buzzing through her body. Evidently Gabe had no intention of easing into this relationship. But then that wasn't him. He went full-out at everything. It was his style and what had made him so successful in business. He went after what he wanted with single-minded determination. And now she was the thing he wanted.

She sipped at the wine just to have something to fill the awkwardness. She didn't know if she wanted to slow way down and take her time with her meal to buy her more time, or if she wanted to dive in and finish quickly so they could move on to . . . dessert.

Gabe finished before her and sat back, looking unfazed as he sipped at his wine. His gaze never left her, and he watched her every movement. He looked cool and aloof. Until she looked into his eyes. There, it was a completely different story. His eyes burned with impatience and simmered with heat.

Leaving only a small portion, she pushed her plate back and

carefully leaned back in her own chair. Though she didn't speak, the *what now?* floated almost tangibly between them. Gabe surveyed her lazily and then said, "Go to the middle of the living room and stand, Mia."

Swallowing and then sucking in a deep breath, she rose as gracefully as she was able, determined that she would be poised. And confident. This man wanted her. *Her.* Not some other woman. It was time to act like she belonged here.

She walked across the hardwood floors, her heels clicking in the silence. When she got to the middle of the room, she slowly turned, only to see Gabe walk over to the armchair that was situated catty-corner to the leather couch.

He sank into the chair and angled one leg over the other in a casual pose that signaled how relaxed he was. She wished she could say the same for herself. She felt like she was on an auction block, standing before him as he devoured her with his stare.

"Undress for me," he said, his voice vibrating over her skin.

She stared back at him, eyes wide as she processed the command.

He lifted an eyebrow. "Mia?"

She started to slip out of her shoes, but he halted her.

"Leave the shoes on. Just the shoes."

She lifted her hands to the three buttons in front and slowly unfastened them. Then she pulled the shoulders down and let the dress slide down her body, leaving her in only her bra and panties.

Gabe's pupils flared. Raw hunger ignited and his features became primal. An uncontrolled shiver worked up her spine. Her nipples hardened, pressing against the silky material of her bra. The man was lethal and he hadn't so much as touched her yet. But his gaze. It was like being brushed with fire when he raked his stare down her body and back up.

"Bra or panties first?" she asked huskily.

He smiled. "Why, Mia, I do believe you're quite the tease. Panties first."

She hooked her thumbs into the lacy, thin waistband and slowly pulled downward. It was instinctual to try to cover herself, to preserve what little modesty she had, but she forced herself to let the tiny scrap of material drop to the floor. She stepped free and slid the panties away with the toe of her shoe.

Then she raised her hands again, pushing back her hair and then arranging it over one shoulder so she could reach the clasp of her bra. She unhooked it and the cups loosened, baring the underswell of her breasts.

"Move your hair back now," Gabe murmured.

One hand holding her bra over her breasts, she pushed her hair back with the other hand. Then she carefully lowered the bra, allowing the straps to slide down her arms. She pulled it from her body and then let it fall to the floor with her other clothing.

"Beautiful," Gabe said, his voice a low growl of appreciation.

She stood, vulnerable, as she awaited his next command. It was clear he was in no hurry whatsoever and he intended to savor seeing her unclothed for the first time.

Her arms crept around her middle and then up toward her breasts.

"No, don't hide from me," Gabe said softly. "Come here, Mia."

She took a trembling step forward. And then another. Until she stood before him, merely inches away.

He took down his leg and widened his knees, leaving a gap. There was a discernible bulge between his legs, straining at the denim fly. He held out his hand, beckoning her.

She stepped between his thighs and took his hand. He pulled her forward and then motioned for her to crawl onto his lap.

Her knees dug into his sides, her legs wedged between him and the arms of the chair. She settled her behind on the backs of her heels and waited. Breathless. Her muscles coiled and taut as she anticipated what he'd do next.

Sliding his hand around to her nape, he gripped her and pulled her to him, crushing her lips against his. His breath whispered over her face, hot and rapid. His fingers slid higher, into her hair, wrapping the strands around so his grasp on her was even tighter.

And then, just as quickly, he pulled her away, his hand still wound tightly in her hair. His breaths were sporadic and his chest heaved. His eyes burned brightly with lust, enough to make her shiver with the raw heat emanating from him.

"I wonder if you have any idea just how much I want you," he murmured.

"I want you too," she whispered.

"You'll have me, Mia. In every conceivable manner."

The promise slid over her like silk, warm and inviting. Husky and so sinfully sexy.

He loosened his hold on her hair and then placed his palms on her belly, sliding them upward until he cupped her breasts. Holding them, he lowered his mouth, sucking one nipple between his lips.

She moaned and quivered beneath his touch. She braced her hands on the arms of the chair and tossed her head back as he ran his tongue around the puckered crest.

Alternating between the mounds resting in his hands, he teased and toyed. Sucked and licked, nipping lightly at the taut peaks until they were rigidly erect and straining outward, seeking more of his touch.

He released his hold on one breast and ran the tips of his fingers down her rib cage, and then lower to her belly and between her spread thighs. His touch was delicate as he delved through the curls and to the sensitive flesh of her pussy. One finger danced over her clit, and her entire body tightened in response.

He teased over the damp flesh, circling her entrance with a finger while his thumb gently stroked the tiny bundle of nerves.

"Gabe," she whispered, his name more of a moan.

She lowered her head just enough that she could see him past half-lidded eyes. His mouth on her breast, sucking at her nipple, was exciting and erotic, fueling her already out-of-control desire.

His finger slid inside her and she moaned again. His thumb applied more pressure, moving in a circular motion as his finger stroked deeper. Then he nipped at her breast, grazing his teeth over the puckered ridge.

Her hands flew to his shoulders, her fingers digging deep, anchoring herself more firmly against him. She stirred restlessly, her orgasm building. It was impossible to remain still. Her entire body was taut, tension coiling low in her abdomen.

"Come for me, Mia," Gabe said. "I want to feel you come in my hand."

His finger slid deeper, pressing against her G-spot. She gasped as his thumb pressed over her clit and he sucked her nipple into his mouth once more. She closed her eyes and cried out his name as the first wave swept over her. Tumultuous and overwhelming.

"That's right. My name, Mia. Say it again. I want to hear it."

"Gabe," she breathed.

She arched up, frantic as he relentlessly pushed forward, taking her higher. She twisted in his hold and then slumped forward, catching herself on his shoulders, holding tight as she sucked in deep, steadying breaths.

Slowly he withdrew his hand and then wrapped his arms around her, pulling her in to his body, his warmth. She rested her forehead on his shoulder and closed her eyes, wrecked by the intensity of her orgasm.

He slid his hands up and down her bare back, soothing and stroking, his touch gentle and comforting. Then his hand tangled in her hair and he pulled just enough that her head came up and their gazes met.

"Hold on to me," he said.

She'd barely wrapped her arms around his neck when he pushed forward and then stood, lifting her into his arms.

"Wrap your legs around my waist."

He hoisted her higher, his hands sliding underneath her bottom to hold her as she hooked her ankles around his waist. He strode from the living room and down the hall into his bedroom.

Leaning over, he landed her softly on the bed and then just as quickly withdrew, tearing at his clothing. She lay there, dizzy with exhilaration, her body still humming in the aftermath of her release. Her pussy throbbed and ached. She wanted more. She wanted *him*.

She lifted her head as he unfastened his jeans and yanked them down his hips. He was so freaking hot, standing there, his erection straining, his eyes burning over her with blazing heat. His desire for her was right there to see, in every inch of his tightly coiled body. She could stare at him for *hours*. He was beautiful and all brooding, alpha-in-control male, his muscles bunching as he reached for her. He grasped her legs, pulling her roughly to the edge of the bed, spreading them as he positioned himself between them.

"I can't go easy, Mia," he said, his voice strained and edgy. "I want to be inside you more than I want to breathe right now. I have to have you. *Now.*"

"I'm okay with that," she breathed out, her voice a husky whisper as she stared into those intense blue eyes.

He hauled her the rest of the way to him and she felt the head of his cock push into her swollen heat. He paused only for the briefest moment before he surged fully into her, seating himself deeply into her body.

Her gasp mingled with his. The shock of his entry nearly sent her over the edge. How could she possibly orgasm again so soon?

The sensation of him inside her was overwhelming her. She was filled. Completely. So tight around him she wondered how he could possibly even move. Or how he'd managed to go so deep.

His fingers dug into her hips and then his touch gentled, almost as if he were reminding himself to take care. He stroked and caressed, sliding his hands to her belly and then up to her breasts, palming them and tugging at her nipples.

"Did I hurt you?" he rasped.

Even as seemingly out-of-control as he was, how desperate he was to possess her, there was concern in his voice. She knew without a doubt that if she wanted him to stop he would. No matter how crazy for her he was in the moment.

And oh man did she love that he was this crazy. Over her. To have *her*.

She shook her head. "No. Not at all. Please. Don't stop."

And it *was* begging. If he stopped now she'd die.

Her hands went to his wrists where his hands covered her breasts. She let them slide up his arms, reveling in all that strength he possessed. She could touch him forever.

His hands moved to hers, covering them for the briefest moment. And then he yanked her arms over her head, her eyes widening at the ferocity in his face, at how his eyes narrowed as a low growl rumbled from his throat.

Her hands went flat against the mattress just above her head as he leaned down, his palms flush against her, holding her down, holding her in place so she couldn't move. Couldn't resist.

It sent a thrill deep into her belly and fluttered outward until it was almost as if a drug had invaded her body. She was high on him. His power and control over her. His dominance.

This was what she craved. Him on top of her, deep inside her, him having absolute power. She couldn't even draw a breath. She was light-headed from exhilaration and anticipation.

He withdrew and thrust forward again, jolting her body with the force of his reentry.

His gaze seared into hers, so intense that she shivered. His voice was guttural and so damn sexy as he rasped out his next words.

"Hell no, I'm not stopping. Not when I've waited this long to have you."

This long to have you. God, but that nearly made her come on the spot. The idea that this man, a guy so far out of her league, had spent any time lusting over her was insane. Never had she imagined that he could possibly reciprocate her fixation.

She was reaching. *Fixation* was a strong word to ascribe to him. She had no idea what his feelings or fixation was with her, only that she'd spent a long time fantasizing about just being right here. Underneath him, pinned beneath his body, his cock buried so deep that she didn't even know how she'd managed to accommodate him.

She wouldn't say he was *freakishly* endowed. Certainly not mammoth, but he was definitely larger than any of her previous lovers, and holy crap but Gabe knew exactly what to do with what he had.

He released his hold on her hands, and when she would have moved them, he gave her a look—fierce—and pushed them back down again before once more releasing her. It was a command that didn't need to be voiced, and she complied, leaving her hands where he'd placed them, her gaze riveted to him as she waited breathlessly for what he'd do next.

He reached down, grasped her legs and pushed them upward to wrap around his waist—and again that *look*. That shivery, sexy look he sent her that told her to leave her legs just as he'd put them. Then his hands slid down, underneath her ass, and he began to push into her, hard, forceful, a steady rhythm that sent waves of pleasure singing through her body.

It was instinctive to reach for him. She needed something to anchor her in the storm that was his possession of her. But his eyes snapped to her again, and his jaw tightened. She let her hands fall back to where they'd been.

"I'll tie them next time," he said. "Don't push me, Mia. I call the shots. I own you. You're mine. You don't fucking move those hands until I tell you. Understand?"

"Yes," she whispered, her body so taut, so very close to the edge that it was all she could do to even breathe.

Her pulse accelerated, nearly exploding, tripping erratically at the sexy, badass look on his face. His gaze was full of promise. Of all the things he'd do to her. All the things he would make her do. And God help her but she couldn't *wait*.

He pounded into her again, shaking her body with the force of his reentry. She closed her eyes, clamping her teeth together to call back the cry that threatened to burst free.

"Eyes," he snapped. "On me, Mia. Always on me. You don't come with your eyes closed. I want to see everything you have when I'm inside you. You don't ever shut me out."

Her eyes flew open, finding him instantly, her breath exploding in a violent rush.

He withdrew and then surged forward again, his hands tightening on her ass. She'd wear his fingerprints for sure. He held her, spread her even wider as he hammered into her. She couldn't last. Wouldn't last. It was too overwhelming. It was too . . . *everything*.

"Say my name, Mia. Who owns you? Who do you belong to?"

"You," she gasped. "Gabe. You. Only you."

Satisfaction blazed in his eyes. His expression was fierce and possessive, strain evident in his jaw.

"That's right, baby. Mine. You say my name when you come."

He slipped a hand between them, finding her clit and stroking as he continued to thrust into her.

"Come," he demanded. "One more. Give it to me, Mia. I want to feel you go all wild around my cock. Soft and so silky. So very tight. It's fucking heaven."

She let out a sharp cry, her arousal at a fever pitch. Her orgasm flashed, explosive and intense, even harder than before. He was deep. Impossibly deep. So far inside her that she could feel nothing else but his pulsating hardness as it drove through her snug tissue.

His thighs slapped against her bottom, shaking her. She arched, wanting more, needing more. And still he thrust, his face a mask of strain.

"My name," he ground out. "My name when you come, Mia."

"Gabe!"

His eyes glittered, a look of triumph as she writhed beneath him, her orgasm quaking through her body with an intensity she hadn't imagined possible.

She went limp on the bed, boneless, exhausted and sated as he continued to press into her. He slowed his thrusts, as though he wanted to savor every moment. He closed his eyes, stroking deep and then shallow. Then he pressed his lips together and began to move with renewed power. Deep. *Hard.*

And then he went taut against her, every muscle in his arms and chest straining, coiled tight. His hands moved from her ass and back to where her hands still rested above her head. He pressed his palms into her, pushing them deeply into the mattress as he lowered his body until it was nearly flush with hers.

"Mine," he gritted out. "Mine, Mia."

She went slick around him as he pulsed wetly into her. He continued to thrust, jetting deep inside her. His release seemed to go on and on. She could feel the dampness between them, could hear the wet sounds as he sank into her over and over.

And then he went deep and held himself there, slowly lowering his body the rest of the way until he covered her completely. His chest heaved and his breaths were hot against her neck. He was still wedged tightly within her. He was still hard as a rock even after coming so hard for so long. God, but he felt so good.

"Can I touch you?" she whispered. She needed to touch him. She could contain herself no longer. It was an overwhelming urge she couldn't control.

He didn't respond, but he slid his hands from hers, freeing her, and she took that silent gesture as assent.

Tentatively she slid her hands over his shoulders, gaining more courage when he didn't object. She allowed her hands to roam, luxuriating in the postcoital glow. They slid down his back as far as she could reach and then up again, stroking and offering him the same caresses he'd given to her.

He made a sound of satisfaction that made her entire body clench. He groaned in reaction when she squeezed around his cock, and then he pressed a kiss to her neck just below her ear.

"Beautiful," he whispered. "And mine."

Pleasure consumed her, at his calling her *beautiful* but most especially that he'd staked his claim. For however long their arrangement would last, she was his. Truly his. In a way most women don't belong to a man.

There wasn't a part of her body that didn't feel the stamp of his possession. She was tired, sore and completely satisfied. Moving wasn't an option, and so she waited, content to lie there, him surrounding her and still deeply embedded in her.

chapter nine

Gabe lay next to Mia listening to the soft sounds of her breathing. She was warm and soft against him and he was gripped by an odd . . . contentment. Her head was pillowed on his arm, which was growing numb, but he refused to move because he liked the feel of her nestled against his side.

He was *not* a cuddler. Not since he was married had he ever devoted any time to the more intimate parts of lovemaking. Not that he hadn't let women sleep over, but there was always a distinct separation, almost an invisible barrier between him and the other women.

Mia hadn't given him much choice in the matter. As soon as he'd withdrawn from her body and cleaned them both, she'd snuggled into his side and fallen asleep. And he hadn't done anything to rectify the matter.

Instead, he lay here pondering the volatility of their coming together.

Guilt plagued him. He'd promised her that he'd be patient and ease her into the physical aspects of their relationship. He should have gone slower, been more gentle. He should have made certain that he had more control.

But the simple truth was that from the moment she walked into his apartment, he'd been instantly seized with the primal urge to have her. Nothing about their sexual encounter had been slow or gentle. He'd fucked her hard and with an urgency that he couldn't even explain.

He glanced at her closed eyes, at her tousled hair and the swell of her breast pressed solidly into his side. He'd imagined that after sating his initial lust for her, he would gain control of this seeming obsession, that he'd be able to settle and treat this as he did all his other partnerships with women. If anything, this first encounter had only sharpened the edge of his arousal. He was hungry for more. In no way had fucking her diminished his burning need for her. He wanted her again. Goddamn it but he wanted her now.

Forgotten were all his promises to ease her into his lifestyle, to take it slow with his demands. He wanted to tie her up and fuck her until they both passed out. He wanted to do about a million things with her, none of which included going slow or easing her into anything. The only thing he wanted to ease was himself. Inside her. Only it wouldn't be easy. He wanted to fuck her hard, deep and long, until she had absolutely no doubt that she was his.

She stirred beside him, made a sleepy noise as her arm slid over his chest. His hand came down over her arm in a caress, the simple need to touch her overwhelming him. Her eyelids fluttered open and she stared up at him, her eyes hazy.

"How long have I been asleep?"

"Not long. Maybe an hour."

She started to push herself upward, uncertainty flashing in her eyes.

"Sorry. I mean I didn't intend to fall asleep. I should probably be going."

He scowled and pulled her roughly back down and let his hand travel up her body, over her curves and to her breast. The hell she was going anywhere. What hadn't she understood about the fact that she was his? And being his didn't include crawling out of his bed the minute the orgasm was over.

"Call your roommate and have her prepare you an overnight bag. I'll send a car for it and you can ride in to work with me tomorrow."

Mia's expression became troubled. "How is that going to look if we show up to work together?"

His frown deepened. "It won't look like anything other than we met for breakfast to discuss your employment and we came in to work together."

She went silent but nodded.

"Use the phone by the bed and call Caroline."

He loosened his hold so she could roll away, and he watched for a long moment, letting his gaze roam over her bare back and her rounded ass. God, she was beautiful.

Forcing his stare away from her, he turned to grab his cell, and while she spoke in low tones in the background to her roommate, he placed a quick call to his driver and gave him instructions to pick up Mia's things from her apartment.

When he turned back over, Mia was sitting up on the bed, her expression still one of uncertainty and awkwardness.

What he wanted to do was pull her underneath him and plunge into her. He was hard as a rock, and the sheets were bunched around his waist, so at least she couldn't see just how aroused he was. Not that she wouldn't know very soon. And yet, he didn't want to haul her underneath him just now. And he couldn't even explain that particular thought since his overwhelming need was to get back inside her—as soon as he could part those gorgeous thighs and bare that pretty pussy of hers.

If it were any other woman he'd either take his pleasure or suggest they both sleep, and he'd turn away, isolating himself from any intimacy. But with Mia he found he had other . . . needs.

Needs he didn't even understand. Nor did he particularly want to analyze them or dig too deep. He wasn't certain he'd like what he discovered.

"Come here," he said, offering his arm so she could lie as she'd done before.

Mia pulled the covers up and snuggled into his side, resting her head on his shoulder.

For a long moment they were both silent and then Mia stirred, turning her head so she could look up at him.

"You aren't going to make me call you *master* or anything like that are you?"

His eyebrow went up and he glanced down to see a mischievous twinkle in her eye. He shook his head. She amused him, and he found himself wanting to laugh. "No. It sounds ridiculous, doesn't it? I'm not much on the appearances of a certain lifestyle or stereotype."

"No *yes sir* or *no sir*?"

He relaxed into their playful banter and smacked his hand over her ass. He was comfortable around her, and he found he enjoyed this . . . moment. Or whatever the hell it was. He should be fucking her again, and yet he was savoring just being here in bed and watching her smile and flirt. Holy hell, but if she turned that flirty, innocent smile on another man he wouldn't be responsible for his actions.

"You're already a disrespectful little baggage. And no, don't call me *sir*. It makes me sound like your father and I already have enough reservations over our age differences to not want to draw even more attention to that parallel."

She lifted herself up, her hair falling over his chest as she stared down at him. Jesus, but she was beautiful. All that gorgeous hair spilling over him. Suddenly he was beyond the playful-banter stage, and he was seized all over again by the need to roll her underneath him and fuck her for another four hours.

"Does my age bother you so much? If it does then why would you want . . . this. I mean *us.*"

He sighed, resigning to control himself at least a few minutes longer. His dick was screaming at him, but Mia was in the mood to talk and he'd accommodate her for now.

"It bothered me in the past. It doesn't bother me as much now. But there *are* fourteen years between us. You're much younger. A whole world away from where I am in my life."

She frowned a bit and a pensive look entered her eyes.

"What are you thinking?" he asked, curious at her hesitation.

Her chest rose with the forceful inhalation of her breath. "You've hinted that you've wanted me for . . . a long time. How long, Gabe?"

He was silent a moment as he pondered how to put his words. The entire conversation turn made him uncomfortable, but he'd pursued the question in her eyes. He couldn't very well refuse to give her an answer when he'd encouraged her to ask.

"I think it was when you came back from Europe, when you took a break in your studies to go overseas. I hadn't seen you much as it was. Just on the occasion when you were with Jace or at holidays. And then when you graduated college. No longer did I see you as a girl, Jace's baby sister. I saw you as a desirable woman. One I wanted to possess. It caught me completely off guard."

"Why now?" she asked softly. "If not then, why now?"

He had no answer for that, other than seeing her on the street the day he'd taken the photo. It had been a fist to his gut. All of the desire and need he'd suppressed had come roaring to the surface. She was an itch under his skin he couldn't rid himself of. Even now that he'd had her, the itch wasn't alleviated. It was more intense than ever.

"It was time," he said simply. "And you, Mia? When did you decide you wanted me?"

She flushed and averted her gaze. Color bloomed in her cheeks making them a delightful shade of pink. "You were my teenage crush. I've fantasized about you for years but you've always been so far out of my league."

Something in her tone alarmed him. It shook him. And he realized just how disastrous this could be if she weren't able to separate her emotions from their physical relationship. Perhaps it was why he'd held off for as long as he had. Aside from the difference in their ages, there was the fact that she was a girl. A young woman who hadn't had the emotional experience that the other women he'd associated with had.

"Don't fall in love with me, Mia," he warned. "Don't take this for anything more than it is. I don't want to hurt you."

Her lips twisted in scorn and her eyes narrowed. She leaned back, putting more distance between them. He didn't like it. He wanted her close. Touching him. Where he could feel her softness and warmth against his skin.

He leaned up, curling his arm around her, and then pulled her back until she landed against his chest. She had no liking for that. Too bad. She could say whatever she wanted to say with him touching her.

Her mouth scrunched into a frown. It was adorable and cute, but it would only piss her off if he said as much. His own mouth twitched, threatening to smile, but he quashed that urge and stared expectantly at her as he waited for what she had to say.

"That's awfully presumptuous of you, Gabe. Not to mention arrogant and assholish. You've been clear in your expectations of our arrangement. I'm not an idiot. Do you assume every woman you meet falls head over heels in love with you and can't live without you?"

He lost the battle not to smile, and she didn't look pleased with the result. She looked like a pissed-off kitten whose claws had just come out. Relief settled into his chest. Yes, he'd gone out of his way to make certain she knew the terms of their agreement, but he still didn't like the idea of hurting her. And his friendship with Jace may not ever recover if Gabe broke Mia's heart. He didn't *want* to break her heart. She was more than just another woman he had sex with.

"Point taken," Gabe conceded. "I won't bring it up again."

She cast him another frown and inserted her hands between them, pushing back so there was space between them. Oh hell no. He pulled her back down so she landed forcefully on his chest once more, her mouth just inches from his.

He kissed her and then growled when he found her lips stiff and unyielding. He slid his hand down her belly, between them, and into the soft, velvety flesh of her pussy. He stroked over her clit until she gasped, opening her mouth to his tongue.

"That's better," he said against her mouth before ravaging her sweet lips once more.

"What about your driver?" she gasped out between kisses.

"We have time."

He reached for her hips, lifting her and then positioning her astride him. He tore at the sheets, pushing them out of the way. His need for her was fierce. *Painful.*

"Put your hands on my shoulders and push yourself up," he growled.

When she complied, he grasped his cock and placed his other hand on her hip, guiding her down onto his straining erection.

"Ride me, Mia."

She looked so uncertain that he moved his hands to her waist and then arched up, thrusting deeply into her. Holding her in place, he guided the rhythm, helping her find her own. He knew it would be quick, hot and out of control. He didn't seem to *have* any control when it came to her.

"That's it, baby," he breathed. "Perfect."

He loosened his hold as she gained more confidence and began to take over. She was hot, liquid and silky soft around him. So tight, squeezing him like a vise. Son of a bitch but he was ready to come now, and he knew she wasn't even close.

As if reading his mind, she leaned down, for the first time taking the initiative, and kissed him. And God it was so sweet. He could taste her on his tongue, feel the luscious softness of her lips against his. Hell yeah, she was his. No doubt about that. And he didn't have any plans to let go of her until he was completely and utterly sated.

"Don't wait for me," she whispered.

He palmed her face, holding her in place as their mouths fused hotly. He arched his hips, wanting more as she rose and then slid back down his cock. His hands fell and he grasped her hips, knowing she was going to wear the marks of his possession the next day. But that idea only fueled his desire even more, until it was a raging inferno burning him from the inside out.

He erupted within her, his release painful in its intensity. He could barely contain his cry, a roar of satisfaction, of victory. As if he'd conquered his prey. She was here, in his arms, his dick buried inside her. His. No more waiting. No more primitive obsession. He'd captured her completely and now she was at his mercy, his to do with as he liked.

They were crazy thoughts filling his mind, swamping him. Images of her tied, hand and foot, as he slaked his lust, of him taking her from behind, of sinking into her mouth, of consuming her until she had no other thought than the fact that she belonged to him.

He wrapped his arms around her, pulling her down so she was flush against his chest. She rose and fell with the force of his breathing, her hair tangled on his face. He slid one hand down to cup her behind and arched once more, seeking to go even deeper, keeping them connected in the most intimate way possible.

God, but he had no defense against a desire this powerful. He'd never experienced anything that compared and he wasn't sure he liked it. It unsettled him and made him unsure of himself. Made him second-guess all his intentions.

He was a selfish bastard. There was no question about that. He took his pleasure, took what he wanted. Always. But Mia made him want to be . . . better. He didn't want to be this savage monster that took without giving. He wanted to be gentle with her, to ensure her pleasure above his. He wasn't sure he knew how, but damn it, he wanted to try.

If she didn't run from his bed after tonight, he couldn't imagine why. He'd ravaged her, not once but twice. Fucked her almost brutally without consideration, and the second time she hadn't even found her own satisfaction.

He closed his eyes and tried to collect himself, and he lay there with Mia atop him, his arms full of sweet, soft woman.

Finally, he rolled, taking her with him, slipping from the heated clasp of her pussy. He kissed her forehead awkwardly, not knowing what to say, and so he didn't say anything at all as he retreated from the bed.

Her gaze followed him as he stood, naked, by the bed. He couldn't discern anything from her stare. There was no judgment, no condemnation, but neither was there acceptance. She simply watched, and that thoughtful gaze made his skin prickle.

He turned away, saying as he reached for his clothing, "Stay here. I'll get your things when they're brought up."

"Okay," she said softly.

He pulled on his pants, knowing he must look a wreck. Far from the remote, untouchable persona he always projected. He didn't want anyone to see him this way. Especially not Mia.

chapter ten

Mia had dozed off, sated and in her warm, hazy cocoon, images of Gabe vivid in her dreams. And then she was roused from sleep as the very real, not-dream Gabe pulled the covers from where she'd tugged them up to her chin.

He had this look, a completely and utterly delicious look in those piercing blue eyes that made her stomach clench, and her immediate reaction was to clamp her thighs shut to alleviate the instant ache that bloomed.

"On your knees."

Holy hell, but the way he made that command made her go weak.

She wasn't entirely certain what he meant. Did he want her literally on her knees, like upright? Or did he mean *hands and knees*? And if he meant hands and knees . . . She shivered as she imagined the hands *and* knees option.

When his eyes narrowed with impatience, she hurried to roll from her back to her side and then onto her belly. Before she could push herself up to her knees, he planted his hand in the middle of her back, holding her firmly against the mattress.

"Stay there a moment. It will be easier if I do this now."

Do what now?

Her heart thudded against the mattress and she squinched her eyes shut, figuring if she wasn't looking at him that it was okay for her to close her eyes.

Gently he pulled at first one wrist and then the other, tugging both hands behind her until they rested at the small of her back. Her eyes flew open when she registered that he was coiling . . . *rope* . . . around her wrists, binding them together.

Oh shit, oh shit, oh shit. He hadn't been kidding about the bondage and restraint stuff she'd read in the contract!

She hadn't realized how tense she'd gone until Gabe leaned down, his lips brushing the back of her ear.

"Relax, Mia. I won't hurt you. You know that."

That whispered promise made her muscles go lax again and she melted into the bed, her brain in overload. She was excited, nervous, scared, but mostly really excited. Her senses were on hyperalert. Her nipples were hard, poking into the mattress, and her pussy had clenched, quivering in anticipation.

Then he hoisted her ass up so that her knees went beneath her, and he positioned her so her cheek was down on the mattress while her ass was perched in the air, her hands solidly bound behind her back.

His hands smoothed over her behind, caressing and soothing, and then his finger trailed down the cleft of her ass, pausing just at her anal opening. His voice was gravelly, a rough edge to his tone when he spoke.

"I'm looking forward to fucking this sweet ass, Mia. And I will. You're not ready yet, but you will be and I'm going to enjoy every second I'm balls deep inside your pretty ass."

She shivered uncontrollably, chill bumps dancing across her exposed flesh.

"For now, I'm going to fuck your pussy, that tight little ass perched high while I imagine it's your ass I'm fucking."

She bit into her bottom lip as lust rolled hot through her, leaving her flushed, excited, desperate for his touch and his possession.

Then the bed dipped and his body pressed into her. His hands glided up her back and then down to settle on her bound wrists. He stroked her clenched fingers and then tugged experimentally at the rope as though he were checking to make sure she was securely tied.

She couldn't breathe. Couldn't process the bombardment of sensations. She was utterly helpless and yet she knew she was safe. Knew he wouldn't hurt her. He wouldn't take her too far.

Keeping one hand securely around her bound hands, he slid his other hand between her legs to cup her pussy. Then he left her long enough to position his cock, the tip teasing her entrance, spreading it as he pushed in the barest inch.

"You're so fucking beautiful," he said in a rough voice. "In my bed, on your knees, hands tied behind your back so you have no choice but to take whatever I give you."

She was ready to scream in frustration. She was so on the edge and he still hadn't done more than remain just inside her pussy, the head nestled right at her opening. She tried to push back against him, tried to force him deeper inside her.

Her mouth fell open against the sheets when he administered a sharp smack to her ass. Then he chuckled. He laughed!

"So impatient," he said, amusement in his voice. "We do this my way, Mia. You forget so easily. I want inside you as badly as you want me there, but I'm enjoying every second of having you tied up and in my bed. As soon as I get my dick inside you, I'm not going to last long so I'm going to savor every second."

She closed her eyes and groaned.

He chuckled again and then pushed forward another inch, opening her wider to his advance. She sighed, tense, waiting, anticipating, her entire body quivering and clenching, her pussy sucking at his cock, wanting it deeper. She wanted all of it. She wanted *him*.

"You want all of me, Mia?" he asked in a husky voice that danced across her skin.

God yes.

"Yes," she croaked out.

"I can't hear you."

"God yes!"

"Ask me nicely," he said in a silky voice. "Ask me for what you want, baby."

"I want *you*," she said. "Please, Gabe."

"You want me or you want my cock?"

"Both," she said in a strangled voice.

"Good answer," he murmured, just before he leaned down to brush a kiss across her spine.

His grip tightened around her bound wrists and he plunged forward. She gasped, her eyes widening, her mouth remaining open as a silent cry echoed through her head.

"Damn good answer," he whispered closer to her ear this time.

His body covered her, blanketing her, pressing into her tied hands. She twitched, bucking upward, unable to help her desperation for more.

Never would she have imagined having so many orgasms in one night. In just a few hours! This was so insanely over-the-top, so out of the realm of even her wildest fantasies regarding Gabe that her mind was completely blown.

Finally he withdrew, dragging his cock through her swollen, slick walls, pulling until the very tip of his erection was barely perched at her opening.

"Gabe, please!"

She was begging. She sounded hoarse and desperate and she didn't care. Didn't care if she was breaking the rules, didn't care if it earned her a reprimand. God, she even hoped he'd smack her ass again, because anything, anything at all at this point would send her hurtling over the edge and into oblivion.

"Shhh, my baby," he soothed in that husky sweet voice that could make a woman come just by the sound of it. "I'll take care of you now. Trust me to do that for you."

"I trust you, Gabe," she whispered.

She turned her face at that moment, just enough that she saw savage satisfaction light fire in his eyes. It was as if those simple words had hit him right in the gut. And he *liked* them.

Both hands went to her bound wrists, gripping, restraining them even though she had no way of moving them. Using them as a handhold, he began to thrust. Deep, hard, *long* thrusts.

Her entire body began to shake. Her legs went weak from the strain of holding herself up. Her knees dug into the mattress and she could feel herself inching downward, her muscles jelly as they spasmed in her impending orgasm.

Flutters rose deep in her belly, spreading, taking wing and invading her veins. He was a drug. Sliding through her body, slow and sweet, intoxicating her with heady, blissful pleasure.

Soft moans rose in the air and she realized they came from her. She was helpless to silence them. They came from somewhere deep inside her, a part of her that had been locked away until now.

Then one of his hands left her wrists and tangled in her long hair. He wrapped the tresses around his fingers as if he enjoyed the feel of the strands. Then his grip tightened and became fiercer. He tugged lightly and then he loosened his hold only to delve deeper, closer to her scalp.

His hand was fisted in her hair, and he pulled until her head was angled so he could see her face.

"Eyes, Mia."

The command was sharp, a demand she wasn't to disobey. Her

eyes came open. She could see him in her periphery, and his expression took her breath away.

There was something savage about his features. His eyes glistened as her entire body shook with the force of his thrusts. Each time he withdrew, her head came back just a little because his hand was wrapped so tightly in her hair.

It didn't hurt. Or maybe it did and she was too drunk off pleasure to know the difference. She was aroused by the way his hand was twisted up in her hair, how he pulled her head back so he could *see* her when she came.

He wanted her eyes.

And so she angled her head even further, determined he would see what he wanted, and she focused on the beauty that was his face, angular, so very masculine and contorted with immense satisfaction. Pleasure. She was giving him that.

Their gazes locked and held and there was something in his eyes that hit her deep. Like a shot to her soul. This is where she was supposed to be. This was where she belonged. Right here, in Gabe Hamilton's bed. At his command and mercy. This is what she craved.

And it was all hers.

"How close?" Gabe said, his voice strained and edgy.

She looked at him in confusion.

He softened his voice. "How close are you to coming, baby?"

"Oh God, I'm right there," she panted out.

"Then come for me, beautiful. Let me see it in your eyes. I love how they go all liquid and hazy. You have such expressive eyes, Mia. They're a shot right to your soul and I'm the only damn man who gets to see them when you come. Understand?"

She nodded, the knot in her throat too big for her to speak.

"Tell me," he said in a lower voice. "Tell me those eyes are mine."

"They're yours," she whispered back. "Just yours, Gabe."

He loosened his hand in her hair and gradually withdrew it, allowing the strands to flow over his fingers until he reached the ends. Then his hand glided down her spine, his touch warm and soothing. He curled his arm around her waist, his fingers wandering lower, to the juncture of her thighs.

He rubbed over her clit and she cried out as a bolt of electricity arced through her body.

"That's it, baby. Let go. Let me have you. I want it all, Mia. Everything you have. It's mine. Give it to me now."

He began to thrust, his hips pounding against her ass as he lightly brushed his fingers over her taut clitoris.

"Oh God," she breathed. "Gabe!"

"You learn fast, baby. My name, your eyes, when you come."

She almost broke eye contact. Everything went blurry. She screamed his name, not recognizing her own voice. It was hoarse, loud, like nothing she'd ever heard before. It was full of need, desperate need. It was a plea for him to give her what she needed.

And he did.

He took care of her. Gave her what she wanted. What she needed.

Him.

She went hot and slick around him as he bathed her pussy in his release. No longer able to maintain eye contact, she went limp, resting her cheek on the mattress. She didn't have the strength to keep her neck turned, even at the slight angle she'd had it. Her eyes closed and she wasn't sure if she was even fully conscious, because she hovered on some other place. Like she was shitfaced, but in the most beautiful place in the world.

Floating. Euphoric. Completely sated.

And *happy*.

Utterly content.

But there was no reprimand. Just soft kisses pressed up her

spine and then to her ear. Murmured words she didn't even understand drifted softly over her ear. And then he withdrew and her protest was immediate. She was rudely yanked from her warm haze and instantly cold and bereft without him.

"Shhh, baby," he whispered. "I need to untie you and take care of you now."

"Mmmm," was all she could manage.

It sounded so very nice. Him taking care of her. She was good with that.

A moment later her hands came free and Gabe took each one in turn, gently massaging them, slowly lowering each arm to the bed so she wouldn't suffer any discomfort. Then he turned her, pulling her forward and into his arms.

He backed off the bed and then picked her up, cradling her against his chest. She was curled into a tight ball, molded to him, her arms wrapped around his neck as if she'd never let go.

God, she felt so vulnerable. So . . . open. She was completely shaken by what had happened tonight. She'd come expecting sex, sure. But this? This wasn't just sex. How could a simple three-letter word that was attributed to any sort of lovemaking possibly describe the raw, fierce, explosive inferno that had just occurred?

Earth-shattering. And she'd had good sex before, but nothing ever earth-shattering.

He walked her into the bathroom and turned on the shower until steam poured from the stall. Then he carried her inside and, still holding her tightly against him, allowed her to slide down his body as the spray covered them both.

When he was sure she was steady on her feet, he separated long enough to get soap and then he proceeded to cover every inch of her body using his hands. He left no part of her untouched, uncaressed, uncared-for.

By the time he finished, she could barely keep her balance. As he moved away to step out of the shower, she nearly face planted. He lunged for her, a curse echoing in her ears. He picked her up again and then set her on the counter beside the sink while he reached for one of the folded towels on the shelf by the shower.

He enfolded her in its warmth and she sighed, leaning her forehead against his damp chest.

"I'm okay," she murmured. "Dry off. I'll just sit here."

When she looked up, his mouth was quirked into a grin and his eyes gleamed with amusement. But still, he kept a cautious eye on her as he reached behind him for a towel.

He made quick work of drying his body, and she enjoyed every single second of the show. The man was fine. Gorgeous with a capital G. And his ass. She hadn't really paid much attention to his ass because she'd always been way more focused on the front side of that particular portion of his anatomy. Because the man had a beautiful cock.

Yeah, it was weird to consider a penis beautiful because in reality they were pretty damn ugly. But Gabe's? He was just beautifully and perfectly formed. Even his penis. She was having some pretty vivid fantasies about having it in her mouth. Tasting it. Making him every bit as crazy as he'd made her.

"What the hell are you thinking about now?" Gabe murmured.

She blinked and realized that he was in her space. He'd moved in between her legs and was looking down, his gaze inquisitive and searching as he explored her face. Heat suffused her cheeks, which was pretty stupid considering the fact that she'd just had torrid, kinky sex for the last few hours, and now she was blushing because she'd been caught thinking about giving him a blow job?

Clearly there was no hope for her.

"Do I really have to answer that?" she blurted.

He lifted an eyebrow and amusement glittered in his eyes.

"Yeah, you really do. Especially now that you've gone all pink with embarrassment."

She sighed and banged her forehead against his chest. "I was checking you out."

He grasped her shoulders, pulling her away so he could look at her again. "That's it? You were checking me out and that embarrassed you?"

She hesitated and then sighed. "You have a really gorgeous cock, okay? I was admiring it."

He choked back his laughter. Well, almost. A strangled sound escaped his throat and she groaned.

Before she lost what remaining nerve she had, she blurted out the rest.

"And I was fantasizing about . . ."

She could *feel* her cheeks getting even hotter.

And then Gabe was up close, spreading her thighs even farther apart as he pressed into her space. He tipped her chin up with his fingers and his fierce gaze penetrated her.

"Fantasizing about what?"

"Having you in my mouth," she whispered. "Tasting you. Making you as crazy as you've made me."

His entire body tightened against her. Lust blazed in his eyes. Like an inferno.

"You'll get your chance, baby. I can guaran-damn-tee that."

Once again her head exploded with images. Really vivid images of her lips locked around that huge cock and licking every inch of his length.

He lowered his mouth to her lips, pressing a gentle kiss to the bow of her mouth.

"We need to get some sleep," he murmured. "I didn't intend . . . I didn't intend to take things so far tonight. You're going to be tired at work tomorrow."

He said that last in an almost regretful tone. He stroked her chin and grazed her cheek with the backs of his fingers. Then he kissed her again. One of those sweet, tender kisses that was a direct contradiction to the raging out-of-control furor he'd demonstrated earlier.

"Come on, baby," he said in a husky voice. "I'm going to take you to bed so you get a few hours of sleep."

chapter eleven

Mia opened her eyes to see Gabe leaning over her, his hand gently shaking her shoulder.

"Hey, time to get up and head to work," he said.

She rubbed her eyes in an attempt to remove the fog. "What time is it?"

"It's six. If you want to shower and get dressed, we'll grab breakfast on the way into the office."

As she became more aware, she saw that Gabe was already dressed for work. She hadn't even noticed when he'd gotten out of bed. She could smell the crisp, clean essence of his soap and the tantalizing aroma of his cologne. He was wearing slacks and a button-up shirt with a tie, although the tie was still loose around his neck and the top button was unfastened.

He looked . . . untouchable. Cool and composed. A direct contrast to the man who'd taken her repeatedly the night before.

She pushed herself upward and then maneuvered to the edge of the bed. "I won't take long."

"Take your time. I'm not in a hurry this morning. I have a meeting at ten. Until then I'm free."

She stumbled into the bathroom and took a look at herself in the mirror. Other than signs of fatigue, she didn't look any different. Somehow she expected for the world to be able to see on her face all that she and Gabe had done the night before.

For a long moment she sat on the closed toilet seat while the shower ran, just needing a few minutes to collect herself. She was sore. She'd never had a marathon sex session before. Her encounters had always been a great deal slower and one orgasm for all.

Gabe had taken her four times over the course of the night. At the very end he'd apologized gruffly, like it pained him to do it. There was genuine regret in his eyes. He said he wanted to be more gentle with her, to keep his promise to go slow in the beginning, but that he couldn't hold back, that he wanted her too much.

Was that supposed to upset her?

Having a man be so crazy for her that he couldn't control himself wasn't exactly a bad thing. He hadn't hurt her. Yes, she was sore. She had marks and small bruises from his hands and his mouth. But she'd loved every minute of it even if she'd spent most of the time completely overwhelmed.

She got into the shower and stood, allowing the hot water to rush over her face. Mindful that Gabe was already dressed and ready to go, she quickly washed her hair and soaped her body before climbing out to wrap a towel around her.

It was then she realized she hadn't brought her clothing in with her. She didn't even know what Gabe had done with the bag the night before. After wrapping her hair in a towel, she opened the door to peek out.

Gabe was sitting on the bed, her clothing laid out next to him. As she moved toward him, he picked up a pair of panties and dangled them off the end of his finger.

"You won't have need for these," he said.

Her eyes widened.

"No panties at work. They'll just get in the way," he said, his eyes gleaming as he stared at her.

She glanced at the skirt and top on the bed, and then back at Gabe. "I can't wear a skirt and no underwear!"

He lifted an eyebrow. "You'll do as I want, Mia. That's the agreement."

"Oh dear God. What if someone sees?"

He laughed. "How will they see unless you show them? I want to look at you and know you're wearing nothing underneath this skirt. And it makes it much easier to just hike it up and slide my dick into your pussy."

She swallowed. She'd realized that her job was a front. A means for Gabe to have her at his beck and call during work hours. But she hadn't quite counted on him wanting sex in his office. The idea of someone walking in on them made her want to crawl under the bed and hide.

"And Mia, that's every day. No underwear. If you wear them anytime you're with me, I'll take them off and you'll wear my handprint on your pretty behind."

Her entire body tingled in reaction. She stared wordlessly back at him, shocked by the fact she was aroused by the idea of him spanking her. What kind of a freak did that make her?

He collected her skirt, top and bra and held them out to her.

"Better get moving. We leave in half an hour."

Numbly, Mia took the clothing and hurried back to the bathroom, her mind alive with images of Gabe fucking her in his office. Of his hand on her ass. It troubled her that she wasn't as horrified as she *should* be. While she certainly didn't want anyone popping in unannounced when Gabe had her bent over his desk, the *idea* that they could be discovered at any moment excited her.

What the hell was wrong with her?

She dressed and nearly died when she pulled on the skirt over her bare bottom. It just felt weird not to have underwear on. Not that a thong offered much more protection than a pair of panties, but even having *something* covering her was better than nothing.

She dried her hair and brushed it out. There wasn't much hope for it this morning, and she didn't have time to mess with it, so she twisted it into a knot and put on a large clip to secure it. After applying enough makeup to cover the smudges under her eyes, she took a deep breath and inspected her reflection in the mirror.

She wouldn't win any beauty pageants, but she'd do.

After brushing her teeth and applying her lip gloss, she left the bathroom to retrieve her shoes from the bed. She stuffed her clothing from the night before in her overnight bag and then left the bedroom in search of Gabe.

He was standing at the bar in the kitchen drinking a glass of juice. When he saw her, he emptied the rest of the contents of the glass and put it in the sink.

"All set?"

She took in a deep breath. "Yes."

He motioned her toward the door and then reached for her bag. "We'll leave this here. No need to take it into the office. That *would* be advertising that we spent the night together and I don't think that's what you want. I'll send it over after work if you like."

She nodded and handed it over and then waited as he summoned the elevator.

The ride down was quiet, though she noticed that he kept glancing her way, his weighted stare raking over her. She kept her gaze averted, her nerve deserting her. Why she would be nervous now after the night they'd spent together, she had no idea, but she was seized by awkwardness and somehow making small talk seemed way too forced. So she remained silent as they departed the building and got into the waiting car.

"We'll eat at Rosario's and then walk to the office," he said, referring to an eatery just two blocks from his office building.

She was famished. And she was already dragging and the day

hadn't even begun. If Gabe planned more nights like the last, she was going to be a walking zombie at work.

To her surprise, he reached across the seat and curled his hand around hers, lacing their fingers together. He squeezed, almost as if he were reaching into her thoughts and reassuring her.

She turned and smiled at him, warmed by the gesture. He smiled back and said, "There, that's better. You were so somber. I can't have everyone thinking on your first day that you'd rather be anywhere else."

Her smile broadened and she relaxed, allowing some of the tension to ebb from her body. It was going to be all right. She could do this. She was smart and capable. She could think on her feet, even if Gabe reduced her to a blithering idiot at times. This job would be a challenge, but one she would embrace. Yes, she had no illusions that Gabe had hired her for her brains, but there was no reason she couldn't prove to be a valuable asset outside of the bedroom.

They ate a leisurely breakfast, and at eight thirty, they walked the two blocks to his office building and rode the elevator up to his floor. She experienced a bout of nerves as they stepped off and walked past Eleanor.

"Good morning, Eleanor," Gabe said in a formal voice. "Mia and I will be behind closed doors until my ten o'clock meeting. I'll be getting her up to speed on her job duties. See that we aren't disturbed. When I attend my meeting, I want you to take her around and introduce her to the rest of the staff."

"Yes, sir," Eleanor said briskly.

Mia had to stifle her laughter as she was reminded of her conversation with Gabe about *master* and *sir*. He sent her a quelling look as he directed her down the hall to his office.

When they went in, she was surprised to see a desk on the opposite wall from where his was situated. Furniture and fixtures had been rearranged to make room for the new desk, and two bookcases had been completely removed.

"This is where you'll work," he said. "Since you'll be working so closely with me, I saw no need to give you your own office." His voice lowered to a velvety, seductive timbre. "You'll remain close to me at all times."

She shivered at the sensual promise in his voice. How the hell was she supposed to get any work done with him sitting across from her and her knowing that at any moment he would get the urge to have sex with her?

And then all trace of innuendo disappeared and he was brisk and businesslike. He went to his desk and pulled out a folder thick with documents. He handed it to her and said, "These are files on investors, business colleagues and other various people important to this business. I want you to read over their profiles and commit them to memory. There are details of their likes, dislikes, their spouses' names, their children's names, their hobbies and interests, et cetera. It's important you retain all of this information and can bring it to mind when you meet them at functions or in a meeting. I'll expect you to be personable and warm and be knowledgeable of them as individuals. It goes a long way in business to know everything you can and use every advantage. As my assistant, you'll aid me in charming these people. We want their money and backing. There's no room for mistakes."

Her eyes widened and she took the folder, feeling its weight. There was a lot of information here and she swallowed back her panic. She could do this. She could totally do this.

"I'll leave you to your reading," he said. "I need to catch up on e-mails and messages before my meeting. When I'm done, we'll go over some of your other job duties."

Nodding, she turned away and headed for the desk assigned to her. She settled into the sumptuous leather executive chair and pulled herself forward to begin memorizing the huge amount of data before her.

chapter twelve

"Mia?"

Mia looked up from the pile of papers she was reading over to see Eleanor standing in the doorway of Gabe's office.

"If you're ready, I'll take you around and introduce you to the staff."

Mia pushed back and rotated her stiff neck, all the information swirling around, jumbled in her brain. She smiled in Eleanor's direction.

Eleanor was nice and she'd been HCM's receptionist forever. Though Mia had only been into the offices a few times before, she'd spoken frequently on the phone with Eleanor. Usually when Mia was calling for Jace or when Jace had Eleanor phone her with a message. Usually that he was running late for one of his dates with Mia.

Mia had watched closely for speculation in Eleanor's eyes. Or even surprise that it was Gabe and not Jace Mia had come to work for. But either Eleanor wasn't surprised or she was very good at hiding her emotions. That wouldn't likely be the case with the rest of the office staff.

Even if she didn't know them, they'd know who she was as soon as she was introduced. The next while wasn't going to be the most comfortable of moments.

Mia stood and straightened the documents before stuffing them back into the folder. Then she self-consciously slid her hand down the back of her skirt, praying that no one would be able to tell she had no panties on. She walked around the desk and met Eleanor in the hallway.

"I'll take you down the other corridor where the offices are located and then we'll hit the wing on the opposite side of the floor where all the cubicles are."

Mia nodded and fell in behind Eleanor as she walked briskly through the reception area and to the opposite hallway. At the first door, she paused and stuck her head in.

"John? There's someone I want you to meet."

John lifted his head as Eleanor and Mia entered. He was a younger man—older than her, but younger than Gabe—with glasses and dressed in a polo shirt. When he stood, she saw the casual slacks. Gabe obviously didn't hold the rest of his staff to his same dress code.

"This is Mia Crestwell, Mr. Hamilton's new personal assistant," Eleanor said.

John's eyebrows lifted in quick surprise, but he didn't offer a comment.

"Mia, this is John Morgan, our marketing director."

He held out his hand to shake Mia's. "It's a pleasure, Mia. I think you'll enjoy working here. Mr. Hamilton is a great boss and a super person to work for."

"It's nice to meet you too," Mia said, offering a smile.

"I'm sure we'll be working closely together since you're Mr. Hamilton's personal assistant."

Mia smiled and nodded, not knowing what else to say. She was terrible with casual chitchat.

As if sensing her unease, Eleanor was quick to retreat.

"Well, we'll leave you to your work, John. I'm sure you're busy, and I still have to take Mia around the office."

"I'll see you around," John said. "Welcome to the team."

"Thank you," Mia murmured.

She followed Eleanor out and then repeated the process with five other employees, all in various positions of management within the company. The CFO was an impatient, fidgety man who seemed preoccupied and irritated at the distraction. Even Eleanor was brief and hurried Mia away.

The two vice presidents Mia met next were women, one who looked to be in her thirties with a warm smile and intelligent eyes. The other was slightly older, maybe forty or so, and she was a talker. It took several attempts before Eleanor was able to pull Mia away and cross the parallel hall to the other side of the building.

There, she met a myriad of people whose names she had no hope of remembering. Several looked speculatively at her when she was introduced as Gabe's personal assistant. She couldn't blame them really, as Gabe hadn't had one in years. And there was the fact that she was Jace's sister, and as soon as her name came out of Eleanor's mouth, there had been instant recognition. And just as instant were the wheels turning in their heads as they'd stared at Mia.

Oh yeah, she was definitely going to be the gossip du jour.

When they were finally done with the meet and greet, Eleanor took her to the lounge and showed her the refrigerator and fully stocked kitchen. There was an eating area with an array of snacks and easy-to-prepare foods, and a cabinet with a variety of drinks, as well as a water cooler.

Eleanor turned and waved with her hands. "And that's the grand tour. Oh, and the ladies' bathroom is between the lounge and the cubicle section."

Mia smiled warmly. "Thank you, Eleanor. I appreciate your taking the time to show me around and for your kindness."

"Anytime. If you need anything at all, don't hesitate to let me know. I'm going to get back to my desk and relieve Charlotte."

Mia followed her out but went in search of the bathroom instead of returning immediately to Gabe's office. She needed to pee and freshen up. She was still feeling the effects of the night before and she was certain she looked hungover.

She went into the stall at the very end and closed the door behind her. Almost immediately, she heard the door open and more than one person enter. Ugh, she hated peeing around others. But the other women evidently weren't going down to the stalls. The sound of a faucet running gave her time to do her business, and she was prepared to finish up and exit when she went still.

"So what do you make of Gabe's new personal assistant?"

The woman's voice was filled with amusement—and disbelief. Mia wanted to groan. Not even here half a day and she was already the topic of gossip. Which was to be expected, but she'd hoped not to have to hear it firsthand.

"Isn't she Jace Crestwell's little sister?" another woman asked.

"Uh-huh. Guess we know how she landed that job."

"Poor thing. She probably has no idea what she's gotten herself into."

"I don't know. I think I could go for some of that," the first woman said. "I mean, *hello.* He's rich, he's gorgeous and I've heard he's a beast in bed. Literally. Did you hear the rumor that he has a contract he makes all his women sign before he goes to bed with them?"

"Wonder which employment contract the new girl signed," the second woman said in a knowing voice.

There was laughter from at least three people. Great. Girls' meeting in the bathroom and Mia was trapped. She pulled up her feet so no one could see and just prayed they never made it down this far.

"I'd rather be the filling in a Jace and Ash sandwich," one of the women said. "Can you imagine having two dominant billionaires in your bed?"

Mia rolled her eyes and shuddered. Like she wanted to hear all of this about her brother?

"What do you think the story is behind those two?" the first one asked. "They always seem to go for the same woman. It's kind of weird if you ask me. I mean not that I would mind having a threesome with them, but for them it's a regular thing."

"Maybe they're bisexual."

Mia's mouth fell open. *Holy shit.* Not that she gave gossip much credence, but apparently the rumor mill was that Jace and Ash had some major kink of their own going on, and Gabe wasn't the lone ranger in this company.

She *so* did not want to imagine her brother in those kinds of situations.

"Ten-to-one, Gabe's fucking Jace's sister. Can you imagine if Jace finds out? Everyone knows he's way overprotective of her."

Mia sighed. It was probably too much to hope for that she could come to work and not have instant speculation.

"Maybe he knows and doesn't care," another woman offered. "She's an adult."

"She's way younger than Gabe, and if he made her sign a contract, I don't see that going over well with Jace."

"Maybe she's into that sort of thing."

"Uh, guys," a new voice piped up in a hesitant voice. "I kind of know the contract thing is real. I snuck into his office one night when I was working late. I was curious. You know, because of the rumors and stuff. He had a boilerplate contract in his desk. Very interesting reading. Let's just say that if a woman goes to bed with him, she basically signs her life over to him for that period of time."

Mia's head dropped to her knees with a thud.

"Get out! Are you kidding?"

"Are you *insane*? Do you know what would have happened if he had caught you? You would have been fired on the spot and God only knows what else he would have gone after you for."

"How the hell did you get into his office? I know for a fact he keeps it locked."

"I, uhm, picked the lock. I'm pretty good at it," the newer woman admitted.

"Girl, you've got a death wish. I wouldn't be doing that shit again if I were you."

"Shit guys, we need to get back to work. That report's due at two, and Gabe is not as understanding as Ash is about tardiness. I wish Jace and Ash would hurry up and get back from wherever it is they are. They're much easier to work for than Gabe."

There was a flurry of activity and the sounds of scurrying feet, paper being pulled from the dispenser and then finally the sounds of retreat. The door squeaked shut and Mia let out a long sigh of relief.

She scrambled off the toilet and hurriedly fixed her skirt. She opened the door to the stall and peeked out and then fled to the sink, doing a quick wash. At the door, she hesitated, cracked it open just an inch and peered down the hall.

The coast was clear so she bolted out and hurried back to Gabe's office.

Oh, the things you learned at work.

Gabe would be so pissed if he knew his office had been broken into and his personal documents had been read. Not that she was going to be a tattletale on her first day of work. She didn't even know which woman was the guilty party. All the names and voices had run together during the introductions.

Thankfully Gabe had not returned from his meeting, and Mia sank into her chair. She opened the folder again and the words swam in front of her eyes. It was a lot of information to process.

She jumped when her phone rang. She eyed it nervously and then hesitantly picked up the receiver.

"Mia Crestwell," she said by way of answering. *Hello* seemed unprofessional, and she didn't want to come across as a complete idiot.

Gabe's voice filled her ear, warm and sensual. "Mia, I'm running a little late. I'd intended for us to have lunch together, but I'm going to be delayed. I'm having Eleanor order in lunch for you."

"Okay. Thank you," she murmured.

"Did she take you around the office?"

"Yes, she did."

"And? Everything go well? Was everyone polite to you?"

"Oh of course. Everyone was great. I'm back in the office, obviously, since I'm talking to you. I'm working on the folder of stuff you gave me this morning."

"Just don't forget to eat," he said, admonishment in his voice. "I'll see you after lunch."

Before she could say *bye*, the line went dead. Ruefully, she replaced the receiver and turned her attention back to the folder.

Thirty minutes later, Eleanor popped her head in the door and Mia waved her in. Eleanor carried a takeout bag with her and placed it on Mia's desk.

"Mr. Hamilton said you like Thai, and there's a really good place down the block that delivers so I ordered you the special. If you'll give me an idea of your likes and dislikes, I'll make note so that in the future I make sure and get you something to your taste."

"Thai is perfect," Mia said. "Thank you. You didn't need to do this."

Eleanor frowned. "Mr. Hamilton was very specific that I was to order in lunch for you and also to make certain you eat. Oh, and if he didn't tell you already, he has a stocked minifridge here in his office with an array of drinks, so help yourself. It's over underneath the cabinet."

"Thank you, Eleanor. You've been very kind."

Eleanor nodded and then turned and disappeared from the office.

So far Mia wasn't entirely certain this was working out the way it was supposed to. She was Gabe's personal assistant, which meant she assisted. It didn't mean that other employees were supposed to wait on her hand and foot. She hoped he didn't give others in the department the same kind of directive. If he had, her name would be mud and no one would believe they weren't sleeping together and that she wasn't here merely to provide Gabe sexual services.

Even if that was indeed her primary job duty.

Gah. It made her sound like a prostitute. And maybe in essence she was. She was contracted for sex. If that didn't make her a call girl, what did it make her?

The only consolation she could take was that he wasn't paying her for sex.

She groaned when she realized just how stupid that assertion was. He *was* paying her. A lot! For a nonexistent job with duties so far that amounted to memorizing details of key people. She was on his payroll and somehow she didn't think she'd find "sex toy" on her personnel file. But they both knew that was precisely what she was. A paid sexual submissive.

Her head hit the desk and she sighed. She didn't think herself particularly submissive. Not that she couldn't be. In the right situation. But it certainly wasn't something deeply ingrained within her. A need that she was compelled to fulfill in order to be happy.

It was . . . a kink. When she'd never imagined she had any. She still wasn't sure exactly where she stood on the whole idea of bondage and submission and all the other eye-opening items in that contract.

But she'd agreed. She'd signed her name willingly. So she was sure as hell about to find out.

chapter thirteen

Mia was buried in her work when the door opened and Gabe walked in. She looked up, drinking in the sight of him. His gaze connected with hers and there was a flare of appreciation that gave her a giddy thrill. There was an instant shock of awareness, tension that was nearly tangible in the spacious office.

Lust coiled in his eyes and her stomach bottomed out as all her girly parts came to life. *Whoa,* but this was some intense chemistry now that they'd allowed it to be unleashed.

"Come here."

The order was quick and imperious and she stood automatically, responding to the brusque command. She met him in the middle of the floor and he pulled her roughly into his embrace.

His kiss was desperate and aching, as if he'd thought of nothing else but her in his absence. It was a fanciful thought, but one that seemed validated by the way he devoured her mouth. Their tongues met, hot and damp. Her lip gloss would be shot, but the idea of seeing her color on his mouth only intensified the quick desire he'd fueled.

She may wear his marks, but in a way, he'd wear hers too, even temporarily. Her stamp. Her brand. She may be his, but he damn well also belonged to her for however long their agreement lasted.

She caught a whisper of perfume on his clothing, and was

seized by fierce jealousy, no matter how unreasonable the emotion was.

The instant possessiveness caught her by surprise. She hadn't ever considered herself a possessive or jealous person. The idea that some other woman had been close to him made her want to bare her teeth and snarl. He needed an invisible sign that said *Hands off. He's mine.*

He reached down, grabbed her hand and then dragged her toward his desk. She wasn't at all sure what he was about to do, but her senses were on high alert.

He sat in his chair, pushing it back just a bit from his desk.

"Take off your skirt," he said bluntly.

She glanced nervously back at the door and then quickly back at him.

"The door is locked, Mia," he said impatiently. "Now take the skirt off."

Swallowing back her hesitation, she slowly began to pull down the skirt, baring the naked lower half of her body to his avid gaze.

To her surprise, he didn't tell her to take her top and bra off; rather, he took her hand again and pulled her between his thighs. She gave a gasp of surprise when his hands then circled her waist and he lifted her onto his desk so she was perched on the edge.

He pushed her back enough so she was securely situated, and then he scooted forward in his chair.

"I was negligent last night," he said in a gruff tone.

She was baffled and she was sure her expression said as much.

"I'm not normally so selfish during sex. My only excuse is that you make me burn, Mia. I had to have you."

He sounded as though he didn't want to be admitting any such thing. There was reluctance in his eyes, but his words rang with sincerity.

"Lean back," he said in a softer tone. "Brace your palms on my desk while I enjoy dessert."

Oh hell. Her breath caught and hiccupped roughly from her lips. She did as he commanded and positioned herself accordingly. He carefully spread her thighs, baring her pussy to his gaze and touch.

He ran one finger down the seam of her folds and then using two fingers, he spread them, baring more of her most intimate flesh. Then he lowered his head and her entire body went taut, anticipating that first touch.

It was like receiving an electrical charge. His tongue swept over her clit, and her hands nearly slipped as she jerked in reaction.

He toyed with the sensitive peak repeatedly, swirling his tongue around and then sucking at it with gentle tugs. Desire pooled low in her belly, spreading like fire to every other part of her body. Each swipe of his tongue had her more on the edge, building quickly and higher until she was gasping for breath.

He nuzzled lower, kissing and licking a path to the mouth of her pussy. He rimmed the entrance, flicking his tongue expertly and then delving within, fucking her with his tongue.

She was to the point of pain, her body straining, tightening with every stroke, her orgasm swelling until she was desperate for release. But he was in no hurry. He seemed to be completely in tune with her body. He'd work her to the very edge of frenzy and then he'd slow and work her back down again with reverent kisses and light brushes of his tongue.

Never had anyone gone down on her with such practiced skill. Gabe may be demanding and selfish—as he'd termed himself— but he was no stranger to pleasuring a woman. He knew exactly what he was doing, and he was driving her to absolute madness.

"Gabe, please," she whispered. "I need to come."

He chuckled, the sound vibrating over her clit. Even that small movement nearly sent her over the edge. He pressed a kiss to the tiny bud and then eased one long finger inside her pussy.

"Not yet, Mia. So impatient. I call the shots here. You come when I allow it."

The power and seductive edge in his voice brought on a full-body shiver that had her straining to maintain control.

"You taste so damn sexy," he said in a low growl. "I could eat your sweet pussy all afternoon."

She wouldn't survive all afternoon. She was close to begging as it was. Her lips clamped shut, and she held back the plea. But he knew. Oh yes, he knew.

"Beg me, Mia," he said, his finger working deep inside her. "Ask me very prettily and I'll let you come."

"Please, Gabe. I need you. Let me come."

"Who owns you?"

"I belong to you, Gabe. You own me."

"And whose pussy is this I'm devouring?"

"Yours," she gasped, her entire body shaking now.

"And if I want to fuck it when I'm done, that's my right, isn't it?"

"God, yes. Please just do it, Gabe!"

He laughed again and then plunged two fingers inside her as he sucked harder at her clit. The explosion was bright and earth-shattering. She came completely apart. Her palms slipped and suddenly she was flat on her back on the desk, and then Gabe rose up over her, his expression fierce and darkly seductive.

He unzipped his pants, pulled out his cock and in one forceful thrust, he plunged into her still-orgasming body. He hauled her legs upward, yanking her back to meet his thrusts. God, he was so deep, even deeper than the night before, almost as if her body had made the adjustment and could accommodate him now.

"Give me your eyes," he demanded.

Her gaze snapped to his, locking on to his face.

There was nothing slow or tender about his possession. He fucked her even more forcefully than he'd done the night before. Her body moved up and down his desk as he pounded into her, his pelvis slapping loudly against her ass. And then suddenly, he pulled out, circling his cock with his hand.

He worked his erection up and down, leaning forward as his release erupted onto her mound. His eyes were closed and his face showed the same signs of strain that invaded her entire body. It was almost an expression of agony, but then he opened his eyes, and they glowed warmly with satisfaction.

There was a raw edge to his gaze that made her prickle in awareness all over again.

The warm splash of his release on her pussy glistened in the light. He let out a sigh as the last jet burst from his rigid cock, and then he slowly stepped back to tuck himself back into his pants.

His hands slid up the insides of her thighs and then over her hips. He stared at the evidence of his possession on her skin and his eyes glinted with triumph.

"I love how you look right now," he said. "On my desk, your pussy red and swollen from my dick and my cum all over your skin. I'd love to keep you here all afternoon just so I can see you."

He walked away, and she wondered if indeed that was what he intended. To have her remain there, wet with his cum, her pussy bared and still quivering. But then he returned a moment later with a warm cloth and carefully wiped the fluid from her skin. When he was finished, he leaned over and helped her up and then lifted her down from his desk.

She stood, unsure of whether she should dress or remain as she was. He settled the matter when he reached for the skirt on the floor next to his chair and held it open so she could step into it.

He pulled the skirt back up her legs and then arranged her top, smoothing the rumpled look.

"My private bathroom adjoins my office. No one will bother you there. You can freshen up and then return to your desk."

Dismissed.

She walked away on shaky legs and opened the door a few feet from his desk. The bathroom was small and obviously catered to a man, but she could at least put herself back together so she didn't broadcast to the entire universe what had just transpired.

She ran cool water and splashed her face. When she got back to her desk, she could reapply makeup and do touch-ups.

When she reentered the office, Gabe was on the phone, so she went quietly to her desk and pulled out her bag, using powder and lip gloss, did her touch-up and went back to work. The problem was, she was still fully aroused, even after the mind-blowing orgasm Gabe had given her with his mouth.

But his rough possession of her had fueled another and now she was fidgety and tingly and she kept repositioning herself on the chair. Her pussy was hyperaware. Every time she moved, a curl of pleasure went winging through her belly.

This had to be a version of hell. Having Gabe across the room and needing to come again.

In an effort to distract herself, she tuned in to Gabe's conversation. He was discussing an event—tonight? And telling whomever he was on the phone with that he would certainly be there, and that he looked forward to it. That was probably a lie. Gabe hated social events even if he was perfect at them.

He was too blunt and impatient to genuinely enjoy being congenial and cordial, but it was part and parcel of the business. He wooed investors, charmed them right out of their wallets.

Ash was the more outgoing, natural charmer. He had it in spades. Mia always wondered why, of the two best friends her brother had, she drifted toward Gabe. Ash was gorgeous. Right to his toes. And he had a killer, charming smile that slayed women everywhere.

But it wasn't him she was attracted to. She viewed him more in the same vein as Jace. Indulgent big brother. Now Gabe? Never,

ever had she looked at him as a sibling. Her thoughts toward Gabe weren't even legal in most states, she was sure. Maybe it was simply because Gabe was more remote, more mysterious. A challenge.

Not that she was stupid enough to ever think she could conquer that particular mountain. Gabe was Gabe. Unapologetic. Hardass. Never going to change. Which was too bad, because it meant she was going to have to spend a lot of time finding another man who lived up to him.

She could imagine herself forever comparing every man after Gabe to him. Not fair to the new man, and a useless waste of her time. There was only one Gabe. Enjoy him for the present and then get over him.

She let out a sigh. It sounded so much simpler than she knew it was going to be. She was half in love with him already, and that was before sleeping with him. Some crushes just never went away. They built, instead, into something permanent, obsessive and all consuming.

Even though she knew better, she couldn't control the wash of emotions he evoked within her. Was it love? She wasn't sure. There were a lot of words she could use to describe her fascination with Gabe. She hadn't viewed any of her prior relationships as long-term. Nothing close to love entered the picture. They were fun. She mostly viewed her previous lovers with affection. But nothing came close to the way she felt about Gabe, and she had no idea if this was love or simply obsession.

Not that it mattered anyway. Love was just an entanglement she'd do well to veer as far away from as possible because Gabe would never return the sentiment. But the heart didn't always listen, and this was one thing she might not have any control over whatsoever.

Caroline would tell her to suck it up, enjoy the ride and not worry over the future. Live in the now. It was good advice, some she would do well to heed. But she also knew herself and that she would fret endlessly trying to analyze Gabe's every word, every action and emotion, and make the relationship into something it wasn't.

She sighed as the words she was trying so hard to concentrate on blurred before her. As first days went, she wasn't setting the world on fire with her work ethic. Unless giving the boss great sex on his desk counted.

"I hope you've studied up on those profiles."

Gabe's voice jerked her to awareness and she yanked her head up to see he was off the phone and staring across the room at her.

"We have an event to attend tonight. A cocktail party put on by a potential investor for our California resort. Mitch Johnson. He's in that stack of papers. You need to know everything you can about him and his wife, their three children, their interests and whatever else I've detailed. There will be others there as well, so make sure you familiarize yourself with the other names in that folder. But the most important is Mitch."

It took everything she had not to let her panic show. Talk about jumping straight from the frying pan and into the fire!

"What time? And what should I wear?"

"What do you have? And I don't mean that scrap of a dress you wore to the grand opening," he said with a scowl. "I'd prefer something that covered more of you. I'll be wearing a suit."

She frowned, mentally going over her wardrobe. It wasn't as though Jace wouldn't have bought anything she wanted, but other than the apartment he'd purchased for her, she'd tried very hard not to run to him with frivolous things. Her wardrobe was modest at best, and the dress she'd worn to the grand opening was the only thing suitable for a more formal occasion.

Gabe checked his watch and then leveled another stare in Mia's direction. "If we leave now, we have time to go buy you something appropriate."

She shook her head. "That's not necessary, Gabe. I'm just thinking over what I have that's suitable for a party like this."

He rose, ignoring her objection. "That's part of the deal, Mia. You're mine. I provide generously for what belongs to me. You'll need more than just one new dress, but that's all we have time for today. Perhaps the saleslady can ascertain your tastes, decide what looks good on you and gather other aspects of your wardrobe for us to pick up at a later date."

She blinked in surprise and when she continued to sit there, Gabe shifted impatiently and gave her a look that told her in no uncertain terms to get moving.

She grabbed her bag, straightened her skirt and hurried toward him, her knees still shaking from their earlier explosive fuck on the desk. And that was only the first day! She couldn't begin to imagine that if he were being patient and moving slowly what the future would bring.

chapter fourteen

Watching Gabe manage the saleslady was a bewildering experience for Mia. He cut through the selections with amazing precision, quickly vetoing the ones he didn't like while immediately picking up on the ones he did.

She'd honestly never been on a shopping trip for herself where she didn't make any of the choices. It was weird, but fascinating all at the same time.

It was obvious that Gabe had a definite eye for what flattered a woman. It was also obvious that he had no desire for her to wear anything remotely revealing. Sexy, yes. He'd picked out several selections that looked to die for and she could hardly wait to try them on. But there was nothing comparable to the dress she'd worn to the grand opening.

And when she did finally try on the dress he'd selected for her to wear tonight, she nearly fainted at the price tag. It was obscene. She tried to block it out as she surveyed her reflection in the mirror, but it was as if there were a neon sign blaring the price on the tag.

Still, she had to hand it to Gabe. The dress fit her like a dream and complemented her body and coloring. It was a red sheath that molded to her hips and then hugged her legs to just a few inches above her knees. It was sleeveless, but the bodice wasn't low cut, and while it bared her arms, it bared nothing of her front or back.

She never wore red. Maybe she considered it too . . . brazen. In your face. But the color looked fabulous on her. She looked like a sexy siren without baring her cleavage, though the material hugged her chest and clearly outlined the rounded mounds.

She looked . . . sophisticated. It was a look she liked. It made her feel like she belonged in Gabe's world.

"Mia, I'd like to see it."

Gabe's impatient voice filtered into the dressing room. She was surprised he hadn't just stripped her down in the retail area. The saleslady had closed the boutique for Gabe's visit and Mia and Gabe were the only two customers inside the store. For what Gabe was shelling out, it didn't surprise Mia that the woman was only too eager to comply with his wishes.

She opened the dressing room door and hesitantly slipped out. Gabe was sitting in one of the comfortable chairs in front of her room and his eyes blazed with immediate appreciation when his gaze settled on her.

"It's perfect," he said. "You'll wear that tonight."

He turned and motioned for the saleslady, who hurried over.

"Find her shoes to match this dress. You can put together the rest of the items we decided on along with any others you think will suit her and have them delivered to my home."

The woman beamed. "Yes, sir." Then she glanced at Mia's feet. "What size are you, Miss Crestwell?"

"Six," Mia murmured.

"I think I have the perfect pair of heels. I'll go get them now."

A moment later, the saleslady returned with a pair of silver heels that looked to be about five inches high. Before Mia could tell her there was no way in hell she could walk in those, Gabe frowned.

"She'll kill herself in those. Find something a little more reasonable."

Undaunted, the saleslady hurried away again and returned shortly with a pair of sleek, sexy black heels that at least didn't look as though they were held up by toothpicks.

"Those are perfect," Gabe said.

He glanced at his watch, and Mia could see he was ready to be done. Without a word, she ducked back into the dressing room and slipped out of the dress, careful not to wrinkle it. After she put her clothes back on, she handed the dress out to the saleswoman to wrap along with the shoes.

When she walked out of the dressing room, Gabe was standing, waiting for her. He put his hand on her back as they walked toward the front of the store, and it was like being scalded. Would her reaction to him ever diminish? Would there ever be a time he could touch her without eliciting a bone-deep shiver? It didn't seem likely given the intensity of the attraction between them. They were like two magnets inexorably pulled together.

After taking care of the purchases with the saleslady, Gabe ushered Mia outside to the waiting car and they began the ride back to his apartment. Knowing Caroline was going to wonder what the hell happened to her, Mia pulled out her phone and texted her friend.

With Gabe. Not sure if I'll stay over again tonight. Have an event to attend. Just went shopping, OMG. Will catch you up later.

Gabe glanced curiously at her but didn't comment. She slipped the phone back into her purse but mere seconds later, it rang. It was Jace's ring tone and she dug through her purse again.

Jace, she mouthed to Gabe.

Gabe nodded.

"Hey, Jace," Mia said as she answered the phone.

"Mia, how are things going? Everything all right?"

"Yes, of course. What about you? When are you and Ash going to be back?"

It was an answer she dreaded because she knew when Jace returned there was no way for her to hide that she was working for Gabe. And no way to know how much speculation or gossip Jace would hear regarding her and Gabe. She wasn't prepared to face Jace with this yet. Maybe never.

"Day after tomorrow. Things are going well here. I just wanted to check in on you and make sure you were doing okay."

In the background, Mia heard the soft laughter of a woman and Ash's voice. Her eyes widened as she remembered the chatter she'd overheard in the bathroom.

"Where are you?" she asked.

"In the hotel suite. We have one more meeting tomorrow and then we're attending a social event for potential local investors tomorrow night. We'll catch an early flight out the next morning and be back in New York by early afternoon."

If they were in the hotel suite, it was obvious that there was indeed a woman with Jace and Ash. It was clear there was a lot she hadn't known about her brother. It was weird and kind of icky to suddenly know aspects of her brother's sex life. No, thank you. She didn't want to imagine him in some illicit threesome with Ash and another woman.

"Okay, I'll see you then."

"Let's plan dinner together when I get back. I hate that I missed you at the grand opening. I haven't seen much of you lately."

"I'd like that."

"Okay then. It's a date. I'll call you when I get in."

"Love you," she said, feeling a surge of affection for her older brother. He'd been such a vital component of her life. Not quite a father figure, but definitely a steadying, supportive presence from a very early age. Not many men would have stepped in and taken care of a much younger sister when he himself had been so young when their parents died.

"Love you too, baby girl. See you soon."

Mia disconnected the call and sat for a moment staring down at the phone, guilt flooding her. There was the argument that she was an adult and fully capable of making her own decisions. But there was also the fact that Jace and Gabe were best friends and business partners. Coming between them wasn't something she wanted at all. And yet she couldn't turn away from the uncontrollable pull between her and Gabe.

"Something wrong?" Gabe asked.

She glanced up and offered her best effort at a smile. "No, not at all. Jace wants to have dinner when he gets back in. Then she paused and frowned because Gabe had exclusive rights to her time. "I'm assuming that's okay?"

Gabe sighed. "I'm not some bastard who's going to isolate you from your friends and family, Mia. Especially not Jace. I know how close the two of you are. Of course you're free to go to dinner with him. Afterward, though, you come to me."

She nodded, relieved at his easy acceptance. Gabe was possessive and controlling. She knew this before the contract had been produced. She had no way of knowing just how far he'd take things or how literally the contract would be interpreted.

"Tell me something, Gabe."

He looked at her in question.

"This job, as your personal assistant, is it just fluff? I mean I was introduced to everyone as your PA but then Eleanor is ordering in lunch for me and catering to me. It could be awkward for me. There's already talk—"

He held up his hand, his eyes suddenly fierce. "What talk?"

"I'll get to that in a minute," she said impatiently. "What I want to know is if my job is going to have any real substance. You're paying me a lot of money and I'd rather earn it and not just on my back."

He raised his eyebrows in surprise. "You're not some whore, Mia. I'll spank your ass if you ever suggest such a thing again."

It was a relief to hear him say it even if she never thought that that's how he viewed her. Perhaps it was more of the way she viewed herself, and she didn't like how it made her feel.

"As for your question, just because I didn't overwhelm you on your very first day doesn't mean that you won't have plenty to do. I'll work you into my routine and familiarize you with how best to assist me. You have to remember, this is new territory for me as well. I'm not used to having a personal assistant and it will be an adjustment for me."

"I just want to earn that salary, Gabe. It's important to me. You were all about how my talents and education were wasted at La Patisserie. I don't want to rely solely on my sexual favors to get me through this job."

"Understood. Now what the hell are you talking about with the gossip? Did anyone say anything to you? I'll have their asses."

"Not to me. Just within my hearing. And it wasn't intentional. I'm sure they would have died if they knew I was within hearing distance. I don't know who said what. I could barely process all the names and faces when I was introduced and I couldn't see who was talking because I was in the bathroom hiding in the stall."

Gabe looked at her incredulously. "Hiding in the bathroom?"

"They came in when I was using the bathroom," she said in exasperation. "The minute they started talking, I wanted to make sure they didn't know I was around. Talk about awkward."

"And what did they say?"

"Nothing that wasn't expected."

"Mia," he growled. "Tell me what was said."

"They wondered if you were fucking me. They also had quite

a bit to say about Jace and Ash, and after the phone call just now, I'm wondering how accurate their speculation was."

"I am fucking you," he said matter-of-factly. "That's not going to change. And they don't know for sure. We already discussed this. They'll think what they want to think and we can't change that. I'm damn sure not going to go out of my way to dissuade them of that notion because if they have their minds made up, nothing you or I do will change that. I don't give a fuck what they think. But they will be respectful of you and if I hear anything or if anything is said directly to you, I'll terminate the person responsible immediately."

There wasn't much left to say about that.

She purposely left off the part about the person breaking into his office, although she felt a twinge of guilt. Shouldn't he know that his personal life was being rummaged through? For that matter, shouldn't he know that this contract issue was now public—or at least office—knowledge?

The whole thing made her uncomfortable. Her loyalty was to Gabe. She didn't know those other women. She owed them nothing. If Gabe found out she knew and hadn't told him, he would be furious.

She sighed, hating the position she was in.

"What's wrong?" Gabe demanded.

She glanced up guiltily and then let out yet another sigh. "There's something you should know, Gabe."

"I'm listening."

"That wasn't all that was said in the bathroom today."

His frown intensified.

"There was a group of women, so no, I don't know who they are. I wouldn't have a clue. But they were discussing your . . . contract. There was speculation and then one of the women spoke up and confirmed that she'd seen the contract so she knew it was real."

"How the hell would she know something like that?"

It was clear Gabe didn't believe her, and he was going to be seriously pissed when she told him how the woman knew. She just hoped it didn't ruin the entire evening, because dealing with a pissed-off, brooding Gabe wasn't on her list of top ten favorite ways to spend the night.

"She says she broke into your office—picked the lock—because she was curious, and she went through your desk."

"What the fuck?"

The sound was explosive in the car, and she flinched at the whipcord lash of his voice.

"Let me get this straight. She says she picked the lock to my office and went through my desk because she was curious whether gossip about my personal life was true?"

The fury in his voice made her wary. He was seething, his entire body bristling with anger.

"That's what she said," Mia said in a low voice.

"I'm going to address this tomorrow. If I have to fire every single employee, I'll do it. I refuse to have people I can't trust working for me."

Mia closed her eyes. This was the last thing she wanted to happen. All she wanted was for Gabe to be aware so he could be more careful. Maybe even consider *not* housing personal, damning information in his office.

And then Gabe's hand closed around hers, squeezing reassuringly. "You don't have to worry, Mia. You said they had no knowledge of your presence in the bathroom. She won't know you told me. She'll think one of her officemates betrayed her."

"It still doesn't bring me any comfort knowing I'm responsible for someone losing their job," she said quietly.

"You're too softhearted, Mia. If she betrayed me in such a fashion, she doesn't deserve to work under me. I don't tolerate disloyalty of any kind."

Mia supposed that was true, but she wished it wasn't her who'd had to tell Gabe.

The car pulled to a stop outside Gabe's apartment building, and they got out. Gabe retrieved her boxes from the store and they headed up to his apartment.

As soon as they were inside his door, he tossed down the boxes and herded Mia into the living room and onto the plush, thick lambskin rug.

"On your knees," he said brusquely.

Disconcerted, she did as he ordered, sliding to her knees on the soft rug.

He began to unfasten his slacks, opening the fly and pulling out his semi-erect cock. He stroked, up and down, watching her all the while, his eyes fastened greedily on her mouth.

She watched in fascination as his erection stiffened and became engorged, rigidly hard and long. His hand over the length, pleasuring himself, was beautiful and erotic. The bite of anticipation was sharp in the air. She could feel his excitement, the edgy desire coiling through his body.

His hand slid to the head, squeezing lightly before pulling back toward his groin, making the distinction even more apparent of just how large he was. She knew, even before he spoke, what he would command her to do. It was all she could do not to squeeze her thighs together to quench the overwhelming ache. Her mouth watered in anticipation of having him on her tongue and tasting him.

He'd told her she'd get her chance. Now it was time.

"Today was all about you, Mia. Now it's all about me. Open your mouth."

She barely had time to process his demand before he was sliding, hard and deep, into her mouth. The shock of the contrast of hard and velvety soft brought her to greater awareness. She inhaled deeply, savoring his scent and the taste of him on her tongue. She ached for him, wanted him, wanted this possession. She couldn't get enough of him.

His hands tangled in her hair, gripping her head, holding her as he withdrew and then pushed into her mouth again.

"Ah, Mia. Your mouth is so sweet. I've been dreaming of this. Of fucking those pretty lips and coming all over your mouth."

She closed her eyes, her entire body quivering as his movements became more forceful. She was by no means an expert at giving head, but she wasn't a complete newbie when it came to oral sex either, and she was determined to make Gabe forget about any other woman who'd ever had her lips around his cock.

She sucked and licked, allowing him to slide in and out of her mouth as she lavished attention on his rigid length. His moan filled her ears, satisfying, fueling her confidence as she took the initiative and sucked him deeper.

"Goddamn," he groaned. "That's it, baby. Take me deeper. Harder. Love the feel of you. Love the way your throat convulses around my dick. Take it. Take more. All of me. That's it."

His fingers curled more tightly in her hair, until it was impossible for her to move. She realized he wanted control. He wanted to drive the action. And so she acquiesced and let him have his way.

Relaxing, she tilted her head back so she could take him deeper, and forced herself to take whatever it was he wanted to give her. She wanted him to be satisfied. She wanted to rock his *fucking world.*

He thrust, forcing himself deeper than before, and then he held himself at the back of her throat, her nose pressed into his groin. Just when she would have struggled for air, he released her, withdrawing and allowing her time to breathe.

Then he guided himself back to her mouth, still holding her hair tightly in his grasp. He rubbed his cock over her lips and then thrust hard and deep.

"Jesus, what you do to me," he said in a ragged voice. "Just kneel there, Mia. I'm going to come in your mouth and I want you to swallow every drop."

Already she could taste precum on her tongue, and she knew he was close. His entire body bristled with tension, a sign of his impending orgasm. This was no slow, sensual dance to completion. It was down-and-dirty, quick pleasure.

He began to thrust fast and hard, wet sucking noises echoing in her ears as her cheeks hollowed with each surge forward. Even though she knew his release was imminent, the first jet of semen still caught her by surprise.

Hot and salty, it spilled into her mouth, filling it as he continued his frantic pace. She swallowed, trying to catch up, but he kept coming and coming, the forceful jets hitting the back of her throat just before the head of his cock did. His hand tightened in her hair to the point of pain, but she ignored it. Then he lifted up on tiptoe, pushing into her until she was nearly overwhelmed by the depth of his entry. For a long moment, he held himself there as the last of his release pumped into her mouth. Finally his grip on her hair eased and he slowly allowed his cock to slide from her mouth.

She swallowed and coughed and then swallowed again, her eyes watering, but she forced her gaze to him, wanting to see his satisfaction. His approval.

But his eyes were filled with regret when he reached down with gentle hands to lift her up. His hands smoothed up and down her arms, from her wrist to her shoulders as he stared down at her.

"There's no hope for me with you, Mia. I make you promises I can't keep. I'm not myself when I'm with you. I'm not even sure I *like* myself right now. But I can't stop. God, even if it makes you hate me, I can't stop. I won't stop. My need for you consumes me and it's not going away."

Shocked by the frank admission, she could only stare up at him, her heart pounding at the implications. He touched her cheek with a gentle caress, regret still a shadow in his blue eyes.

"Go now and get dressed for tonight. We won't stay too long and then we'll go out for a late dinner."

chapter fifteen

Gabe was silent and brooding as they rode to a jazz club in the Village where the cocktail party was being hosted. Mia kept sending him seeking glances, and he could see the uncertainty in her eyes, but he couldn't bring himself to offer her reassurance. How could he?

He was unhinged. It embarrassed him how little control he exerted around her. With no other woman had he ever shown such a lack of restraint. His actions and responses were always precise. With Mia, he had none of the calm and distance that had been a part of his life since he was a teenager.

Hell, he'd all but mauled her. He'd raped her mouth, for God's sake. He'd hurried her into his apartment, shoved her onto her knees and then forced himself down her throat. His self-loathing knew no bounds, and yet he couldn't regret it. Worse, he knew he'd do it again. And again. He was already itching to get home later so he could have her in his bed, underneath him.

He'd been furious over the lack of respect shown to Mia in the office by the other employees, but he was a huge hypocrite. He'd shown her a far greater lack of respect by treating her like the whore she feared she was. Not that he ever, even *once*, considered her any such thing. But his actions hadn't mimicked his thoughts so far. His dick was doing all his thinking for him and

it didn't give a fuck that he wanted to slow down and not overwhelm her from the start. His dick wanted more. His hands and
mouth wanted more. His lust for her was all consuming and it
hadn't shown any sign of waning thus far. If anything, it increased
every time he made love to her.

Made love. He wanted to laugh. That was a much softer term
for what he'd done. Maybe he thought it in an attempt to make
himself feel better. He'd fucked her senseless. He'd danced a very
thin line in brutalizing her, and yet for all the remorse he felt, he
knew that next time wouldn't be any different no matter his intentions. He could say one thing all he wanted, but he was a damn
liar and he knew it.

"We're here, Gabe," Mia said, softly touching his arm.

He pulled himself from his thoughts to see they were parked
at the corner by the club. Recovering quickly, he got out and then
went around to open Mia's door and helped her from the car.

She looked fucking amazing, and he had a sinking feeling that
no matter the fact he'd chosen clothing for her that was purposely
unrevealing, there would be no less attention than if she'd shown
up in the dress she'd worn to the grand opening.

Mia was a beautiful woman, and there was something special
about her that drew people to her. She'd even stand out in a crowd
wearing a burlap sack.

Cupping her elbow in a casual manner, he guided her toward
the entrance. It took every bit of his restraint not to haul her into
his side and put his stamp of possession on her for the world to
see, but he wouldn't embarrass her, and he wouldn't threaten her
relationship—or his—with Jace. Knowing she was his behind
closed doors was enough. But he'd be damned if he watched other
men fawn over Mia tonight either.

As they reached the entrance to the room reserved for the
cocktail party, Gabe put a respectable distance between himself
and Mia. Every instinct screamed to have her close, to put the in-

visible *hands off* to any other man, but he forced himself to remain cool and distanced. She was here in a business capacity. Nothing else. She wasn't here as his date, his lover, his woman. Even if they both knew differently.

As soon as they walked in, Mitch Johnson saw them through the crowd and nodded before making his way toward where Gabe and Mia stood.

"Showtime," Gabe murmured.

Mia did a quick survey of the crowd and then focused in on Mitch, who was nearly to them. She put a genuine smile on her face and stood attentively at Gabe's side as they waited.

"Gabe, glad you could make it on such short notice," Mitch said, extending his hand.

"I wouldn't miss it," Gabe said smoothly.

He turned to Mia. "Mitch, I'd like you to meet my personal assistant, Mia Crestwell. Mia, this is Mitch Johnson."

She extended her hand with a warm, inviting smile. "It's a pleasure to meet you, Mr. Johnson. Thank you for having us."

Mitch looked delighted with Mia, a fact that made Gabe want to scowl, but he forced his composure to remain intact. Mitch was happily married. He wasn't the type to stray. But he was looking at Mia, and it pissed Gabe off.

"The pleasure is all mine, Mia. Please do call me Mitch. Can I get you two drinks? Gabe, there are several people I'd like you to meet."

"Nothing for me," Mia murmured.

Gabe shook his head. "I'll get something later, perhaps."

Mitch gestured toward the crowd. "If you'll come with me, I'll make the necessary introductions. I've been speaking with several business colleagues. They're very interested in your California venture."

"Excellent," Gabe said in satisfaction.

He and Mia followed Mitch through the crowd and Mitch took them to meet various parties, made introductions. The entire time business was discussed, Mia stood at Gabe's side, her expression one of interest. She was good. This had to be boring as hell for her, but she didn't let on if she was.

She completely surprised him when, in one of the conversation lulls, she looked at Trenton Harcourt and said, "And how is your daughter doing at Harvard? Is she enjoying her studies so far?"

Trenton looked taken aback and then beamed. "She's doing very well. My wife and I are very proud of her."

"I'm sure business law is a tough curriculum, but think of how useful she'll be to your own endeavors when she graduates. Always nice to have connections within the family," Mia said, a twinkle in her eye.

The group laughed and Gabe felt a surge of pride. Apparently she *had* studied up.

Then he watched as she took over the gathering, addressing personalized comments to the other men present. She maintained a steady flow of conversation and had the men completely in her thrall. He watched closely, waiting for any inappropriate look or remark, but the men were courteous and seemed utterly charmed by Mia's sweetness.

"Are you any relation to Jace Crestwell?" Mitch asked, when the conversation paused.

Mia went still but maintained her composure. "He's my brother." Her tone was almost defensive, just an edge that Gabe caught, though he doubted the others picked up on it.

"I got her first," Gabe said lazily. "She's smart and perfect for the position as my PA. I don't mind fighting Jace for who brings her into the business."

The others laughed.

"Smart man, Gabe. Always a hardass in business. But hey, to the victor goes the spoils, eh?" Trenton said.

"Exactly," Gabe replied. "She's a valuable asset and one I have no intention of allowing to slip through my fingers."

Mia's face bloomed with color but the pleasure in her eyes was well worth Gabe's making the effort to ensure he made it clear he valued Mia as an employee.

"If you'll excuse me and Mia, I see a few other people I need to say hello to," Gabe said smoothly.

He cupped her elbow and steered her away from the group, and started across the room to get them both a drink when he came to a complete stop, his gaze riveted on the doorway. He uttered a curse beneath his breath, but Mia heard it, and she glanced up, her brows furrowed. Then she followed his gaze to the door and grimaced.

His father had just entered the room, a gorgeous, much younger blonde wrapped securely around his arm. Damn it. What was his father doing here? Why hadn't he let Gabe know so that at least he'd be prepared? After seeing his mother over the weekend and doing all he could to lift her spirits, it angered him to see his father here with his latest arm candy.

Mia touched his arm, her face a wreath of sympathy. There was no way to avoid the confrontation. His father had already seen him and was making his way through the crowd in Gabe's direction.

"Gabe!" his father said, his eyes brightening as he approached. "Glad I caught you here. It's been too long since we saw each other last."

"Dad," Gabe said shortly.

"Stella, I'd like you to meet my son, Gabe. Gabe, this is Stella."

Gabe nodded curtly but didn't extend a warm greeting. His skin itched and he only wanted to be away from this situation. All he could picture was his mother's face, the sadness in her eyes. The confusion and betrayal she still felt after her husband of thirty-nine years had abruptly left her.

"It's a pleasure," Stella said huskily, her gaze drifting with lingering precision over Gabe.

"How have you been, Son?" his father asked. If he noticed the awkwardness, he didn't react. Or maybe he was completely oblivious to all the hurt he'd caused his family by his actions.

"Busy," Gabe said shortly.

His father waved his arm. "Like that's anything new. You should take some time off. Take a break. I'd love to have you out to the house. It would be nice to catch up on all that's going on with you."

"What house?"

Gabe's voice would have frozen fire.

"Oh, I purchased a house in Connecticut," his father said airily. "I'd love for you to see it. We could have dinner. Are you free any night this week?"

Gabe's jaw clenched until it ached. Mia softly cleared her throat and then stepped forward, a gentle smile on her face.

"Would you like something to drink, Mr. Hamilton? I'm going to run to the ladies' room a moment, but on my way back I'd be happy to get you and Gabe something."

Gabe's father looked at her in puzzlement a moment before recognition flared in his eyes. "Mia? Mia Crestwell? Is that really you?"

Gabe's father had only met her on two occasions, when Mia was much younger, and only briefly. He was surprised his father even remembered.

Mia nodded. "Yes, sir. I'm working for Gabe now as his personal assistant."

His father smiled and leaned over to kiss Mia's cheek. "My how you've grown up. The last time I saw you was years ago. You've grown into quite a lovely young lady."

"Thank you," Mia said. "Now about that drink?"

"Scotch on the rocks," his father said.

"Nothing for me," Gabe said flatly.

Mia sent Gabe a look filled with sympathy and then hurried

away in the direction of the ladies' room. He couldn't blame her. There was so much tension in the air that it was extremely awkward.

He watched her retreat and realized how much he wanted to be away from this place. In his apartment, behind closed doors, Mia in his arms, him losing himself in her over and over.

"So how about that dinner?" his father persisted.

Mia escaped into the ladies' room in relief. Since she had no need of the facilities and it was just an excuse to escape the uncomfortable situation between Gabe and his father, she touched up her lipstick and surveyed her reflection in the mirror.

To her surprise, the door opened and Stella walked in, positioning herself at the mirror next to Mia. Stella glanced over conspicuously before reapplying her lipstick as well.

"So, tell me," Stella began, still intent on her lipstick application. "Is the gossip true about Gabe Hamilton and the expectations he has for his women?"

Startled, Mia nearly dropped her lipstick and fumbled to tuck it back into her small clutch. She turned to Stella, taken aback by her brazenness.

"Even if I knew the details of Mr. Hamilton's personal life, I would most certainly not betray such a confidence."

Stella rolled her eyes. "Come on, give a girl the inside track. I'd love to get up next to him and if he's the beast I suspect in bed, bring it on."

Mia shook her head. "You're here with his *father*."

Stella waved her hand dismissively. "Money. But Gabe has a lot more and he's younger and more virile. If you can have the younger Hamilton, why wouldn't you go for it? Got any tips for me? You work for him. Surely you've had to deal with his past women at some point."

Mia shouldn't have been shocked, but frankly she was befuddled by the straightforward, unapologetic grasping of the other woman. Not knowing how to begin to respond, she simply turned and exited the bathroom. She shook her head as she headed toward the bar. She couldn't believe the woman's daring!

She ordered the Scotch and then waited as the bartender poured the drink. After, she turned, seeking Gabe and his father in the crowd. They were still standing where she'd left them, and Gabe looked anything but happy.

His face was cold, his eyes hard. It was as if he were facing an opponent he fully intended to wipe the face of the earth with.

She blew out her breath. She knew it had to suck to have your parents split up after so many years. Gabe had grown up in a healthy, stable home environment while she and Jace had struggled to pull the pieces back together when their parents were killed. In a way, Gabe's parents' divorce was much like losing them, even if they were still alive, because nothing would ever be the same again and he'd be forced to view his parents as separate entities now.

She grimaced when she saw Stella return to where Gabe and his father stood. The woman had no hesitancy whatsoever as she looped her arm through Gabe's, turning up her one-hundred-watt smile as she blatantly flirted.

Her tinkly laughter drifted to Mia as she neared with the drink. To Mia's surprise, Gabe returned Stella's smile, one of those seductive, killer smiles that immediately put Mia's back up. It was a smile Gabe used when he was on the prowl. A smile that told the woman there was no question he was interested.

What the ever-loving hell?

Mia stood a few steps in front of the men, unnoticed, as she attempted to control the vicious jealousy—and anger—that surged through her veins. She wasn't a jealous person, she reminded herself.

To hell with that. She was insanely jealous and she wanted nothing more than to tear the blonde's hair out by the roots. Was Gabe out of his mind? Was this the sort of woman who appealed to him? One clearly out for only what she could gain?

But then he preferred no emotional entanglements in his relationships. He demanded it. But over her dead body was he going to flirt with some floozy when he had a contract with Mia. She'd kick both their asses if that's what it took.

She shoved forward, extending the drink to Gabe's father.

"Thank you, my dear," Mr. Hamilton said with a warm smile.

Stella turned a pout up at Gabe. "Dance with me, Gabe. The music's just going to waste and I'm ready to move."

Gabe chuckled and it grated on every one of Mia's nerves.

"If you'll excuse us," Gabe said to his father. He didn't even look at Mia as he guided Stella toward the section marked for dancing.

Mia stared in absolute astonishment as Gabe pulled the blonde into his arms—way too damn close for some casual dance—and he smiled down at her. Smiled! He rarely smiled at anyone.

And he'd left her with his father, which was awkward enough given the fact that Gabe had just walked away with his father's date. She couldn't very well escape to the bathroom again. She'd already used up that excuse.

She noticed Mr. Hamilton's frown as his gaze drifted to where Gabe and Stella were dancing. She was helpless to avert her own gaze, her anger growing by the minute when she saw Gabe's hand suggestively slide down the woman's body.

To hell with this. She wasn't going to stand around while Gabe felt up some other woman—his father's date no less! She'd done her duty. She'd been nice and personable. She'd schmoozed his investors and rattled off all that useless trivia she'd spent the afternoon memorizing.

She had better things to do. Mainly go home and vent to Caroline.

chapter sixteen

"What a jerk," Caroline said. "I can't believe he let that skank attach herself to him like that. Especially when he has you!"

Mia smiled at the fierce loyalty in her friend's voice. The two were slouched on the couch after Mia had rid herself of the dress that just stood as a mockery of her entire evening. Fat lot of good it had done to look fabulous when Gabe's attention was directed elsewhere.

No one knew of her relationship with Gabe, which meant no one knew of her embarrassment, but it hadn't prevented the heavy cloak of humiliation she suffered.

"Who knows what he's thinking," Mia said wearily. "But I wasn't going to hang around there and watch those two make goo-goo eyes at each other. It was nauseating."

"And you shouldn't!" Caroline exclaimed.

Her eyes gleamed with sudden light, and that was a signal to Mia that she should probably run.

"So is he as good as I imagine him to be in the sack?"

Mia sighed in exasperation. "For God's sake, Caro."

"Hey, give me something to work with here. All I have are fantasies. You have the real thing."

"He's a god, okay? He blew me away. Nothing to compare it

to, and I've had good in the past. I've just never had holy-shit good before."

"Day-um," Caroline said in a mournful voice. "I knew it was some heavy shit when you called to have me get a bag ready for you. Didn't even work for him a day before you had a sleepover. The dude moves fast. You have to hand it to him."

Mia scowled. "Yeah, he moves fast all right."

"So you want to order takeout and gorge ourselves on the ice cream in the freezer? Or did you already eat?"

Mia shook her head. "We were supposed to have dinner after the cocktail party. That was until Blondie hit the scene."

Caroline reached for her phone. "Pizza sound good?"

"That sounds heavenly," Mia breathed.

As Caroline was looking through her contacts, the buzzer sounded. Mia got up, motioning for Caroline to stay put. "You call the food in. I'll see who it is."

She went to the intercom and pressed the button. "Yes?"

"Mia, get your ass down here right now."

Gabe's furious voice filled the apartment. Caroline dropped her phone, her eyes wide.

"What's the point, Gabe?" Mia said, allowing her irritation to bleed through.

"Swear to God if you don't get your ass down here right now, I'll come up there and haul you out myself, and I don't give a damn if you're dressed or not. You have three minutes to make an appearance."

Mia shut off the intercom, anger bristling over her. She walked back to where Caroline sat and flopped down.

"Well," Caroline said, drawing out the word. "If he's here, demanding your presence, he's not with Blondie obviously."

"Are you suggesting I answer that arrogant summons?" Mia asked incredulously.

Caroline shrugged. "Well, let's put it this way. I absolutely think he'd find a way to come up here and drag you out of this apartment. Might be better to go peacefully and figure out the Blondie situation firsthand. After all, he's here and she's not." She checked her watch. "But now you only have like two minutes before he tears the building apart."

Mia sighed and then bolted for her bedroom, unsure of why she was even giving Gabe the time of day after the scene at the cocktail party. It was enough to turn her stomach. Still, she hurriedly dressed in jeans and a T-shirt, and as an afterthought, shoved clothes to wear to work the next day in her bag. Better to be prepared than sorry.

After collecting her toiletries, she hurried back past Caroline and blew her a kiss.

"Text me and let me know you're still alive or I'll assume he's killed you and I'll start looking for the body," Caroline said.

Mia waved over her shoulder and let herself out of the apartment, hurrying toward the elevator. When the doors opened, Gabe was standing a few feet away, his jaw bulging and a look of fury in his eyes.

He stalked toward her, not giving her any time to advance on her own. He was one big ball of pissed-off alpha male, and he was coming right at her.

She took one step off the elevator and his hand closed around hers, yanking her past the alarmed-looking doorman toward the entrance to the apartment building. Mia managed a reassuring smile at the doorman, not wanting him to call the cops, before she turned her attention back to Gabe. His grasp was tight and uncompromising, and his anger rolled in hot waves from his body.

What the hell did he have to be so pissed off about? It wasn't like she hooked up with some other guy in front of him at a cocktail party they were at together.

She sighed when he stuffed her in the back of his car and then walked around to the other side. As soon as he slid in next to her, the car pulled away.

"Gabe . . ."

He turned to her, his expression fierce. "Just shut up, Mia. Don't say a goddamn word to me right now. I'm too pissed off at you to be reasonable. I need to calm down before I can even think about discussing this with you."

She lifted a shoulder in a careless shrug and turned away, refusing to meet his stare any longer. She could feel the burst of frustration from him, heard his low growl of impatience and irritation. But she ignored him, continuing to focus on the passing lights and the city all a twinkle with the colors of night.

She should have just remained at her apartment, but she wanted this confrontation. She'd simmered with anger all evening and now that Gabe was forcing the issue, she was armed and ready.

They rode in silence, though his anger was a force all on its own. She never once looked in Gabe's direction, refusing to show any weakness. And she knew it only pissed him off more.

When they reached his building, he yanked open her door, grasped her hand and hauled her out. His fingers wrapped firmly around her upper arm, he walked her into the building and onto the elevator.

As soon as his apartment door shut behind him, his lips tightened and he seemed to be working to maintain his temper as he stared down at her.

"In the living room," he ordered. "We have a lot to talk about."

"Whatever," she muttered.

She wrested her arm from his grasp and walked into the living room. She flopped onto the couch and then stared expectantly at him.

He paced back and forth in front of her, stopping to glare at her. He sucked in his breath and then shook his head. "I can't even talk to you right now I'm so pissed."

She arched an eyebrow, unimpressed by the fact that he was the one angry. She was pissed. She had a right to be.

"*You're* pissed?" she asked incredulously. "What the hell for? Did your floozy turn you down after all? I can't imagine that to be the case. She was pretty hot to get into your pants."

Confusion wrinkled his brow. "What the hell are you talking about?"

When she would have been more than happy to explain, he raised his hand, cutting her off. "First you're going to listen while I explain just why I'm so goddamn pissed off. Then, when I've had a chance to calm down, I'm going to redden your ass."

"The hell you will," she snapped.

"You disappeared," he bit out. "I had no idea where you went, what happened to you, if some asshole had taken you or if you were sick or hurt. What the fuck were you thinking? Did it ever occur to you to give me the courtesy of an explanation? If you had said you wanted to go home, I would have taken you myself."

She surged to her feet, angry at his obliviousness. Was he really that thick?

"If you weren't so glued to your father's date, you might have noticed!"

Understanding flashed in his eyes, and he shook his head as he sighed. "So that's what this is about. Stella."

"Yeah, Stella. Or whatever the hell her name is."

He shook his head again. "You were jealous. For God's sake, Mia."

"Jealous? You're so damn arrogant and self-centered, Gabe. It has nothing to do with jealousy and everything to do with respect. You and I are in a relationship. It may not be a traditional one. But we have a contract. And by God you damn well belong to me and I'm not sharing you with some blond bimbo."

He looked completely startled by her vehemence. Then he threw back his head and laughed, which only served to piss her off more. His shoulders still shaking, he said, "You just managed to curb the edge of my anger enough that I'm going to spank that pretty ass of yours. Get in the bedroom, Mia. And strip."

"What the fuck?"

"And watch your mouth. Jace would wash it out with soap."

"Don't be a hypocrite. You and Jace have toilet mouths."

"Bedroom, Mia. Now. For each minute you delay, you get an extra five smacks, and if you don't think I'm serious, try me. You've already earned twenty."

She openly gaped at him, but when he glanced down at his watch, she bolted for the bedroom. She was insane. She should *so* be out the door, and yet here she was, stripping down to nothing in his bedroom so he could spank her.

A shiver worked up her body. Anticipation coiled in her belly. Anticipation? It made no sense to her. The idea of being spanked was repugnant, and yet somehow it all seemed so . . . enticing and erotic. His hand on her ass. Marking her. Exerting his dominance over her.

She was out of her damn mind. But that wasn't a new thought. Signing the contract in the first place made her sanity questionable.

When Gabe entered the bedroom, she was naked and sitting on the edge of the bed, hesitant and worried, her mind fried over what was to come. She wasn't at all sure she was going to like this. She was fairly certain she wouldn't. But there was that small part of her that was intrigued and aroused by the idea of his hand on her ass.

Her heart leapt into her throat when he stopped in front of her, his presence powerful and consuming.

"Get up, Mia," he ordered calmly, all traces of anger gone.

Shakily, she rose and he went to the bed to sit. He scooted to the headboard, leaning back against the pillows, and then he held out his hand to her. She climbed onto the bed, and hesitantly took his hand. He pulled her across his lap, positioning her facedown, her belly over his thighs so her ass was perched within easy reach.

He caressed the plump cheeks, rubbing lightly over the entire expanse of flesh.

"Twenty blows, Mia. I expect you to count them. At the end, you will thank me for spanking you and then I'm going to fuck your brains out."

Her mind exploded with *whoa* and *what the fuck* and *oh, yes please*. All at the same time. She was crazy. There was no other explanation for it.

The first smack startled her and she let out a brief exclamation. She wasn't sure if it was because it hurt or if it just surprised her.

"You get one more now," he said grimly. "Count them out, Mia."

Oh shit.

He rubbed his hand over her ass and then the next smack came.

"One," she choked out.

"Very good," he purred.

He soothed the area with his palm and then smacked a different part of her ass. She nearly forgot to say the count and rushed to say, "Two," before he tacked on yet another.

Her entire ass tingled and after the initial burn, arousal hummed, sweet and deep, coiling in her belly. Her pussy clenched, and she shifted restlessly to alleviate the unrelenting ache.

Three. Four. Five. By the time she got to a dozen, she was breathless, overheated. Squirming all over Gabe's lap. His caresses drove her insane. A contrast to the harder blows of his hand. And yet he never struck her too hard. He used just enough bite to deliver the edge, and by the sixteenth blow, she was begging for . . . more. Harder.

Her entire ass was on fire, but the burn was beautiful. Intensely pleasurable. Never before had she experienced anything like it. She was so close to orgasm, and she would have never dreamed that she could achieve release with a mere spanking. Or that she would actually revel in the experience.

"Be still and don't you dare come," Gabe warned. "You have two more, and if you orgasm, I'll damn well make sure you don't enjoy the next spanking nearly as much."

Sucking in a deep breath, she closed her eyes and made her entire body go tense, staving off the orgasm that threatened to swallow her whole.

"Nineteen," she said, so breathless it came out as a whisper.

"Louder," he demanded.

"Twenty!"

Oh God, it was over. She sagged onto the bed, her entire body heaving with exertion, from the pressure of holding her breath and working desperately not to come. Her pussy was on fire. It was as if he'd spanked her there, as if she'd felt every single swat to her clit. It pulsed and tightened and she knew if he were to so much as breathe on it, she would go off like a rocket.

And it pissed her off. Her lack of control. The fact that he'd made her love something she should find abhorrent.

He let her lie there a moment, until her breathing calmed and she didn't lurk so close to the edge of release. Then he gently lifted her and rolled her to her back. He came with her, looming over her as he yanked at his fly and at his clothing.

His mouth found her breasts, tugging with his lips, sucking as he wrestled with his clothing. When his shirt came off, she expected him to spread her and fuck her hard, but instead he levered himself off the bed and then took hold of her legs, pulling her to the edge of the bed.

He spread her legs, positioned his cock at her entrance and

stared down at her with intense, glittering eyes. "Enjoy your spanking, Mia?"

"Fuck you," she said rudely, still pissed over her reaction. He unsettled her. He made her question everything about herself, and she didn't like that feeling one bit.

His jaw tightened at the blatant disrespect in her voice. "No, Mia darling. That's fuck *you*."

He pushed in deep with one forceful shove. She gasped and arched her back, her hands balling into tight fists, clenching the covers with her fingers.

"Thank me for spanking you," he said.

"Go to hell."

He withdrew, pulling out until just the head of his cock rimmed her entrance, stretching and teasing.

"Wrong answer," he purred. "Say thank you and make it pretty."

"Just do it. Finish it," she said, her desperation mounting. She didn't want to be this weak, begging person, but she was perilously close to losing any semblance of pride when it came to him.

He kissed her. But it was a punishing kiss, meant solely to remind her that she was nowhere near in charge. And still, it made her that much hungrier for him. Her need was all consuming. She was crazy with it.

"You forget who calls the shots here, Mia darling," he murmured as he grazed her jawline. "I own you. Which means it doesn't matter what you want. Only what I want."

Her eyes narrowed and her lips pursed. "Oh bullshit, Gabe."

He withdrew slowly, dragging his cock through the swollen flesh of her pussy. "I have a contract that says I do," he said silkily. He drove deep again, shocking her with the force and speed of his possession.

"I could tear up that contract at any time," she said crossly. She was tempted to do so now, just to piss him off as much as she was pissed off. But it wasn't what she wanted, and they both knew it.

He went still, his body tense over hers, his lips halting on its path down her neck where they'd eventually slide over her breasts. Her nipples hardened in anticipation and she arched upward in a silent plea. She wanted his mouth on her. She was so on the edge. So ready. And so very pissed off.

"Yes, you could," he said lazily. "Is that what you want, Mia? You want to tear up the contract and walk away right now? Or do you want me to fuck you?"

Damn it but the man made her crazy. He knew damn well what she wanted, but he was going to make her say it. He was going to make her beg.

His gaze grew more piercing. He thrust hard and held himself still within her. She pulsed and twitched around his cock, a silent plea for him to continue. But he remained still, waiting.

"Say it, Mia."

She was near tears of frustration. She was so close. So on the edge. She couldn't even remain still, so hyperaware was her body.

"Thank you," she muttered.

"Thank you for what?" he prompted.

"Thank you for spanking me!"

He chuckled. "Now tell me what you want."

"I want you to fuck me, damn it!"

"Say please," he said, a smirk toying at his mouth.

"Please, Gabe," she said huskily, hating the desperation in her voice. "Please fuck me. End this please."

"Good things happen when you obey me. Remember that, Mia. Remember that the next time you think to take off without so much as a word to me."

He leaned over, threading his hands through her hair. He gripped her head, then let his hands slide down to her shoulders where he dragged her back to meet his forceful thrusts. He pounded into her, setting a relentless pace that blinded her to everything else but him, his cock driving in and out of her.

She had no idea what she cried out. *Stop. Don't stop.* She was begging. Hoarsely pleading. Tears streamed down her face as she bowed her back completely off the bed.

And then Gabe was there, surrounding her, his arms gathering her close. He murmured soft, soothing words to her. Stroked her hair as he pulsed wetly into her body.

"Shhh, Mia darling. It's okay. It's okay now. I've got you. Let me take care of you."

She was utterly wasted and bewildered by what had just occurred. She wasn't this person. She wasn't into kink and spankings and forceful sex. She liked it slow and tender. Leisurely. Taking her time. Sex with Gabe was like an inferno. He was a force like she'd never encountered, and she knew she never would again.

He was unpeeling her layer by layer, exposing a part of her she wasn't familiar with. It made her feel vulnerable and uncertain. What was she supposed to do with this new Mia?

He lay atop her, kissing her temple as he stroked through her hair with soothing motions. She cuddled into him, seeking his warmth and his strength. He was a safe haven when so much was in turmoil. Her mind, her body, her very heart.

When he found her lips, this time he was exquisitely tender where before he'd been possessive and demanding. Sweet, so very sweet. Like they were lovers, reconnecting after an emotional round of lovemaking. Only she could hardly count having her ass spanked and then fucked long and hard as lovemaking.

Sex. It was only sex. Hot, mind-blowing, toe-curling, emotionless sex. But sex all the same. And it was a dangerous mistake to ever consider it anything else.

chapter seventeen

Gabe lay in the darkness, his gaze fixed sightlessly on the ceiling as Mia lay nestled in the crook of his arm. He knew she was awake. She hadn't yet settled into the soft breathing and limp body he associated with her rest. But she lay there quietly, curled into his side, almost as though she were processing everything that had occurred.

He was a bastard. He knew it. Suffered some regret. But he knew he wouldn't stop. He'd broken every promise he'd made to her so far, and yet he knew he'd continue to break them. There was no easing her into his lifestyle. No gentleness. No patience. She made him crazy. She unhinged him.

He opened his mouth, then closed it again. He owed her an explanation for tonight and yet his pride wouldn't allow him to tell her why. It pissed him off that she'd walked out in a huff, and yet at the same time, it amused him and he felt pride that she'd basically said *fuck you* to him and left.

If it were any other guy she was involved with, a stunt like he pulled tonight would be grounds for him to cheer her actions. He'd be the first one to tell her to run far, far away as fast as she could. Then he'd want to kick the bastard's ass who used her in such a fashion.

But if she tried to walk away from him, he knew damn well he wouldn't let her escape. He'd go after her with everything he had, and short of tying her to his bed and holding her captive, he wasn't letting her go. Not yet.

"Tonight wasn't what you thought," he said, surprising himself when the statement slipped from his lips.

Goddamn it. He didn't want to get into this with her. Not any time. If she couldn't stick around long enough to see for herself what happened, then why should he have to explain it?

Because she's different. You've been a dick. You owe this to her.

Mia stirred against him, lifted herself up to her elbow, her hair falling in a curtain over her shoulder. He reached for the lamp, his urge to see her nagging at him. The soft glow illuminated her features and her dusky skin shone in the low light.

She was beautiful. There was no other word for it. There was a sweetness to her that inspired a physical ache. Except maybe when she was pissed off at him, but he had to admit, he'd been hugely turned-on when she got all scornful and puffed up like a ticked-off kitten. He'd wanted to fuck her right then and there and let her use those claws on his back.

"I thought it was pretty obvious what was going on," Mia said, her eyes narrowing. "Blondie cornered me in the bathroom and made it plain she'd prefer the younger, richer Hamilton over the older, less wealthy version, and she wanted pointers on how to get you in her bed. Next thing I know, the two of you are glued together on the dance floor and your hand's on her ass, not to mention a few other places."

She paused and took in a deep breath. He could tell she was getting angry all over again, but he admired that she put it out there. She wasn't afraid of him, and he liked that. He didn't want a meek mouse, no matter that he wanted someone utterly submissive. There was a difference between submissive and spineless.

He wanted a strong woman with a mind of her own, but one who wouldn't chafe under his dominance. Mia may well be the perfect match for him, and he wasn't sure what to make of that.

"I know our relationship isn't public. I get that I was there in a professional capacity. No one knows about us. There should have been no embarrassment involved for me. But I was humiliated and there was nothing I could do about it. I wanted to crawl under a table and die because I kept thinking, we have a contract. I belong to him, but damn it, if I belong to him then he goddamn well belongs to me too, and there you were all cozy and touchy-feely with Blondie. You *smiled* at her, Gabe. And you don't smile at *anyone*."

His chest twisted at the edge of pain in her voice. At the accusation in her tone.

"It pissed me off and it humiliated me because all I could think was that you weren't satisfied with me and that I wasn't woman enough for you. We've been together, what, a few times and you're already shopping for your next contract?"

"That's bullshit," Gabe said, angry that she'd been hurt by his actions. "Complete and utter bullshit. Look, I danced with her. I let her make her play for me because I wanted my father to see what he was tangled up in. She wasn't subtle at all and I wanted my dad to see that. It pissed me off when he walked in with her and it made it worse that she was putting the moves on me with my dad right there. I haven't gotten over my parents' divorce. I'm not used to seeing my dad with a new woman every week. My mother is at home grieving for her marriage while my dad doesn't seem to give a fuck. So yeah, I let her make her play and I made it obvious what she was doing, because my dad needs to see what kind of woman he replaced my mother with."

Mia's eyes softened and some of the anger left her as she touched Gabe on the arm. "It hurts you to see him with all these other women."

"Hell yes it does," Gabe bit out. "I looked up to them my entire fucking life. I was humiliated when Lisa and I divorced. I felt like the biggest damn failure because here my parents had kept it together and worked through their differences for almost *forty years* and I couldn't keep my marriage together for *three*. They were an example of what marriage could be. They were proof that love does exist in this day and age and that marriages can make it if people work at it. Then all of a sudden, my dad walks out and they're divorced within months. I still don't understand it. It makes no goddamn sense. And I *hate* what it's done to my mom. I'm so goddamn furious with my father and yet I love him. He let me down. He let our *family* down. And I can't forgive him for that."

"I understand," she said gently. "When my parents died, I was so angry with them. How stupid is that? It wasn't their fault. They certainly didn't intend to get themselves killed. They were the victims of a drunk driver. And yet I was so angry with them for leaving me. If it weren't for Jace, I don't know what I would have done. He was my rock. I'll never forget all he did for me."

Gabe squeezed her to him. He knew she'd had a very difficult time after her parents had died. Jace had despaired of how to help her, of what to do. She was angry and grief stricken, and she'd seemed unreachable. It had driven Jace crazy as he tried to reach her, to take care of her and offer her love and support.

Jace had raised her, like a substitute father. Only he'd been everything to Mia. Father, mother and brother. Protector, sole source of support. Not many men would have done what he did, pushing everything to the side, any possibility of a family or relationship in order to take sole responsibility for a younger sister. Gabe admired him for that.

Mia hesitated and then put a small distance between her and Gabe, a fact he didn't like, but he resisted the urge to anchor her more firmly against him. The action seemed too desperate, too needy. And he didn't want to need anyone.

"Gabe . . ." She broke off, her expression filled with uncertainty. She seemed to battle whether or not to pose the question burning in her eyes.

He waited, unsure himself of whether he wanted her to ask whatever it was she was working up the nerve to say.

"What happened with you and Lisa? I know it hurt you—damaged you. I know she was the one to leave and that it had far-reaching ramifications."

Gabe was silent a long moment. The very last thing he wanted was to discuss Lisa, or the betrayal he'd felt over the way they'd split up. Did he owe it to Mia to explain? No. He didn't owe anyone a damn thing. But still, he felt himself loosening, wanting to explain to her so that maybe she would understand why the contract, why the exacting requirements. He'd never once explained himself to any of the women he'd been with since his divorce. It wasn't a habit he wanted to get into. But Mia was different, and he realized this even as he grappled with the knowledge that her being different was dangerous.

"I'm sure the contract seems . . . extreme . . . to you," he began. "Even cold. Heartless. Domineering. It probably makes me a huge asshole. There are a lot of words that come to mind."

She didn't respond, but he could see the knowledge in her eyes. There was no quick denial. No attempt to make him feel better, and he liked that about her. But there was no judgment either. Just . . . curiosity.

"Lisa and I shared a relationship in which I had complete control. I don't want to delve into the whys and wherefores. Some things just are. It was—is—a need that I have. I don't have some traumatic childhood that makes me the way I am. No emotional instability. It's a kink, but more than that, it's who I am. I can't change that for anyone. I don't want to change. I'm comfortable with who I am and what I want and need."

She nodded. "I get that."

"I don't know why she left. Maybe I no longer satisfied her. Maybe she no longer wanted the kind of relationship we shared. Hell, maybe she only agreed in an effort to make me happy. Maybe she was never truly happy. I don't know. At this point I don't care. But when she left, she made a lot of baseless accusations. She crucified me in divorce court and to the media. She told anyone who would listen that I abused her and my power over her. She painted the relationship as nonconsensual, which was bullshit, because I let her know from day one what my expectations and needs were. I was very careful that she went into our relationship and marriage with her eyes wide open."

Mia's eyes became troubled and instantly on the heels came a look of sympathy. He hated that. He didn't need anyone's pity. It wasn't why he was spilling his guts in some sappy, postcoital, snugly moment. He just wanted Mia to understand.

"If that kind of relationship no longer worked for her I wouldn't have held that against her. All she had to do was be honest and say she wanted out. I would have provided generously for her. I would have supported her decision. Instead, she went on the attack and painted me as some abusive monster. That I'll never forgive. I learned a very hard lesson with my marriage to her. I never went into another relationship without means of protecting myself from those kinds of accusations. It may be viewed as extreme, but I don't enter into a single relationship without signed, detailed contracts. I don't do one-night stands. I don't have casual sex. If a woman is going to be in my bed, she has all the facts and she's signed a contract that protects both of us."

"Maybe she needed to convince herself that you were this terrible person in order for her to be able to leave," Mia said softly. "I can't imagine walking out on a marriage is ever easy."

Gabe snorted. "Tell that to my dad. You're naïve, Mia. Sweet, but naïve. People walk out of marriages every day. I've always wondered what makes someone wake up one morning and say,

'Hey, this is the day I'm going to ditch my husband or wife.' Loyalty should count for something. Nobody wants to work it out nowadays. It's too easy to get a divorce lawyer and move on."

She put her hand on his chest, the gesture infinitely soothing. He liked her touching him. God help him, but he wasn't sure he'd ever get enough. He'd take and take from Mia until there was nothing left. Until she became a Lisa and could endure it no longer. He never wanted another woman to feel as Lisa had evidently felt. It was far better to take his pleasure and move on. The very thing he accused Lisa and his father of. Maybe he was no better than they were after all.

"Not everyone will betray you, Gabe," she said quietly. "There are many who are loyal to you. You can't control everything. You can't control how someone feels about you. Or what makes them tick. You can only control how you react, how you *act*, how you think and feel."

"You're amazingly wise for someone as young as you are," he said wryly. "Why do I just feel like I've been schooled by someone fourteen years younger than me?"

She leaned over, surprising him with her kiss. Her lips lingered over his, warm and so damn sweet. Her bare breasts brushed over his chest, and God help him, his dick hardened instantly.

"You're too hung up on this age thing," she murmured. "Maybe I'm just smart."

He chuckled and then claimed her lips again, his body already revving to life now that she was pressed against him again. But she hesitated and pushed back against him, her face going serious. He didn't like that. He wanted her next to him, but it was clear she had one more thing she wanted to get off her chest.

"We need to get something straight now. I get the point you were trying to make to your dad. Giving me a heads-up wouldn't have been out of line, just so you know. It pissed me off to see you wrapped around Blondie, and if that kind of crap ever happens again, I'll walk out just like I did tonight. Only next time you won't be able to sweet-talk your way back into my good graces. I get that you have all the power in this relationship, but that doesn't mean I'm going to stand by and watch you feel up another woman while I'm forced to watch."

She regarded him warily, like she was certain what she'd said was going to make him angry, but he threw back his head and laughed. When he looked back at her, she looked bemused and a little disgruntled over his reaction.

"You're cute when you're pissed," he said, still grinning. "Maybe you aren't as smart as you think if you agreed to this insanity."

"Or maybe it's the best decision I ever made," she replied, her tone suddenly serious, her eyes regarding him somberly.

"That's debatable, but I'm not going to spend time questioning my good fortune," he said.

He wrapped his arms around her and rolled her beneath him, his cock already probing between her legs. He hoped to hell she was ready for him, because he couldn't wait. Couldn't spend another second outside her body.

But something about the conversation, the look in her eyes, the way she seemed so accepting, made him hesitate. Damn it, he'd take it slow this time. Give her what she deserved instead of a hard fucking that made him little better than an animal.

He didn't have to be this cold, mistrustful person. For once he could concentrate on someone else's pleasure instead of being selfish. For Mia he could do this. He wanted to do it. She deserved nothing less.

Instead of plunging into her, he kissed her. Softly. Without as much aggression as he had before. He nibbled delicately at her lips, feeding on them, coaxing her to open under his advance. His tongue swept over hers, teasing, flirting. Just the briefest touch and then he followed it with another. And another.

He slid his mouth down her jawline to her ear where he toyed with the lobe, swirling his tongue around the shell and then sucking lightly just below on the sensitive skin of her neck. He felt her shiver, felt immense satisfaction that he was bringing her pleasure.

Chill bumps rapidly broke out and raced across her flesh, hardening her nipples until they poked at his chest.

Unable to resist that particular temptation, he kissed a line down her chest, between her breasts, and then he lapped at the underswell, getting closer and closer to her straining peaks.

"Gabe . . ."

His name came out as a breathy sigh, and it had a volatile reaction to his already-aroused body. The head of his cock was nestled in her sweet heat, but he hadn't pushed in yet. He wanted to make damn sure she was just as aroused as he was, and then he would take his time. He wanted her as wild for him as he was for her. He'd settle for nothing less.

Reaching between them, he grasped his dick and rubbed up and down her damp folds, over her clit and then back to tuck barely inside her entrance. He licked at one nipple, running his tongue slowly and leisurely across the puckered bud.

"You like this?" he murmured.

"Oh yes," she breathed. "Suck them, Gabe. I love it when you put your mouth on my breasts."

God he loved it too. He trembled he was so on edge. He needed her. Needed to possess her. He wanted to drive deep and hard, remind her without words who she belonged to. It was hell battling those instincts, but he forced himself to maintain control.

He nipped gently at one nipple and then followed it with a light lick before finally sucking the crown into his mouth. He held it there, working it with his mouth, enjoying the feel and taste of her on his tongue. There was nothing sweeter. Nothing as exquisite as having her underneath his body, his mouth and hands on her, tasting, touching, exploring. And she was his. All his. He could have her any time he wanted as many times as he wanted. It was like putting a feast before a starving man and telling him to have his fill. He wanted everything at once. To lose himself in her and forget everything else.

Her hand slid into his hair, gripping his scalp, her nails digging in as she held him to her breasts. It was the first time she was remotely aggressive in bed, and he liked it. He liked it a damn lot. It told him she was there with him, sharing this mind-blowing, crippling obsession. He wasn't alone.

She arched her hips, pushing herself at him, trying to maneuver his dick inside her. Wetness bathed the head of his cock, and he knew she was more than ready, but he still didn't make that final move. He wanted her mindless. Wanted to bring her pleasure like she'd never experienced.

Kneeling up, his erection bobbing, he kissed a path from her breasts to her belly. She flinched and moaned when his tongue delved into her navel. He played there a moment, enjoying her restless movements as her desire rose.

He kissed his way to her pelvis and then over to one hip where he lavished her skin with sweet, gentle kisses. He ran his tongue down her leg, to the inside of her thigh and precariously close to her pussy. But he stopped before he reached her most intimate flesh.

Her sigh of frustration made him smile.

He sank his teeth lightly into the inside of her thigh and then followed it up with a soothing swipe of his tongue before venturing lower, grazing his teeth down the inside of her leg, past her knee and lower still to her ankle.

Her toes were tiny, painted pink, a delightful shade that complemented her well. He sucked her big toe into his mouth and suckled at it as he'd done her nipples. Then he treated each toe to the same, working his way across her foot.

"God but you make even the simplest things unbelievably hot," she choked out. "I've never had my toes sucked. I would have said *gross*, but your mouth is pure sin."

He gazed at her over her raised foot. "*Gross?*"

"Forget I ever said anything. Carry on."

He laughed and then lowered her leg and began all over again at her other hip, licking and kissing a path to those tiny, delectable toes. He sucked each and every one into his mouth, licking the pad and then sucking more strongly.

He loved that she was unapologetically feminine, and yet she had a strong personality and she didn't take shit lying down. She was going to be a challenge. A welcome challenge, and a change from the women he was accustomed to. She may very well keep him on his toes over the coming weeks.

He wanted to spoil and pamper her shamelessly. Let her indulge in all the girlie delights she wanted. He wanted to see her smile—be the one who made her smile. He wanted that shine in her eyes to come from him. If that made him a selfish, egotistical, self-serving bastard, he could live with that.

He took hold of both feet and pushed forward, doubling her legs and then spreading them as he knelt between her thighs. She was splayed wide open to him, the soft, pink flesh of her pussy glistening in the low light.

Resting one foot against his shoulder, he reached and trailed a finger down the seam of her pussy and then slid it inside, feeling the snug tissues hug him. Sweat broke out on his forehead. He wanted inside her so badly he was about to come.

He leaned down and licked from her entrance to her clit in one rough swipe that had her bowing off the bed. Her cry escaped. His name. An urgent demand for satisfaction. He could sense that she was at the end of her patience, and that was fine with him because he couldn't hold off another second.

Moving in closer, he grasped his erection and fitted it to the mouth of her pussy. For a moment he toyed, sliding it in and out the barest inch until she growled at him in frustration.

A smile curving his lips, he eased forward, inch by inch, enjoying the thrill of her enveloping him and pulling him deeper.

"You're such a damn tease," she said crossly. "God, Gabe. Fuck me already!"

He let her legs fall and then leaned over her, angling himself so he could thrust deeper. He kissed her, still smiling. "So demanding," he mocked.

She reached up, grasped his head and yanked him down into a forceful, demanding kiss that firmly proved his point.

He plunged through her wetness, sliding past swollen, tight tissues until his hips met hers.

"Fuck me, what you do to me," Gabe said in a tortured whisper.

She wrapped her legs around him, hooking her ankles at his ass. She lifted herself upward, wanting more. Hell, he wanted more. It would never be enough.

Planting his hands on either side of her head, he began to pump in and out. He pushed and undulated deep, holding himself there at the deepest possible point before sliding back out, retreating, only to advance again in an erotic, tantalizing rhythm.

"Tell me what you need," he managed to grit out. "How close are you, Mia? What do you need?"

"You," she said simply, that one word tearing to the very heart of him. "Just you."

He didn't have to tell her to give him her eyes. Her gaze was solidly fixed on him, sweet and understanding, the glow of arousal warm in her depths.

He sped up his thrusts, plunging, rocking against her. She fluttered and convulsed around him. He felt the start of her orgasm as she rippled along the length of his cock and then squeezed him so tight that it initiated his own.

It was like being turned inside out. The rush was nothing he'd ever experienced before. The ultimate adrenaline surge.

The first jet of semen erupted from his body, painful and so intensely pleasurable that he lost sense of everything but his dick diving into her over and over. She was limp on the bed, her eyes on him when she came—as her chest rose and fell in rapid succession. Even when the last of his release had left his body, he still fucked her, not wanting that feeling to go away.

Her arms circled his shoulders and her hands rubbed up and down his back, her nails lightly scouring his flesh. He moaned and shuddered from the toes up. He pushed inside her and stayed, lowering his body so it rested atop hers.

He slid his hands underneath her ass, pulling her tighter against him, not wanting to lose that connection. If it were up to him, he'd remain a permanent part of her, his dick wedged in her pussy. There was no better feeling on earth.

"Mmm, that was decadent," Mia said in a sleepy, completely satisfied voice.

He had nothing to say because there weren't adequate words to convey just how wrecked he was right now, and he didn't want her or anyone to know just how vulnerable he felt at the moment.

He kissed her temple, careful not to move so he remained inside her. He wasn't leaving her until he had to. It was twisted, but he liked the fact that she was apparently every bit as possessive of him as he was of her.

She was snuggled tightly into his body and they were still connected, their bodies entwined intimately. He thought she'd already drifted off to sleep when he heard her quietly say his name.

He picked up his head just enough that he could see her, and he thumbed a thick strand of hair from her forehead.

"What's on your mind?" he asked. They'd already talked about way more than he was comfortable with. And something in her gaze told him this wasn't something small.

"The contract," she whispered.

He tensed and then levered himself upward even more as he stared down at her in question. He was still hard inside her, still solidly a part of her and he remained that way, wanting her underneath him, pinned down and possessed by him. Especially if they were going to discuss the damn contract.

"What about it?"

She sighed. "I just wondered. I mean, about the 'other men' thing. Is that a for-sure thing or is that a just-in-case thing?"

The very last thing he wanted to talk about—or imagine—when he was balls deep inside her and she was naked and sated in his arms, was another man touching her.

But there was also curiosity in her gaze. Not fear. Just genuine question. Almost as if she were wondering about it . . .

"How do you feel about that?" he asked bluntly. "Does it turn you on? The idea of another man touching you while I watch?"

She started to move her gaze from his.

"Eyes," he commanded. "You look at me while we're having this conversation."

Her gaze flickered back and he could see the flush on her face.

Then she licked her lips and he could feel her nervousness, her hesitation.

"Okay, yes, I admit, I do wonder about it. I mean I can't tell you if it's something I'd like or not, but I do think about it. I know that Jace and Ash . . ."

Gabe winced. "I don't really want to hear about Jace and Ash nor do I want to discuss anything that remotely involves them being naked."

Mia laughed, her eyes sparkling. But she also relaxed in his arms as some of her tension fled.

"I just mean that I know they have threesomes with women and I guess I wondered about that. Not about them. God, no." She shuddered. "But about the concept in general. I mean when I first read that in the contract, my immediate reaction was shock and a resounding *hell no*. But then I began to wonder what it would feel like."

She trailed off in a whisper, her expression anxious as she stared up at him.

"Does that make you angry?"

He sighed. "I'm not going to get pissed at you for wondering about something I said was a possibility, Mia. There's nothing wrong with your being curious. And I'm glad you're not afraid. Does it excite you? Having someone else touch you while I'm watching and commanding the scene?"

Slowly she nodded. Her nipples hardened and her pussy clenched around his dick, sending a wave of pleasure through his groin. Yeah, the idea obviously excited her. He just wasn't sure it was something he could ever give her. He wasn't sure if he could stand by and watch another man touch what was his.

He leaned down to kiss her, not voicing any further thoughts on the matter.

He was really beginning to hate that fucking contract.

chapter eighteen

Gabe's line buzzed, and he frowned at the interruption. Mia was across the room at her desk—a distraction in itself—but he was putting together financials for a proposed island resort, and he'd specifically told Eleanor he wasn't to be disturbed.

"What," he barked into the intercom.

Eleanor's nervous voice wavered over the line. "I know you said you weren't to be disturbed, Mr. Hamilton, but your father is here to see you. He says it's important. I didn't think it wise to send him away."

Gabe's brow crinkled and his frown deepened. Across the room, Mia looked up from her work, worry in her eyes.

"I'll come out," Gabe said after a moment's hesitation. He didn't want whatever was on his father's mind to be aired in front of Mia.

"I can leave, Gabe," Mia said softly as he rose.

He shook his head. He much preferred her here in his office. Away from the gossip and speculation of others. He'd already uncovered the person responsible for breaking into his office—it hadn't taken much encouraging on his part to get her coworkers to out her—and he'd terminated her on the spot without a reference. He wanted Mia as far away from that kind of environment as possible.

He strode out to the reception area to see his father standing a short distance from Eleanor's desk. His father looked thoughtful and ill at ease. Gabe had never seen him look so uncomfortable. Especially around Gabe.

"Dad," Gabe said in greeting. "What can I do for you?"

His father's expression grew even more somber. There was a hint of regret that shadowed his eyes.

"There used to be a time when I'd come to see you and you didn't ask me such a thing. You were glad to see me."

Guilt dampened some of the irritability that plagued Gabe.

"You usually call. I wasn't expecting you. I was concerned that something was wrong," Gabe said.

His father hesitated a moment, then shoved his hands into the pockets of his expensive slacks. "There is. Can we go somewhere and talk? Have you had lunch yet? I was hoping you'd have time for me."

"I always have time for you," Gabe said softly, echoing a sentiment he'd offered his mother. Used to be he could spend time with them both and not have to split it between them.

Relief dimmed some of the worry in his father's eyes.

"Let me call for my car," Gabe said.

He turned to Eleanor. "Have the car pick us up outside. And make sure Mia eats lunch. Let her know I'm not sure when I'll return and that if I'm not back by four to go ahead and leave for the day."

"Yes, sir," Eleanor said.

"Shall we go?" Gabe asked his father. "The car should be around by the time we get out front."

The two rode the elevator down in silence. It was awkward and stilted but Gabe made no move to right it. He wasn't sure what it would take to mend the breach between them. He'd acted like a bastard at the cocktail party. His father was probably embarrassed by the quick defection of his date. That hadn't been

Gabe's intention. No matter his anger or confusion when it came to his father, he loved him and he had no intention of hurting him. He only wanted his father to see the kind of woman he'd chosen to associate with.

They waited a brief moment before Gabe's car pulled up and the two men got in. Gabe directed the driver to Le Bernardin— one of his dad's favorite places to eat.

It wasn't until the two were seated and their orders placed that Gabe's father broke the silence. It was as if he couldn't remain silent a moment longer and the words came bursting out, his face a mask of sadness and regret.

"I've made a terrible mistake," his father admitted.

Gabe went still. He put the napkin he'd been unfolding just to have something to do down on the table. "I'm listening."

His father scrubbed a hand over his face and it was then that Gabe could see just how weary he looked. He seemed older. Aged overnight. There were shadows in his eyes, and the wrinkles at his eyes and brow were more pronounced.

His father fidgeted a moment and then took a deep breath, his entire face crumpling. To Gabe's horror, tears shone in his dad's eyes.

"I was a fool for leaving your mother. It's the worst mistake of my life. I don't know what I was thinking. I just felt so trapped and unhappy and I reacted to that. I thought if I did this or I did that or if I started over that it would fix everything—that I'd be happier."

Gabe blew out his breath. "Shit," he murmured. This was the last thing he'd expected to hear.

"And it wasn't your mother's fault. She's a damn saint for putting up with me all these years. I think I woke up one day and thought to myself that I'm *old*. I don't have much time left. I panicked and then I freaked out because I started blaming your mother. God. Your mother! The one woman who's stuck by me all this time, who gave me a wonderful son. And I blamed her because I saw an old man staring back at me in the mirror. A man who thought he had to turn back the clock and get back all those years. I wanted to feel young again. Instead I feel like a bastard who shit on his wife—his family—you, Son. I shit on you and your mother and I can't tell you how much I regret that."

Gabe didn't even know what to say. He was agog at all his father had just thrown at him. All of this because of some fucking late-in-life crisis? Coming to grips with inevitable age? Jesus.

"I hate to even come to you with this, but I don't know what else to do. I doubt Matrice would even give me the time of day now. I hurt her. I know that. I don't expect her to forgive me. If the positions were reversed and she did to me what I did to her, I doubt I could ever forgive her."

"Goddamn, Dad. When you fuck up, you go big."

His father fell silent, his gaze fixed on his drink, sadness rimming his eyes.

"I just want to go back—take it back—so it never happened. Your mother is a good woman. I love her. I never stopped loving her."

"Then why the hell have you been doing your damnedest to shove all these other women not only in her face but mine?" Gabe snarled. "Do you have any idea how badly you hurt her?"

The older Hamilton's face went even grayer. "I have an idea. Those women didn't mean anything to me."

Gabe held up his hand in disgust. "Stop it. Just stop it, Dad. God. You're spouting the oldest cliché in the book. You think Mom gives a flying fuck if those women meant shit to you? Do you think it'll make her feel better at night knowing that while you were out fucking some chick half your age—or younger—that you were really thinking about how much you loved her?"

His dad flushed and quickly looked around as Gabe's voice rose. "I didn't sleep with those women," he said in a low voice.

"Not that Matrice will ever believe me. But I'm telling you that I didn't betray my marriage vows."

Gabe's temper simmered and he fought to keep it from erupting. "Yeah, Dad, you did. Whether you slept with them or not, you betrayed Mom and your marriage vows. Just because it wasn't physical adultery doesn't mean it wasn't emotional adultery. And sometimes emotional adultery is the hardest to get over."

His father rubbed a tired hand over his face and resignation bled into his features. "So you think I don't have a chance of ever winning her back."

Gabe sighed. "That's not what I said. But you need to understand what you did to her before you can ever think to make it right. She has her pride too, Dad. And you damaged it. If reconciliation is what you really want, then you have to be in it for the long haul. She's not going to take you back overnight. You can't quit after one try. If she means anything at all to you, then you have to be willing to fight for her."

His dad nodded. "Yeah, I get it. And I do want her. I never didn't want her. It's all so stupid. I'm a fool. An old, deluded fool who messed up."

Gabe softened. "Talk to her, Dad. Tell her everything you told me. And you have to be patient and listen to her when she goes off on you. You have to listen while she calls you every name in the book. You deserve it. You have to give that to her and you have to take it."

"Thanks, Son. I love you, you know. I hate that I hurt not only Matrice, but you as well. You're my son and I let you both down."

"Just make it right," Gabe said softly. "Make Mom happy again, and that will be enough for me."

"Hey Gabe, need to talk to you about . . ."

Mia looked up to see Jace standing in the doorway of Gabe's

office. Her heart leapt and her adrenaline spiked. He wasn't supposed to be here yet. This wasn't how she intended to break the
news to him that she was working for Gabe.

Ash pushed in behind him and his eyebrows rose when he
saw Mia sitting at her desk.

Jace's face darkened and he looked between her desk and
Gabe's as if expecting it all to make sense.

"What the hell are you doing here?" Jace asked.

"Nice to see you too," Mia said dryly.

Jace strode across the floor toward her desk. "Damn it, Mia.
You caught me off guard. I wasn't expecting to see you here." He
perched on the edge of her desk, his gaze scrutinizing as he took
in the papers scattered over the surface and the laptop she was
working on.

Ash sauntered in behind Jace, standing a short distance away,
but no less interested.

"What are you doing here? Where the hell is Gabe?"

The confusion was evident in his voice. Mia took in a deep
breath and plunged ahead, knowing the best thing to do was get
it out of the way and in the open so nothing seemed suspicious.
The longer she drew it out, the guiltier she'd look anyway. She had
no poker face whatsoever—a fact that had kept her in trouble in
her early teenage years. She'd never been able to lie to Jace with a
straight face so she prayed his questioning didn't get too in depth
here or she was fucked.

"I'm working for him," she said calmly.

Ash's lips formed a silent O and then he turned back toward
the door. "I'll just wait outside."

Jace's face was the poster child for *what the fuck*. As soon as the
door closed behind Ash, he turned back to Mia, his jaw tight.
"Okay, what the hell is going on? You're working for him? In what
capacity? And why am I only just finding this out?"

"What's going on is Gabe offered me a job. I'm working as his personal assistant. And you've been gone, and this isn't the sort of thing I'd simply tell you on the phone."

"Why the hell not?"

She rolled her eyes. "Because you'd react just like you are now and you'd be on the first flight home determined to figure it all out."

"When did this happen?" he asked bluntly.

She lifted her shoulder in a shrug. "About the time you and Ash left for California. I saw Gabe at the grand opening. He told me to come into his office. Voila. Here I am."

"Just like that," he said skeptically.

His eyes narrowed and he studied her intently as if trying to peel back her skin and see inside her head.

"Gabe was right. Working at La Patisserie was a waste of my education and all the money you spent sending me to college. I was comfortable and maybe a little scared to bust into the real world. This job gives me an opportunity to get my feet wet."

Jace's expression softened. "If you wanted a job, why didn't you come to me? You have to know I would have taken care of you."

She chose her words carefully, because she didn't want to seem ungrateful. She dearly loved Jace. He'd sacrificed a lot for her and still managed to build a successful empire, all while dealing with a much younger sister.

"I wanted to do this on my own," she said quietly. "I know you would have given me a job. And maybe it's no different that Gabe has hired me. I'm sure everyone will say the same as if you'd done the hiring. That I'm Jace Crestwell's little sister and this is nepotism at its finest. Besides, I couldn't work for you and you know it." She grinned mischievously at him. "We'd kill each other after a day."

Jace chuckled. "Okay maybe. But only because you're so hard-headed."

She shook her head. "I'm not stubborn. My way is just better."

"It's nice to see you by the way, baby girl. I missed you in California."

"Which is why you're still buying me dinner tomorrow night," she said cheekily.

He grimaced. "Can we do it the next night? Ash and I have this thing. Part of the reason we're back early. Investor dinner. Boring as hell. Lots of ass kissing."

"Okay, *that's* a date," she said. "And you're not getting out of it."

"Bet your ass. It's a date. After work, run home and change if you want and I'll pick you up at your apartment."

Then he frowned.

"How are you getting to and from work anyway?"

She was careful to make her voice casual, like it was perfectly normal for Gabe to provide transportation for her. "Gabe sends a car for me and has it bring me home."

She conveniently left off the part about them leaving work together most of the time and of her spending the nights at Gabe's apartment. Now that Jace was back, they were going to be forced to be a great deal more circumspect. He'd flip out if he knew what went on behind closed doors between her and Gabe.

Jace nodded. "Okay good. Don't want you walking or taking the subway." He checked his watch and then angled his gaze at her. "Do you know what time Gabe is due back? Where the hell is he for that matter? I thought his calendar was clear today."

"He, uh, left with his dad. Not sure when he's getting back, or if."

Jace grimaced. "Say no more. That's a fucked-up situation."

And Jace didn't even know the half of it.

He reached over and tousled her hair. "I'll let you get back to work. Gabe's a hardass to work for. I hope you know what you're getting yourself into. Maybe we should have put you to work for Ash. He has a huge soft spot for you."

She laughed. "I'll be fine. Stop worrying. Don't you and Ash have someone else to pester?"

"Yeah, investors," Jace muttered. "Take care, baby girl. I'll look forward to our dinner. We have a lot of catching up to do."

As soon as he left Gabe's office, she sagged in relief. Her pulse was beating a mile a minute and she leaned forward, putting her face in her hands. That had gone better than expected.

When Gabe got out of the car at his office building, he hadn't taken three steps toward the entrance when Jace came out, a deep frown on his face. It was obvious that he'd evidently been waiting on Gabe. *Shit.* He wasn't supposed to be back until tomorrow. He hoped to hell Mia had handled things well between her and Jace. But judging by the look on his friend's face, whatever it was she'd said or how she'd explained the situation hadn't satisfied him.

"We need to talk," Jace said curtly when Gabe drew abreast of him.

"Okay," Gabe said calmly. "What's up? Problems in California?"

"Don't play dumb with me. It just pisses me off. You know good and damn well why I met you out here."

"Mia," Gabe said with a sigh.

"No shit. What the hell is going on, Gabe? Any reason you didn't tell me of your plan to hire my little sister?"

"I'm not having this conversation with you on the street," Gabe bit out.

"My office will do," Jace said.

Gabe nodded and the two men reentered the building and got on the elevator. There were several others in with them and they remained silent as they rode up to their floor. When they got off, Gabe followed Jace into his office just down the hall from his own.

Jace shut the door behind him and then paced to the window before turning to stare at Gabe. "Well?"

"I don't understand what you're pissed about," Gabe said mildly. "I told you I saw her at the grand opening. She was looking for you. I danced with her, we talked, I told her to get her ass into my office the next morning, and then I sent her home in a car."

"You could have filled me in on those developments. Hell, I saw you the same morning you told Mia to come into your office."

Gabe nodded. "But I had no idea how she'd respond to my offer. No sense getting you worked up if she refused. I don't need your permission to hire a personal assistant."

Jace's expression darkened. "No, but you damn well need my permission where it concerns Mia. She's mine, Gabe. All I have left. The only family I have left and I'll protect her with my dying breath. She's not in your league."

"Oh for God's sake. I'm not some heartless bastard who's going to skin her alive. I've watched her grow up too, Jace. I'm not going to be mean to her."

Even as he said it, guilt flooded him. He was so going to hell. Burn in hell. For an eternity.

"Just make sure you don't hurt her," Jace said in a carefully controlled voice. "And I mean in any way, Gabe. You keep your hands off her. You respect her absolutely. Don't ever cross the line with her. You'll answer to me if you do."

Gabe swallowed back the surge of anger at Jace's threat. He couldn't blame Jace for protecting Mia. In his place he'd be doing the same. But it irritated him that Jace had so little faith in him that he thought he'd destroy an innocent.

But wasn't that what he was doing? Using her for his own pleasure? Uncaring of anything but the fact he possessed her?

"Understood," he said through clenched teeth. "Now if we're done, I have work to get to."

"Ash and I have an early dinner tonight. Business thing. We'll wrap up early, though. Want to meet for drinks after?" Jace asked casually.

It was a peace offering. After the dressing-down, Jace was attempting to smooth it over. Let Gabe know that things were cool. *Fuck.* Gabe had plans with Mia. Nice dinner. And fucking was definitely on the agenda.

Hell. But he didn't want to fuck things up with Jace and Ash either. If he was going to pull this off he had to find a very delicate balance between keeping his time with Mia secret and also not withdrawing from Jace and Ash.

"Make it later. Nineish," Gabe said, already working it out in his head how to handle it with Mia.

Jace nodded. "Works for me. I'll let Ash know."

chapter nineteen

Mia looked up when Gabe entered the office and a flutter began deep in her belly when he locked the door behind him. She knew what that meant. She regarded him cautiously as he stalked toward her, his eyes glittering with lust—and need.

"Gabe . . ." she began. "Jace is here. I mean he's back early."

He never paused. He hauled her out of her chair and propelled her toward his own desk.

"Neither Jace nor Ash will disturb me when my door is closed. They're busy making plans for their business dinner tonight."

The sentences were clipped, as if he didn't like having to explain himself. Well fine, but she wasn't going to be blindsided by her brother trying to get through the door when Gabe was doing God knew what to her behind that locked door. Jace and Ash were both used to having unfettered access to Gabe's office. She had no idea how he was going to continue their office debauchery with her brother lurking.

He reached underneath her skirt and his hand froze when he encountered panties. Damn it. She'd forgotten. She hadn't even given it any thought. Putting on panties was second nature. Who actually gave thought to not wearing them? She'd been tired from Gabe's ceaseless demands the night before, and it had slipped her mind to leave the underwear off.

"Take them off," he demanded. "The skirt too, and then bend your ass over my desk. I told you what would happen, Mia."

Oh shit. Her ass was still sore from the previous night and now he planned to spank her again?

Reluctantly, she tugged down her underwear, letting them fall to the floor. Then she slipped her skirt off, leaving her naked from the waist down. With a sigh, she leaned forward on his desk.

"Lower," he ordered. "Lay your cheek on the wood and perch that ass in the air for me."

Closing her eyes, she complied, wondering for the hundredth time if she'd lost her fucking mind.

To her utter shock, his fingers slipped between her ass cheeks, well lubricated as he pressed against her anal opening. His fingers left and then returned with more lubricant as he gently worked the opening.

"Gabe!" she gasped.

"Shhh," he reprimanded. "Not a word. I have a plug I'm putting in your ass. You'll wear it for the rest of the day, and before you go home, you'll come to me so I can remove it. Tomorrow morning when you come into work, the very first thing you will do is present that pretty ass for me so I can put it back in. You'll wear it the entire time you're at work and only remove it at the end of the day. Each day I'll go up a size until I'm satisfied that you can take my dick in your ass."

He followed his words with the blunt end of the plug, pressing against her tight ring.

"Relax and breathe out, Mia," he said. "Don't make it harder than it needs to be."

Easy for him to say. No one was bending him over shoving foreign objects up his ass.

Still, she sucked in her breath, let it out and tried to relax as best she could. As soon as she did, he shoved inward with one firm push. She gasped as she was instantly assailed by a burning sense of fullness. She squirmed and wiggled, but all she got was a smack on her ass for her efforts. And God that smack was overwhelming because it jarred the plug.

She heard him walk away. The sound of an opening cabinet. Then he was back again, his footsteps close. Her breath caught in her throat when she felt the tip of . . . leather? . . . slide across her ass in a sensual glide.

Then fire exploded over her ass and she yelped, bucking upward.

"Back down," he ordered sharply. "Stay put, Mia. You take your punishment like a good girl and you'll be rewarded."

She squeezed her eyes shut and whimpered when he landed another blow with the crop. It had to be a crop. It snapped and felt like a belt, but it was small and didn't cover much of her ass at one time.

A low moan escaped as he peppered her ass. The plug was making her insane. Stretched around it, the sting of the swats. It was turning her on and that infuriated her. She was so wet it would be a miracle if she weren't dripping.

He paused a moment and then tugged lightly at the plug, pulling it barely out of her body before sending it back inside. She couldn't remain still. It was driving her insane. She burned. She itched. It was like being on fire with no relief.

She braced herself for another swat but it never came. She heard the rasp of a zipper as it was being undone. Then rough hands on her legs, turning her over so her back was flush against the desk. Her legs hung over the edge and he gathered them, looping them over his arms as he positioned himself between her legs.

Oh my God. He was going to fuck her with that plug up her ass.

It was like having two cocks at once, and never in her wildest fantasies had she even gone there.

The blunt head of his dick pressed against her opening made smaller by the plug. He pushed, forcing his way inside her body.

"Touch yourself," he said in a strained voice. "Use your fingers, Mia. Make it easier for me to take you. I want this to be good for you. I don't want to hurt you."

She reached down, sliding her fingers over her clit. God, it felt so good.

"That's it," he purred. "You're taking me, baby. Keep touching yourself. Make it feel good."

He pressed in halfway and then lunged forward, forcing himself the rest of the way in. She nearly came up off the desk and the cry lodged in her throat. She had to take her hand away because she nearly orgasmed on the spot. And she wanted this to last. She wanted to enjoy every second.

It was down and dirty, a race to completion. He fucked her long and hard, riding her in a relentless, forceful rhythm that had her gasping with every breath.

"If you don't hurry up I'm going to leave you behind," he rasped out. "Get there, Mia. I don't have long."

She hurried to finger her clit again, pressing in and rotating in a tight circle. "Oh God, oh God," she chanted.

"That's it, baby. That's it. I'm going to come all in you. The only thing better will be when I get to come inside that sweet ass."

Those dirty, illicit words sent her hurtling right over the edge. Her back bowed and her other hand slapped the desk as she exploded around his cock in a wet rush. Hot semen splashed into her pussy, making his entry easier. He fucked her until his cream ran down to where the plug was firmly wedged in her ass. Sweat beaded his brow and exertion showed on his face. But when he opened his eyes, they glowed with primal heat.

For a long moment he stood there, looking down at her, pumping his hips against her ass. Then finally he pulled out, leaving her limp and sated on the desk.

"Fucking beautiful," he growled. "My cum running down

your ass. It's dripping on the floor. Your pussy is swollen and full of my cream. Just like it should be."

Oh man she loved it when he talked dirty. She shuddered and her pussy squeezed, forcing more of the liquid onto the floor.

"Jesus, Mia. You're so fucking hot. I can't wait to fill that ass with it."

He lowered her legs and then reached for her arms, pulling her up so he could lift her down from the desk. His semen slid down the insides of her legs the moment she stood, and she wobbled unsteadily as she tried to gain her footing.

"Go clean up," he said huskily. "Leave the plug in until I take it out."

On shaking legs, she went into his bathroom, the plug burning and arousing her all over again as she walked. The pressure was overwhelming and wonderful.

The minute she walked back out of the bathroom, Gabe was there waiting for her. He hauled her against his chest and gave her a punishing kiss that left her breathless.

"Do not disobey me again," he warned.

"Sorry," she said softly. "I forgot."

His eyes gleamed as he stared down into her face. "Bet you won't forget next time."

chapter twenty

Sulking was juvenile and immature but damn if she wasn't pouting like a damn two-year-old. The damn man knew precisely what he was doing to her and she was having serious fantasies about all the ways she could make *him* suffer.

Even after the mind-blowing orgasm he'd given her, she was restless and on edge. She needed to come again! That damn plug was driving her insane, and he knew it.

He just sat across the room at his desk, acting like they hadn't just fucked like monkeys on that same desk.

His intercom went off, not an unusual occurrence, and Mia typically ignored him and focused on whatever task Gabe had set to her for that particular day. But when she heard what Eleanor said, she immediately tuned in while trying to appear as though she weren't paying the slightest bit of attention.

"Mr. Hamilton, uh, Mrs. Hamilton is here to see you, sir."

Gabe straightened, a frown marring his face. "My mother? Send her in, of course."

There was a light, uncomfortable cough. "No, sir. She says she's your wife."

Mia barely controlled her mouth before it fell open. Wow, that took some balls to show up at her ex-husband's office claiming to be Mrs. Hamilton.

"I don't have a wife," Gabe said icily.

There was a sigh and Mia felt sorry for Eleanor. This had to be incredibly awkward for her.

"She says she won't leave until you see her, sir."

Oh shit. This couldn't end well.

She glanced up, expecting Gabe to be furious. But he looked cool and unflappable. As if his ex-wife coming by his office were an everyday occurrence.

"Give me a minute and send her in," Gabe said flatly.

He glanced up at Mia. "If you'll excuse us, please. You can wait with Eleanor or go take a break."

Mia rose, only too glad to be out of his office. The temperature had dropped a good twenty degrees. She walked as fast as she was able with that damn plug up her ass. She'd just stepped out the door when Gabe's ex came down the hall.

Mia had seen her before. She'd seen pictures. Lisa was a beautiful woman. Tall and elegant without a hair out of place. The perfect wife for a man such as Gabe. She looked as polished and wealthy as Gabe himself.

They made a striking couple, Mia had to admit. With Lisa's silver-blond hair and Gabe's nearly black hair, they provided a perfect contrast. Lisa's eyes were a cool green while Gabe's were a rich, deep blue.

Lisa walked by her, smiling lightly in Mia's direction as she passed. It was mortifying for Mia to be standing there with a plug Gabe had inserted not long before as his ex-wife paraded by. Her face had to be on fire.

"Thank you," Lisa murmured.

Mia shut the door behind her and waffled a moment over the ethics of what she was contemplating.

Fuck it. What's the worst that could happen? Another spanking?

She placed her ear against the door and then glanced nervously down the hall to make sure no one could see her. She was dying of curiosity, and okay, maybe she was a teensy bit threatened by Lisa's visit. It made her feel insecure and . . . jealous. She could admit to jealousy regarding the other woman. After all, she'd had what Mia didn't and would never have.

Gabe's heart.

She listened intently and finally she caught their words as their voices rose.

"I made a mistake, Gabe. Can you not forgive that? Are you willing to turn your back on what we had?"

"You were the one who walked out," he said, his tone so cold that Mia shivered. "That was your choice. It was also your choice to lie about our relationship and to make a mockery of everything we shared. I didn't turn my back on you, Lisa. You turned yours on me."

"I love you," she said in a softer voice that had Mia straining to hear. "I miss you. I want us back together. I know you still have feelings for me. I can see it in your eyes. I'll grovel, Gabe. I'll do whatever I have to in order to convince you that I'm sorry."

Damn it but they must have moved farther from the door. She couldn't hear!

"What in the world are you up to?"

She stood straight up, bolting upward in fright. "Damn it, Ash! You scared me to death!"

He crossed his arms over his chest and regarded her in amusement. "Is there any particular reason you have your ear glued to Gabe's door? Did he lock you out? Already raised the boss's ire? See, this is why you should come to work for me. I'd pet you and love you and be nice to you."

"Oh for God's sake, Ash. Shut up. I'm trying to eavesdrop here."

"That much is evident," he said dryly. "Who are we eavesdropping on?"

"Lisa came to see him," she hissed. "And keep your voice down or they'll hear us!"

Ash's smile fizzled and a frown replaced his amusement. "Lisa as in his ex-wife Lisa?"

"That's the one. I was trying to hear what was going on. All I got was that she's sorry and she wants him back."

"Over my dead body," Ash muttered. "Move over so I can hear."

Mia scooted back enough that they could put both their ears to the door. Ash held a finger up for Mia to be silent. Duh! She was the one trying to get him to shut up.

"Ah shit, she's crying," Ash muttered. "A crying woman is never a good thing. Gabe can't stand it. He's toast when a woman cries and that bitch knows it."

"Don't you think you're being a bit harsh?" Mia murmured.

"She f— uh, she screwed him over royally, Mia. I was there. So was Jace. If you ever have any doubt, ask Jace how messed up he was when she went public with her lies. He's a dumbass if he doesn't toss her out of his office."

"Well, that's what I'm trying to find out if you would be quiet," she said patiently.

"Right," Ash said and fell silent as the two strained to hear once more.

"I won't give up, Gabe. I know you love me and I still love you. I'm willing to wait. I know you have your pride."

"Don't hold your breath," Gabe bit out.

"Oh shit, they're coming this way," Ash said. He grabbed Mia's arm, dragged her down the hallway and then thrust her through the open door of his own office. "Sit," he directed. "Act like we've been having a good ole time."

He hurried around behind his desk and planted his butt in his chair before propping his feet on top of the polished surface. Not three seconds later, Lisa strode past, her face red with tears. She was putting on her sunglasses to hide the evidence as she disappeared.

"Just hang out here," Ash said softly. "I wouldn't want you to go back into the lion's den so soon after that confrontation."

A noise outside made them both look up again to see Jace start to walk by. He halted when he saw Mia and did a double take. He entered the office, a frown on his face, and Mia silently groaned. This was beyond awkward. She was stuck in Ash's office with Jace and she had an anal plug up her ass while Gabe was next door fending off advances from his ex-wife.

"What's going on? Why is Mia in here?"

Ash shook his head. "Am I not allowed to say hello to my best girl?"

"Knock it off, Ash. Don't be a dick," Jace growled. "Was that Lisa I saw walking through the lobby?"

"Yep," Ash replied. "Hence the reason Mia is in here with me. I'm sparing her Gabe's ire when he's so fresh off his meet and greet with his ex."

"What the fuck is she doing here?" Jace demanded.

It was clear that neither Ash nor Jace had any love for Lisa. Their loyalty to Gabe was strong and they'd banded together, closing ranks around Gabe after the divorce.

"Ash and I were eavesdropping outside Gabe's door," Mia said.

Jace lifted one eyebrow. "And you want to keep your job? Gabe would have your head and even I wouldn't be able to save you from that."

"Do you want to know what we heard or not?" she asked impatiently.

Jace stuck his head out the door, looked down toward Gabe's office and then pushed back in, closing Ash's door behind him. "Spill."

"She wants him back," Ash drawled. "She put on quite the show too."

"Ah hell," Jace muttered. "I hope he told her to fuck off."

"I'm not sure what he told her," Mia murmured. "Someone wouldn't shut up so I could hear."

"I guarantee you that Gabe didn't fall for that line of shit," Ash said, leaning back and crossing his arms over his chest.

Mia wasn't so sure. After all, Gabe had been married to her. The breakup of their relationship had formed the basis of every single relationship that had come after, including her own with him. That said a lot about how affected he'd been. He may well be angry—she didn't dispute that for a minute. But it didn't mean he didn't still love her and it didn't mean he wouldn't attempt to work things out if it meant having her back on his terms.

"I'll kick his dumb ass," Jace muttered.

He glanced at Mia and then reached over to ruffle her hair. "We still on for dinner tomorrow night? What time you want me to pick you up?"

"What? And I'm not invited?" Ash asked in horror.

"Don't you have someone else to bother?" Jace asked.

Ash's expression stiffened for a moment and then he muttered, "Family get-together. I'm bailing."

Mia's heart softened and even Jace grimaced in sympathy. Ash's family and Ash were not on speaking terms. Not in any way. Ash didn't even make a pretense. If his family was involved, he made it a point to be somewhere else. And most of the time it was with Jace or Gabe.

"Oh, let him come," Mia said, keeping her tone light so Ash didn't pick up on what she was doing. "It'll keep you from lecturing me on God knows what. Ash sticks up for me."

"See, she likes me better," Ash said smugly.

"Okay, what time do you want us to come pick you up?" Jace said in mock resignation.

"Six is fine. Will that work for you guys? I won't need long to change and get ready. Are we eating casual or what?"

"I know this great pub that serves food that's right up your alley, baby girl. Wear jeans and we'll hang out there," Jace said.

Meaning he was doing this for her because hanging out in pubs wasn't exactly Jace's thing.

"Perfect."

The door opened and Gabe stuck his head in, a frown creasing his forehead. "Hey, have you guys seen . . ."

He halted when he saw Mia sitting in front of Ash's desk and then he glanced at Jace and Ash with suspicion. "Am I interrupting anything?"

"Not at all," Ash said nonchalantly. "We were just keeping Mia company while you kissed and made up with your ex."

Mia's eyes widened at Ash's daring. Holy shit but he was going to get them both in hot water with Gabe.

"Shut the fuck up, Ash," Gabe snarled.

"Nice," Jace muttered. "Now you're sending Mia back in there with him when you were supposedly rescuing her from that fate."

Mia rose, hoping to head off any further snarkiness from Ash.

"I'll see you guys tomorrow night for dinner," she said hurriedly as she nudged Gabe back through the door.

She shut the door behind her, effectively sealing off Gabe from Jace and Ash and any further comments either of them would make. Without waiting for Gabe, she walked down to his office and entered.

Gabe came in behind her. She could feel his presence, overwhelming. Could feel the heat radiating from him. He was like a seething lion. Appropriate since Ash had been so convinced she was heading back into the lion's den.

"You're going to dinner with both of them?"

She turned, her brows drawn at the odd note in his voice. "Yes. Ash invited himself. Jace is picking me up at six. I'm going straight to my apartment after work."

He closed in on her, his gaze intense and brooding. "Just don't forget who you belong to, Mia."

She blinked in surprise and then she laughed. "You can't seriously think that Ash . . ." She shook her head, unwilling to even voice such a ludicrous idea.

He tipped her chin up, forcing her to meet his gaze. "Maybe you need a reminder."

There was something in his tone, in the raw power flowing from his body that made her remain silent and accepting.

"Get on your knees."

She sank to her knees, awkwardly situating herself so that the plug remained intact. He fumbled with the zipper of his pants and pulled out his semi-erect cock.

"Suck it," he ordered. "Make me come, Mia. I want that gorgeous mouth of yours wrapped around my dick."

He tilted her head back, dug his hands into her hair and then pulled her toward his growing erection. The tip bounced against her lips and then he pushed, forcefully opening her lips to his advance.

Then he was inside her, pressing deep, rubbing back and forth over her tongue. He was even more intense than usual, and she wondered just how affected he'd been by Lisa's visit. Was he even now trying to erase her presence in his office?

But then she caught the look in his eyes and she softened all over. He was angry. Not at her. There was need. Almost desperation in his gaze. His hands roamed freely over her head and then to her face, caressing, touching, almost as if he were apologizing for that desperate need.

She reached up and wrapped her hand around the base of his cock and then gently pushed him away with her other hand so she could lever up further on her knees. She slowed his pace, taking him in long, leisurely sucks.

This would be no mindless release for him. She would show

him her love, even if he didn't want it. He needed it. He needed her. Even if it was the last thing he'd ever tell her.

Her hand coaxing up and down in time with her mouth, she gripped him, working from base to tip, letting the tip dangle precariously on her lips before sucking him in whole again.

"Goddamn, Mia," Gabe breathed. "Goddamn, what you do to me."

His hips bucked forward and the warm, salty burst of his release filled her mouth, and still she sucked him deeper, wanting all of him, taking all of him. She lavished every bit of love and attention on him, taking him sweetly, moving slowly, and forgoing the frantic pace of earlier.

She licked from the head to his balls, leaving no inch of him untouched.

Finally she slid her mouth down and allowed him to slip from her lips. She stared up at him, a picture of perfect submission—of acceptance. And she allowed him to see her. Really see her.

He flinched and then he lowered himself to his knees in front of her so they were nearly eye level. And then he pulled her into his arms, holding her tightly as his body heaved from the ease she'd given him.

"I can't be without you," he whispered. "You have to stay, Mia."

She stroked her hands over his back and then up to his head and held him lovingly.

"I'm not going anywhere, Gabe."

chapter twenty-one

Mia bent over Gabe's desk, palms flat on the surface, her skirt hiked up as Gabe withdrew the plug. She closed her eyes and breathed out her relief. She'd been on the edge the entire afternoon. Now maybe she could come down off that edgy high.

Gabe carefully cleaned her bottom, taking his time smoothing the cloth over her flesh before lowering her skirt and giving her a light pat.

"Go get your things. We'll run by the apartment to change and then we'll go to dinner."

She wanted to sag onto the desk and lie there for the next fifteen minutes while she recovered from teetering on the edge for so long. Instead of reprimanding her for not immediately following his order, Gabe slid his hands over her shoulders and then lifted her upward, pulling her into his arms.

She snuggled into his embrace, inhaling his spicy scent and his warmth. He kissed the top of her head and murmured, "I know I push too hard, but God help me, I can't seem to do anything else."

She smiled against him and hugged him, wrapping her arms around him to squeeze. He seemed surprised by the gesture. He went still but then he squeezed her tighter against him and buried his face in her hair.

"Don't let me change you, Mia," he whispered. "You're perfect the way you are."

But he had changed her. Irrevocably. She'd never be the same.

When he let her go, he turned away, almost as if he loathed the fact that he'd whispered what he had. She straightened her clothing and pretended not to see his discomfort. She went to her desk, grabbed her purse and then turned back to Gabe, a bright smile on her face.

"Shall we go?"

Gabe held out his arm and she went ahead of him, his hand pressed to her back as he let them out of his office. They said their good-byes to Eleanor who was preparing to leave as well and then they ran into Ash at the elevator.

Mia's heart plummeted. Wasn't he supposed to be at a dinner meeting with Jace? God, what if he'd tried to go into Gabe's office? Had he been there and found it locked? Worse, could he have heard anything?

"Ash, I thought you were with Jace," Gabe said easily.

Ash grinned and Mia marveled at how damn good-looking the man was.

"Forgot a folder with important info on the people we're meeting for dinner. Jace is schmoozing and giving my excuses for being unavoidably detained."

Mia snorted. "Jace schmoozing? That's your forte, Ash. How on earth did you finagle being the one to retrieve the folder? He's probably about to crawl out of his skin right now."

Ash chucked her on the chin and then pulled her into a squeeze. "Missed you, kiddo. And yeah, I didn't give Jace a choice. I cut and run before he could be snarly."

She hugged Ash back, comforted by his obvious affection for her. Until today, it had been a good while since she'd been with Ash or Jace. She missed that. Missed their steady, reassuring comfort. "Missed you too. It's been too long, Ash. I was beginning to think you didn't love me anymore."

They got onto the elevator and Ash gave her a look of mock horror. "Not love you? I'd slay dragons and lay them at your feet. I adore you."

She rolled her eyes. "Don't overdo the charm. You wouldn't want to use it all up because it's totally wasted on me."

He slung an arm over her shoulders, grinning the entire while. "It doesn't hurt to dream." He gave a dramatic sigh. "One day, you'll be mine."

"Yeah, right after Jace removes your balls," Gabe said darkly.

Ash winced, which only made him even more damn sexy. It was a shame she wasn't attracted to him because he would be so good in bed. Flirty. Fun. Full-on down-and-dirty sex. But if the rumors were true and he and Jace tended to have sex with the same woman, that would be incredibly awkward . . .

She shuddered at the thought. There were just some things she didn't need to know about her brother for God's sake. And picturing him naked with Ash may well have ruined any appreciation she had for Ash. Which was sad, because the man did fuel some sigh-worthy moments.

"See you later tonight, Gabe," Ash said as he broke from the elevator. "Jace awaits and if I don't get there soon, he'll run off the investors before I have a chance to charm them."

Gabe held up a hand in a wave and Mia called back a good-bye. Then Gabe ushered her into his car for the ride to his apartment.

"You're seeing Ash tonight?" Mia asked when they settled in for the ride. "So are we not going out?"

Gabe's lips tightened. "You're going to dinner with me, as planned. I have to meet Jace and Ash around nine for drinks."

"Oh," she said, wondering what that was about. But it wasn't as if it weren't a normal occurrence. When all three were in town and not traveling in different directions, they spent a lot of time together.

And she supposed if that changed all of a sudden along with the timing of her coming to work for Gabe, it may set off some alarms with Jace especially.

"What should I wear?" she asked, changing the topic.

Gabe's gaze fell on her, sweeping up and down until she may as well have been naked.

"One of your new dresses. The black one with the slit up the thigh."

She lifted her eyebrows. "Going fancy tonight?"

He didn't react. His expression was inscrutable. "I'm going to take you for a nice, quiet dinner and dancing. Good music, good food, beautiful woman. Not much more a man can ask for."

She went warm with pleasure at his compliment. Her smile was quick and his lips quirked almost as if he couldn't help but react to her pleasure.

Then his expression grew serious. "You're not just a beautiful woman, Mia. I don't want you to ever forget that. You're more than that. Don't ever let me take so much there's nothing left."

His cryptic warnings were growing in frequency. She wasn't sure what to make of them. Was he warning her or himself? Gabe was an enigma. She never really was certain what he was thinking unless they were having sex. That was a no-brainer. She knew exactly what his thoughts were then.

When they arrived at his apartment, they went up and Mia disappeared into the bathroom to ready herself. If they were going fancier, she wanted to wow Gabe. She wanted to appear sophisticated. Like she belonged at his side.

She curled her hair and then arranged it in an elegant up-sweep, allowing a few curls to fall loosely at her nape and down the sides of her neck. She applied light makeup, going with mascara and a pale lip gloss that made her lips shine but not appear overly dramatic. There was something to be said for less is more. The art of wearing makeup was to appear as though you were wearing none at all.

Her dress was wow worthy. She still couldn't believe how she looked in it. With the tall heels, she had enough height to carry off the long dress with the daring slit. Her legs appeared long and shapely with the aid of the shoes.

Even though Gabe had bitched about the backless dress she'd worn to the grand opening, he'd chosen this dress that only had two strings crisscrossing the back. The rest was bare and it dipped daringly low to hover just above her ass. The small of her back was enticing, just inviting a man's hand to rest there.

She wore no bra and the bodice was form fitting enough she had no worries there, although the neckline dipped, as did the back of the dress, to hint at the upper swells of her breasts.

Evidently Gabe was in an interesting mood. He was usually quite snarly about anyone—especially other men—seeing her in anything remotely revealing. But tonight she looked and felt like a sexy beast. She liked the confidence it gave her.

When she exited the bathroom, Gabe was sitting on the edge of his bed waiting for her. His eyes flared with instant appreciation, causing her to do a twirl. She turned around, hands up, and then faced him again.

"Will I do?"

"Fuck yeah," he growled.

As he stood, her gaze drifted appreciatively over him as well. The expensive three-piece suit made her mouth water. On another man, it would be boring. Staid almost. But on Gabe? It was divine. Black slacks. Black coat. White shirt with the top button unfastened. He looked expensive casual, like he didn't give a fuck what anyone thought, and that just made him even sexier.

"I take it where we're going a tie is optional?" she teased.

One half of his mouth turned up. "They bend the rules for me."

And who wouldn't? Who could possibly say *no* to Gabe Hamilton? Apart from the fact that he had more money than God, he had a natural charisma that drew women and men alike. They responded to him. Some feared him, others hated him, but everyone respected him.

"Would you like something to drink before we go?" Gabe asked.

She slowly shook her head. The longer they remained in his apartment, the more likely they were never to make it out to dinner. And she was looking forward to an actual date with him. So far there had been sex and work and not much else.

He held out his hand to her and she slipped her fingers through his. He tugged her toward the elevator and they rode down to get into his car.

On the way over, she battled over whether to bring the thing with Lisa up. She was dying of curiosity but she didn't want to open a big can of worms either.

She glanced sideways at him and he caught her gaze, lifting his eyebrows in question.

"What?" he asked.

She hesitated and then figured she may as well take the plunge. He wouldn't leave her alone until she spilled what was on her mind anyway.

"Uhm, Lisa . . ."

Before she could continue, Gabe's face became like ice and he held up his hand, halting her in midsentence.

"I refuse to ruin a perfectly good evening by discussing my ex-wife," he bit out.

Well. And that was that. And really, she wasn't going to complain. She didn't want to ruin their evening either. Even if she *was* dying of curiosity over what Gabe thought about the whole thing. And maybe a little frightened . . .

At the restaurant, they were taken to one of the back tables in a private alcove. It was perfect. The interior was dimly lit but candles burned at each of the tables, and an array of Christmas lights was strung through decorative shrubs, lending a festive, holiday feel. It made her long for Christmas.

She loved the holidays in the city. Jace had always taken her down to Rockefeller Center for the lighting of the Christmas tree. It was one of her favorite memories of him and her together.

"What are you thinking of?" Gabe asked.

She blinked and focused her attention on him. He was watching her, a curious expression on his face.

"You looked very happy. Whatever occupied your thoughts must have been good."

She smiled. "I was thinking of Christmas."

"Christmas?"

He looked baffled.

"Jace always took me down for the lighting of the tree. It's one of my favorite memories with him. I love all the lights and the hustle and bustle of Christmas in the city. Love window-shopping and looking at all the displays. It's the very best time of the year."

He looked thoughtful for a moment and then shrugged. "Lisa and I always spent it in the Hamptons, and then when she and I divorced, I just worked through the holidays."

She gaped at him. "Worked? You work during Christmas? Gabe, that's terrible. You sound like Scrooge!"

"Pointless holiday."

She rolled her eyes. "I wish I would have known. I would have made you spend it with Jace and me. No one should be alone at Christmas. I assumed you'd spend it with your parents."

She broke off, biting her lip in consternation for bringing up a sore subject.

"I'm sorry," she said quietly. "I wasn't thinking."

He gave her a rueful smile. "It's okay. Apparently my father has decided he's fucked up and now he wants my mother back. Lord only knows how that's going to go down."

Her eyes widened. "He said that?"

"Oh yeah," Gabe said with a weary sigh. "Over lunch when he came to the office. The day after his date was trying her best to get into my pants."

Mia scowled and Gabe laughed.

"So what's your mother going to do?" Mia asked.

"Hell if I know. If I had to guess, he hasn't yet gone to grovel or I would have heard about it by now."

"I don't know that I could forgive him sleeping with all those women," Mia said unhappily. "That had to hurt your mother terribly."

"He says he wasn't unfaithful."

Mia gave him an *oh please* look.

He waved his hand. "I have no idea what he considers being unfaithful and I'm not sure it even matters if he didn't sleep with them. The entire world thinks he did. My mother thinks he did. It's not humiliation she's going to get over soon."

"This must be so difficult for you," she said in a soft voice. What a sucky day all around. First his dad dropping the bomb, and then his ex-wife showing up just hours later.

He looked uncomfortable with her sympathy and glanced away, his eyes lightening with relief when the waiter approached with their entrees.

The seafood smelled divine as she sniffed appreciatively. The waiter set her grilled shrimp in front of her and Gabe's blackened mahimahi in front of him.

"*Ohhh*, yours looks awesome," she said.

He smiled and forked a bite, holding it over the table to her. She closed her mouth over it, holding it for just a moment as their gazes caught and held.

It was surprisingly intimate, his feeding her just that one bite.

He was staring at her mouth as he lowered his fork back to his plate.

She cut a piece of her shrimp and then offered him a sample as he'd done for her. He hesitated a moment but then allowed her to slide the bite into his mouth.

A little unsettled by how deeply affected she was by the exchange, she lowered her gaze to her plate and focused on eating her meal.

"Good?" Gabe asked several long minutes later.

She glanced up and smiled. "Delicious. I'm nearly stuffed!"

He lifted his napkin from his lap and dabbed at his mouth before tossing it down on the table. As soon as she lowered her fork and pushed back her plate, he rose and extended his hand to her.

"Let's dance," he murmured.

Feeling as fluttery as a teenager on her first date, Mia allowed him to pull her to her feet and lead her through the maze of tables to the area reserved for dancing.

He turned her toward him and tucked her tightly against him. There wasn't an inch between them, and his hand splayed wide on her bare back, settling possessively just above where the material rested.

She let out a contented sigh and closed her eyes as Gabe rested his cheek to her temple. They were barely moving. Softly swaying to the strains of the music, wrapped up in one another. She could stay this way forever. She could fool herself into thinking that Gabe was truly hers. That their relationship transcended just sex.

It wouldn't hurt to pretend for a little while. It may hurt later, but right now she was determined to live the fantasy.

His hand didn't remain still just above her behind. He stroked and rubbed, caressing as they danced, his body molded tightly to hers. She turned her nose toward his neck, inhaling his scent. She was so tempted to nibble at his ear and at the column of his neck. She loved the taste of him and she hadn't had many opportunities to indulge because Gabe was always solidly in control when they had sex. Oh what she wouldn't do for one night to explore him at will.

One song bled into another and they remained locked together, neither willing to break the intimacy that surrounded them, concealing them in the small space the two occupied.

She closed her eyes dreamily, swaying along with the music as Gabe held her tightly, his hand roaming her body. They were practically making love on the floor. Not sex. Not this torrid, all-consuming obsession that gripped them every time the clothes came off.

This was sweeter. Softer. More intimate and she loved every second.

She could fall in love with this Gabe. *Was* falling.

"I wonder if you have any idea how much I want you right now," he murmured next to her ear.

She smiled and then lifted her mouth to whisper in his ear. "I'm not wearing any underwear."

He stopped right in the middle of the dance floor, not even making an effort to make it look like they were dancing. His hold tightened on her and his body went rigid against hers.

"Jesus Christ, Mia. What a thing to say right here in the middle of the goddamn restaurant."

She smothered another smile and blinked innocently up at him. "I just thought you'd want to know."

"We're getting the hell out of here," he growled.

Before she could say anything, he grabbed her hand and hauled her toward the exit, his other hand reaching for his cell phone. Thank goodness she hadn't brought a purse or it would have been left at the table!

In terse tones, he told his driver they were ready.

Outside on the sidewalk, Gabe retreated closer to the building, holding her protectively against his side, away from the passersby.

"Gabe, what about the bill?" she asked, mortified that they'd just walked out.

He gave her a patient look. "I have an account with them. I'm a regular here. I even have a standard tip added to each of my bills. So don't fret."

The car pulled up and Gabe hustled her inside. As soon as the doors were closed and the car pulled away, Gabe pushed the button for the privacy screen between the front and back seat.

Anticipation fizzed in her veins until it felt like she was a shaken-up bottle of carbonated soda.

He reached for the fly of his slacks, rapidly unfastening it. A second later, he pulled out his long, beautiful cock and stroked it to utter rigidity. Her gaze was glued to him, the masculine ruggedness of his body.

"Pull up your dress and get on my lap," he said, reaching for her hand.

Maneuvering up into the seat, she hiked up her dress, baring most of her thighs, and then Gabe scooted to the middle of the seat so she could straddle him.

He reached underneath her dress and slid his hand up the inside of her thigh to her bare pussy, and he smiled in absolute satisfaction.

"That's my girl," he purred. "God, Mia. I've fantasized about fucking you in this dress and those killer heels ever since you walked out of the bathroom at my apartment."

He slid one finger inside and then pulled it back out and up between them. It glistened with her wetness. Slowly he slid his tongue up one side of his finger and she nearly came on the spot. Holy shit, but the man was lethal. Then he put his finger to her mouth.

"Suck it," he said huskily. "Taste yourself."

Mortified but morbidly curious, she tentatively parted her lips, allowing him to slide his finger inside and over her tongue. She sucked lightly and his pupils dilated. His cock surged upward, touching the mouth of her pussy in an impatient gesture.

He reached down with his other hand to grasp his dick, and then he withdrew his finger from her mouth so he could grip her waist. Then he lowered her down, guiding his erection into the very heart of her.

Oh but it was decadent watching Manhattan fly by, the glow of the lights, the noise of traffic, while Gabe was fucking her in the backseat of his car.

Positioning both hands at her waist, he began to thrust upward, holding her in place as he arched up and then withdrew. Faster. Harder. It was a race to see if he could get them both off before they arrived at his apartment.

She came first. A frenzied, bright flash that blew over her with the force of a hurricane. She was left panting as he continued to plunge into her over and over. She gripped his shoulders, holding on for dear life. And then the car began to slow.

Gabe erupted inside her, hot, spurting deep into her body. He pulled her all the way down onto his cock until there was no space separating them as he flooded into her. The car halted in front of his apartment and Gabe hit the intercom.

"Give us just a moment, Thomas," he said quietly.

Gabe sat there a long moment, his cock still pulsing and twitching inside her. He raised his hands to cup her face and then he kissed her. It was a direct contradiction to the frenzied way he'd just taken her. It was long and sweet. Warm and so very tender. As if he conveyed by actions what he could never say in words. Would never say in words.

He pulled her to him and held her against his body as he stroked her hair. For several long moments she lay against him as he softened within her.

Finally he lifted her upward and angled her into the space beside him. He pulled a handkerchief from his pocket and pressed it between her legs before cleaning himself. Unhurried, he tucked himself back into his pants and refastened the fly, straightening his clothing while she pulled her dress down.

"Ready?" he asked.

She nodded, too shaken, too wrecked to say anything at all. Anything she said wouldn't make a bit of sense anyway.

He opened the door and got out and a moment later came around to open hers.

"You're staying over again," he said as they walked toward the entrance.

It wasn't a request, but there was none of the usual arrogance in his voice. He said it matter-of-factly as though there were no other conceivable possibility. But then he looked at her, and brief uncertainty—so brief she wasn't even sure if that was what she saw—flashed in his eyes.

But she nodded, confirming his dictate.

"Of course I'll stay," she said softly.

They rode up the elevator and as they stepped off, he pulled her back against him, using his body to block the doors.

"Wait for me in bed," he said in a husky voice. "I won't be too late."

She leaned up and brushed her mouth across his lips. "I'll wait."

There was immediate satisfaction in his eyes. Then he nudged her forward and stepped back into the elevator so the doors could close.

chapter twenty-two

Not surprisingly, the venue for drinks was at Rick's in Midtown, a popular gentlemen's club where Gabe, Ash and Jace were regular visitors. Jace and Ash were already there when Gabe strode into their VIP suite, and there were two waitresses flirting heavily with Jace and Ash. Their gazes immediately snapped to Gabe, interest flaring in their eyes.

He dismissed them with a glance, tersely ordered his drink, and they scurried away.

"Bad day?" Ash asked when Gabe took his seat.

He wanted to laugh. *Bad day* didn't begin to cover it. It was one for the record books. He didn't think twice about sharing. Jace and Ash were the only two people he ever trusted with anything personal.

Gabe grimaced. "Dad came to the office today wanting lunch."

"Shit," Jace muttered. "Sorry, man. I know that sucks. How's your mom doing anyway?"

"I had dinner with her over the weekend. Had to drag her into the city. She's been at that monstrosity of a house licking her wounds. I'd even thought to talk her into selling the house and moving into an apartment in the city. Though I guess that's probably not going to happen now."

Ash lifted an eyebrow. "Why?"

Gabe let out a long breath. "Dad's decided he fucked up and he wants Mom back. That was the reason for lunch today."

"Holy shit," Ash said.

Jace frowned. "What the fuck? He's fucked his way through half the gold diggers in Manhattan. What is he thinking?"

"According to him he didn't fuck any of them and they didn't mean anything."

Ash rolled his eyes. "Wow. That's the lamest line in the book."

"Tell me about it."

"Jesus, your day *did* suck," Jace muttered. "First your dad and then Lisa."

"Yeah. Mom's been blowing up my phone bitching about all the women my dad's been seen with. Now she'll be blowing up my phone over Dad's latest brain fart."

"You want them back together?" Ash asked curiously.

"I never wanted them apart," Gabe said in a dark tone. "I have no idea what the hell possessed my dad. It sounds like total bullshit when he tries to explain it. I don't think he even knows what the hell happened. So yeah, I'd like to see them back together, but I want them to be happy, and if he's going to pull this kind of stunt down the road, I'd rather they just quit now and call it good. I don't want my mom going through that all over again."

"Yeah, I hear you," Jace said.

"So speaking of reconciliation," Ash said casually. "What the ever-loving fuck was Lisa doing in your office?"

Gabe's jaw tightened and his teeth ground together. The very last thing he wanted was to discuss Lisa, but he also knew his friends were going to be curious. They'd been there when Lisa had left him. They'd stood by him when she pulled her crazy-ass shit. It was only natural they'd be concerned when she started sniffing around again.

"Did you kick the crazy bitch out and tell her to fuck off?" Jace asked with a scowl.

Gabe chuckled, his mood lightening. He could always count on Jace and Ash to shoot straight.

"I made it clear I had absolutely zero interest in rehashing the past."

"She wants money," Jace said darkly. "I made a few calls. She's already gone through most of the settlement, and the alimony payments you fork out every month are barely keeping her head above water."

Gabe's eyebrow lifted. "You checked up on her?"

"Hell yeah. Not going to let her fuck you over like she did last time," Jace bit out. "She's still living like she's married to you. Hasn't downgraded in that department. High-maintenance bitch."

Gabe grinned. "No worries there, man. I'm not dipping back into those waters."

"That's good to hear," Ash said, relief evident in his voice.

Gabe's eyes narrowed. Had there been any doubt? Then he realized. Jace and Ash *were* worried.

"I can handle Lisa," Gabe said easily. "She's a manipulative, grasping bitch. Lesson learned."

Jace and Ash nodded their agreement. The waitresses came back with the drinks and spent several minutes flirting with Jace and Ash. They left Gabe alone. Maybe they sensed he wasn't in the mood. He had zero interest in these girls when he knew Mia was in his bed waiting.

Drink in hand, Jace turned to Gabe when the waitresses disappeared. "So how are things working out with Mia?"

Gabe was instantly on alert. He'd already had one come-to-Jesus moment with Jace over this. He didn't want it to be a bone of contention between them. Before he could say anything, Jace continued.

"I know I busted your balls about it, and yeah, I probably overreacted. It just caught me off guard. I didn't like Mia working in that damn pastry shop, but I figured she just needed time to figure out what she wanted to do. She worked hard in school. She probably just needs a break to sort herself out, and I'm not in a hurry for her to do that. She has me. I'll provide anything she needs and I don't want her to feel pressured."

A huge surge of guilt hit Gabe right in the gut. He'd definitely pressured Mia. No doubt about that. Not that he regretted it. He'd be a damn liar if he said otherwise. But still . . .

"She's working out great, Jace," Gabe said in a casual tone. "She's smart and she's motivated. She's already finding her place. She works her ass off and she has her shit together. She wowed investors at the cocktail party she attended with me. Everyone at work seems to like her and has responded well to her presence. I'm sure many of them figure she got the job because of who she is, but she's proven she deserves to be there."

"Well, and who can't like her?" Ash cut in. "She's sweet and friendly. Not a mean bone in that girl's body."

"If anyone says shit to her I want to know about it," Jace bit out.

Gabe held his hand up. "I have this, man. And if you think about it, it's a hell of a lot better for her not to work for you. This way she can prove she deserves the job because she's not working for her big brother. I'm not going to be a hardass with her but I'll expect her to do her job. You'd just coddle her and baby her to death."

Ash burst into laughter. "He totally nailed you with that one, man. If she had so much as a hangnail, you'd be sending her home."

Jace grinned. "Okay, okay, you both have a good point." Then he grew more serious. "I just want what's best for her. I want her to be happy. She's all I have."

Gabe and Ash both nodded. "I get it," Gabe said. "In your position, I'd feel the same. But lighten up. Let her spread her wings a bit. I think you'll be surprised at just how much she can do without you hovering over her."

Then in an effort to move the conversation away from Mia so Gabe wasn't in such an awkward position, he glanced at Jace and Ash with a half grin. "Brunette history or what?"

Ash groaned and Jace just looked pissed.

Gabe raised his eyebrows. "That bad?"

"Batshit crazy," Ash muttered. "Not one of our better decisions to hook up with her for a few days. Hell, she even knew it was temporary. Very temporary."

Jace kept silent, his face still dark.

"Let's just say she didn't take it too well and she definitely did not get the message. She blew up both our phones for a few days."

Gabe's brow furrowed. "You gave her your cell numbers? Are you out of your minds?"

"Fuck no," Jace exploded, speaking for the first time. "She called the office. Repeatedly. Had to threaten to report her for harassment before she finally chilled out."

Gabe laughed. "You two sure know how to pick them."

"Crazy," Ash muttered again. "I don't know how much clearer we could have been."

Gabe lifted his shoulder in a shrug. "Be more discerning next time."

Jace snorted. "Maybe we should just have contracts like you. Get all that shit sorted out before sex."

Ash choked on his drink and Gabe scowled at them both.

After an hour of drinks, more joking, and definite babe checking out on the part of Ash and Jace, Gabe glanced at his watch and saw it was close to eleven. Damn. He'd told Mia he wouldn't be that late. To wait up for him. And he was stuck here bullshitting with Jace and Ash.

He'd give it fifteen more minutes and then make up an excuse.

He was saved when Jace and Ash became riveted by a private performance. Gabe didn't have any interest. Not when he had something as sweet and gorgeous as Mia waiting for him at home.

And damn if that didn't give him a huge measure of satisfaction.

She was at home, in his bed. And she was waiting for him.

That was all the motivation he needed to stand and say his good-byes, citing an early morning, and head for the exit. Jace and Ash were distracted, muttered an appropriate "later," and then turned their attention back to the dancers.

It was a short drive to his apartment building, and he found himself hurrying to the elevator, an itch under his skin he couldn't alleviate.

He walked into his apartment to find that Mia had left the foyer light on for him. He smiled at her thoughtfulness, his chest tightening at the thought that he didn't need physical light. She was light. A ray of sunshine on a cold day.

He was already stripping out of his clothing as he entered his bedroom and he stopped, the smile broadening when he saw her curled in the middle of his bed, covers to her chin and her head resting on his pillow.

Sound asleep.

His cock was already rigid and straining, trying to break free from his pants.

"Down boy," he murmured. "Not tonight."

His dick didn't pay attention. It saw what he wanted and it was demanding ease.

Ignoring the urge to awaken her by thrusting deeply into her body, he instead quietly undressed and then carefully pulled the covers back so as not to awaken her.

He slid in next to her, pulling the sheets back up. She didn't awaken, but as if she sensed his presence, she immediately snuggled into his body, throwing her arm possessively over his side.

He smiled again as he settled more firmly against her and pulled her into his arms. Yeah, he wanted her, but this was . . . nice.

chapter twenty-three

Mia woke the next morning to a hard body pressing her into the mattress, her thighs firmly spread. And then a cock thrust deep into her body. She gasped and came fully awake, Gabe's eyes boring into hers.

"Good morning," he murmured just as his mouth claimed hers.

She couldn't even form a coherent response. She was on fire, her arousal sharp and rising higher with every single thrust.

He held her hips in his firm grasp, pressing her into the bed so she was pinned, unable to move. All she could do was lie there and take what he gave her.

It was quick. No lazy climb to release. He thrust hard and fast, his hips slapping against hers. He nuzzled her neck and then nipped at her earlobe. Chill bumps danced across her skin and she moaned, already so close to her own orgasm.

"Give me your eyes, baby. And get there."

The guttural command fueled her arousal into a full-fledged inferno. She locked her gaze to him, her body tense, every muscle coiled tight.

"My name," he whispered.

"Gabe!"

Eyes locked, his name tumbling from her lips, he leaned down, pressing his body to hers and surged into her, spilling himself deep.

For a long moment, he blanketed her, his body heaving, warm and comforting over hers. Then finally he propped himself up on his forearms and kissed her nose, his eyes warm as he stared down at her.

"Now that's the way I like to start the day," he murmured.

Then he rolled off her, patted her hip and said, "Hop into the shower, baby. We have to get to work."

Damn chipper man.

As crazy as the previous day had been, Mia was almost afraid to see what today held in store. Despite their bout of hot morning sex, as soon as they got into the office, he inserted another plug.

She never imagined the damn things came in so many sizes! There couldn't be many more because the one he used today was huge! She felt like she waddled, which only made her more self-conscious about letting anyone see her walk anywhere, so she spent the majority of the day sequestered in Gabe's office, suffering as she sat and fidgeted in her chair.

And damn if Gabe wasn't insanely busy. Three conference calls. Two meetings, plus countless other calls he had to return. So there was no crazy-hot office sex to alleviate the burn.

She was back to sulking, even as ridiculous as that made her feel.

By quitting time, she was hugely relieved. She wanted to have this damn thing out of her ass, and she wanted to get the hell out of the office. She was going stir crazy. At least she had dinner with Jace and Ash to look forward to.

Mia rode with Gabe at his insistence. He had his driver take her by her apartment before going on to his. The ride was mostly silent, but he kept hold of her hand the entire time. Almost as if he just needed that contact. And it was true, they'd seen little of each other that day. The only alone time they'd shared was when he inserted the plug in the morning and when he removed it in the afternoon.

His thumb smoothed up and down her palm, rubbing in a pattern as he stared out the window. She wasn't sure he was that in tune with her or her presence, and yet the one time she'd tried to move her hand, he'd clamped down and curled his fingers tightly around hers.

Maybe he'd missed her as much as she'd missed him. It was a stupid thought, but it didn't mean it didn't have a firm hold in her brain.

As they neared her apartment, she realized they hadn't made plans for *after* her dinner with Jace. She had no idea what Gabe expected. Would he want her to come to his apartment afterward? Or was she simply to go in to work on her own the next day?

The car pulled to a stop in front of her building, and Mia started to get out, but Gabe halted her.

"Have a good time tonight, Mia," he said softly.

She smiled. "I will."

"I'll see you at work in the morning. The driver will be here for you at eight a.m."

Well that answered her question. Evidently she'd been dismissed for the evening. And yet, as she got out, Gabe didn't look happy that she was spending the night away from him.

"See you tomorrow," she murmured.

She shut the door and watched as the car rolled away, wondering what Gabe was thinking. With a sigh, she went into her building and up to her apartment. She only had an hour to change and get ready before Jace would be there.

When she walked through the door and into the living room, Caroline popped her head out of her bedroom, her eyes wide with surprise.

"You're home! Holy shit. I was beginning to wonder if you'd moved in with Gabe."

Mia smiled. "Hello to you too."

Caroline walked over and grabbed Mia in a hug. "I've missed you, girl. All the girls have. Want to grab takeout tonight and watch movies?"

Mia winced. "Sorry, I can't. Jace is coming over, which is why I didn't go home with Gabe. Jace and Ash are taking me to eat tonight. Catch-up, because Jace has been out of town. I'm sure he's going to grill me about Gabe too since he now knows I'm working for Gabe."

Caroline's face fell. "Damn. It sucks not seeing much of you anymore. I worry about you getting in over your head on this one. It doesn't seem like you ever spend any time away from him."

Discomfort gripped Mia as she stared back at her friend. It was true she hadn't seen Caroline or the girls since the inception of her relationship with Gabe. Not that it had been forever, but she and her friends spent a lot of time together, and they were used to going out as a group.

"Club. Friday night," Caroline said firmly. "I'll round up the girls and we'll go out and have some fun."

"I don't know," Mia hedged. She had no idea what Gabe's plans for her were.

Caroline's gaze sharpened. "Tell me you're not pondering asking his permission to go out with your girls. He doesn't own you, Mia."

Mia barely controlled the guilty flinch. Gabe *did* own her. He had contractual rights to her body, her time, her everything. Not that she wanted to share that particular bit of knowledge with Caroline. Her friends would never understand.

She sighed, knowing the best thing to do would be to go and spend the evening with them. She didn't want to shut herself off from her friends because when Gabe moved on, she'd need them.

They were going to be the ones who stuck by her through thick and thin, and if she didn't take care, there would be no one left for her down the road.

She'd simply have to tell Gabe that she had plans Friday night, and hope to hell he was reasonable about it.

"Okay. Friday night," Mia relented.

Caroline's face lit up and she danced around Mia. "We are going to have so much fun! I've missed you, Mia. It's not the same without you around."

Mia felt another surge of guilt. It had been her idea for Caroline to move in. Aside from the fact that Caroline needed a place to stay, Mia had wanted the company. And now she was spending very little time in her apartment or with Caroline.

"I'm going to go call the girls so they don't make other plans. Will I see you after your dinner tonight?"

Mia nodded. "Yep. I'm spending tonight here."

"Awesome. Tell you what. Don't eat dessert. I'll make fudge and get a movie. We'll veg on the couch when you get home."

Mia grinned. "Perfect!"

Caroline made a shooing motion. "Okay, go get ready. I'll get out of your hair."

Mia ducked into her room and pulled out her favorite pair of jeans. Holes in the legs, sequined pockets and low-slung hip-hugging. They were her favorite comfort item, and she'd worked diligently to make sure they still fit even after three years of owning them. No better incentive to keep her weight down than to be able to remain in her jeans, right?

She snagged a cami and an off-the-shoulder top, and then went into the bathroom to repair her hair and makeup.

She was looking forward to her night out with Jace and Ash. They made her comfortable, and they enjoyed an easy relationship. Instead of one older brother, it was like having two, even if Ash flirted endlessly with her. He was perfectly harmless—to her at least. He was lethal to other women, but he was too firmly entrenched in her mind as a family member. Gabe was a whole different matter . . .

And the more she thought about it, the more she looked forward to her night out with the girls. Caroline had it right when she'd said that Mia hadn't been around since she'd taken the job with Gabe. Gabe was . . . Well, he was an obsession that was all consuming. And there was the matter of the contract she'd signed giving up her time to him to do with as he wished.

If the girls knew of that particular caveat, they'd be checking her into an institution.

She brushed on another layer of mascara and touched up her lipstick, a shiny pink that matched her toes, and then she pulled her hair up into a messy bun and secured a large clip to hold it in place.

By the time she made it back into the living room, the decadent smell of chocolate filled the air.

"Oh my God, Caro, that smells divine," Mia groaned.

Caroline looked up from the stove and grinned. "I'm even sacrificing the nuts just for you."

"You are too good to me."

Mia perched on the bar stool across the island from where Caroline was cooking, and rested her arms on the countertop.

"So how is work going?"

Caroline stopped stirring a moment and then reset the temperature before laying the spoon to the side. She wrinkled her nose and made a face.

"Boss is still a dickhead. He spends more time trying to get into my pants than he does actually working. As soon as I have enough money saved up, I'm going to start looking for another job."

Caroline took a deep breath and glanced up at Mia.

"I met this guy . . ."

Mia leaned forward. "Oh do tell. Is this someone I should know about?"

"Well, maybe. I'm not sure yet. We're just talking. Texting. God, I feel like I'm in high school or something. And I'm paranoid. You know, after Ted."

Mia sighed. Caroline's last relationship had been a disaster. She'd met Ted, fell instantly in lust and love only to find out after six months of strange meeting times and dates that he was married with two kids. It had made her question herself in a huge way.

"So you think he's married or something?" Mia asked.

Caroline's lips turned downward. "I don't know. Something's off. Or maybe I'm just screwed up after what happened with Ted. Part of me wants to just walk away before we become involved, but the other part of me wonders if I'm being stupid and if I should give him a chance."

Mia pursed her lips and looked thoughtfully at Caroline. "You know, Jace runs background checks on every man I've ever seen. I could always have him do a little checking on your guy. Wouldn't hurt to have some info before you take the plunge."

Caroline gave her a look of incredulity. "Are you serious?"

Mia laughed. "Unfortunately, yes. If a guy so much as expresses interest, he launches a full investigation."

"Wow. That's heavy. I'm not sure how I'd feel about doing a check on Brandon." She wavered a moment, clear indecision written on her features. "But if he's married or otherwise attached I don't want to get involved, you know?"

"Give me some more details," Mia said. "I'll speak to Jace about it tonight. No harm in doing a little digging. It's not like we're stealing his identity, although I'm sure Jace could manage it."

"He's a bouncer at the club we're going to Friday night. You know, my in with the passes. His last name is Sullivan."

"Okay, I'll see what I can do," Mia said. She reached over the counter to squeeze Caroline's hand. "It'll be fine."

Caroline let out a long breath. "I hope so. I don't want to be made a fool of again."

"You weren't a fool for loving someone, Caro. He was the fool. Not you. You went into the relationship in good faith."

"I don't like being the other woman," Caroline said, cringing as she remembered.

The wife in question had confronted Caroline outside Mia's apartment building. It hadn't been pretty. Caroline had been completely blindsided and devastated by the revelation as well as the horror of facing an irate, jealous wife.

Mia's cell phone rang with Jace's ring tone. She reached for it and brought it to her ear.

"Hey you," she said in greeting.

"We're just pulling up. Are you ready or do you want us to come up?" Jace said.

"No need. I'll be right down."

"Okay, see you in a few."

She hung up and then slid off the stool. "See you later, Caro. Can't wait for that fudge!"

Caroline waved as Mia left the apartment and headed for the elevator.

A moment later, she walked out to see Jace's car waiting at the curb. He drove a sleek, black BMW that still looked as it had on the showroom floor.

Ash got out and waved, smiling broadly as he opened the door to the backseat for her.

"Hey, beautiful," he said, kissing her cheek just before she ducked inside.

"Hey, baby girl," Jace greeted once she was inside.

Oh but this car just smelled of expensive male awesomeness.

Ash settled back into his seat and Jace pulled away.

"So how was Gabe after he hauled you out of my office after the incident with Lisa?" Ash asked. "My big mouth didn't get you into trouble, did it?"

She worked hard to suppress the heat from flaring into her cheeks and even harder to sound casual.

"He was fine. Silent and brooding. We didn't speak much before I left."

Jace shook his head. "I hope he doesn't let her get into his head. She's bad news all the way around. I imagine the only reason she's sniffing around him now is because she's out of money."

Mia arched an eyebrow. "You know this for sure? Didn't she get a lot from him in the divorce?" Like a whole lot. Gabe had money. A lot of it. And from what she figured out from gossip and bits and pieces of overheard conversations was that Lisa got a very healthy divorce settlement. Nothing that would cripple Gabe, of course, but Lisa had walked away with enough to last someone a lifetime. Or at least a normal person.

"I have a pretty good idea after placing a few calls after she left the office."

Whoa, that was interesting. First, that Lisa was having financial issues and second, that Jace had been so quick to check into the matter. Not that it should have surprised her. Gabe, Jace and Ash were tight. And they had each other's backs. Always.

Jace and Ash had closed ranks around Gabe after the divorce and while it seemed ludicrous that Gabe would need any sort of support, she knew that an unbreakable bond existed among the men. She only hoped to hell it was unbreakable enough to survive the fallout if Jace ever found out about her relationship with Gabe.

And then she remembered Caro's plight.

"Hey, speaking of," Mia said, leaning up to stick her head between the front seats. "Can you do a background check on a guy named Brandon Sullivan? He's a bouncer who works at a club called Vibe. Just general info. You know, like whether he's married, shacked up with someone or has a criminal record."

Jace braked for the red light and then both he and Ash turned to stare at her, deep frowns on their faces.

"Is this someone you're seeing?" Jace demanded.

"A bouncer, Mia? You can do much better than that, sweetheart," Ash chided.

Mia shook her head. "Not me. Caroline. I told her I'd ask you to check. She's paranoid after what happened with the last guy she was involved with."

Jace's expression became thoughtful as he accelerated down the street. "Oh yeah, wasn't she involved with a married guy a while back? I remember you saying something about that."

"Yeah, that's the one," Mia said with a sigh. "It messed her up pretty bad. Caro's not like that. I mean she would have never gotten involved with a married man. She's so sweet and trusting and this guy screwed her over royally. I just don't want to see that happen to her again."

"I'll take care of it," Jace said. "Tell Caro not to worry. I'll have him checked out first thing tomorrow morning."

"You're the best," she said.

Jace smiled indulgently at her in the rearview mirror. "I've missed you, baby girl. We haven't spent much time together lately."

"I've missed you too," she said softly. And she had. Lately, though, it seemed they'd gone their separate ways, even before the thing with Gabe. Jace had been busier than ever with work. It was why she'd purposely gone to his grand opening. A night that had changed the course of her life. Looking back, she'd never have imagined how the decision to go to something as innocuous as a boring cocktail party would change everything so dramatically.

They had to park a block away from the pub, and Ash opened her door, offering his hand to help her out. Jace and Ash flanked her as they made their way down the busy street as dusk settled around them.

The pub was still relatively quiet. It was early to eat yet, and the pub wouldn't fill to capacity until later in the night. Ash directed them to a corner booth that overlooked the cross street, and a peppy waitress was extremely fast to pick up their table. She eyed Ash and Jace like they were her next meal and she was about to dig in.

She was younger than Mia. She had to be. She looked to be maybe twenty. Probably a college student waiting tables for extra money. Which meant there was an even bigger age gap between her and Jace and Ash. Eighteen years? Not that it was that much more than the difference between her and Gabe, but it just seemed creepy to watch as someone who looked like a teenager flirted with her brother and his best friend.

They managed to get their food ordered after the flirt session. Mia was in the mood to indulge. Since fudge was waiting for her at home, why not just let it all hang out? While she may eat a salad with Gabe, she had no reservations with Jace and Ash and she ordered nachos fully loaded.

That didn't stop her from mooching off Jace's and Ash's plates.

They laughed and joked and talked about everything and nothing. After she'd shoved her plate forward, so stuffed she could barely breathe, she impulsively leaned over and hugged Jace.

"Love you," she said fiercely. "Thank you for tonight. It was just what I needed."

Jace hugged her back and kissed her temple. "Everything okay with you?"

She pulled away and smiled. "Yeah. Perfect."

She hadn't lied. Tonight had been exactly what she'd needed. Her relationship with Gabe was intense and all consuming. It was easy to get so caught up in him and his demands that she lost sight of everything else. Her family—Jace. Her friends—Caroline and the girls. *Herself.*

"Are you sure everything's okay with you, Mia?" Ash asked.

She glanced over to see him studying her, his shrewd stare boring into her.

"Are you happy at work?"

Jace picked up on Ash's question with a frown. "Is there something going on I don't know about?"

"Jace, I'm fine," Mia said.

She was utterly sincere. Maybe she wasn't always absolutely certain about her direction. Of where she was going with Gabe. But she knew she was fine. Whenever the ride was over, she'd be okay. She'd be better than before.

"You'd tell me if you had a problem," Jace said in a soft voice, his gaze solidly fixed on her.

It wasn't a question and it wasn't voiced as one. It was a statement of fact he wanted her reinforcement on.

"You'll always be my big brother, Jace. That means, unfortunately, that I'll always run to you to fix things for me."

She finished with a wistful smile, remembering all the times when she was a girl that he'd been so patient with her. She always wondered if the reason he hadn't married and had kids of his own was because he'd spent so much time raising her. It saddened her because he would make such an amazing father. But he'd shown no signs of settling down with one woman. And well, if he and Ash were always in bed with the same woman at the same time, she supposed it would make it a little awkward to forge a more traditional relationship.

"There's no 'unfortunately' to it, baby girl. I wouldn't have it any other way."

"And hey, just so you know. My office is always open if Jace isn't around," Ash interjected.

They were genuinely concerned. Was it so evident that she was unsettled? Did she wear the evidence of her association with Gabe on her face? She didn't feel different. Didn't think she looked different. But everyone around her had sensed her disquiet.

"You're both sweet," she said. "But I'm good. Gabe was right. I was hiding by working at La Patisserie. I needed that jolt he gave me to get me moving in the right direction. I'm not saying I'll work as a personal assistant forever, but Gabe gave me the opportunity to gain some experience that wasn't about refilling a coffee cup."

"As long as you're happy," Jace said. "I just want you to be happy."

She smiled. "I am."

They sat and talked for a while longer before Jace motioned for the check. After the waitress dropped it off, Jace took out his credit card. As he slid it inside the leather folder with the check, a tall brunette walked purposefully in their direction.

At first Mia thought she was going to the bathroom, but her gaze was locked on Ash and Jace and it became apparent that she was on a mission.

"Oh shit," Ash murmured.

Jace looked up and the brunette halted at the table, her eyes glittering and a fake fourteen-karat smile plastered on her face. But then she turned to look at Mia and her gaze became frigid.

"Ash. Jace," she said in a clipped voice. "Slumming tonight?"

Mia's eyes widened. *Holy shit* but she'd just been royally insulted. She glanced down. She didn't look that bad, did she?

Jace's face grew cold. It was a look that had always scared Mia because when he got that quiet and that glacial, it meant he was seriously pissed off.

"Miss Houston," he said tersely. "This is my sister, Mia, and you owe her an apology for your rude, crass behavior."

The brunette's cheeks bloomed with instant color. She looked mortified. Mia could almost feel sorry for her except . . . well, she didn't.

Ash looked as pissed as Jace did. He reached over, picked up the check holder and then waved it at the waitress, looking beyond the brunette as if she weren't standing there.

"Forgive me," the brunette said huskily. But she wasn't looking at Mia when she uttered the apology. Her stare was still fixed on Jace and then Ash in turns. Mia may as well have not even been there.

"You never returned my calls," she said.

Ugh, this was starting to get ugly. Mia cringed for the woman. She wanted to tell her to have some pride and walk away.

"We said all that was necessary when we parted," Ash said, before Jace could respond. "Now if you'll excuse us, we're having a night out with Mia and we'd like to get our check from the waitress who's standing behind you."

Mia didn't need it spelled out to her that this was obviously one of Jace and Ash's threesome women. The way Miss Houston looked at both men told of her intimate knowledge of both.

Jace stood, his face brooding and dark. "Have some class, Erica. Go home. Don't make a scene in public. You'll regret it tomorrow."

He reached back for Mia's hand, pulling her up so she stood on his other side, away from Erica.

Erica's face hardened and her eyes narrowed.

"The only thing I regret is that I wasted my time with the both of you."

She pivoted on her very high heels and stalked out of the pub, leaving Jace, Mia and Ash standing by the booth they'd occupied.

"You guys have a stalker?" Mia murmured. "Kind of weird that she'd show up in the exact same place we're eating out of all the possible restaurants in Manhattan."

Neither man looked inclined to comment. They both looked like they wanted the matter to disappear. Mia could find it funny if they both weren't so pissed off.

They walked back to Jace's car and when they got in, Jace glanced up in his rearview mirror. "Sorry about that, Mia."

She smiled. "Women flocking to you two isn't anything new. And hey, if you guys ever want to go slumming again, call me. The food was awesome. I probably gained five pounds tonight and I'm going home to gain another five eating the fudge Caroline made."

Ash groaned. "For God's sake. You could let us forget she made the slumming comment. What a bitch she was. I can't believe she insulted you like that."

Mia shrugged. "I don't think it would have mattered if I were dressed to the nines. She would have found some way to take me down a few notches. How dare I be out with you two!"

Jace grimaced and fell silent as he and Ash exchanged quick, uneasy glances. She wanted to laugh. Yeah, she knew about them and it was funny to see them worry about just how much she knew.

They drove her to her apartment and Jace let her and Ash out front so Ash could walk her up while Jace circled the block and came back for him.

"Thanks for dinner, Ash. It was a lot of fun," she said when they were inside the building.

He kissed her on the cheek when the elevator door opened and then waved as she got inside.

"See you tomorrow at work," he called.

She waved back, and then he disappeared as the doors closed.

How very interesting the evening had turned out. She mulled over the scene at dinner as she rode up the elevator.

Her phone went off, and she dug into her purse as she got off the elevator and walked toward her apartment door. She punched the button to retrieve the text message and saw it was from Gabe.

Hope you had a nice dinner with Jace and Ash. Text me to let me know you made it back to your place safely.

Her heart fluttered and her chest tightened as she stared at his words. His concern, or rather his possessiveness—she wasn't sure which it was—warmed her to her core.

She sent back a quick text, smiling as she entered her apartment. I'm back just now. Had fun. See you tomorrow.

chapter twenty-four

Gabe's phone rang as he entered his office building the next morning. He was earlier than usual. It had already become a habit, a routine he found pleasure and comfort in, for him and Mia to ride in together after she'd spent the night at his apartment. Last night had made him restless and edgy, and he'd spent the majority of the evening brooding in silence as he imagined Mia in her bed alone just as he was alone in his.

He didn't like feeling this way. Hated that he was somehow dependent on Mia for the peace of mind he only felt when she was near. It made him feel like a needy, grasping fool, and with his age and experience he shouldn't be responding like this.

He grimaced when he saw that it was his mother calling. He let it go to voice mail as he got onto the elevator, resolving to call her back in the privacy of his office. What she had to say wasn't a conversation he wanted to have in public. Or what he imagined she would say.

The offices were empty and silent as he made his way down the hall to his own. Mia wouldn't be in for another hour and a half, and already he was antsy with anticipation. He flexed his hands, curling them as he sat behind his desk. He should have just gone by her apartment on his way in. He should have just sent a car for her after she got finished with her dinner with Jace. But he'd been determined to prove to himself that he didn't need her. That he didn't think about her when she wasn't with him. He needed this space between them, because she was fast becoming an addiction he had no hope of surviving.

Yeah, that wasn't working out so well for him so far.

He picked up his phone and dialed his mother's number, waiting as it rang.

"Mom, it's Gabe. Sorry I didn't answer. You caught me on my way up to the office."

"You won't believe this," she said, distress clear in her voice. She wasted no time getting to the heart of why she'd called.

He sighed and leaned back, already knowing what was coming. But still, he asked, pretending ignorance. "What's going on?"

"Your father said he wants to reconcile! Can you believe that? He was *here* last night."

"And what do you want?" he asked softly.

She sputtered a moment and then there was a long silence. Clearly she hadn't expected him not to react. Or maybe she hadn't even thought about what she wanted yet.

"He says he didn't sleep with all those women. That he loves me and wants me back and that he made the biggest mistake of his life," she raged. "He bought a house, Gabe. A house! Does that sound like a man who hasn't moved on and isn't over his marriage to me?"

"Do you believe him?"

There was another distinct pause. Then he could hear her sigh heavily, and he could picture her sagging, her face crumbling.

"I don't know," she said, upset radiating from her voice. "You saw the pictures, Gabe. Everyone thinks he was with those women even if he wasn't. And now he comes crawling back to me because he made a mistake. After all the humiliation I've suffered and all he's put me through, he expects me to just simply forgive and forget and move forward like he didn't walk out on me after thirty-nine years of marriage."

Gabe held his tongue because there was nothing he could say. It wasn't a decision he could make for her, and he couldn't very well advocate her taking his father back because Gabe knew all too well how she felt. How ironic that his own ex-wife had come to plead her case at the same time his father was pleading his. There was no way in hell he'd ever take Lisa back so he understood his mother's reluctance where his father was concerned. He'd be a huge fucking hypocrite if he nudged her in that direction. He wouldn't do it, even if in his heart he wanted his parents back together. His family. Two people he'd looked up to his entire life.

"I understand why you're angry," Gabe said. "I don't blame you. But you have to do what you want, Mom. Decide what makes you happy and damn what anyone else thinks or says. Do you still love him?"

"Of course I do," she said in agitation. "That doesn't go away in a month or two or even a year. You don't give thirty-nine years of your life to a man and get over him just because he decides he no longer wants you."

"You don't have to make a decision right away," he pointed out. "You're in the driver's seat on this one, Mom. He's got a lot of making up to do with you. There's no crime in taking your time and weighing your options and your feelings. No one says you have to take him back overnight."

"No," she agreed. "And I wouldn't. There's too much we'd have to work out. I love him, but I also hate him for what he did and for the way he did it. I can't forget all the pictures of him with those other women. I can't look at him without seeing him with someone else."

"I just want what's best for you," Gabe said gently. "Whatever that is. You know you have my full support no matter what you decide."

There was another sigh, and then he could hear the tears in her voice. It made his jaw clench and his fist curl in anger. Damn his father for what he'd done to her.

"I appreciate that, Gabe. Thank God for you. I don't know what I would have done without your support and understanding."

"Love you, Mom. I'm here any time you need to talk."

This time he heard her smile as she returned his love.

"I'll let you get back to work," she said. "But you're in awfully early this morning. I think you should consider taking that vacation we discussed. You work way too hard, Son."

"I'll be fine. You just take care of you. Okay? And call me if you need me, Mom. You know I'm never too busy for you."

They rang off and Gabe shook his head. So his dad had made his move. He hadn't just experienced a brief moment of regret resulting in his confession to Gabe. He'd gone to Gabe's mom and began the long, winding path to reconciliation.

He busied himself with e-mails, keeping an eye on the clock. The closer it came to the time when Mia would arrive, the edgier he got. Twice he nearly sent her a text to ask where she was, but he put his phone down each time, determined that he wouldn't sound so goddamn eager.

In his desk was the last plug he intended to use on her to ease her into anal sex. The image of her bending over his desk, her cheeks parting as he inserted the plug, made him grow achingly hard. He couldn't wait to slide his cock in her ass instead of a plug. He was growing impatient. He wanted full access to her body. He'd given her enough time to adjust to his demands. It was time to indulge fully in every dirty, hedonistic fantasy he'd conjured around the two of them.

He was already thinking ahead to the weekend. Next week

she'd accompany him on a business trip out of the country. Before that he wanted a few days where it was only the two of them. Her full initiation into his world.

Anticipation licked up his spine, his entire body growing heavy with lust as he imagined her tied and spread before him. Of him plunging into her ass from behind. Of fucking her mouth until his cum spilled down her lips. Of sinking so far into her sweet pussy that there was no separation between them.

He'd already claimed Mia. He'd fucked her tirelessly. But what was to come was his removing any doubt from her mind that she belonged fully and completely to him. He wanted every time she looked at him for her to have the knowledge in her eyes of his possession. For her to remember him taking her and marking her in vivid detail.

If that made him a primitive asshole, oh well. It was who he was, and he was helpless to control his need for her or the fierce urge to dominate her wholly.

At eight thirty, his door opened, and Mia walked in.

His body leapt to life, relief hovering over him like a cloud.

"Lock the door," he commanded in a quiet voice.

She turned to do as he'd ordered and then she swiveled back around, staring at him across the space. She was too far from him. He needed her next to him, his touch like a tattoo on her skin.

"Come here."

Had it only been since yesterday afternoon that he'd seen her? It seemed forever, and he was only interested in reestablishing his dominance over her. Or reminding her whom she belonged to.

He reached in his desk for the plug, and today, instead of having her bend over the desk and raise her skirt, he motioned for her to follow him to the sofa along the wall. He sat and then patted his lap, pulling her down to lie over his legs.

She rested her cheek against the soft leather and turned so that she could see him out of the corner of her eye. Her hair tumbled around her face, and her eyes had a sleepy look that glowed with desire.

Sliding a hand underneath her skirt, he was satisfied when he encountered the smooth, naked flesh of her ass. He pushed upward, baring her to his gaze, and then he reached for the lubricant, knowing today she'd need more because this plug was the largest yet.

He teased her opening, stroking it with his fingers as he liberally applied the gel. She went tense over his lap and he caressed her bottom, sliding his hand up her spine.

"Relax," he murmured. "Trust me, Mia. I won't hurt you. Let me make you feel good."

She let out a sigh and went limp over his lap. He loved that she was so responsive. So sweetly submissive.

He began to work the tip of the plug inside her opening, stretching the small ring as he gently stroked back and forth, gradually gaining depth. Her fingers flexed and then formed tight balls. She closed her eyes, and a soft moan escaped her full lips. Lips he had every intention of availing himself of. Or perhaps he'd sink into her pussy. She would be exquisitely tight with the plug nestled inside her.

She gave a small cry when he finally lodged the plug fully inside her. He immediately caressed and stroked her behind and her back, soothing and comforting her.

"Shhh, baby. It's done with now. Take deep breaths. Don't fight it. It will burn a moment and feel tight and full, but just breathe."

Her chest rose and fell in quick succession, her entire body heaving over his lap. After giving her a moment to gain control of her senses, he eased her upward. After instructing her to stand between his knees facing away from him, he reached to unfasten his fly and he pulled out his dick.

He scooted to the edge of the couch, and then reached up to

put his hands on her waist, guiding her down onto his waiting cock.

She gasped when he sank into her pussy and her ass came to rest on his lap. Oh hell yes. She was tight and quivering around him. Liquid heat, surrounding him and sucking him deeper.

After fucking her this way for a few strokes, he pushed her upward and then rose to stand behind her. He turned her and positioned her on her hands and knees, her ass perched high in the air, her knees on the very edge of the sofa.

Her pussy was spread and bared to him, the pink flesh glistening welcomingly. Like nectar he couldn't wait to dive into.

He pushed inside her, stroking deep into her wetness. He loved taking her from behind. It was one of his favorite positions.

Grasping her hips, his fingers digging into her flesh, he held her firmly in place and began driving forcefully into her. His hips slapped against her ass, the noise loud in the silence of his office.

He glanced down, watching as his dick disappeared into her pussy and then as it withdrew, slick with her juices.

"Touch yourself, baby. Finish yourself off. I'm not going to last," he said in a strained voice.

It was a familiar thought and statement. It was one he seemed to make every time they made love. He simply couldn't control himself around her. He only knew one speed when it came to Mia. All out.

Her pussy clutched around him like a fist. She went soft and silky, instant liquid, dissolving around him. It made him crazy. He closed his eyes. They nearly rolled back in his head. His release built, coiling in his balls and then racing up his length until it burst from his cock and splashed deeply within her body.

She felt so damn good. Nothing had ever felt better. No one had ever made him feel this crazy and out-of-control, but in a totally good way. He couldn't even explain it.

She just did it for him.

She was his drug. His addiction that he was helpless to break. Moreover he had no desire to ever break it.

He leaned into her, remaining inside her warm clasp for several long moments. When he eased away, he helped her to her feet and sent her into the bathroom to freshen herself while he straightened his clothing.

He'd just had one of the most mind-blowing orgasms of his life and yet he was ready to go again the minute she walked out of the bathroom. He sucked in his breath and returned to his desk, determined to act with a little class and not be reduced to a rutting beast.

As he glanced over his calendar, he realized he hadn't yet told her of their trip to Paris the next week. He'd wanted to surprise her and he hoped she'd light up as he imagined she would.

"I'm traveling to Paris next week on business," he said casually.

Mia's head came up at her desk. "Oh? How long will you be gone?"

Was it disappointment he heard in her voice or was it merely wishful thinking on his part?

He smiled. "You're coming with me."

Her eyes widened. "Really?"

"Yes. We leave Monday afternoon. I assume your passport is still valid?"

"Yes, of course."

There was excitement in her voice and her entire face had lit up.

"We'll spend the weekend together and I'll take you shopping for anything you may need for the trip," he said indulgently.

She sobered and her gaze dropped for a moment. He couldn't tell if she looked guilty or if she was merely avoiding his eyes. His brows furrowed as he continued to stare at her. Waiting for what she'd reacted to.

"I have plans Friday night," she said in a husky voice. "They were made before. I mean before you and I . . ."

It was on the tip of his tongue to ask her *what plans* and to press her further. It was certainly within his right. But she looked so uncomfortable that he didn't want to put her on the defensive, and he damn sure didn't want her to lie to him. And she may well if he cornered her.

"I assume it's only Friday night then?" he said in a short tone. She nodded.

"Okay then, be at my apartment Saturday morning. You'll spend the weekend with me and then we'll leave Monday afternoon for Paris."

Relief flashed in her eyes and she smiled that thousand-watt smile again.

"I can't wait," she said. "Paris sounds so exciting! Will we have a chance to see anything?"

He smiled at her enthusiasm. "Probably not, but we'll see what happens."

His phone rang and he checked his watch. Time had slipped away from him and it was time for his conference call. He waved his hand for Mia to go back to what she was doing, and then he got comfortable in his chair before answering the call.

chapter twenty-five

"Tell Jace thank you for checking up on Brandon for me," Caroline said as the two rode in a cab to Vibe. "It was really sweet of him. I feel horrible that I even let you do this for me, but after Ted, I just have this horrible, sick feeling every time I even look at a guy with interest, you know?"

Mia reached over to squeeze her friend's hand. "It will get better, sweetie. And hey, from everything Jace reported, Brandon sounds like a hardworking, honorable guy. Most importantly, he's single and he lives alone."

Relief was evident in Caroline's face and she twitched eagerly as they approached the club.

"Yeah, that helps a lot. I guess we'll see what happens, huh?"

Mia smiled as the cab slowed. It was nine o'clock and she was tired after her day at work. She'd rather be with Gabe at his apartment, having a quiet dinner and whatever else he had in store for her. She hated that she'd effectively lied to him about what her plans were for the night. Not that she'd blatantly told an untruth, but she hadn't been open with him. Somehow telling him she was going clubbing made her worry over his reaction. What if he told her *no*?

It wasn't that she wouldn't have gone anyway. Yes, they had a contractual agreement—God, she was tired of that word. She was getting to the point where she hated the very thought of that piece of paper she'd signed. Not because she regretted any part of her relationship with Gabe, but because of what that contract represented. Or rather what it didn't represent.

She simply hadn't wanted that confrontation with Gabe. She wasn't out guy shopping tonight. She was going to have fun with her girls and spend time with them—time that had been a precious commodity ever since Gabe had taken over her life.

Yes, she could see why Caroline would be worried. If one of her friends had entered a relationship where she spent all her free time with the guy to the point of excluding everyone else in her life, Mia would be concerned about the relationship. She'd question whether it was healthy for one of her friends.

And maybe her relationship with Gabe wasn't healthy. She knew damn well her emotional dependence on him wasn't. She was headed for a serious fall, and when that happened, she'd need her friends more than ever, and that was why she couldn't shut them out now.

But whatever this was between her and Gabe was what she wanted. She craved it. She wasn't in denial of her circumstances. She had a very good idea of what was going to eventually happen. But she was going to enjoy every moment—savor every minute— until the time he set her free.

She'd survive. Or maybe that was the part she was in denial over. She wasn't entirely certain she would survive when Gabe walked away.

"Hey, we're here," Caroline said. "Earth to Mia."

Mia blinked and looked up to see Caroline already out of the cab. Mia dug into her pocket for the cash to pay the cabbie and then she scrambled out after Caroline.

Chessy, Trish and Gina were waiting outside the club in the Meatpacking District, and a long line had already formed down the block. They all ganged up on Mia, hugging and exclaiming over her. Mia laughingly fielded their affection and some of her anxiety eased. This would be fun. And an evening away from Gabe was probably a good thing. It was too easy to get caught up in the alternate universe he'd created for them. But this . . . this was real. These were her friends and this was her life.

It was time to cut loose and have some fun for the night.

Caroline herded them toward the VIP entrance and it was then that Mia got her first look at Brandon. He was a tall, heavily muscled man. Bald, with a goatee, a diamond earring flashed in his left lobe. As soon as his gaze lighted on Caroline, he lost the menacing, badass look of a bouncer, and he looked as though someone had just put a puppy in front of him.

He visibly melted, and if Mia had any reservations that this guy was genuinely interested in Caroline, they were gone.

He positioned himself between the line of people and the door and motioned for Caroline.

Mia and the others followed Caroline and Brandon reached into his pocket to pull out five VIP passes.

She couldn't hear what Brandon said to Caroline over the street noises. He leaned in close to say something in Caroline's ear. Whatever it was had Caroline suffused with color and her eyes danced with delight. He smiled gently at her and then motioned her and her friends through the entrance.

"He's hot, Caro!" Chessy exclaimed when they got inside.

Gina and Trish were quick to agree even as they gazed around at the crowded club. Music pulsed and vibrated off the walls. The dance floor was huge—and packed. There was an electric look and feel to the place. Mostly dark but with neon underglow at the tables and the bar. Laser beams danced across the floor, bouncing off the moving, gyrating bodies.

"I vote we get totally hammered," Trish said. "Good music, dancing, drinks and hopefully some hot guys."

"I'm in," Chessy declared.

"Me too," Gina said.

They turned to look at Mia. "Bring it on," she said.

They all whooped and then waded in to find the table Brandon had reserved for them.

Caroline tugged Mia back a step and then leaned in by her ear so Mia could hear her.

"I'm going home with Brandon afterward. Is that okay? Will you be okay getting back to the apartment by yourself? He said he'll get a cab for you."

Mia's eyebrows rose. "You sure, Caro?"

Caro nodded. "We've been talking for a while now. I'm not even saying we're going to sleep together. Our work schedules are completely opposite, so we haven't been able to hook up until now."

"Then go. Just be careful, okay?"

Caroline smiled and nodded.

They found their table, ordered drinks and waited. The frenetic beat of the music invaded Mia's body and she found herself wiggling in time as they stood by their table. Chessy joined in and soon the girls had their own section of the dance floor right at their table.

Before their waitress arrived with their drinks, two guys came over, their smiles charming, and began talking to Chessy and Trish. Mia purposely stayed to the back of the table where it abutted the rail overlooking the dance floor. In no way did she want to advertise she was looking, and she didn't want to have to deal with any awkward brush-offs. Instead, she turned to face the floor and bopped along with the music.

A few minutes later, their drinks were delivered and the two guys had disappeared. They collected their glasses from the tray and then Caroline held hers up in a toast.

"Here's to an awesome night!" she yelled.

They clinked glasses, and the drinking began.

Mia paced herself. She didn't have the tolerance for alcohol that her friends had. They bounced back and forth between the dance floor and their table, and their waitress kept a steady supply of drinks delivered to them.

By midnight, Mia was feeling the effects of the alcohol, and she slowed her intake while the others continued to whoop it up. Chessy had hooked up with a guy who stuck to her like glue the entire night. Where she went, he went, and he made certain the girls had what they wanted.

Brandon came by after a while to check in on them and he spoke to Caroline for a few minutes to the side. When he left, Caroline's smile was huge and her eyes sparkled. She was excited— flush with the newness of a potential relationship when everything was shiny and exhilarating. Mia was happy for her. Caro deserved happiness after her last relationship. Maybe Brandon would be the one.

By two in the morning, Mia was ready to drop, and she was more than a little intoxicated. Since Caroline was riding home with Brandon, Mia saw no reason for her to stay any longer. She pulled Caroline to the side and told her she was heading home. Chessy and the others were still on the dance floor, but they'd all hooked up for the night and were occupied with their respective guys. They wouldn't miss Mia.

"Let me get Brandon and we'll walk you out to a cab," Caroline said above the music.

Mia nodded and waited as Caroline ducked away. A moment later, she returned with Brandon in tow and Mia followed them out of the club. Brandon motioned for one of the taxis that was parked at the corner and then opened the door for Mia to get in.

"I'll call you tomorrow," Caroline said as she leaned down into the backseat.

"Be careful and have fun," Mia said.

Caroline grinned and shut the door.

Mia gave her address to the driver and then leaned back in the seat. She still had a major buzz going even though she'd stopped drinking almost an hour before. Her phone went off and she frowned. It was past two o'clock. Who the hell would be texting her at this hour?

She pulled her phone from her pocket where it had lain forgotten all night, and winced when she saw she had over a dozen missed calls. All from Gabe. And then there were the texts. The last one had just been sent a few seconds ago.

Where the fuck are you?

While there was no way to discern tone from a text, she could positively see Gabe bristling with anger. There were several other texts, all demanding to know where she was and how she was getting home.

Shit. Should she call him? It was awfully damn late—or early—but he was obviously up and he was obviously pissed or worried or both—at her.

She'd wait until she got home and then text him back. At least then she could say she was at her apartment.

It took far less time to get home, as traffic wasn't a factor at this hour of the morning. It wasn't long until the cab pulled up to her building. She paid him and then got out, bobbling a bit as she got her legs underneath her.

The cab pulled away and she started toward the door to her building when she saw him.

Her breath caught in her chest and her pulse accelerated until the alcohol in her stomach swirled, making her queasy.

Gabe was standing outside the door of her building, and he looked pissed. He strode rapidly toward her, his expression dark and those eyes glittering dangerously.

"It's about goddamn time," he bit out. "Where the hell have you been? And why the hell didn't you answer my calls or my texts? Do you have any idea how worried I've been?"

She weaved unsteadily and he cursed, grabbing her arm to keep her from falling.

"You're shitfaced," he said grimly.

She shook her head, still not having found her voice. "N-no," she finally managed to stammer out.

"Yes," he said.

He propelled her inside as the doorman opened the door and hustled her toward the elevator. He took the key she was holding in her hand, and pried it from her fingers as they entered and he punched the button for her floor.

"Can you even walk?" he asked, his gaze flicking over her like a whip.

She nodded, although she wasn't so sure now. Her knees were shaking and more and more she felt the urge to vomit. Her face paled and sweat broke out on her forehead.

Gabe cursed again as the elevator doors opened. He grabbed her hand and then pulled her into his side, supporting her as they walked to her door. He jammed the key into the lock, opened the door and then swept her inside. He slammed the door and then rushed her into the bathroom.

Not a moment too soon.

Her stomach rebelled and she leaned over the toilet just in time.

Gabe gathered her hair in his hands and pulled it back, holding it away from her face. Then he slid one hand up and down her back in a soothing, calming manner.

He didn't say a word—a fact she was grateful for—while she released the contents of her stomach. When the retching finally eased, he left her only long enough to dampen a washcloth in the sink and then he returned, wiping gently at her face and forehead.

"What the hell were you thinking?" he demanded. "You know you can't tolerate alcohol that well."

She sagged and leaned her forehead onto his chest, closing her eyes as she sucked in deep breaths. All she wanted was to lie down. Even after puking so much, she was still way impaired. And she wasn't certain why. She hadn't drunk that much. Had she?

The entire evening was somewhat of a blur to her. Dancing. Drinking. Dancing some more. Or maybe it had been drinking some more.

"Want to brush my teeth," she mumbled.

"Are you sure you can stand up for that long?"

She nodded.

"I'll go get your bed ready so you can lie down," he said.

Gabe left the bathroom, anger still a tight knot in his gut. More than anger, however, had been fear. A sensation that still gripped him right by the balls.

If she weren't so damn drunk, he'd tan her ass right here and now. Of all the irresponsible, idiotic things to pull.

He pulled back her covers, fixed the pillows and then arranged the sheets so he could slide her into bed. If she wasn't so sick, he'd haul her over to his apartment right now and she'd stay there until they left for Paris.

He walked back toward the bathroom, frowning when he heard nothing but quiet.

"Mia?" he asked as he stepped to the doorway.

He shook his head at the sight that greeted him. Mia was sitting on the floor in front of the toilet, her arm propped on the seat. Her head was resting on her arm and she was passed out cold.

With a sigh, he bent down and lifted her into his arms. He carried her into her bedroom and laid her on the bed so he could undress her. When she was naked, he stepped back long enough to undress to his boxers, and then he climbed into bed next to her, arranging her so she was comfortably resting against his body, her head pillowed on his arm.

They were going to have a long damn talk in the morning whether she had a hangover or not.

chapter twenty-six

When Mia opened her eyes, it felt as though someone put an ice pick right through one of her eyeballs. She groaned and turned from the source of light shining through her window only to see Gabe standing in the doorway of her bedroom.

He was dressed in jeans and a T-shirt, his hands shoved into his pockets as his gaze trailed down her body. She didn't know if it was because she rarely saw Gabe in jeans that she reacted so strongly to the sexy-as-hell sight or if he just looked incredibly hot in denim.

"Feels like shit doesn't it?"

She didn't pretend to misunderstand what he meant. She nodded, the motion hurting her head all the more.

He pushed off the doorway and walked to the bed, settling on the edge next to her.

"The car is waiting out front. Get dressed so we can go."

Her brow furrowed. "Where are we going?" She didn't want to move. She wanted about another six hours of sleep. Maybe then she'd wake and her head wouldn't hurt so badly.

"My apartment," he said shortly. "You have five minutes. Don't keep me waiting."

Her lips turned up into a snarl as he moved away and disappeared from her bedroom. If he was only going to give her five minutes, then he couldn't expect her not to look like death warmed over. She needed a hot shower and time to put herself together.

Hell, she still didn't even know what bug he had up his ass from last night. For that matter, she didn't even remember getting to bed. All she remembered was brushing her teeth. And then waking up.

Gabe had spent the night, but had he slept?

She pushed herself out of bed, groaning as she trudged to her closet. She yanked out a T-shirt and a pair of jeans, not even bothering with bra or underwear. It wasn't as if Gabe liked her wearing panties anyway.

She did pack a quick bag with a few changes of clothes along with the things she'd forgone—bra and panties—and then she went into the bathroom to throw her toiletries in the bag.

When she walked into the living room, she saw that Gabe was standing by the window staring out. He turned when he heard her.

"You ready?"

She shrugged. She wasn't really, but whatever.

He pulled her into his side and then put his hand to her back as they headed out of her apartment. A few moments later, he bundled her into the waiting car and got in beside her. As soon as the car took off, he motioned for her to come to him.

He tucked his arm around her, and she sighed as his warmth seeped into her body. She nestled her head on his chest and closed her eyes. She'd expected him to lecture her. Or rant about whatever he was pissed at her for. But he'd been surprisingly quiet, almost as if he knew just how badly her head hurt.

His mouth brushed over her head, and he kissed her hair as he smoothed the strands with his hand.

"When we get to my apartment, I have something you can take for the headache," he murmured. "You need to eat something as well. I'll make you something that isn't hard on your stomach."

A thrill began low in her belly and worked its way into her chest. It was so easy to lose herself in the fantasy of being with Gabe because he *made* it easy. He took absolute care of her. He saw to her every need. Was he demanding? Hell yes, but he wasn't selfish. He took. He was ruthless in his demands. But he gave her back so much. Not just materially but emotionally, though he'd likely deny he did any such thing.

She was nearly asleep when they rolled to a stop in front of Gabe's building. Gabe got out, and to her surprise, he reached in and lifted her into his arms, carrying her through the doorway to the elevator.

She burrowed her head underneath his chin and enjoyed the strength of his hold on her. He carried her into the elevator and had her insert the card to get to his floor and then they rode up, her nestled solidly in his arms.

In his living room, he lowered her onto the couch, and then went to get pillows and a blanket from his bed. He tucked her in and then went into the kitchen a moment. He returned with a glass of milk and a pill. She frowned when she saw it and raised her gaze in question.

"It'll help your head," he said. "But drink some milk first. It will make you woozy and it will be worse if there's nothing in your stomach."

"What is it?" she asked suspiciously.

"Take it, Mia. I wouldn't give you anything that would harm you. And since I can assure you that you won't be randomly drug tested at the office, you're perfectly safe to take it."

She smiled as much as her headache would let her and then took the pill. She drank half of the glass of milk before swallowing the pill, and then she drank down the rest, handing the glass back to him.

"Get comfortable. I'll make us something and we'll eat in here," he said.

Content to let him wait on her hand and foot, she tugged the blanket up to her chin and then laid her head in the nest of pillows he'd arranged. If this was going to be her treatment every time she pissed him off, she'd have to make sure she did it more often. Not that she even knew what he was angry about.

She was just starting to feel the effects of the medication he'd given her when he walked back in carrying a breakfast tray. The pain had eased and in its place warm euphoria sludged through her veins.

"Feeling better yet?" he asked in a low voice as he sat beside her.

"Yeah. Thanks. You're very good to me, Gabe."

Their gazes locked and held for the longest time. Then his lips thinned. "You likely won't say that after I tear into you for that stunt you pulled last night."

She sighed. "What did I do? Granted I don't remember much, but when I got to my apartment you were there and you were pissed. Why?"

He shook his head. "I can't believe you'd even have to ask that." When she tried to speak again, he held up his hand. "Eat, Mia. We'll discuss the matter once you've finished and are feeling better."

He handed her a plate with a toasted bagel and cream cheese and a small bowl of diced fruit.

She stared dubiously at it, unsure whether her stomach would take anything at this point. She took a tentative bite of the bagel, deciding dry bread would be more appealing than the moist fruit.

As soon as she took that first bite, her stomach roared to life.

She hadn't eaten the evening before and then all that alcohol on an empty stomach? No wonder she'd been so trashed.

"Starving," she mumbled.

He sighed impatiently. "Did you even eat last night before you drank that much alcohol?"

She shook her head, bracing herself for his reaction.

"Damn it, Mia."

He looked as though he wanted to say more, but he shut his lips together in a firm line and then directed his attention to his own breakfast.

She was honest enough with herself to admit she took her sweet time eating even though she wanted to consume everything in one bite. The longer she took to eat, the longer it would be before Gabe tore a strip off her hide.

"You may as well finish up," Gabe said. "You're only delaying the inevitable, Mia."

She grumbled under her breath, and then leaned forward to put the plate on the coffee table. "I guess I don't understand what you're so pissed about. So I had a little to drink. I'm sure you've done the same a time or two."

He put his own plate down and then sat forward so he could stare into her face. "You think that's what I'm pissed about?"

She shrugged. "Either that or because I went out to the club with my friends. Either way, your reaction seems extreme."

"Extreme." He sucked in his breath, simmering with anger. He shoved a hand through his hair and shook his head. "You have no clue, do you?"

"Enlighten me then because I'm lost."

"I knew you were going out, Mia. Why you couldn't have just told me the truth to begin with I'm not sure. Did you think I wouldn't allow you to go? I know you have friends."

"Is that why you're angry? I don't know why I didn't just say exactly what I was doing, Gabe. Maybe I did worry you wouldn't want me to go."

"Hell no that isn't why I'm furious," he bit out. "I get a call from my driver because he was never called to pick you up. Nothing. You weren't at your apartment so I could only think you'd taken a cab. You and your friends, out to a club. No protection. Getting into some cab with God knows who and then coming home drunk off your ass, alone, in a cab, at two o'clock in the damn morning."

She blinked in complete surprise. That wasn't at all what she thought he'd say.

"This isn't about me controlling you or you needing my permission to go out, Mia. It's about you being careful. It's about me being worried out of my mind because I had no idea where you were, if you were safe. You weren't answering my calls or texts so I couldn't even send the driver to where you were to wait on you. Hell, since you weren't answering my calls or my texts, I was imagining you dead in a dumpster somewhere!"

Guilt hit her hard. Damn it, he was right. He'd been worried— really worried about her—and she'd been out drinking and having a good time while he worried about her being hurt—or dead. *Ugh.*

"I'm sorry," she said softly. "I didn't think. I mean, it didn't even occur to me."

He frowned. "And you came home by yourself. What if I hadn't been there, Mia? Would you have even made it to your apartment or would you have fallen and passed out on the sidewalk?"

"Caroline went home with someone else," she said quietly. "He got me the cab."

"Well at least he did that much," Gabe said in disgust. "You should have called me, Mia. I would have come to get you no matter how late it was."

Warmth filled her heart. There was genuine worry in his eyes along with the anger and frustration. He'd been worried about her. She leaned forward putting her hands to his face. Then she kissed him.

"I'm sorry," she said again. "It was thoughtless of me."

He slid his hands up her neck and into her hair, holding her there just inches from his mouth. "Just don't let it happen again. I assigned a driver to you for a reason, Mia. It doesn't mean he just takes you to work and back when you aren't with me. If you need to go somewhere—anywhere—you call him. Understand? If you ever find yourself in a situation like that again, you call me. I don't give a fuck what time it is, you call me. If you can't reach me then you goddamn better well call your brother or Ash. You understand?"

She nodded.

"We both need a nap," he said, stroking her face with his hands. "You didn't sleep well and I didn't sleep. Right now I want to take you to bed and hold you while we rest. When you're feeling better I'll redden that pretty ass for worrying the hell out of me."

chapter twenty-seven

Mia sat cross-legged on Gabe's bed, devouring the pizza he'd had delivered. It was oh-my-God good just the way she liked it. Extra cheese, light sauce and thick crust.

He watched her in amusement as she licked her fingers clean before sinking back against the pillows with a sigh.

"That was wonderful," she said. "You're spoiling me, Gabe. There's no other word for it."

His eyes gleamed devilishly. "I'd wait until later before you start saying how much I spoil you."

Her body did an instant clench as heat surged through her veins. Try as she might, she couldn't muster any dread of the coming spanking he'd promised her. If anything, she was buzzing with anticipation.

She caught his gaze and she sobered. "I really am sorry about last night. I had no idea you were so worried. If I would have checked my phone I would have called or texted you, Gabe. I wouldn't have ignored you."

"I know you wouldn't," he said gruffly. "The thing I want you to be conscious of is being careful. You and your girlfriends going out alone and getting drunk only invites trouble. Any number of things could happen to a group of girls alone and vulnerable."

That he was so protective of her gave her immense satisfaction.

He had to feel something for her beyond viewing her as a sexual object.

"Now if you're finished, there's the matter of your punishment," he said silkily.

Holy hell. His gaze had gone molten and he bristled with lust and desire. Need sizzled over her skin, burning and edgy.

She pushed the pizza box away and he picked it up, setting it on the nightstand by the bed.

"Strip," he said bluntly. "I want you to have nothing on. When you're finished, get on your hands and knees, ass to the edge of the bed."

She rose on shaky knees and quickly pulled the T-shirt—Gabe's shirt—from her body, leaving her naked to his gaze. She turned her back to him where she faced the bed and then put her knee to the mattress, pushing herself upward to balance her knees on the edge. She planted her palms forward and closed her eyes, breathing deeply as she waited.

Footsteps echoed through the room. The sound of a drawer opening. More footsteps and then items being placed on the nightstand.

His lips pressed to one of her ass cheeks and then his teeth grazed over her skin, eliciting a shiver that produced chill bumps down her legs.

"Don't make a single sound," he said, his voice laced with desire. "Not a word. You'll take your punishment in silence. Afterward, I'm going to fuck that sweet ass of yours."

Her elbows buckled and she nearly lost her balance. She pushed herself back up, locking her elbows once more.

The crop slid across her ass, whispering faintly, deceptive in its softness. It left her skin, and then fire raced across her ass when he administered the first lash.

Her teeth sank into her lip to prevent any noise from escaping.

She'd been unprepared. Too caught up in her desire. She focused this time, preparing for the next blow.

He never struck the same spot twice nor did he draw out the punishment for effect. He peppered her behind with a series of lashes that varied in strength and sharpness. There was no way to know what to expect next because he changed it up each time.

She lost count at seventeen. Her entire body was crawling with need. The initial pain had diminished and in its place, a steady, heated throb had settled in. She lost awareness of her surroundings, floating off to a completely different plane where the line between pleasure and pain was blurred.

The next thing she became aware of was warm lubricant circling her anal opening and then his hands smoothing over her cheeks.

"Your ass is beautiful," Gabe murmured, his voice as silky and smooth as the finest chocolate. "My marks are there. You wear them because you belong to me. And now I'm going to fuck your sweet little ass because it belongs to me and I've not yet taken what is mine."

She swallowed and lowered her head, closing her eyes as his hands gripped her hips and then slid over her ass, spreading the cheeks. The blunt head of his cock nudged against her and then he pushed with more force, opening her to his initial entry.

He went extremely slow, and he was patient. Much more patient than she was. She wanted him inside her. The waiting was killing her.

"Relax, baby," he soothed. "You're way too tense. I don't want to hurt you. Let me inside you."

She tried to do as he instructed, but it was hard when every nerve in her body was on edge and screaming. Instinctively, she pushed back against him, but he put his palms on her ass, halting her motion.

"Be patient, Mia. I don't want to go too fast and hurt you."

He withdrew and pushed forward, performing shallow thrusts. She felt the brush of his knuckles as he gripped the base of his cock and fed it inside her, gaining more depth than before.

The burn was overwhelming. Not even being stretched daily with the plugs he'd made her wear could prepare her for having his entire length inside her. He was thick and rigidly hard. It was like being impaled by steel.

"Almost there," he whispered. "Just a bit more, Mia. Be a good girl and take it all."

She forced every muscle in her body to relax and just as she did, he pushed forward more forcefully and his balls came to rest against the mouth of her pussy.

He was inside her all the way. She'd taken him whole.

"Goddamn you feel so good," Gabe said in a strained voice. "Touch yourself, Mia. Lower your head so you can put your cheek on the bed and use your fingers while I fuck your ass."

The dirty words only aroused her further.

She leaned down, finding a comfortable position as he moved with her, his dick still wedged firmly in her ass. She slid her fingers through the folds of her pussy and began to manipulate her clit with just the right amount of pressure to get herself off.

When she was settled, Gabe eased back, withdrawing nearly all the way before pushing his way back inside. His movements were slow and methodical. Tender. He never got in a hurry and never lost control. He stroked in and out, his balls pressing to her pussy each time he reached his depth.

"I'm going to come inside you, Mia. I want you to be very still and continue to pleasure yourself."

She was so close to orgasming that she had to stop touching herself momentarily or she was a goner.

Gabe's thrusts increased in speed and force, but he didn't overwhelm her and he wasn't rough. Then she felt the first hot jet as he exploded inside her. The next moment, he withdrew and more pulsed onto her skin, at her opening and inside. And still more, until it slid from the opening and down the inside of her thigh.

And then he was back inside her, pushing deep, still hard, forcing his semen deeper. For several long moments he stroked in and out, even after he'd already come.

She lost the battle to control her own orgasm. As soon as she put her fingers to her clit, her release surged, sharp and unrelenting. It crashed over her and consumed her like a tidal wave. Her knees slipped and she went down to her belly, so she was flat on the bed. Gabe slipped out momentarily, but then he hoisted himself higher and thrust back into her.

His body blanketed hers. He lowered himself onto her back, his cock still rigid and thick in her ass. He nibbled at her shoulder and then kissed a path to her neck.

"Have you ever done this before?" he murmured against her ear.

"You're my first," she said, barely above a whisper.

"Good."

There was intense satisfaction in his voice. Triumph.

He lay there for several long minutes, gradually softening, lessening the tension and stretching sensation. And then he withdrew from her ass, rising up and then backing away.

She lay there trying to process what had just happened. Her thoughts were scattered. She was still euphoric after a mind-numbing orgasm. Her ass was sore from his spanking and from his thorough possession. But she'd never been more satisfied than she was right now.

He returned to wipe her clean with a warm washcloth. Then he went back to the bathroom, and she heard the shower turn on. A moment later he was back and gently picking her up from the bed.

He carried her into the bathroom and set her down in front of the shower. Then he stepped in and drew her in behind him. She sighed when the hot water rained down over her. And holy crap, but what a decadent experience to have Gabe take care of her completely.

He washed every inch of her, lavishing attention on her ass where the redness still remained. By the time he was finished going over her body, she was breathless and aching all over again.

After he had rinsed all the soap from her skin, he cleaned himself and then turned off the water. He stepped out first and then held out a towel for her to walk into. He wrapped her fully and hugged her to his chest.

"God, you spoil me," she breathed.

She lifted her head just in time to see a smile curve his lips. The man was absolutely sinful.

He finished drying her body and then allowed her to wrap the towel around her hair.

"Don't bother getting dressed," he called as she walked back toward the bedroom.

She smiled at the promise in his voice. No, she wouldn't need anything to wear for quite a while, she imagined. It was only Saturday night and they had nowhere to be until Monday morning.

chapter twenty-eight

"Gabe, I have to run these documents down to John so he can look them over before we leave for Paris. I also have to pick up the marketing plans from him. I thought I'd grab us lunch so we can eat in the office."

Gabe glanced up to see Mia standing close to his desk, question in her eyes. He checked the time and saw that indeed it was past time for lunch. He and Mia had been working the entire morning in preparation for their trip to Paris this afternoon.

Part of him was tempted to keep her sequestered in his office where he could see and touch her at all times. Have someone else go get lunch for them. It was an urge he had to fiercely restrain.

Even after spending the entire weekend with her in bed, exhausting them both, he hadn't had enough of her.

"That's fine. Don't go far. The deli down the block is fine. You know what I like."

She smiled, her eyes gleaming suggestively at his remark. The little tease did know exactly what he liked in exacting detail. And if she didn't leave now, he was going to be helpless against his reaction.

"Go," he said in a husky voice laced with need. "If you don't stop looking at me that way, we'll never get to Paris."

Her soft laughter filled the air and his ears as she turned to walk from his office. He experienced a moment of panic when she closed the door behind her, leaving him alone in the now-empty office.

It wasn't the same when she wasn't here, occupying the same space as he was. It was like having clouds move in on a sunny day.

He refocused his attention on the information in front of him, refusing to watch the clock and wait for Mia's return.

Eleanor buzzed him, interrupting his concentration, and he frowned.

"What is it, Eleanor?"

"Sir, Mrs. Hamilton is here to see you. Uh, Lisa Hamilton."

Gabe blew out his breath and closed his eyes. Not now for God's sake. Had the world around him gone insane? His father was pursuing his mother and now Lisa was sniffing around again. He'd made it clear to her the last time she'd dragged into his office that he had no desire to see her again, and over his dead body would they ever reconcile.

Maybe he hadn't been quite as clear as he thought.

"Send her in," Gabe bit out.

Evidently he was going to have to get his point across in a way she couldn't possibly misunderstand.

A moment later, Lisa opened his door and walked in, perfectly made-up, not a hair out of place. But then she'd always looked and acted perfect.

His gaze narrowed when he saw that she was wearing her wedding rings—rings he'd given her. It disgusted him to see any reminders of his possession of her.

"Gabe, we need to talk," she said.

She settled into the chair in front of Gabe's desk without waiting for him to issue the invitation or to toss her out, either one.

"There's nothing for us to discuss," he said mildly.

Her brow furrowed and the first sign of emotion flared in her eyes.

"What do I have to do, Gabe? How much do you want me to grovel? Tell me so I can do it and we can move on."

He tempered his impatience and sat a moment so he didn't react too harshly. And then he wanted to laugh at the idea that he could act too harshly. She'd skewered him. She'd betrayed him. And he still didn't know what had made her snap.

"There is nothing you can do or say that will ever change my mind," he said in clear, concise words. "We are over, Lisa. That was your choice. You divorced me. Not the other way around."

Her face fell and she dramatically wiped at a nonexistent tear.

"I know I hurt you terribly. I'm so sorry, Gabe. I was such a fool. But we still love each other. It would be a terrible waste for us not to at least try. I can make you happy. I made you happy once. I can do it again."

He was close to losing his temper, and he chose his words carefully.

"I don't love you," he said bluntly.

She flinched, and this time she didn't have to fake the tears welling in her eyes.

"I don't believe you," she said huskily.

He sighed. "I don't really care what you believe. That's not my problem. You and I are in the past and that's where we are staying. Stop doing this to yourself—to me—Lisa. I have work to do and I can't get it done with constant interruptions."

"So how does a club on sourdough sound?" Mia said as she entered his office, arms full of the takeout bags.

She came to a screeching halt when she saw Lisa, and her eyes widened.

"Oops. Sorry," she said awkwardly.

She hastily backed from his office and disappeared, bags in hand. He had to bite his lip to keep himself from commanding her back. Damn it, he wanted Lisa gone, not Mia.

When his gaze returned to Lisa's, her eyes were narrowed and recognition flashed.

"It's her isn't it?" Lisa said softly.

There was accusation in her stare. She rose to her feet, fists clenched at her sides.

"It's always been her. I saw the way you looked at her even when we were married. I played it off. She's Jace's little sister and so I thought you viewed her with a measure of affection afforded someone her age. But God, you wanted her even then, didn't you, you bastard? Are you in *love* with her?"

Gabe stood, his anger sharp and explosive. "That's enough, Lisa. You will not say another word. Mia works for me. You're embarrassing yourself."

Lisa made a sound of derision. "I never had a chance, did I, Gabe? Even if I hadn't been the one to walk out."

"That's where you're wrong," he said in a clipped tone. "I was faithful to you, Lisa. I would have always been faithful. I was committed to our marriage. It's too bad you weren't."

"Don't keep fooling yourself, Gabe. I saw the way you looked at her then and how you looked at her just now. I wonder if she has any idea what she's getting into. Perhaps I should warn her."

Gabe came around the desk, no longer able to control the anger biting at him.

"If you ever so much as breathe in Mia's direction, I'll ruin you, Lisa. All the money you still receive from me? Gone. And I won't hesitate or feel one moment's remorse over it. You're a cold, calculating bitch. Mia's worth ten of you. And if you don't think I'm enough of a threat, let Jace find out your intentions toward Mia. I guarantee he won't be as nice or as patient as I've been."

Lisa's eyes became calculating. "How much is it worth, me not going to your little assistant?"

And now she got to the real point of this bullshit reconciliation attempt. He was livid, but he managed to hold on to his temper. Barely.

"Blackmail won't work with me, Lisa. You of all people should know that. I know why you've come sniffing back around. You're broke and barely making ends meet on your alimony payments, which by the way, you should know I've contacted my lawyer. I'm going to court to have them reduced. I was more than generous in our divorce. Maybe it's time you got off your ass and worked, or find some other sucker to support you because I'm done."

She turned away, clutching her handbag like a lifeline. "You'll regret this, Gabe."

He remained silent, refusing to rise to her bait. It was done as far as he was concerned.

When she paused at the door, he said, "You won't be allowed in here again, Lisa. So don't try it. You'll only cause a scene and humiliate yourself. I'm going to alert security that you are never to be allowed back, and I'll tell Eleanor to alert them if she sees you anywhere near my offices." His voice dropped to a dangerous level. "And so help me God, if you go anywhere near Mia, I'll make you very sorry. Understand me?"

Lisa shot him a look filled with so much venom and hatred that he knew everything he'd suspected was absolute truth. She was broke and looking to get back on the money train.

"How the mighty Gabe has fallen," she said softly. "In love with his best friend's little sister. Wonder if she'll break *your* heart."

With that, she flounced out of his office, her hair bouncing off her shoulders. He hoped to hell it was the last time he saw the back of her.

He was about to go in search of Mia when she popped her head back through the door. He motioned her in and she carried the bags over to his desk.

She was silent as she took out the box containing his sandwich. She set up everything for him and then retreated to her own desk with her meal.

He watched her as she ate and read through several of the reports he'd given her to memorize for their trip. His own appetite had diminished. Lisa's accusations swirled in his mind, and he couldn't put them out of his head. He didn't like what she'd implied, but he couldn't immediately discount her observations. And that pissed him off all the more.

Gabe was brooding and silent the entire flight from New York to Paris. But then he'd been that way ever since Lisa had departed his office. Mia wasn't certain exactly what had transpired between them, but Gabe had made it clear to his staff and to security that Lisa was never to be allowed in the building again.

He'd been curt and short as he and Mia had left for the airport, their bags already packed. They'd ridden in silence, and Mia had been only too happy to preserve that silence as they'd boarded.

As soon as she was able, she pulled out her iPod and earphones and leaned back in her seat, closing her eyes to listen to her music. It was a long flight, and she was exhausted from her weekend with Gabe. If she didn't sleep now, she was in for a long day. They were landing in Paris at eight in the morning local time, which meant it would be fourteen hours before she'd be able to sleep.

She wasn't certain why she was going. Gabe was meeting with prospective bidders, front-runners he expected would be the top three for the new hotel project. If all went according to plan, they'd break ground in the spring. Along with the bidders, Gabe was also meeting with local investors.

There was really no reason for her to be here. She certainly couldn't add anything to the mix. The only thing she could come up with was that Gabe didn't want to be without sex for that long.

Halfway through the flight, she drifted off, music still playing in her ears. The seats were heavenly, and being able to fully recline made it easy to give in to fatigue.

The next thing she knew, Gabe was shaking her awake and motioning for her to right her seat. She pulled the earphones from her ears and stared groggily over at him.

"We're preparing to land," he said.

Had he slept at all? He still wore that brooding, grim expression he'd had when they departed New York. This trip was going to suck if his mood didn't improve.

They touched down and taxied to the gate. After an hour to get through customs and collect their luggage, they got into a car and headed for the hotel.

It was curious to Mia why they were staying in their biggest competitor's hotel, but Gabe had explained that he liked to keep up with what his competition was doing, and the best way to do that was to stay at their facilities.

The suite was luxurious and took up half of the top floor. The panoramic view was absolutely breathtaking with the Eiffel Tower and the Arc de Triomphe in sight from their huge picture window.

Mia flopped onto the sumptuous couch and sagged. Even though she'd slept half the flight, she was still feeling grubby. Traveling did that to her. She needed a hot shower and bed, in that order. But she wasn't certain what Gabe's plans were.

Gabe set up his laptop and typed steadily for half an hour before he finally looked up to where Mia was wilted all over the sofa.

"You're free to rest if you want," he said. "We don't have anything planned until this afternoon. We're having dinner, and afterward, we're having drinks here in the suite with a few people. I've e-mailed you detailed outlines on each of the individuals so be sure to read up before we go out later."

His tone was dismissive, and she figured he still hadn't dug out whatever bug was up his ass, so she got up and left the living area of the suite. There was only one bedroom or she would have taken up residence in separate quarters, and there was only one bed. Oh well.

She hit the shower, and spent a full thirty minutes soaking under the heated spray. By the time she got out, the chill had left her bones and she was pink all over from the hot water.

She still had hours yet, and she'd already committed to memory every single detail Gabe had given her on the people they were meeting. Ironically, of the three who were expected to be the top bidders for the construction of the new Paris hotel, only one was French. Stéphane Bargeron was a wealthy French developer who was renowned in Europe. The other two, Charles Willis and Tyson "Tex" Cartwright, were American developers with European presences.

Charles was younger, handsome. Maybe Gabe's age or a little older. He'd inherited the business from his father when the older Willis had passed away, and he was struggling to build his own reputation. He was hungry, and Gabe fully expected him to submit a very competitive bid. He needed this project. It would boost his standing and enable him to land other lucrative jobs.

Tyson Cartwright was a Texas billionaire in his forties, and he'd built his company the old-fashioned way. From the ground up. His story was impressive. Mia had read up extensively on him, and he'd been on his own working his ass off since he was in his teens. By his early twenties, he already owned a small construction company in East Texas and he'd only expanded from there. His was truly an American success story. Hard work. Resolve. Success.

Stéphane Bargeron she knew less about, simply because his was a family business that many Bargerons were involved with. He was the guy sent in to do the ass kissing while his father and brothers did most of the hard work. He was the polish and they were the brains.

All three would be back in Gabe's suite for drinks after tonight's dinner. She wasn't sure in what capacity she was supposed to act, but looking at four really good-looking men couldn't be that much of a hardship, right?

She knew what she needed to know, so she wasn't going to drag out her laptop and rehash it all.

Not when a perfectly good nap awaited.

chapter twenty-nine

Gabe watched as Mia charmed the group of men over dinner. She smiled, chatted and conversed with ease, and she had every single one of them under her spell.

The question was, did she have him under it as well?

Lisa's question echoed over and over in his mind.

Are you in love with her?

He couldn't quite explain the anger or the helplessness he felt over such a question. He'd brooded the entire day, in turns angry and frustrated over his inability to put distance between himself and Mia.

It infuriated him that he hadn't been able to immediately refute Lisa's angry question.

He'd thought to end their agreement right then and there, walk away, terminate her employment with him. But he hadn't been able to, and that made him only feel more helpless. He needed her. God help him, he needed her.

His gaze drifted over the potential bidders—men who would be coming to his suite later. They obviously lusted after Mia— what red-blooded, heterosexual man wouldn't? It made Gabe want to grit his teeth, but he choked the urge away and instead embraced the opportunity for what it was.

A chance to prove to himself that his obsession with Mia wasn't unbreakable. That he didn't love her. Didn't need her.

Such a thing was provided for in their contract, though he'd never thought to actually hand her over to another man before now. The very idea sent rage and fierce jealousy surging through his mind. It did so now. But she'd expressed curiosity over the idea. He knew she wasn't adamantly opposed. And it was certainly something he'd done in the past.

He could do this.

He would do this.

He only hoped to hell he survived it and it didn't destroy him—or her—in the process.

Gabe's mood had shifted from brooding and pissed off to . . . She wasn't sure what his mood was exactly. It worried her because now he stared at her, when before he hadn't looked much at her at all. And that stare was something new, as if he were looking at her in a whole different light. Like his expectations had taken a dramatic shift, only she had no idea what those expectations were.

Where before she'd embraced the silence between them, not wanting to delve into the reason behind his moodiness, now it made her distinctly uncomfortable. She wanted something from him. Some kind of reassurance, though why, she wasn't certain.

They rode back to the hotel, the tension welling until she nearly choked with it. She wanted to ask him, wanted to question him, but there was something in his steady gaze that made her fear what she would learn.

As soon as they were inside the suite, Gabe closed the door and focused that glittering gaze on her. He bristled with dominance where before he'd always demonstrated patience and tenderness with her.

"Strip."

She blinked at his tone. It wasn't angry. It was more . . . determined. Unease drifted over her and she hesitated, which only made his eyes narrow.

"I thought . . ." She swallowed hard. "I thought they were coming up for drinks." Had the plans changed?

He nodded. "They are."

Oh God.

"Don't make me tell you again, Mia," he said in a soft, dangerous voice.

Her hands shaking, she reached down and lifted the hem of her dress and pulled it over her head, letting it fall to the floor beside her. She kicked out of her heels, sending them skittering across the wood floor.

There were a thousand things she wanted to say, a thousand questions burning in her mind, but he looked so . . . forbidding . . . that she clamped her lips shut and removed her bra and panties.

"Go and kneel on the rug in the middle of the room," he said.

As she walked slowly to the rug, he began to pick up her clothing and her shoes and then he disappeared into the bedroom, leaving her to follow his command. She sank to her knees, feeling the plush thickness of the lambskin rug against her knees.

When she heard his footsteps, she looked up, and she let out a gasp when she saw the rope in his hands. It wasn't traditional rope, the braided kind you'd find in a hardware store, but rather it was satin covered, a deep mauve. It looked sexy and soft, and yet there was no mistaking it was meant to restrain her.

He coiled it around his hands, letting the ends hang down as he stalked in her direction. He bent where she knelt and wordlessly pulled her hands behind her back. She closed her eyes, her heart thundering in her chest as he began to wind the rope around her wrists, tying them tightly together. To her further surprise, he looped the ends around her ankles, effectively ensuring she couldn't move, couldn't stand, couldn't do anything more than kneel there and take whatever it was he intended to do.

And that idea excited her. It bewildered her, this desire, this curiosity and edgy need that invaded her. She was by turns nervous as hell, but also tantalized by the forbidden. Other men touching her, doing God only knew what under Gabe's direction. Surely that was what he intended? It wasn't as if they hadn't discussed it.

As he finished, there was a knock on the suite door, and she jumped, her pulse accelerating so rapidly that she became lightheaded.

"Gabe," she whispered, uncertainty bleeding into that one simple plea.

He tugged at the last knot and as he rose, he threaded his hand into her hair, stroking downward in a comforting gesture.

That little touch heartened her in a way nothing else could. Relief settled in as he walked toward the door.

She'd known from the beginning of his desires, his proclivities. He'd outlined them in stark detail. And she'd signed her name to a contract agreeing that she was his to do with as he wished.

Maybe she hadn't really thought he would. Maybe a secret part of her *hoped* he would.

Whatever the case, she was kneeling, tied hand and foot, naked, and other men were about to see her.

Gabe opened the door and ushered the three gentlemen they'd had dinner with inside. Their gazes fell on her immediately, and what struck her most was that there was no surprise. No shock. There was only lust and appreciation reflected in their eyes.

Had they known? Had Gabe told them what to expect? Had he told them that she was tonight's entertainment?

Gabe didn't immediately direct any attention to her. She sat there quietly while he conversed with the men and poured drinks.

It was only after a few moments that they entered the living area, drinks in hand.

Business was being discussed. Gabe went over his ideas for the new hotel and explained the backing that HCM already had and what further backing they were looking for. It was all very businesslike and polite. Except for the fact that she was trussed like a turkey and didn't have a stitch of clothing on.

She watched the men, all handsome, virile. She saw the way their gazes skated sideways to her, even in the midst of their business conversation. They definitely knew she was there, and anticipation was a living, breathing thing in the room. The air was thick with it.

And then Gabe moved in her direction, his hands going to the fly of his trousers. He unzipped them and let the lapels hang down as he ran his hands through her hair, framing her head before caressing her cheeks. He ran a finger over the seam of her lips and then pressed inside, wetting it on her tongue.

The other men watched intently, their gazes fixed on Mia as they waited, lust clearly marked on their faces.

Gabe pulled out his cock and then palmed her forehead, tilting her head back so she was at an appropriate angle.

"Open," he commanded.

She was flush with nervousness but excitement also danced in her veins. She was aroused by the fact that he was going to fuck her mouth right here in front of these strangers. She was experiencing so many conflicting emotions that it was hard to know exactly what she thought or felt about the situation.

But she trusted Gabe, and that was enough to make her relax and give herself into his hands and his care.

Her lips parted, and he slid inside her mouth, probing deeply as the tip of his cock brushed the back of her throat. Her cheeks hollowed and then plumped outward as he withdrew and then plunged inside again.

He was surprisingly gentle given his intense mood. She'd expected him to be rougher, more demanding. But he framed her face with his hands, brushing his thumbs over her cheeks as he pushed in with long, slow strokes.

"Beautiful," he murmured.

"Yes, she is," one of the men said from behind Gabe.

His voice startled her, pulling her out of the moment. She'd been able to forget their presence because she was consumed by Gabe. Only Gabe. Now she was very aware that they were there—watching. Lusting after her. All wanting to be Gabe as she pleasured him.

"Focus only on me," he whispered as he thrust again, filling her mouth with his rigid length.

It was an easy command to obey. She closed her eyes and lost herself in Gabe's dominance.

He began to move faster and with more force. He thrust and then held himself deeply, locked against the back of her throat. Then he released her and smoothed his hands over her face while he waited for her to catch her breath.

"She's fucking hot," Tyson breathed.

"I want some of that," Charles said, his voice strained with lust and envy.

Gabe's hands tightened on her face. He thrust again and then began pushing hard and fast. He erupted against her throat, onto her tongue, spilling onto her lips as he withdrew and thrust forward again.

"*Merde*," the Frenchman muttered.

The wet sucking sounds rose in the room, erotic and almost harsh against the silence.

"Swallow it," Gabe ordered. "Lick me clean, Mia."

He continued to rock against her, giving her time to obey his dictate. She licked and swallowed, until finally he withdrew, his cock shining with moisture from her mouth.

He reached down and fumbled with the knots at her wrists, loosening the silken rope from around her hands and ankles. Her arms and legs screamed their protest when he pulled her to her feet. He stood there holding her a long moment, allowing her to regain her strength. Then he lifted her into his arms and carried her to the long coffee table in front of the couches.

He laid her down, spreading her legs, and then he raised her arms above her head and slipped the rope around each wrist before binding them to the legs of the coffee table underneath her head.

When he stood again, his gaze was directed at the man nearest to Mia.

"You can touch her. You can pleasure her. Do *not* hurt her in any way. Do not frighten her. This is all about her. You keep your dick in your pants and do not penetrate her in any way. We clear?"

"Hell yeah," Charles said as he rose.

chapter thirty

Gabe backed away from where Mia lay tied to the coffee table. She was an irresistibly erotic sight, her long dark hair tousled and tumbled over the edge, her eyes wide, lips puffy from his possession.

Charles Willis circled her like a waiting vulture, his eyes feasting greedily on Mia's naked body. Gabe's stomach clenched when Charles's fingers trailed over her belly and up to her breasts. Charles circled one taut peak, teasing it to rigidity.

Stéphane and Tyson closed in but stood just back to give Charles his turn. They waited, like predators stalking prey, for their opportunity to touch her.

This was wrong. So very wrong. His gut screamed at him. His mind protested. She was *his*. No one should be touching her but him, and yet he'd set this up. As what, a test? Something to prove to himself?

He brooded as Charles continued his exploration of Mia's beautiful body. A body that belonged to Gabe. He was a possessive man—he knew this—and yet he'd never had a problem allowing another man to pleasure a woman under his care. He was . . . indifferent to it. Not so with Mia.

He hated every goddamn minute of this.

Lisa's taunt echoed over and over in his ears.

Are you in love with her?

He turned away, unable to bear the sight of Charles's hands on Mia's body. Her soft gasps filled the air. He stood tense, hands shoved into his pockets, across the room, not wanting to see or hear the results of his foolishness.

He was a fool. And a complete bastard. A cowardly asshole.

This wasn't *right*. He couldn't allow this to continue. All he'd proven to himself was that he'd never share Mia with another living soul, and he'd be damned if he allowed another man to touch what was his.

This had to end. They had to leave.

He was about to turn and order them all out when he froze, his blood turning to ice.

"No!" Mia cried. *"Gabe!"*

His name was a terrified cry for help.

He whirled around to see Charles with his fly unzipped, his hand curled roughly in Mia's hair as he tried to force himself into her mouth.

Rage exploded, a volcanic force erupting. He charged forward and to his horror, Charles, enraged by Mia's refusal, backhanded her across the face. Mia's head snapped back, her eyes wide with shock. Blood immediately seeped from the corner of her mouth.

Gabe went crazy.

He threw Charles away from Mia. He hit the couch and Gabe went after him. The other two men scrambled up and away, one of them hastily refastening his fly.

Gabe doubled Charles over with a fist to his gut and then flattened him with another to Charles's jaw.

Gabe loomed over him, murderous fury sizzling through his veins. "Get out. Get the fuck out of here and I better never see you again. I'll fucking ruin you."

He wanted nothing more than to beat the man to a pulp, but

he had to see to Mia. Mia, whom he'd betrayed horribly. Mia, who had trusted him. Mia, whom he'd acted reprehensibly toward. All because he was a coward unable to face the truth of what she meant to him.

The other two men helped pick Charles up and they fled the suite, slamming the door behind them.

Gabe flew to Mia, dread weighing on him with suffocating force. Her lips and chin quivered and tears shone in her eyes. She looked scared and embarrassed. Shame shone bright in her tear-filled eyes and it gutted him.

And blood. God. There was blood where that bastard had *hit* her.

He knelt down to untie her hands, his fingers shaking as he fumbled with the knots. He pressed his mouth to her hair and her temple, kissing her over and over.

"I'm so sorry, baby. I'm so sorry. Oh God, Mia. I didn't mean for this to happen."

She was silent, and he wasn't sure if it was because she was in shock over what had happened or if she was too pissed at him to speak. He couldn't blame either reaction. This was all on him. He'd done this to her. He'd hurt her.

When she was free, he gathered her in his arms, pulling her off the table. He carried her into the bedroom and crawled onto the bed, still holding her tightly. She turned into his chest, burying her face against his neck. The shock of her hot tears on his skin ripped his heart right out of his chest.

God he was such a bastard. A complete and utter asshole. He clutched her to him, desperation crawling up his spine and seizing him by the throat.

"I'm sorry, Mia. God, I'm so sorry."

It was all he could say. Over and over. Panic hit him right in the gut. What if she walked away? He certainly couldn't blame her. Hell, she should be running, not walking.

"Please, baby. Please don't cry. I'm so sorry. It will never happen again. I shouldn't have allowed it."

He rocked her back and forth in his arms as she clung to him, her body still shaking. Whether it was fear, upset or anger, or a combination of the three he wasn't sure. He deserved whatever she threw at him. He'd failed her utterly. He hadn't protected her. He hadn't taken care of her as he'd promised. All because he was trying to distance himself, trying to prove some stupid point to himself that he didn't need her.

It was such a lie. He did need her. She was his obsession, his fix, a craving that went soul deep. Never had he felt such an overwhelming, fierce possessiveness as when another man put his hands on what Gabe considered his. But he hadn't treated her like she was his. He'd treated her like she was a thing. A toy, not a woman he cared about.

He stroked his hands down her trembling back. She was shaking harder now and he was desperate to comfort her, to offer her what he hadn't given her before.

She clutched at his shoulders and tried to pull away, but he held her fiercely, afraid to let any space between them. He had to touch her, had to feel her in his arms. He was afraid if he let her go, he'd never get her back.

"I want a shower," she choked out. "Please, I need it. I just want to be clean. He . . . *touched* me."

Desolation swept through Gabe like a winter storm, cold and stark. Of course she felt violated. Not only by Charles, but also by him. He'd given her the ultimate betrayal in allowing this to happen. He'd not only allowed it, he'd encouraged it. How the hell could he ever get past something like this? How could she?

"Let me go start it," he said, wiping her hair from her face.

Her cheeks were damp with tears, and her eyes were wounded as she stared back at him. Blood still oozed from the corner of her mouth. Then she looked away, unable to meet his gaze, and his stomach dropped.

"Stay right here, baby. I'll go start it and then you can take your shower."

He backed away from the bed, his instincts screaming not to let her go even for the moment it took to start the water running. His chest felt empty and panic clawed at his throat. Never had he experienced such emotional devastation. It unhinged him. Made him crazy.

Not when Lisa had walked out on their marriage. Not when she'd smeared him in the media and spouted her lies. Nothing had even come close to this and the fear that had him in its vicious hold.

He hurried to the bathroom and turned on the shower, testing the water until it was the right temperature. He pulled out a bathrobe and a towel, his haste making him clumsy. He cursed when the towel fell off the counter, and he bent to pick it up, folding it back up and making sure it was within reach of the shower.

He went back into the bedroom to find Mia sitting on the edge of the bed, her legs drawn protectively to her chest. She hugged her knees to her chin, her face down, her hair spilling down her legs. She looked so damn vulnerable that Gabe wanted to die on the spot.

He'd done this to her. Not Charles. Not some other man. *He* had done it. There was no getting around that fact.

He touched her shoulder, allowing his fingers to twine in her silky hair. "Mia, baby, the shower is ready." He hesitated before he said the rest, worried that she'd reject him, knowing he deserved it if she did. "Do you want me to help you?"

She turned her face up to him, her eyes still haunted. But she didn't say no. She didn't say anything at all. She just nodded.

Relief surged through him, leaving him weak and shaken. He

had to wait a moment to collect his strength. She hadn't rejected him—yet.

He gathered her in his arms, lifting her protectively, holding her as closely as he could as he carried her into the bathroom. He set her down in front of the shower, taking just enough time to strip out of his own clothing before he opened the door and went in before her. He reached back, taking her hand, guiding her into the shower with him.

For a long moment, he simply held her, both standing under the hot spray. Then he began to wash her, lavishing every inch of her body with the scented soap. He left no part of her untouched, gently rinsing away any reminder that another's hands had been on her.

He soaped her hair, gently massaging the shampoo into her scalp, and then he rinsed each strand. Then he pulled her into the protective embrace of his arms, holding her as they stood, silent under the steady stream of soothing water.

Finally he reached up to turn off the spray and opened the shower door, reaching for the towel so she didn't get cold. He wrapped the towel around her body, keeping her close as he dried her skin and her hair. He didn't bother with himself, using the chill to punish himself. She was what was important. Not him. He just hoped he hadn't realized it too late.

When she was completely dry, he wrapped the towel around her head and then helped her into the thick, plush robe. He tied the ends securely around her waist, covering her body so she didn't feel vulnerable. So she felt safe. Even from him.

He grabbed one of the other towels as he ushered her back into the bedroom, and only after he had her tucked into bed did he then dry himself and pull on his boxers. He reached for the phone and tersely ordered hot chocolate. Then he sat on the edge of the bed and urged her upward so he could finish drying her hair.

The silence stretched between them as he rubbed the moisture from the strands. When he was satisfied that most of the dampness was gone, he took the towel into the bathroom and collected her comb. He returned to see her sitting just as he'd left her.

He climbed onto the bed and pulled her between his legs, positioning her so he could comb out the tangles. He was infinitely patient, combing strand by strand until her hair began to dry and hang limply down her back.

After he set the comb on the nightstand, he grasped her shoulders and leaned his head down to press a kiss to her neck. She shivered as he continued to rain gentle kisses down the curve of her shoulder and then back up again.

"I'm sorry," he whispered.

She tensed slightly underneath his mouth and then a distant knock sounded. Reluctantly he pulled away, climbing out of bed.

"I'll be right back. Make yourself comfortable. I'll bring the hot chocolate in here."

She nodded and as he moved away, she settled back against the pillows he'd been leaning on and pulled the covers to her chin.

He took the tray from the room service attendant and wasted no time returning to the bedroom where Mia lay. He set it on the desk against the wall and then carried one of the steaming mugs to Mia.

She grasped it with both hands as if seeking its warmth, and then brought it to her lips where she blew over the steaming chocolate before tentatively taking the first sip. She winced when the hot liquid hit her wounded lip, and she pulled the cup away with a grimace.

He hurriedly took it from her grasp, furious with himself because he hadn't thought. He hadn't considered that the hot chocolate would hurt her injured mouth.

"I'll get you some ice," Gabe said. "Don't move, baby."

He stalked back into the living room, grabbed the ice bucket the room service attendant had left and then wrapped some of the ice in a towel. When he went back into the bedroom, Mia was still sitting just as he'd left her, her eyes vacant and distant.

Taking a chance, he sat down beside her and carefully pressed the ice pack to her mouth. She flinched and tried to move away, but he persisted, his voice gentle and low.

"Mia, darling, you need the ice so it won't swell."

She reached up, taking the towel from him and then put a foot of space between them. He didn't blame her and he didn't fight her. It was far less than he deserved. He rose from the bed and paced a short distance away before turning to look at her again.

Gabe stood back, anxious and worried. Insecure. God, he wasn't an insecure person and yet with Mia, he was riddled with uncertainty. He was seized by the enormity of his fuck-up. This wasn't an *oops I'm sorry*, forgive and forget situation. He'd placed her in harm's way. He'd allowed another man to *abuse* her when she was in his protection.

He didn't know if he could or would ever forgive himself so how could he expect her to do the same?

He was still hovering when she loosened her hold on the towel and allowed it to slide down her neck. Her gaze was weary and defeated. It made him wince to see the light extinguished from her beautiful gaze.

"I'm tired," she said softly.

And she did look utterly drained. Fatigue shadowed her face and dulled her eyes.

He'd wanted to talk to her. To beg her forgiveness. To explain to her that it would never happen again. But he wouldn't push her. Not until she was ready. And it was evident that she had no desire to talk about the matter tonight. Maybe she was still coming to terms with it herself. Or maybe she was just working up the nerve to tell him to fuck off.

He nodded, a knot solidly lodged in his throat. He went to turn the lights off, leaving only the lamp at his bedside on.

Then he got into bed, unsure of whether she'd want him to touch her or not. When he was beneath the covers, he reached back to turn off the lamp, dousing the room in darkness. Only the glow from the city lights illuminated the curtains.

He turned back over, automatically reaching for her. But she'd already turned on her side, facing away from him. She didn't reject his touch, but neither did she embrace it. Still, he curled his arm around her middle, locking her solidly to his chest. He wanted her to know he was here. And God, more than that he needed the assurance that she was here.

After a moment, she let out a breathy sigh and he felt her relax into his hold. Her soft even breathing filled the room signaling her sleep. Or at least that she was on her way.

But he didn't sleep. Didn't close his eyes. Because every time he tried, all he saw was the look on Mia's face when another man had forced his touch on her.

chapter thirty-one

The next morning when Mia awakened, Gabe wasn't in bed with her. She felt the loss, but she was also relieved because she wasn't sure she could face him yet. There were too many things she had to say and she wasn't entirely certain how she was going to say them. Maybe that made her a coward. But she knew that what she had to say could very well mean the end of her relationship with Gabe.

She was still lying under the covers, hugged up to Gabe's pillow, deciding whether to move or not when Gabe appeared in the doorway, a breakfast tray in his hands.

"Are you hungry?" he asked in a quiet, serious tone. "I ordered breakfast."

She was surprised by how nervous he seemed. There was worry in his eyes and genuine concern for her. And regret shone, darkening his gaze every time he looked at her. Her heart twisted and she closed her eyes to block out images from the night before.

"Mia?"

She opened her eyes to find him standing by the bed still holding the tray. She pushed herself upward, propping pillows behind her back so she could sit up to eat.

"Thank you," she murmured when he placed the tray across her legs.

He eased down on the bed beside her and thumbed over her bruised lip. She winced when he hit a particularly tender spot, and his gaze was immediately apologetic.

"Will you be able to eat?" he asked in a low voice.

She nodded and then looked down and picked up her fork, no longer able to hold his gaze.

"I've cancelled all our business engagements."

Her gaze shot upward, a frown gathering her brows. Before she could respond, he continued, as if she hadn't reacted at all.

"I've arranged our flight back home for tomorrow morning first thing. But today, I'm going to take you to see Paris. The Eiffel Tower, Notre Dame, the Louvre and whatever else you want to see. I have reservations for dinner at seven. A bit early by Paris standards, but we depart early and I want you to be rested."

"That sounds wonderful," she said huskily.

The joy and relief in his eyes was staggering. He opened his mouth as if to say something further, and then he clamped it shut again.

She couldn't imagine why he'd cancelled his business engagements. The sole purpose of their visit was business and the up-coming hotel. But a day in Paris with Gabe was something straight out of one of her fantasies.

No business. No strange men. Nothing but the two of them having fun and enjoying their time together. It sounded like heaven. And for a brief time, she could ignore the strain between them. She could pretend that last night didn't happen.

It wouldn't go away. It had to be addressed. But she'd take the respite offered, and she'd face what it was she needed to say to Gabe later. Because when that time came, it might well be the end of their relationship.

While Gabe watched, his gaze lingering on her, worry still evident in his eyes, she hurriedly ate, wanting to have as much time to explore the city as possible. One day to take in Paris? Impossible. But she'd take as big a chunk out of it as she could.

After she finished, she dressed and pulled her hair back into a clip. She didn't bother with makeup. She'd brought her favorite pair of jeans and now she was grateful she had.

"It's cold out this morning. Did you bring something warm to wear?" Gabe asked.

He was leaning against the doorframe of the bathroom, watching as she pulled on her jeans.

"We can always go buy what you need. I don't want you to be uncomfortable."

She smiled. "I have a sweater. And if we're walking a lot, that'll keep me warm."

His breath left his throat in an audible rush. "God you're beautiful when you smile."

Surprised by the compliment and by the absolute sincerity in his voice, she smiled more broadly and then ducked her head self-consciously.

After pulling on her socks and her tennis shoes, she retrieved the button-up sweater and put it on, leaving it open in the front.

Gabe was dressed and ready, and they headed down to the lobby of the hotel where Gabe got a map and spent a few moments speaking to the concierge. After that, they were on their way.

They left the hotel, and Mia sucked in her breath at the beauty of the day. There was a crispness to the air that immediately refreshed her. There couldn't be a more perfect day to sight-see in Paris. The sky was brilliantly blue without a single cloud to mar it.

After the first block, Mia shivered when a brisk wind with a biting chill blew down the street. Gabe frowned and then broke away, heading for one of the vendors that lined the block.

He chose a brightly colored scarf, handed Euros to the man and then returned to where Mia stood on the sidewalk. He looped the scarf around her neck, covering the lobes of her ears with the warm material.

"Better?" he asked.

She smiled. "Perfect."

He gathered her to his side, holding her tightly against his body as they continued their walk. Mia sucked in deep breaths, reveling in the sheer beauty of the city. She stopped often, looking into the windows of shops or taking time to browse the street vendors. Through it all Gabe was patient and attentive. If Mia so much as looked as though she liked something, Gabe was quick to purchase it. As a result, they now carried several shopping bags with them.

The view from the Eiffel Tower was magnificent. They stood staring down at the city of Paris, the wind ruffling Mia's hair and tugging at the ends of the scarf.

Impulsively, she went up on tiptoe and pressed a kiss to his mouth. His eyes darkened with surprise and what looked like relief.

As her heels hit the ground again she grinned ruefully. "It's always been a dream of mine to be kissed on top of the Eiffel Tower."

"Then let's do it right," Gabe said gruffly.

He dropped the bags he was holding and pulled her into his arms. He cupped her chin, tilting her head up so her mouth was angled perfectly for his. Then his lips slid warmly over hers, his tongue brushing lightly, coaxing her to open to his advance.

She sighed into his mouth and closed her eyes, soaking up every second of the experience. Here in one of the most romantic cities in the world, she was fulfilling a teenage dream. What woman wouldn't want to be kissed atop the Eiffel Tower?

The rest of the day was more fulfillment of her most vivid romantic fantasies. They saw the sights, laughed, smiled and took in the wonders of the city. Gabe was so very tender and he spoiled her endlessly.

At one point, he called for a driver to take their bags back to the hotel because they'd become too much for them to carry.

And at the day's end, he took her to a restaurant overlooking the Seine. Dusk had descended, and all the lights twinkled and popped against the skyline. She was tired from all the walking, but there had never been a more perfect day.

As they waited for their entrees, Gabe reached underneath the table and propped her feet on his lap. Unlacing her shoes, he pulled them off and began to massage each foot.

She groaned in sheer pleasure as he pressed into her arches and rubbed the soles.

"We'll take a cab back to the hotel," he said. "You've walked enough today. Your feet will likely hurt tomorrow."

"They hurt now," she said ruefully. "But this has been the most fabulous day, Gabe. I can't thank you enough for it."

He sobered instantly. "No need to thank me, Mia. I'd do damn near anything to make you smile."

His gaze was so serious, his eyes intent. Every time he'd looked at her today, there had been a softness that made her heart squeeze just a bit. Almost as if he cared for her. Beyond just as a sexual object.

Their food came and Mia dug in with gusto, even though they'd snacked on delicious pastries, breads and cheeses the entire day. She slowed toward the end of the meal, because as wonderful as the day had been, she knew that when they returned to the hotel that it would be time to face the issue they were currently avoiding.

She wasn't in any hurry to end the day. It would be a memory she would savor her entire life. No matter what happened in the future, she would never forget her time in Paris with Gabe.

When it came time to go, Gabe took her hand, lacing his fingers through hers, and they walked out to the patio overlooking the river. A dinner cruise floated by, the lights twinkling festively.

It was a gorgeous night. Chilly. Heralding the coming winter.

Overhead, a full moon was rising, just barely peeking over the horizon. She sighed, taking in the view, the boats, the couples walking along the pathway paralleling the river. Yes, it had been a perfect day and a perfect evening.

Gabe pulled her into his chest, wrapping his arms around her to keep her warm as they watched the activity on the river. He kissed her temple and then tucked her head beneath his chin.

An ache began in her chest that wouldn't go away. If only things could be between them this way all the time. It was a hope—a dream—that wouldn't go away. She closed her eyes and savored the moment. The feel of him and their closeness.

He seemed as reluctant as she was to end the evening. He tucked her hand into his and guided her toward the taxi queue just down the block. A few minutes later, they were on their way back to the hotel.

Back to the reality that awaited them.

chapter thirty-two

Mia sat on the bed, one of Gabe's T-shirts pulled down her thighs nearly to her knees. Gabe was in the shower and she waited nervously for him to come to bed. It had taken her time to figure out exactly what she wanted to say. She hadn't wanted to react too quickly when her emotions were scattered. She hadn't wanted to do or say things she'd later regret. This was too important.

But now she'd gathered her courage and she was ready to confront Gabe. Not with an ultimatum. But with the truth.

The door opened and he came out, a towel hung loosely at his waist. His hair was damp and moisture glistened on his upper body. He was . . . beautiful. There was no other word for it.

The towel slipped as he reached into his suitcase for his underwear, and she got a prime view of his ass and when he turned, his cock, impressive even at complete rest.

She averted her gaze, feeling guilty that she was so unapologetically eating him with her eyes. She didn't want to get distracted.

When he came to the bed, she caught her breath and plunged forward. If she didn't get it out there, she'd never say all the things she needed to get off her chest. It was better to just say it, no matter how inelegant her wording.

"I *hated* last night," she said bluntly, her words soft and trembling.

He closed his eyes briefly, pausing in his descent into bed. He perched instead on the edge, keeping a short distance between the two of them.

"I know," he said quietly.

She continued, knowing she still had more to say—more that she needed to say.

"I *hated* him touching me. I know what I agreed to, Gabe. I know I signed a contract. And I know I said I wasn't entirely opposed to the idea, or at least experimenting. But I don't want anyone else but you touching me. I felt violated. I felt *dirty*. And I don't want to ever feel that way about my relationship with you."

"Oh God, baby, no," he whispered.

His expression was stricken and his eyes wounded.

And still she continued, unwilling to let him speak yet.

"I don't give a damn what the contract says," she said hoarsely. "I hate that thing right now. The only man I want even looking at me is you. Not someone you decide to let borrow your plaything."

A strangled noise erupted from his throat but she held up her hand, determined to say her piece. God, she couldn't let him interrupt now or she'd never have the courage to say all she had to say.

"I won't do it again." She shook her head adamantly to reinforce her point. So he would know how serious she was. "I know I agreed to allow it, but I don't want it. I'll *never* want it. I hated every minute of it. If it *ever* happens again, I'm done. I'll walk away and I won't ever be back."

As if he couldn't hold back a minute longer, he reached for her, hauling her into his arms and against his chest. He held her so tightly that she couldn't breathe.

"I'm sorry, Mia. I'm so damn sorry. It will never happen again. Ever. No one will ever touch you. God, I hated every goddamn minute of it. I was going to put a stop to it but then I heard you cry out. Heard the fear in your voice and you saying no. And I swore to you that it was the only word you'd ever need to say for me or anyone else to stop. And then that son of a bitch *hit* you before I could get to you. Sweet mother of God, I'll never forgive myself for that, Mia. *Never.* For that fear, for that bastard making you do things you didn't want."

He shook against her. His hands rubbed up and down her back in agitation. He pulled her head away and palmed her face, staring intently into her eyes.

"I'm so sorry, baby. I don't know if I can ever forgive myself for what I did. I hated it. *Hated* it, Mia."

"Then *why* did you *do* it?"

His gaze dropped and he looked away, his hands sliding from her face. He closed his eyes, disgust simmering in his features. "Because I'm a goddamn coward."

His voice was so low she almost didn't hear what he said, and even so she wasn't sure he said what she thought he said. What did it mean?

Then he reached for her hand, squeezing tightly. He brought it up to his mouth and pressed a kiss to the inside of her palm.

"Know this, Mia. It will never happen again. I'm asking you to forgive the unforgivable. Yes, you signed an agreement, but it wasn't what you wanted. Not last night. Not any night. And I think I knew that even before. I knew it and I still gave that bastard permission to touch you, and I hate myself for that. It's my responsibility to know your wants and desires and place them above my own. I didn't do that last night."

It didn't make sense to her why he'd done it at all. It had come out of the blue. Even though they'd discussed the *possibility*, she hadn't ever gotten the idea that he was going to actually do it.

She had to wonder what was going on in his mind when he'd invited those men back to the suite. He'd been moody and brooding since before they'd left New York City. Did that have anything to do with his decision? Was he trying to make some point she didn't understand? Or did it have nothing to do with her at all?

"I'm sorry, baby." His voice dropped even lower, so much regret seeping into his words. "Please forgive me. Please say you'll stay and not walk out. It's what you should do, absolutely. I don't deserve you. I don't deserve your sweetness or your understanding. But I want it. God help me but I'm not sure I can live without it."

It was the closest he'd ever come to admitting she meant more to him than sex.

She leaned forward, pushing up to her knees, her hands going to his face.

"You don't have to live without it—or me," she whispered. "I'm here, Gabe. I'm not going anywhere. But it has to be just us. You and me. No other men." She could barely contain the shudder that threatened to roll up her spine.

His eyes ignited with relief. Then he crushed her to him, holding on, hugging her tightly. He kissed her temple, her head, every part of her hair, almost as if he could do nothing else but touch her in some way. "Just us," he whispered against her ear. "I swear it."

Then he pulled away just enough that he could rest his forehead against hers.

"Let's go home, Mia. I want to put this behind us. I want you to be able to forget it and wipe it from your memory. I know I hurt you terribly. I swear to you I'm going to make it up to you."

She savored the fervent promise, held tightly to it. He spoke as if they had a future, as if he wanted more than just contractual sex. Was she a fool for believing that?

She looped her arms around his neck. "Make love to me, Gabe. Make our last night in Paris special."

"Ah baby," he said, a catch in his voice. "I'm going to love every inch of you tonight. And then I'll hold you all the way home while you rest on the plane."

. . .

Mia woke in the middle of the night and blinked to adjust to the low light. There was a narrow beam shining from the bathroom, and it illuminated Gabe's sleeping features.

She was tucked securely into his side, his leg thrown over both of hers, effectively trapping her against him. His arm was slung securely over her body. Even in sleep he was intensely possessive.

Only he had been willing to allow other men to touch her, so how possessive could he really be?

But there was no faking the very real regret and agony in his face when he'd apologized profusely to her. She still wasn't sure of the reasons why, but she knew it had done something to him. Something profound. Something maybe even he didn't understand.

She tried to disentangle herself from his hold and he came awake, his eyes bleary with sleep.

"Bathroom," she whispered.

"Hurry back," he murmured, loosening his hold so she could get up.

She went into the bathroom and after peeing she checked her appearance in the mirror. She winced at the still-swollen corner of her mouth and the shadow of an already formed bruise. How on earth was she going to explain this to Jace? He'd freak when he saw her.

Caro would have to work her makeup wonders on this.

Her entire body was tender, but not for the usual reasons. Gabe had been exceedingly gentle with her. Shockingly so. He was always so out of control. Crazy hot for her, which made her crazy hot for him in return. And yet tonight?

He'd taken forever. Teasing, taunting, gentle and so very loving. Her chest still fluttered and butterflies scuttled around her belly at how achingly beautiful their lovemaking had been.

For the first time, she hadn't felt like it was just sex.

Knowing he'd come to find her if she kept him waiting for too long, she went back into the bedroom and crawled onto the bed. Gabe's eyelids fluttered open and he viewed her through half-lidded, sleepy eyes. He reached for her but she didn't go into his arms. Instead she rocked back on her heels, studying him in the low light.

He was so incredibly beautiful, and she'd ached to be able to touch and explore him from day one. She'd never been afforded the chance because Gabe was always, *always* in control.

Gabe frowned, pushing up on his elbow. The action sent the sheet sliding down his body, baring his chest and then lower, bunching around his hips as he stared at her, concern etched into his forehead.

"Mia?"

There was uncertainty in his voice, a thread of fear that surprised her.

"What's wrong?" he asked softly.

"Nothing," she said in a husky voice.

His eyes narrowed. "Then why are you not right here?" He patted the indentation where her body had rested moments earlier.

She shifted up on her knees and crawled closer to him, and then she placed her hands on his chest, carefully gauging his reaction to her advances.

His body was a magnet for her hands. She itched to touch him and explore all the muscled lines and contours.

"I want to touch you, Gabe. Can I touch you?" she whispered.

His eyes glittered brightly in the dim light. He sucked in a discernible breath and then his chest caved at the explosive expulsion. "Hell yes."

She leaned forward until her hair swept over his skin and her face hung just over his. "I want to do more than touch."

He reached up to cup her cheek, his thumb gently brushing over the bruise at the corner of her mouth. "Baby, you do whatever you want to do. I'm not going to complain."

"Well. Okay then," she breathed.

Now that she had him exactly where she wanted, she wasn't entirely certain where to begin. She let her hands roam over his chest, to his shoulders, and then down his arms before going to his taut belly. She traced every line of his six-pack and then lowered her mouth to trace a similar pattern with her tongue.

His hand tangled roughly in her hair and he squeezed, wrapping his fingers tightly against her scalp, holding her down so her mouth stayed in contact with his skin.

Emboldened by his seeming approval, she gained more confidence. She yanked the sheet down, completely uncovering him. His cock was in a state of semi-arousal, long and thick, rising from the dark hair between his legs.

She smacked her lips in anticipation and Gabe groaned aloud.

"For God's sake, Mia."

She threw her leg over his thighs to straddle him, positioning herself just below his cock, which was growing more erect by the second. It strained upward, reaching toward his firm abdomen. Unable to resist the temptation she reached down and wrapped both hands around his thick length.

As soon as she touched him, he jerked convulsively and arched his hips upward, seeking more of her touch.

His erection firmly sandwiched between their bellies, she leaned down to claim his mouth. It was a heat brand against her skin, hard and rigid, pulsing against her stomach. She slid her tongue into his mouth, dueling with his in a teasing dance.

Testing her boundaries, she pulled at his hands, and as he'd once done to her, she planted his hands on either side of his head, her palms pressed to his, holding him down.

He smiled against her mouth. "The kitten has turned aggressor and has become the lion."

"Damn right," she growled. "Tonight I call the shots."

"I like this side of you," he murmured. "Huge turn-on, Mia. You're a tigress. Ferocious."

"Bet your ass," she murmured back.

And then she silenced him, devouring his mouth as he'd done to her so many times in the past. She kissed him until he was struggling for breath. His chest heaved and each exhale was ragged and erratic. She loved it.

He was wild for her. Every muscle in his body was coiled tight, and he quivered beneath her body. His eyes glowed fiercely and yet he didn't try to move his hands. Even after she cautiously lifted her palms from his, he made no effort to take them from where she'd placed them.

He was content to allow her to take the wheel this time.

Exhilarated, she kissed a path down his chest, allowing her hair to slide over his skin. She scooted down his legs until she perched at his knees. Her hands circled his cock once more and for a moment she paused, simply holding him in her hands.

She glanced up at him, found his gaze locked on her, lust and desire blazing in the depths of his eyes.

With a satisfied smile, she lowered her mouth to where she grasped his cock and slid her mouth over the head, allowing her tongue to dance around the ridge and linger along the backside where the plump vein traveled the length of his erection.

A long hiss escaped his lips and he arched upward, seeking more of her mouth.

"God, Mia."

His voice was so strained that his words were barely discernible.

She smiled, a confident, smug smile that said she knew for

once the power had shifted to her. He was right where she wanted him. Putty in her hands. He wanted her desperately and he seemed content to let her do anything she wanted.

Anything.

It was like laying out a chocolate buffet to a woman with PMS.

She sucked him deep, taking him to the very back of her throat. Then she swallowed around the head, squeezing and convulsing around him.

His groan was loud in her ears, and then his hands tangled in her hair and she grinned. It hadn't taken him long to move his hands from where she'd placed them. But that was okay because the feeling of his hands in her hair was amazing. She loved the urgency with which his fingers tightened and pulled at the strands.

But he still let her dictate the action. He didn't pull her down onto his cock. His hands just remained twisted in her hair like he had to have something to do with them or he'd go crazy.

She sucked her way down his length and then glided upward, leaving a damp trail over the silky-soft skin.

"Holy shit," Gabe breathed. "Goddamn, Mia. That's it, baby. Take it deep. Love it when you swallow around me like that."

She took him deep, until her nose met his flesh, and then she made a low sound of satisfaction that vibrated around his cock. His hold tightened in her hair and for the first time, he bucked upward, his entire body so tense that she could feel his muscles twitching.

When she could hold her breath no longer, she slid back up his cock and took deep, gulping breaths, her hand gripping him, fingers wrapped around his length, working him up and down as she stared into his eyes.

His gaze smoldered, blue smoke, filled with so much heat and desire and approval. Oh yeah, he loved what she was doing. With a smile, she kept hold of him and then inched her way forward, working up his thighs until she cradled the base of his cock in the V of her legs.

Then she rose up, tucking the head of his dick to her entrance, and without waiting, she slid down, embedding him deeply inside her with one smooth motion.

Gabe made a strangled sound, his hands going to her hips, his fingers digging deep as she settled more comfortable around his cock.

"God, you're beautiful," he said, his gaze drifting up and down her body.

His hands left her hips and lifted to cup her breasts, molding them in his palms while his thumbs brushed over the taut peaks. But this wasn't about her. Not that she wasn't thoroughly enjoying herself, but this was for him. All him.

She wanted to rock his entire universe. Wanted to firmly implant in his mind that he'd never want to allow another man to touch her—anyone to touch her.

With a sigh and tossing her hair back, she began to undulate, rocking back and forth, rising and then lowering herself. She could feel the tension radiating from him. Could see how taut his body was. How tight his jaw was clenched, and the strain around his mouth and eyes.

And then he closed his eyes.

"Eyes," she said huskily, echoing the command he so often gave her. "I want to see your eyes when you come."

His eyes flew open, pupils dilated and his nostrils flared, his jaw tightening. But his gaze didn't leave her.

"Anything for you, baby."

That made her happy. Really damn happy. A contented sigh whispered past her lips and she went liquidy soft around him.

She increased the speed and force of her movements, taking

him higher and higher and closer to the edge until his jaw bulged, his eyes glittered and something unintelligible escaped raggedly from his lips.

She saw the moment he came. Even before she felt his release, she could see it in his eyes. The immense burst of fire, the way they momentarily blanked. Then his hands settled firmly at her waist and he gripped her so hard he'd leave marks.

But then one of his hands slipped even lower and his finger glided through her folds to her clit, stroking as she continued to rock over him.

When she began to close her eyes, his command was swift, for the first time asserting himself.

"Eyes. On me, Mia. When you come, I have your eyes."

She focused on him, her orgasm rising, billowing with excruciating intensity. She was a restless wild thing atop him and now it was his turn to anchor her. To be that steady calm. He stroked his hand down her body while he gently pressed his fingers to her clit.

It was overwhelming. She didn't even have the strength to remain upright as she began to come apart. She tensed and slumped forward and he gathered her in his arms, pulling her down, cradling her into his chest as her orgasm quaked over her, a sudden, fierce storm.

Gabe collected her against him, his mind reeling with what he'd just experienced. He was in awe. He was humbled. Most of all he was so damn *grateful*.

He had no words to describe what she'd just done for him. She'd made love to him. After what he'd done to her, that he still had her trust, much less her giving the gift of herself so selflessly.

He was overcome by what he held in his arms. Gripped by a possessiveness so fierce that he couldn't comprehend it. He hated himself for what he'd done. And yet she *didn't*. And that was almost more than he could bear.

She touched a part of him he'd thought was inaccessible. A part that had been jealously guarded for years. And she'd gotten there with no effort whatsoever. She'd walked into his life and heart like she *belonged*.

And the hell of it was that he was convinced she *did*.

chapter thirty-three

As traumatic an experience as Paris had been for her, in many ways, that night played a crucial turning point in their relationship. Gabe was even more fiercely protective of her and he displayed a tenderness—an *emotional* tenderness—that had been absent before.

It heartened Mia. Made her dare to dream that they could eventually be more than just a contract. She loved Gabe and she only fell more under his spell with every passing day. Love made her patient. It made her hopeful.

The only thing she regretted was that their relationship was secret. From the world. From Jace. Especially from Jace.

Jace had picked up on Mia's upset when she and Gabe had returned from Paris. She hated having to lie to him when he asked her what was wrong. She'd played it off as a stomach bug and jet lag. Thank God for Caroline's expertise with makeup. She'd been able to hide the evidence of her bruise until it faded.

Thanksgiving was approaching, and Gabe had been invited to his parents' house for the occasion. As much as Gabe had mourned their breakup, he seemed to be struggling with their getting back together as well. There was betrayal in his eyes when he looked at his dad, and he was still fiercely protective of his mother. He blamed his father for hurting his mother.

Mia wasn't sure of her own Thanksgiving plans. Gabe had seemed torn between spending the holiday with his parents and remaining with Mia. She'd insisted that he accept their invitation. It was only for a day. It was likely Mia would spend it with Jace provided he planned to be in town. If not, she'd hang out with Caro and her family.

Gabe didn't like the idea of her spending the holiday away from him, but what was there for him to do about it? Unless he wanted to go public with their relationship—and so far he'd been solidly against that.

"Have you finished putting those bids in a presentation for my meeting with Jace and Ash?" Gabe asked from across the room.

Mia glanced up to see him staring at her, warmth and tenderness lighting his eyes. Yes, he'd definitely changed in his actions toward her. He'd become more . . . human. Someone she believed could love her in return.

"Just finishing up," she said. "There are spots for the other two bids. As soon as I receive them, I'll input the information."

Gabe nodded approvingly. "We'll make our selection this week. It's possible that I'll need to return to Paris closer to Christmas. Would you want to go?"

That was another thing that had changed with Gabe. Before, he'd never asked her what she wanted to do or if she wanted to travel with him somewhere. He told her where he expected her to be. She hadn't had a choice in any of it.

Now? Now he never demanded. Though she could often discern what he wanted her decision to be, he never made it for her.

"I'd love to go to Paris at Christmas," she said, excitement squeaking in her voice.

He smiled, relief welling in his eyes. "I'll make our arrangements and I'll include an extra day so you can see anything we missed the first time."

If she'd felt ridiculously spoiled before, it was to the point of absurdity now. He was a complete dream. So very attentive to her needs. Responsive to anything he perceived she wanted or needed.

It was an experience she thoroughly enjoyed. She savored every gentle touch, every look of concern, every attention to exacting detail where she was concerned.

Gabe's phone rang, and he answered. She realized quickly it was his mother. His entire demeanor changed when he spoke to her.

He'd likely be a while. He and his mother had been talking more and more lately as she navigated the tricky waters of her reconciliation with Gabe's dad. She relied heavily on Gabe for emotional support.

She checked her watch. It was past lunchtime and Gabe had been busy all morning. She doubted he planned to take a lunch break at all and work on through until his afternoon meeting.

Making a decision, she rose and collected her purse. Gabe looked up, his eyebrow raising in question as she started toward the door.

Lunch, she mouthed. *I'll bring you back something.*

He nodded and then slid the phone down his chin so his mouth was free.

"Wear a sweater, Mia. It's cold out. There's a chance of snow, so be careful on the sidewalk."

She smiled, heartened by his concern. She went back to her desk, pulled on the warm sweater she kept there for just such occasions. Then she blew him a kiss that made his eyes gleam.

When she stepped outside the building, an excited thrill raced up her spine. She could positively smell snow in the air. There was a brisk chill and moisture with that gray overcast sky. Perfect holiday weather.

She practically danced her way down the block toward the deli where she and Gabe often had takeout. She loved this time of year. Loved the change in seasons. And she always looked forward to Christmas.

With Thanksgiving a mere week away, many shops were already decorating their windows with Christmas lights and displays.

She hugged her sweater tighter as a gust of wind blew over her. She ducked into the deli and placed her to-go order.

Five minutes later, she collected the plastic bags and pushed her way through the crowded interior to step back onto the sidewalk. A raindrop hit her nose, and she picked up her pace as light drizzle began to fall. She hadn't thought to bring an umbrella. She'd only planned to be a few minutes.

Figures it would start raining now. It couldn't have waited the five minutes it would take her to get back to her building?

She had her head down as she rounded the corner to the front entrance of Gabe's office building when she ran smack into another person. She dropped one of the bags and she bent, apologizing as she picked the food back up. Hopefully it would all still be intact. As she rose, the person she'd run into was still standing there.

Nausea curled in her stomach when she got a good look at the man's face. Charles. The man who'd assaulted her in Gabe's Paris hotel suite. There was no way it could be a coincidence that she'd run into him outside the office building.

She took a wary step back and he grasped her arm, pushing her out of the way of pedestrians and against the stone of the building. She was still several feet away from the entrance. Her gaze automatically took in her surroundings as she pondered the best way to escape Charles's grasp.

"Don't touch me," she bit out. "Gabe will kill you for this."

Charles's face twisted into a snarl. "Thanks to your overreaction, Gabe went off his hinges. He's trying to cut me out of the deal entirely. He won't do business with me, and that's going to hurt my ability to do business with others. I need this deal, and you fucked it up for me."

"I fucked it up for you?" she yelled. "You stupid fuck wad. You assaulted me! And I fucked it up for you? You're a dick!"

"Shut the fuck up!" he hissed, pressing in closer, his grip tightening on her arms.

"Back off," she warned. "Get the hell away from me."

His grasp was tight and cruel, and she knew it would leave marks. She only wanted to get the hell away from this asshole and return to Gabe. Where it was safe. Where he'd never allow anything to happen to her.

Rain sluiced down her face, and she blinked to clear her vision. It was cold and only growing colder as wetness permeated her clothing and hair.

"You and I have something to discuss," he snapped. "I want inside information on the bids. I know you have access to it. My only shot is to be able to come in substantially lower than my competitors so that HCM doesn't have a choice but to go with me. I may lose money in this deal, but it sets me up nicely for the future. I need this deal to happen, Mia, and you're going to get it for me."

"You're out of your mind! I'm not telling you jack. Gabe would kill me and so would my brother. I won't betray either one of them, especially not for a dickhead like you. Now get out of my space or I'll start screaming the block down."

"I wouldn't do that if I were you," he said in a low voice.

He shoved his phone at her, the display screen jumping before she could bring it into focus. She gasped, horrified by what was on the screen. This wasn't happening. It could not be happening!

"Oh my God," she whispered.

Nausea was a vicious knot in her stomach. She was utterly sickened by what she saw. It was *her*. Tied and on her knees with

Gabe's cock shoved into her mouth. Her cheeks were bulging as she took his length.

Charles pushed a button and the next picture was of her bound to the coffee table, her eyes tightly shut, her mouth clamped just as tightly shut as Charles stood above her, his hand on her head, other hand grasping his cock as he attempted to shove it into her mouth. Which meant one of the others had taken the photos. What kind of sick bastard did this kind of thing?

It took every bit of strength she had not to gag and vomit there on the street.

"You sick bastard!" she hissed.

There was no need to ask him how he'd gotten the pictures. They'd been taken in the hotel room in Paris. The idea that someone had these photos, that they *looked* at them, horrified her.

"Now here's the deal, Mia," Charles said. His grasp on her arm tightened as if he knew just how badly she wanted to get away. "You're going to get me the information I want or I go public with these photos. How do you think your brother will like seeing pictures of his baby sister all over the Internet? You'll be famous but not in a way either of you will like."

Cold settled into her bones. So deep that her entire body was a block of ice. She stared numbly back at Charles as devastation crashed over her.

The asshole would do it too. She saw the resolve and desperation in his eyes.

"You son of a bitch!" she said hoarsely. "You did that to me! And you're going to threaten me with pictures of you *assaulting* me?"

"Think about it," he said grimly. "I'll expect your call before this weekend. If you fail to deliver, I'll ensure everyone in the world sees these photos."

He released her arm and strode away, disappearing into

the sea of umbrellas and pedestrians hurrying to get out of the rain.

She stood there a long moment, still in shock over the illicit photos he'd produced. Rain pelted her face, soaking into her clothing, but she was numb to the cold. Numb to everything else but the fact that she was in an untenable position.

If she betrayed Gabe, she'd lose him forever. He'd cut her from his life without thought or regret. If she didn't betray him, those photos would be released. Jace would see them. The world would see them. Not only would Jace's friendship with Gabe end, but it could also very well mean the end of their business relationship. And Gabe's reputation would once again suffer under accusations that he'd abused another woman. Once might be played off, but twice? Where there was smoke, there was fire in the public's eye.

She gathered the soggy bags to her chest and stumbled toward the entrance to the office building. Panic made her clumsy. Her heart was beating painfully, so fast that she couldn't process thought.

She rode up the elevator, dread increasing with every breath. What was she supposed to do?

Yes, she had access to the bids. It would be a simple matter to pass along the information to Charles. It would do her no good, though, because even if he came in substantially lower than his competitors, Gabe would *never* use him. And then, even though she'd done as Charles had demanded, he'd be angry and would likely retaliate by publishing those pictures anyway.

What was she supposed to do?

When she got to Gabe's office, he was off the phone. As soon as she walked in his door, he was on his feet, his expression concerned.

"Mia, what the hell? You're soaked! Did you not bring an umbrella?"

He hurried over to her, cursing when he took in her saturated clothing. He took the bags from her hands and discarded them without a look.

"Are you all right? What's going on? You look like you've seen a ghost."

"J-just c-cold," she stammered out. "I got caught in the rain. It's not a big deal, Gabe. Really."

"You're freezing," he muttered. "Come on, I'll take you home and get you into dry clothing. You're going to make yourself ill."

She shook her head, stepping back, her resistance so adamant that he looked taken aback.

"You have a meeting that you can't miss," she said. "There's no need for you to go with me."

"Fuck the meeting," he said bluntly. "You're more important."

She shook her head again. "Have the driver bring me home. I'll go take a hot shower and get into dry clothing. I promise. I can be back in an hour and a half."

This time it was he who shook his head. "No. I don't want you coming back in. Go on home and get warm. Wait for me there. I'll be home as soon as my meeting is done."

She nodded, cold seizing her more firmly in its grasp. Now when she was out of the rain and in the warmth of his office, she began to shiver uncontrollably. She had to keep it together or he'd know that something had gone terribly wrong.

She smiled brightly and gestured toward the bags. "The food is still good. You need to eat, Gabe. You haven't eaten all day."

He touched her cheek, feathering his hand over her face before leaning in to kiss her cold lips. "Don't worry about me. Take your meal home and take it easy for the rest of the day. I'll be home to take care of you in a little while."

His words made her heart squeeze, but they weren't enough to take away her terror or the enormity of the decision she faced. She needed time to think.

Already the beginnings of a headache plagued her. The dull

throb at her temples coupled with the bone-deep cold was beginning to unravel her.

He went to his desk and retrieved his coat and then wrapped it around her, rubbing his hands up and down her arms.

"Come on," he said grimly. "I'll walk you down and get you into the car. Call me if you need anything at all, okay?"

Her smile was wan. Forced. "I'll be fine, Gabe."

She hated lying to him.

chapter thirty-four

Gabe let himself into the apartment and frowned when he saw none of the lights were on. Had Mia misunderstood and gone to her apartment instead?

Since their return from Paris, she'd spent just about every night with him, except for one time when Jace had taken her to dinner and then dropped her back by her place. Just that one night without her had made him itchy and moody, and he'd gone to work in a black mood the next morning.

He stepped into the living room, and his tension immediately eased when he saw Mia curled up on the couch, sound asleep. His fireplace was on and she was covered from head to toe with blankets.

He frowned. Was she coming down with a bug? Thinking back, she'd been fine before she'd gone out to get their lunch. Sunny, bright and smiling. Cheerful. As beautiful as she always was. It scared the shit out of him just how dependent he'd become on her presence in his office. How integral a part of his day she was. Most people needed coffee in the mornings. He just needed Mia.

As he leaned closer to her, intending to feel her for signs of fever, he saw that her eyes were red and puffy and blotchy. As if she'd been . . . crying. *What the hell?*

What could have happened? What wasn't she telling him? He was tempted to wake her and demand to know what the hell was wrong, but he didn't want to disturb her. She looked tired. Deep shadows rested underneath her eyes. Had she looked this tired the night before? Had he been too hard on her? Too demanding? Was he the reason she was sick?

Dread pitted his stomach. Was this relationship too much for her? He couldn't even promise to ease up, to back off. Instead of time begetting distance, with every passing day she became more of an overwhelming need within him. Time would only sharpen his desperation for her. Not alleviate it. He'd been a fool to ever think allowing another man to touch her would somehow prove that he wasn't emotionally dependent on her. That it wouldn't bother him.

He still wanted to beg her forgiveness every time his mind went back to that night in Paris. She'd already forgiven him, but just remembering had the power to take him to his knees.

He wasn't worthy of her. He knew this well. But damned if he had the power to do the right thing and let her go. It would destroy him.

Checking his watch, he frowned. He was later getting home than he'd intended. It was close to the dinner hour and he wondered if she'd even eaten her takeout. He walked into the kitchen to find his answer on the counter. The bag was untouched. The box inside unopened. He cursed softly. She needed to eat.

He rummaged in his cabinets for a can of soup. His housekeeper kept the staples on hand for him, and he gave her a shopping list on Fridays for any weekend cooking he thought to do. But the simple matter was, he wasn't home often enough to keep a fully stocked pantry.

After deciding he had nothing suitable, he picked up the phone and called down to the concierge to tell him what he required. After being assured the matter would be taken care of immediately, Gabe hung up and searched the medicine cabinet for a thermometer and appropriate medication.

The only problem was, he wasn't certain what she was sick with. Or if she was running any fever. It could be a cold. Could be a stomach bug. How was he supposed to know until he could ask her?

Deciding it could wait until she awakened—he wanted her to rest as long as she needed—he walked quietly back into the living room. The blanket had slid down, uncovering the upper half of her body, so he pulled it back up and tucked the ends around her. Then he kissed her forehead, feeling for any sign of fever.

She was warm, but not overly so. Her respirations seemed fine.

He went to the fireplace, turned up the flame and then disappeared into his room to change into more comfortable clothing while he waited for Mia's soup to be delivered.

There was plenty of work to be done—he'd left right after his meeting and he still had financials to go over in preparation for his meeting with Jace and Ash to discuss the construction bids—but instead he picked up his tablet and settled on the couch across from Mia.

She settled him. Made him think about more than just work and business. He liked just being in her company, doing something as enjoyable as reading a book in the silence.

She'd been thrilled when he'd presented her with a brand-new e-reader—the latest upgrade—along with an entire collection of her favorite books in digital, loaded onto the reader. She'd thrown her arms around him and hugged and kissed him so exuberantly that he'd laughed. But then he did that a lot around her. Laughed.

There was something quite irresistible about her. Her charm was infectious. She was his . . . sunshine. He cringed at how corny that sounded. He was acting and thinking like an overdramatic teenager. Thank God no one could see into his thoughts. He'd never be able to hold his head up at business meetings.

Men like him were supposed to be intimidating. Cold. Un-reachable. Feared, even. If anyone had any clue that a petite bru-nette with a million-dollar smile was his absolute kryptonite, he'd be laughed out of town.

His cell phone beeped, and he dug it out of his pocket to see that the concierge had texted him to say that he was coming up right away with Gabe's order. Gabe rose from the couch to meet the man at the elevator doors. They opened just as he arrived in the foyer. He thanked the concierge and then took the bag into the kitchen.

The soup was still steaming hot, so Gabe didn't warm it fur-ther in the microwave. He poured it into a bowl and toasted two slices of bread. Then he dug into the fridge for Mia's favorite soft drink. Black cherry soda. It was an item he'd told his housekeeper to keep stocked because Mia was addicted to it.

There were a lot of things he kept stocked now because of Mia's preferences. He'd committed them to memory and then made certain he had the things she liked. He didn't want to give her any reason not to want to stay over.

He put the soup, toast and her drink on a tray, and then carried it into the living room, placing it on the coffee table in front of her. He was still reluctant to wake her, but she needed to eat and he needed to determine her condition. If necessary, he'd call his per-sonal physician and have him come over to see Mia here.

"Mia," he said in a low voice. "Mia, wake up, honey. I brought you something to eat."

She stirred, uttered a sleepy protest and then turned her head to the other side, her eyelashes fluttering as she closed her eyes again.

He chuckled. She never did like having her sleep disturbed.

He touched her cheek, tracing a path down to her jaw, enjoying the silky feel of her skin beneath his touch.

"Mia. Wake up, baby. Come on. Open those pretty eyes for me."

She opened her eyes and her unfocused stare encountered his. To his surprise, fear registered, and something else he couldn't quite put his finger on. Worry? Anxiety?

What the hell was going on here?

She yawned and rubbed her eyes, avoiding his gaze as she sat up. She clutched the covers around her in a manner that screamed self-preservation.

He had to bite his tongue to keep from demanding answers right here and now. There was something infinitely fragile about her right now. He hadn't seen her this way since that night in Paris. His gut knotted just thinking about it.

"Hey sleepyhead," he said in a gentle tone. "I brought you some soup. I see you didn't eat your lunch."

She grimaced. "I was cold and just wanted to get warm. Didn't feel like eating."

"Are you feeling okay? Are you unwell? I can have my doctor come see you."

She licked her lips and shook her head. "I'm fine. Really. As soon as I got warm I was so sleepy that I couldn't stay awake. But I feel fine. I promise."

He didn't quite believe her and he wasn't sure why. There was something off about her even if she wasn't ill. And there was the fact that it looked very much like she'd been crying. Maybe he was overreacting. Maybe she'd just rubbed her eyes before nodding off.

"Feel like eating now?" he prompted.

She eyed the tray on the coffee table and then nodded. "Starving."

When she started to get up and move forward, he held out his hand to help her. She laced her fingers through his and pulled herself to a sitting position on the edge of the couch.

"Thanks," she said huskily. "You're so very good to me, Gabe."

It wasn't the first time she'd said such a thing, but every time she did, he was besieged by guilt. If he'd been as good to her as he should have been, he would have never allowed her to be abused by another man.

He watched as she ate, the need to touch her and shield her from whatever had caused her upset growing by the minute. It was an insatiable urge he had no control over. The strength of his attraction to her defied logic. But then when it came to her, it was clear he had no reason. No sanity. No ability to maintain any distance between them.

When she finished with her meal, she pushed back the blanket that was still halfway wrapped around her and to his surprise—and delight—she crawled onto the couch with him and wrapped herself around him.

He put his arm around her and then reached forward for the blanket that had fallen by the wayside. He pulled it over both of them and positioned her so she blanketed him, her body soft and warm against his.

He buried his nose in her hair, content to have her snuggled as close to him as possible.

"Thank you for dinner," she said. "I just want you to hold me right now. It's all I need to feel better."

Her words spoke to the very heart of him. Said with utter sincerity. How simple she made it sound. She'd never asked anything of him. She was very undemanding. She didn't give a shit about his money or what he could buy her. The only things she'd ever truly asked him for were so simple. Hold her. Touch her. Comfort her.

The idea that he held such power over her should have contented him. It was what he wanted, wasn't it? Complete control. Her bending to his will. But instead it made him all too aware of the fact that he had the power to destroy her.

"Want to stay here in front of the fire or do you want to go to bed?" he asked as he stroked her hair.

"Mmmm," she uttered in a sleepy, contented voice. "Here for a while, I think. It's nice in front of the fire. I wonder if it's snowing yet."

He chuckled. "If it is I imagine it's only flurries. We never do get much this early in the year."

"Head hurts," she murmured as she snuggled further into the crook of his shoulder.

He frowned. "Why didn't you say something sooner? How bad is it?"

She shrugged. "Bad enough. I took some ibuprofen when I got home. I'd hoped that when I woke up it would be gone."

He pushed her gently to the side and then disentangled himself from her and the blanket before rising from the couch. He strode into the kitchen, shook out one of the prescription painkillers from the bottle and then returned to Mia.

She frowned. "Those make me so fuzzy."

"Fuzzy is better than you being in pain," he said patiently. "Take it and I'll take care of you. We'll sit on the couch until you get sleepy and then we'll go to bed. If you aren't feeling better in the morning, you're going to stay home."

"Yes, sir," she said, her dimple flashing in her cheek.

He gave her the pill and then handed her the half-empty bottle of black cherry soda and watched as she swallowed the medicine. Then he sat back down, immediately pulling her back into his arms. He settled the blanket over her body and wrapped both his arms around her, holding her securely in his embrace.

She gave a contented sigh as she burrowed her forehead against his neck.

"I'm glad I'm with you, Gabe. I don't regret my decision even for a moment."

She said the words so softly, he almost didn't hear. And when he did realize what it was she said, he was gripped by a satisfaction so fierce that he couldn't immediately respond. But there was also something odd about her statement. Almost as if it were a prelude to a good-bye. He wouldn't even consider that possibility. He'd do whatever it took to ensure she didn't go anywhere but right back to him.

"I'm glad you're here too, Mia," he returned softly.

chapter thirty-five

Mia pulled a jacket on over her shirt as she prepared to leave Gabe's apartment. He wouldn't be happy when she showed up at his office. He'd left this morning with stern instructions that she was to stay home in bed and rest.

He thought she was getting sick, that yesterday had been the prelude to a cold or a stomach bug.

She had spent most of the day numb with shock and fear. She'd been so panicked that she hadn't been able to think about what the best course was for her to take. And time was running out. It was Friday and Charles expected her to cough up the information by the end of the week.

Her stomach was in knots. She was a nervous wreck as she walked down to get into the car that would take her to Gabe's office—her office.

She'd weighed all her options and the only one available to her was to go to Gabe, tell him the entire truth, and hope that he could take care of the matter. Betraying him wasn't an option. She had no idea what kind of future they had, but it was time they took matters into their own hands and told Jace, effectively taking away any power Charles perceived he held.

The night before, she'd left her long-sleeved pajama top on even after going to bed with Gabe, citing that she was cold. In reality, she hadn't wanted Gabe to see the bruises on her arm from where Charles had grabbed her. Gabe would have most assuredly noticed, and she would have had to explain before she'd had time to get things straight in her own mind and come to peace over her decision.

She rubbed over the length of her arm through the leather jacket, and bit her lip pensively as the car wove through late morning traffic.

There was still a drizzle in the air. No snowflakes or flurries. Not even sleet. But it was cold, gray and overcast, and the skies looked ready to burst at any moment.

When the driver pulled in front of the building, Mia ducked out and hurried toward the door so she didn't get soaked again. She rode up the elevator, her anxiety heightening with every floor as she crept upward.

Eleanor looked surprised when Mia walked through the reception area.

"Mia, Mr. Hamilton said you were sick this morning. Are you feeling better?"

Mia smiled wanly. "A bit, yes. Is Gabe in his office?"

Eleanor nodded.

"See that we aren't disturbed until he tells you otherwise," Mia said in a quiet voice. "We have an important matter to discuss this morning."

"Of course," Eleanor replied. "Let me know if you want lunch delivered. I'll see to it."

Mia ignored the last and headed in the direction of Gabe's office, her dread intensifying with every step. It sickened her to have to tell him of the pictures she saw. Of what Charles had threatened. She didn't want to have to rehash what had happened in Paris all over again. She and Gabe had moved beyond that.

When she opened Gabe's door, he glanced up, his brows drawn.

When he saw that it was her, he immediately rose from his desk, a frown curving his lips downward.

"Mia? What the hell are you doing here? Are you all right? You should be at home in bed."

He put his hands to her shoulders and pulled her into his chest, looking down at her face as if examining her for any signs of illness.

"There's something I need to talk to you about, Gabe," she said hesitantly. "It's about yesterday . . . And what really happened."

Gabe pulled away from Mia so that he could see the entirety of her face and expression, and his pulse accelerated as he took in the fear and dread in her eyes. She looked . . . terrible. And she never looked bad. But this morning she looked as though she hadn't slept at all the night before. She looked tired and fragile.

He remembered thinking she looked as though she'd been crying yesterday. And now she was here suggesting that she hadn't told him about something—something big—that had happened yesterday.

"Come sit down," he said, his throat tight.

As he attempted to gently guide her toward the sofa across the room, she shook her head and pulled her hand from his grasp.

"I can't sit, Gabe. I'm too worked up. I just need to tell you this and pray that you aren't pissed—at me."

Now he was really starting to worry. For the life of him, he couldn't put all the pieces together. Everything had been so normal yesterday. Until lunch. When she'd gone out to get them both something to eat. When she'd gotten back, she'd been soaked to the bone, and it was almost as if she'd been in shock.

His brow furrowed further as she stared back at him, vulnerability shining like a beacon in her eyes. She was afraid. It sickened him that she was evidently afraid of him, or at least his reaction to what she would tell him.

In an effort to alleviate her tangible fear and unease, he slid his hands up the sleeves of her jacket and squeezed softly. She flinched and moved one arm away from his grasp, her hand immediately going to cover the spot where he'd grasped.

What the hell was going on here?

"Take off the jacket, Mia," he said in a firm voice.

She hesitated, her breath blowing through her lips. Tears rose in her eyes, stunning him.

No longer willing to wait a moment longer, he stripped the jacket down from her shoulders and held her arm out so he could slide the sleeves down from her arm. She wouldn't meet his gaze the entire time. As soon as the jacket was off, he saw her upper arm, the one she'd flinched over when he'd touched her.

His breath exploded in one huge burst when he saw the purpling bruises that painted the upper portion of her arm. His fingers went to touch the area, but he held back, not wanting to hurt her.

He reached for her other hand and dragged her toward the window where the light was better and he could see the marks.

"What the fuck happened here, Mia?" he demanded.

He ran light fingertips over the bruised flesh, and his pulse started pounding at his temple when he saw that the bruises very much resembled fingerprints. As if someone had roughly grabbed her and held on. Large fingers and hands. A man's hands.

A tear trickled down her cheek and she hastily tried to wipe it away with her free hand. Fear seized him by the balls. What had happened to her? A knot formed in his stomach as dread foamed through his gut.

"Who did this to you?"

His voice was low and menacing and he was barely holding on to control. He wanted to find the son of a bitch who'd put his hands on Mia and kill the bastard.

"Charles Willis," she said, barely above a whisper.

"What?"

She flinched from the explosion of his voice. Then she lifted her hand to put on his chest. He was vibrating with fury and she knew it. Her tear-filled gaze met his and there was pleading in her eyes.

"Yesterday when I went to get lunch, he stopped me on the street. On my way back, not far from the entrance to our building. He said he wanted me to give him information on the bids you've received on the project in Paris. He said his only chance was to undercut his competitors by enough that you'd be forced to go with him despite any misgivings on your part."

A sense of foreboding crept up Gabe's spine. "Did you give him this information?" he asked. Was this why she was so upset and convinced that he was going to be angry with her?

"No!" Mia said, her vehemence unmistakable. She looked devastated that he'd even ask such a question.

"Is that why he put those bruises on you?" Gabe demanded. "I'll kill him for this."

"There's more," she choked out.

She turned away, her shoulders shaking as she wrapped her arms protectively around herself.

"Oh God, Gabe. He made threats. He showed me . . . *pictures*."

"Pictures of what?"

She turned back around, her face a mask of anguish. "Of *us*," she choked out. "From that night. Of me tied and kneeling with you . . . in my mouth."

She shook from head to toe. Her hands were trembling so badly that she looked as though she might collapse.

"And then there was a picture of me on the coffee table with him where he was trying to thrust into my m-mouth."

"Son of a bitch!"

His response was angry and explosive. She flinched and took a step back, her arms crowding around herself once more.

"H-he s-said that if I didn't g-give him the information he w-wanted that he'd go public with the photos. That he'd tell Jace. That he'd ruin you."

Gabe was stunned. He couldn't even form a response, though dozens crowded his lips. He was so angry that he couldn't even think straight. He lifted a hand and pushed it through his hair and then over his face as he tried to process the threat.

Mia pushed forward then, her expression pleading and earnest. "I had to tell you, Gabe. I had to come to you with this. I couldn't—wouldn't—betray you. But he has pictures—God, the pictures he has! He's angry and desperate. He gave me until the end of this week to call him and give him what he wanted."

Gabe's hand fell as he stared at her in utter bewilderment. She hadn't betrayed him. She'd come to him, her eyes begging him to fix this. God, she trusted him, even after what he'd done to her in Paris. He was at fault here. It was *his* fault that this asshole had illicit, damning photographs of her in a position Gabe should have never put her in.

His heart was about to beat right out of his chest. Any other person wouldn't have thought twice about betraying him. Hell, he couldn't have blamed her if she'd turned over the information in an effort to protect herself. But she hadn't done that. She'd come to him, had told him everything—at great risk to herself.

He couldn't wrap his mind around it. He stood there staring at her, unable to breathe, unable to process the enormity of her decision.

She'd chosen him. Him over dishonor, humiliation. She'd chosen him over *Jace*.

God, she'd forgiven the unforgivable, and instead of being hurt and angry when faced with photos that showed, in graphic detail, what Gabe had allowed to happen to her, she'd chosen not to betray him. Instead she'd come to him, trusting him to take care of the matter. Trusting him to protect her!

Such faith baffled him. He was used to people betraying him. Hell, he expected it from most. He wouldn't have blamed her if she had done whatever was necessary to protect herself.

But she hadn't done any of the things he may have imagined. Instead she'd come to him. Hurt, frightened, confused. She'd still come to him when he deserved none of her trust.

No longer able to stand her looking at him with so much uncertainty and panic in her eyes, he roughly pulled her to him, holding her so tightly he doubted she could breathe. He buried his face in her hair and closed his eyes, inhaling her scent, absorbing the sensation of her against his skin.

She was tattooed on every part of his body. Deeper, in his heart, his very soul. A permanent brand that would never wear off.

"Mia, my sweet, darling Mia," he whispered. "I've let you down and yet you still had enough faith in me to come to me with this."

She pushed at him, putting hated distance between them. Her eyes were wild with grief and fear. No wonder she'd been in shock the day before. The bastard had not only hurt her but he'd terrified and humiliated her.

"I couldn't betray you," she choked out. "God, Gabe, I'm in a no-win situation. Do you understand that? If I gave Charles what he wanted, you would have cut me out of your life with the precision of a surgeon's scalpel. If I don't give him what he wants, he'll humiliate us both. Jace will find out, and not only will it affect your friendship, but it could ruin your business partnership as well. Not to mention the things that would be said about you. The way it looks in those pictures . . ."

She trailed off, choking off as a sob welled in her throat. She swallowed, visibly making the effort to pull herself together.

"It looks as though you're forcing me. That you're doing this horrible thing. Those pictures are so *damning*."

Hardened resolve screamed through his mind, roaring like an out-of-control freight train. But Mia needed calm. She needed reassurance. She needed him.

She'd trusted him more than anyone had ever trusted him. She'd given him her unconditional faith. He'd be damned if he let her down now.

"I'll take care of the matter," he said quietly. "I don't want you to worry. I want you to put this from your mind."

Relief simmered in her eyes. There was hope as she stared back at him, damp trails down her cheeks. He lifted his hand and gently caressed away some of the moisture, and then he pulled her to him, lowering his mouth to crush hers.

He kissed her, inhaling her sweetness, savoring it on his tongue. He kissed away all traces of her tears, pressing his lips to her eyelids and then her cheeks, and back to her mouth again.

As he pulled away, a sob erupted from her throat, and it was as if she could no longer maintain her composure. Tears flooded her eyes and her shoulders sagged. It ripped his heart right out of his chest to see her sobbing as though her own heart were breaking.

"Mia, baby, ah honey, please don't cry," he said, reaching for her again.

This time he didn't give her a choice. He pulled her over to the couch and down onto his lap, holding her as she wept against him.

She clung fiercely to him, her arms wrapped around his shoulders as she pressed her face into the side of his neck.

"I'm so scared, Gabe," she choked out. "I don't want my actions to make people I care about suffer. You, Jace. You both could be so hurt by this."

"Shhh, baby. This isn't your fault. Goddamn it. It's *mine*. I was stupid and careless and I didn't protect you like I should have.

None of this would have happened if I hadn't been such a goddamn fool."

"What will you do?" she asked in an aching voice.

Her face was blotchy and red, her eyes swollen from crying. She was pale and she looked ill. Anyone seeing her right now would think she'd been through the wringer.

He cupped her head against him, stroking her soft hair.

"I don't want you to worry about that," he murmured. "I *will* take care of the matter. You have my word on that."

He slid his hand up her arm, over the dark bruises that bastard had put on her. Rage made him crazy. This was twice that Charles had frightened and intended to harm Mia. He was going to take the son of a bitch apart and ruin him beyond repair.

He kissed her hair and then carefully pulled her upright so that he could look into her eyes.

"Listen to me, okay? Freshen up in the bathroom here. Take as long as you need. I don't want anyone to see you this way. It would raise a lot of questions and I don't want anyone to see you so upset. As soon as you're ready, I want you to go back to my apartment and stay there until I get home."

Fear and concern flashed in her eyes.

"Where will you be?"

He put a finger to her lips, indulging in their velvety softness. He traced the bow of her mouth and then followed it with a brief kiss.

"I'm going to ensure that Charles Willis never threatens you again."

chapter thirty-six

Gabe got out of the car on Lexington Avenue in front of the small office building that housed Charles Willis's suite of offices, and he strode toward the entrance, his hands coiled into tight fists.

He'd bundled Mia into a car and sent her home after she'd ridded herself of all traces of upset, and after he'd asked her to describe the photos Charles had shown her in exacting detail.

Charles's office was on the first floor, space he shared with another company because he wasn't often in New York City. His worldwide construction company had many offices around the globe, but Gabe would never do business with the man again. If it weren't for the fact that Charles's company employed a lot of people—good people who depended on him to support their families—Gabe would utterly shut him down and run him out of business.

As it was, he'd never have anything personally or professionally to do with the man again.

Gabe strode past the startled receptionist and opened Charles's door with a bang. Charles looked up, startled, from his desk and Gabe saw a hint of fear flash in the other man's eyes before he rose to his feet and masked his features.

"Gabe," he said in a cordial voice. "What can I do for you?"

Gabe slammed the door shut behind him and stared intently at Charles as he walked forward. He never lifted his gaze, and Charles was visibly uncomfortable with Gabe's scrutiny.

"You fucked up this time, Charles," Gabe said softly. "You touched what is mine. You put your hands on her. You hurt her. You frightened her. You *threatened* her."

Charles battled his obvious panic and then arrogantly shrugged his shoulders. "She's just another whore. What do you care?"

Gabe flew at him in rage, drawing back his fist. He punched the other man in the mouth, sending him reeling into the bookcase behind his desk. Charles's hand flew to his mouth and when it came away, it was smeared with blood.

"I'll have you arrested for assault!" Charles raged. "You can't come in here and hit me!"

"You fucking piece of shit. You're lucky I don't kill you with my bare hands," Gabe seethed out. "If you *breathe* in Mia's direction again, I will ruin you. When I'm finished with you, you will have nothing. No credibility. No backing. No contracts. Nothing at all."

Panic leached all the color from Charles's face.

"I'll go public with those photos!" he threatened, babbling out the words like an incoherent drunk.

Gabe went still, his nostrils flaring. "You do that, Charles. Make those photos public. I'll have you charged with rape. It's precisely what you tried to do to her, and those photos prove it. I don't give a shit what it does to me or my reputation. But I won't have Mia hurt or humiliated by you or anyone else. I'll nail your ass to the wall and you'll spend the next several years in prison being a fuck toy for your cell mate. If you don't believe me, just try me."

His voice was full of menace. And conviction. If Charles didn't believe Gabe, he was a fool. Gabe had never been more serious in his life.

Charles paled and realization set in, his eyes flashing with recognition. Gabe was absolute and Charles knew it.

"I will spend every penny I own ensuring that you lose everything you have," Gabe continued. "And I have a lot of connections. A lot of favors owed to me that I'm more than willing to collect now."

Charles looked as though he wanted to faint. He tried to pick himself up from where he'd slid down the bookcase, but he wobbled and couldn't gain his footing.

"I'm sorry," he blurted out. "I was desperate. I knew you wouldn't give me the bid after what happened. I need that deal, Gabe. I have to have it."

Gabe held out his hand to help Charles to his feet. Charles stared warily at him but finally slid his hand into Gabe's grasp.

As soon as Charles was back on his feet, Gabe flattened him with another punch. He likely broke Charles's nose. Blood splattered over his face as Charles lay dazed against the bookcase.

"That's for putting your hands on Mia. For leaving bruises on her skin. If you ever go near her again, there isn't a rock on this earth you can hide under. I'll hunt you down, and I'll take you apart. I can make you disappear, Willis. No one would ever find your body."

Knowing he'd made his point, Gabe turned and stalked from the office. Charles was stupid, but he was smart enough to know that Gabe was utterly serious. If he made good on any part of his threat to Mia, Gabe would destroy him.

Gabe got into his car and headed for his apartment. He was anxious to be back with Mia so he could reassure her that the matter was taken care of.

It baffled him and brought him to his knees that she hadn't betrayed him. That her first instinct was to come to him and ask for help. To trust him to solve the matter when she stood to lose so much.

What a gift he'd been given in Mia.

His thoughts were consumed with her as he rode through town. There was a lot he wanted to discuss with her—matters he wasn't sure how she'd feel about.

But this situation had brought to him in stark clarity how easily they could be discovered. Was such a deception worth the possible consequences?

Before, he agreed wholeheartedly with Mia in keeping their relationship from Jace. It only made sense because he'd known that whatever their relationship was, it wouldn't last very long. If Jace never knew, there would be no awkwardness. No anger. They could go on as before, pretending his time with Mia had never happened.

Only now . . .

Now, Gabe was reluctant to think of the agreement between him and Mia ending. He wasn't sure when it had happened that he'd started looking at her in a new light. As someone he had no intention of walking away from. At least not any time soon.

Jace needed to be told and then Gabe and Mia would deal with whatever fallout ensued. It was becoming increasingly more difficult for Gabe to pretend distance at the office. To pretend Mia was just an employee. Or that she was just Jace's little sister and someone Gabe viewed with affection.

He wasn't sure how Mia would feel about them going to Jace with the truth—or rather a simpler version of the truth. No one would ever know of their contract. It was a thing that shamed Gabe now, where before he'd lived by it, would never enter a relationship without one. Now? It seemed ridiculous and useless. A product of his overreaction to the past.

More important than any of that right now was ensuring that Mia was reassured, and that he soothed any worry or fear she had with regard to the threats Charles had made.

His hands itched to touch her. He wanted her against him,

breathing the same air as he did. He wanted to taste her and to feel her against his skin.

He silently urged his driver to go faster. He'd been away from Mia for too long. She was his addiction, and he was already suffering from withdrawal.

Mia worried and fretted as she waited for Gabe to get home. She checked the clock countless times, the minutes passing with excruciating slowness.

What had he done? How could he possibly hope to take care of the matter? Had she done the right thing in going to him?

She was weary and her head ached vilely. She'd already raided Gabe's medicine cabinet for ibuprofen, but nothing seemed to ease the pain at her temples and at the base of her neck.

And then she heard footsteps in the foyer, and she lunged up from the couch and met Gabe as he entered the living room.

She flew into his arms and he gathered her close as she all but crawled up his body. He hoisted her up and she wrapped her legs around his waist as she clutched tightly at his shoulders.

His hands palmed her ass, holding her up as he stared into her eyes.

"Are you all right?" he asked in a low voice.

She nodded. "I am now that you're home. I've been so worried, Gabe."

He carried her to the couch and sat down, her still straddling him. He pulled her down into a kiss and then smoothed the hair from her forehead.

"Everything is fine. I want you to trust in that fact. Charles will not ever be a problem for us again. I promise."

Worry flashed in her eyes and her lips pursed. "What did you do?"

"He and I merely reached an understanding," Gabe said calmly. "It's over, Mia. He won't bother you again."

It was then that her gaze fell on his hand, at the scrape on his knuckles and the faint smear of redness, almost as if he'd wiped the blood but hadn't gotten quite all of it.

She glanced back into his eyes, her brows furrowing. "What did you do, Gabe?"

"He put his hands on you," Gabe said sharply. "That's twice he's forced himself on you with the intent of harming you."

"If he presses charges, you'll be arrested," she said unhappily. "Then everything will come out. He's not worth you going to jail for."

A low growl echoed from his throat. "You're worth *everything*. I'd die for you. I'd sure as hell go to jail to prevent some asshole from hurting you."

Shocked to her core by the vehement words, she could only stare at him in utter bemusement. Hope was sharp and overwhelming, fluttering deep in her heart and flooding her veins with soothing warmth. Tears filled her eyes, threatening to spill over onto her cheeks.

She lifted his hand and gently kissed the abrasion.

His gaze softened and he cupped her cheek, rubbing softly over her jaw.

"There's something else I want to discuss with you, Mia."

She could sense the difference in his voice. He was a little less certain, and yet his words were firm, full of determination.

"What?"

"I think we should tell Jace about us."

Her eyes widened in shock.

"He doesn't need to know exact details. But we run the risk of discovery all the time. I'm tired of pretending you don't mean a damn thing to me. You live in fear of him discovering us and what it will do to our friendship and your relationship with him. If we remove that fear, then it won't have any power over us any longer. He may be angry at first, but he'll get over it."

Mia blew out an unsteady breath. This was . . . Well, it was huge. Gabe wanted to go public with their relationship? She dared not hope what that meant. She couldn't afford to read anything into it, to assume that it was anything more than ending a source of considerable strain as they sought to keep their relationship secret.

"Mia? Do you agree?"

She blinked and refocused her gaze on Gabe. Saw the determination etched on his face. Then slowly, she nodded.

"When?" she whispered.

"When he gets back into town. He's supposed to be back Monday or Tuesday. I'll let him know that I have something important to discuss with him."

"Okay," she agreed, her pulse racing.

"Now, this is what I want us to do now that we've gotten all of that out of our way and decided, and the matter of Charles is dealt with," Gabe said.

He touched her face, then threaded his hand through her hair, stroking in sweet caresses.

"I want us to spend the weekend together not worrying about a damn thing other than what pleases us. I'll order in dinner for us, and we'll have a nice meal by the fire and watch the rain turn to snow and sleet."

She sighed and leaned forward, wrapping her arms around his neck in a hug. "That sounds wonderful, Gabe. It's the perfect weekend."

chapter thirty-seven

Gabe kept a close eye on Mia throughout the weekend. She still showed signs of worry and anxiety, and he made every effort to distract her when it was obvious she was brooding over the situation with Charles. He had no doubt he'd made his point with Charles and that he wouldn't be a threat to Mia any longer.

Still, he never assumed anything and so he'd placed a few discreet calls so that Charles's activities could be monitored. But he kept that fact from Mia, not wanting to give her any reason to doubt his assurance that Charles would no longer pose a threat.

Sunday, he took her out for a late lunch, early dinner, and they sat in a restaurant that had already been decorated for Christmas ahead of the Thanksgiving holiday that was in a few days' time. He knew she loved Christmas and everything having to do with it. Her entire face had lit up when they'd walked into the festively lit interior of the eatery.

He wasn't at all certain of what to do for Thanksgiving. A lot would depend on Jace's reaction to his and Mia's relationship when they told him everything this week. His parents had invited him to spend the holiday with them, and as glad as he was that they were on the road to working things out, he still felt awkward around them. Plus, he didn't want to spend the time away from

Mia. And he didn't want to leave her alone if Jace didn't plan to be in town for the holiday.

When they walked out of the restaurant, darkness had settled over the city, and the wet sidewalks glistened in the streetlights and the glow from the traffic lights. Mia turned up her face and laughed in delight as a snowflake swirled down and hit her on the nose.

She posed an enchanting figure in her knit cap and long coat. She spun around, hands held out as a few other flakes danced downward in a drunken spiral.

He was utterly captivated by her.

Before he lost the moment, he picked up his phone and snapped a picture of her, wanting to add it to the other photo of her that he frequently looked at. She never noticed, so absorbed was she in catching the scattered flakes.

"It's freezing out here!" Mia exclaimed.

She ran over and burrowed into Gabe's overcoat, her arms wrapping around his waist as she shivered from head to toe. He caught her against him, smiling at her exuberance.

"Let's get you warm then," he said, guiding her toward the waiting car.

They climbed into the backseat where the seat warmers had already heated the leather. Mia sank into the seat, sighing in utter delight.

"I do love modern conveniences," she said.

He chuckled. "I'm more than happy to keep you warm."

"Mmmm. When we get back to the apartment I'll be more than happy to let you."

He ran his hand up her leg and then back again to the curve of her knee. "I have plans for you when we get back, most assuredly."

She lifted an eyebrow in interest, her eyes glowing with instant fire. "Oh?"

He smiled. "You'll find out when we get there."

She turned her lip down into a pout and narrowed her eyes at him. He just grinned.

Oh yes, he had plans. He was a little nervous given what he had planned, but it was important to him to replace her last memory of bondage with something sensual. Hot. Passionate. Something welcome instead of something distasteful.

He knew with enough time that he could absolutely make the experience incredible for her, but he wouldn't force her to do anything she didn't want to. He would watch her closely, and if she was afraid or uneasy, he'd stop immediately. He'd already screwed up badly with her. He had no desire to ever give her reason to doubt him again.

When they arrived at his apartment, he helped her from the car and held her hand as they rode the elevator up. Once inside, he took her coat, scarf and cap, and she rubbed her hands up and down her arms as she turned to walk into the living room.

He'd left the fireplace burning while they were gone so the living room would be plenty warm when they returned.

After removing his own coat, he followed Mia into the living room to see her standing in front of the fire.

"Stand there and undress," he said, his voice husky with need.

She lifted her gaze and he watched for any sign of reluctance. But all he saw was trust shining back at him.

"I have a few things to get from the bedroom. Stay by the fire and keep warm. I'll be right back."

He strode into the bedroom and retrieved the rope, the anal plug and the vibrator from his closet. When he returned, she was silhouetted by the flames, her skin glowing from the fire.

She was so damn beautiful that she took his breath away.

When her gaze lighted on the items in his hand, her eyes widened and she looked up at him, clear question in her eyes.

Never before would he have stopped to explain himself with

any other woman. They were expected to obey without question. They agreed to anything and everything he could ever wish to do when they signed the contract.

But Mia was different. He wanted her to understand. Wanted her to know what he was thinking. The very last thing he wanted was to frighten her or to make her walk away.

"I want to show you how very pleasurable this can be," he said in a low voice. "I did it for all the wrong reasons in Paris. It wasn't about you then, no matter what I said. It was about me and my reasons—my *stupid* reasons. Give me this chance, Mia. I want to show you how beautiful a woman in bondage can be. And how pleasurable I can make the experience for you. Trust me to make it perfect for you."

Her eyes softened. "I do trust you, Gabe. Only you. No one else. It was never you I objected to. It was the *other* men. As long as only you are touching me, then I'm not afraid."

God but she was so sweet. Never had anyone put so much faith in him. Not his ex-wife. Not any of the other women he'd been with. They had never looked beyond the material things he gave them. Never looked beyond his wealth and status to the man behind it all. And they'd never embraced that man.

Mia had. She accepted him. Wanted him as much as he wanted her. And she was unaffected by his wealth and power. She knew the *real* Gabe Hamilton and she wanted *that* man.

Slowly, he was learning that it was okay to let down his barriers with her and allow her to see a part of him no one ever saw. Just as she trusted him, he also trusted Mia with his most protected asset.

His heart.

He motioned her toward the large leather ottoman, and positioned her on her hands and knees. Then he began to meticulously wind the rope around her body. Underneath and over her breasts, drawing attention to the luscious mounds. Then he looped around to her back and secured her wrists together at the small of her back, while instructing her to lay her cheek against the soft leather.

After binding her hands, he stretched the rope downward and spread her thighs before looping rope around each ankle and stretching it taut between her wrists and ankles.

She was completely and utterly helpless and vulnerable to whatever he wanted to do to her. And there was a hell of a lot he wanted to do.

His cock was hard as stone and straining at his pants, but he was determined to take things slowly. He wanted her with him all the way. Wanted this to be about her and her pleasure when before it hadn't been.

He slid his hand over the curve of her ass and lower to her silky, slick folds. He swirled his fingers teasingly around her entrance and then inserted a finger, feeling the hot clasp surround him and suck him deeper.

He removed his hand, and then took a step so he was positioned at her head. He offered her his finger to suck.

"Taste it," he murmured. "Taste how sweet you are, Mia. And imagine it's my cock you're sucking."

Hesitantly she parted her lips and he slid his finger inside, over the slight roughness of her tongue. She closed her lips around him and sucked gently as he withdrew.

As he took his hand away, he reached for the plug and the vibrator. Her eyes widened when she saw them both, and he smiled.

He applied lubricant to the plug as well as directly to her opening, and then used his fingers to ease the gel around and inside her entrance. Then he pressed the plug to the puckered opening and began to press forward, taking his time, allowing her body to slowly accept the alien sensation.

Watching her widen to accommodate the plug fascinated him, and he groaned as he imagined his dick pushing into her and stretching her opening around it. Her chest heaved with exertion, and she panted as he stretched her further and further. And then he pushed it the rest of the way in and she let out a long sigh as her body sagged onto the ottoman.

"This is only the beginning," he said with a smile.

"I may not survive it," she said breathlessly.

He picked up the vibrator next and turned it on high. As soon as he touched the tip to her clit, she bolted upward, her body quivering in reaction. Tied as she was, she had no choice but to take the intensely pleasurable sensations as he pressed the tip to her again, this time sliding it down the sensitive flesh to her opening.

He pushed in the barest inch and then mimicked fucking motions with shallow thrusts.

She moaned softly, and tension showed in the lines of her face.

He slid the vibrator deeper, making her gasp at the depth of penetration. She was filled completely, ass and pussy, with the plug and now the long, thick vibrator.

She began shaking from head to toe and her ass bucked upward with each thrust. She twitched and writhed until he thought she'd quake right off the ottoman.

"Gabe, please!" she begged.

"You want to come?"

She groaned. "You know I do."

He chuckled lightly and then withdrew the vibrator before kneeling behind her to run his tongue from her clit up to her entrance.

"Oh God!" she exclaimed.

He pressed his face into the softness of her flesh and sucked her clit gently into his mouth. When he felt her tense again and the sudden wetness against his tongue as he licked his way lower, he knew she was very close to her release.

He rose, unzipped his pants and pulled out his erect cock. Positioning himself just behind her, he guided his dick to her pussy opening and plunged deeply.

She cried out. His name escaped her lips in a long, harsh hiss.

Grabbing on to her bound hands, he used them as a handle and began to fuck her with long, hard strokes.

She went liquidy soft around him, a hot sweet rush that bathed him all the way to his balls. It took everything he had not to slake his lust right then and there and come all over her. But he'd sworn this was for her, and so he'd wait. He intended to give her pleasure many more times before the evening was done.

She convulsed around him, and then every muscle in her body tensed and she went completely rigid. She let out a strangled cry and then went limp as he buried himself in her again.

He remained still, waiting for her to come down from the sharp orgasm. Then he carefully withdrew and tucked his cock back into his pants.

While he gave her a chance to catch her breath, he retrieved one of the crops from his closet. When he returned, her eyes were closed as her cheek rested against the ottoman.

He touched the crop to her ass and trailed it over the fullness of her cheeks. Her eyes came instantly open, and she sucked in her breath in anticipation.

"Do you like it when I spank you, Mia?"

"Yes," she whispered.

"Does it feel good? All that sharp, edgy pain that skates a precariously close line to pleasure?"

"Yes!" she said louder.

"Tonight I'm not spanking you for punishment. I'm marking your pretty ass for no other reason than it will bring us both great pleasure. And when I'm finished reddening your sweet behind, I'm going to fuck your ass."

She moaned, and it was a sound that fired his senses. A sound of feminine appreciation, all breathy and sweet.

He bent to carefully remove the plug, and she flinched, making another sound of pleasure as he pulled it free. After putting it away, he once more trailed the end of the crop over her behind before finally administering the first blow.

He was purposely gentle, leashing his strength so he didn't hit her too hard. He wanted to work up to leaving the beautiful red welts that would stripe her ass. If he began too hard, she'd quickly have too much, and he wanted her begging for more, not begging him to stop.

How beautiful she was, bound hand and foot, spread before him, her hair spilling over her body and the ottoman like the darkest night sky.

The red appeared with every blow, remaining a long moment before finally receding, only to start all over again the moment he administered another strike.

She twisted restlessly, straining against her bonds, all the while arching her ass upward as if seeking and wanting more.

By the time he got to the fifteenth blow, he'd increased the strength of the swats and the red remained longer until her entire ass was aglow with a rosy bloom.

Only a few more and then he would sink into her tight ass and lose himself in the beauty of her submission.

As the smack of the next blow sounded, another sound exploded into the room.

"What the *fuck* are you doing?" Jace roared.

Gabe's head jerked up, the haze surrounding him disappearing as he saw Jace and Ash standing in the foyer, the elevator doors closing behind them. Gabe had been so immersed in the scene with Mia that he'd never heard the elevator arrive. Never knew that Jace and Ash were there.

The horror on Mia's face was a fist to Gabe's gut.

"Oh my God, Gabe. What have you *done*?"

Ash's horrified voice drifted to Gabe just as Jace lunged for him, his fist connecting with Gabe's jaw.

chapter thirty-eight

Gabe went flying amid Mia's scream. He hit the floor, Jace on top of him. Jace's expression was murderous. Fury blazed in his eyes and he punched Gabe again.

Pain exploded in Gabe's nose, and he rolled away, but he didn't fight Jace back. He *couldn't*.

Ash was bent over Mia, his expression worried as he worked frantically to untie her. Gabe would have gone to her, would have helped, just so they could explain, but Jace loomed over Gabe, his hands grabbing at Gabe's shirt, yanking him upward as he snarled down at him.

"How could you do this?" Jace roared. "I *knew* it! You son of a *bitch*. I can't *believe* you did this to her."

"Jace, for God's sake," Gabe bit out. "Let me explain."

"Shut up. Just shut the fuck up! What the fuck is there to explain? Jesus Christ! How could you do this, Gabe? Is this what you want her thinking a relationship works like? Do you want her thinking that all your twisted desires are normal? What about when you get tired of her just like you get tired of every other woman? What then? You want her going to another man and seeking out something like this and have the asshole abuse her?"

Guilt swamped Gabe and he couldn't meet Jace's gaze. Every word, every accusation was like a well-aimed dart into his very soul. Weariness assailed him because so much of what Jace said was so very true. He had taken advantage of Mia. He'd pushed her. He'd taken over her life and he'd allowed her to endure unimaginable pain and humiliation. Not to mention the emotional stress of keeping something this huge from her only family.

God, he didn't deserve her. Didn't deserve her sweetness. He didn't deserve to bathe in her sunshine and have his entire world lit up by her precious smile.

Everything having to do with her, he'd done wrong from the very start. That fucking contract. The secrecy. The way he'd treated Mia. And now he was responsible for a huge wedge between her and Jace, and Jace and himself. One that none of them may ever recover from.

Was it any wonder that Jace had gone ballistic? He put himself in Jace's and Ash's shoes for a brief moment and pictured what they'd walked in on. Imagined how it must have looked to them. Jace's baby sister tied and bound, helpless while Gabe was using a crop on her ass. There'd been red welts all over her behind.

He cringed because there was no way for them to understand how it had really been. He recognized that he was damned in their eyes. He couldn't even blame them. And he was ashamed that he'd put Mia in a position where anyone could ever think that she was being abused and ill-treated.

She deserved so much more. Someone who would treat her like a fucking princess, like the treasure she was. Not some twisted, fucked-up, self-absorbed bastard like him.

"How could you take advantage of her like this?" Jace raged. "You offer her a job and put her in a situation where she thinks she has to do whatever you want because you're in a position of power over her? I could kill you for this. That you had no more respect for her, no more respect for our friendship. You aren't the man I thought I knew, Gabe."

Gabe closed his eyes, feeling sick to his soul. Jace was twisting the knife deeper, and the hell of it was that everything he said hit Gabe where he lived. He knew Jace was right. He had no defense. There was none.

Gabe knew he hadn't treated her right. Hadn't given her the respect she deserved. God, what if she had felt like she had to agree to everything because she worked for him, because his obsession with her was so heavy and intense that he gave her little choice in the matter? He'd taken over her life, her body. He'd consumed her until there was nothing left.

The very thing he'd been most afraid of—of him taking her until there was nothing left, and of him changing the very things about her that brought him the most pleasure—was happening.

She'd been deeply upset and traumatized by what had happened in Paris. And it had all been Gabe's fault. And she'd initially agreed to it instead of calling a halt to it because she'd signed that fucking contract giving up all her rights.

She'd felt compelled to do it. She didn't feel as though she had a choice. Yeah, he'd told her she could say no, but at what cost?

How much else had he forced on her?

"Swear to God, I'll never forgive you for this," Jace said hoarsely. "I'm getting her the hell out of here and then you stay the fuck away from her. Don't you *ever* try to contact her again. You forget she even exists."

Ash finished untying Mia, and then he bundled her in his arms before she could do or say anything. He ushered her into the bedroom where he wrapped one of Gabe's bedsheets around her.

He fumbled through Gabe's bathroom before finally coming out with a robe and then he secured it around her, tying the end in a double knot.

"Jesus, Mia, are you all right?" Ash demanded.

No, she wasn't all right. It was a stupid question. She was appalled and humiliated that Ash and her brother had burst in unannounced to Gabe's apartment, and seen her bound and naked.

It was something out of her worst nightmares. And to make it worse, Jace was beating the crap out of Gabe and Gabe was doing nothing to fight back. Nothing to defend himself.

She forced herself to sit there and breathe deeply, to gather her composure when what she wanted to do was run to Gabe and then explain to Jace. Just like they'd planned to do when Jace returned home from his business trip. Just one more day. It was all they'd needed.

She was numb with shock. So numb that she couldn't process the simplest thing. All she knew was that she had to get to Gabe. She had to end this. She had to *fix* this! God, she had to make everything right. All her fears had been realized and now two men who'd been best friends almost as long as she'd been alive were in a terrible fight.

Hot tears pricked her eyelids and she swallowed them back, fiercely determined to maintain her calm, but she was shaking violently. The last thing she wanted was for Ash and Jace to see her upset and think it was because of anything Gabe had done to her.

"Ash, I'm fine," Mia said, her voice quavering. "I'd prefer you go to make sure they aren't killing each other."

Ash's expression was dark. "I'm not stopping Jace if he wants to beat the shit out of Gabe. The bastard deserves it for what we walked in on. Jesus, Mia, are you *crying*? Did he hurt you? Did he force himself on you? Are you all right? Do you need to go to the hospital?"

Mia hastily wiped at her face, horrified by the direction Ash was going with his questions. Did he and Jace truly believe that what was going on was nonconsensual? She supposed it could have looked that way, but surely they were familiar enough with Gabe's preferences to know he regularly indulged in such things.

Or maybe it was because she was their baby sister and all they could see was her tied down naked to an ottoman and being flogged. She winced at the sight she must have presented. She could understand why Jace had lost his mind. Who wouldn't if they'd walked in on what they'd witnessed?

But she had to make them understand.

She was on her feet, determined to go back into the living room, when Jace burst into the bedroom, his eyes blazing. He immediately came to her and enfolded her in his arms.

"Are you all right?" he demanded.

There was an edge to his voice that told her how shaken and angry he was. This was quickly spiraling out of control and she had no idea how to make it stop. How to make them understand. Emotions were high. There was no way for either of them to see reason.

"Jace, I'm fine," she said, forcing her voice to remain level so she didn't worsen the situation. "What did you do to Gabe?"

"Nothing he didn't deserve," Jace said darkly. "Come on. I'm getting you the hell out of here."

He took her hand and dragged her toward the bedroom door. She had no choice but to follow him. And it was fine because she only wanted to go to Gabe.

As soon as they entered the living room, Mia saw Gabe sitting on the edge of the couch, his head buried in his hands. Concern filled her and she started to go to him, but Jace pulled her up short.

"We're going, Mia," he bit out.

She frowned and yanked her hand away. "I'm not going anywhere."

Gabe looked up then, and his eyes were distant and vacant. Carefully encased in ice as he stared at her.

She hurried to Gabe and knelt in front of the couch where he sat. She reached up, tentatively touching his arm, but he flinched and shrugged away her hand.

"Are you okay?" she asked softly, dread filling her chest and her heart until it squeezed the breath right out of her.

"I'm fine," he said in a stiff, formal voice.

"Talk to them," she whispered. "*Explain*. I'm not leaving you, Gabe. We have to make them understand. You can't let them think what they're thinking. Make this right. We were going to tell him anyway. Make him *understand*."

She was pleading with him, but what else could she do? Fear was making her desperate. Irrational. And Gabe was worth her pride. He was worth anything.

Gabe stiffly rose and put distance between himself and Mia. She pushed to her feet, confused by his mood and demeanor. Dread knotted her throat. She didn't like the way he was looking at her. The resignation in his face. The acceptance. Acceptance of what? What had Jace said to him? What had Gabe said to Jace?

And then when Gabe spoke, her blood turned to ice. She froze, too stunned to do more than gape in astonishment.

"You should go," he said in a curt voice. "It's better this way. You were becoming too emotionally attached. I don't want to hurt you. It'll only be harder if we wait. A clean break will be easier and less . . . messy . . . later."

"What the fuck?" Mia demanded, her shocked expletive exploding in the strained silence.

"Mia, let's just go, honey," Ash said in a gentle voice.

She could hear the pity in his tone, knew he felt sorry for her and that he thought she was making a complete fool of herself. They were seeing just another woman in Gabe's life being rejected, cut loose. Shoved away so he could move on to someone else.

To hell with that. She wasn't leaving without an explanation. Without trying to reach the man behind that coldly imposing mask. She knew the real Gabe. Had felt his warmth and tenderness. She knew he cared about her no matter the cluster fuck going on in this room right now.

She shook her head, her refusal adamant. "I'm not going anywhere until Gabe tells me what the hell all that bullshit he just spouted was about."

Gabe looked right through her, his expression and eyes indifferent. Cold and remote. She was sure it was a look many a woman had received from him when it was time to part ways. It was a look that said, "I don't want you anymore. Don't embarrass yourself."

Fuck that. She'd already sacrificed whatever pride she had over this man. There wasn't anything much more embarrassing than having your brother walk in on you during bondage sex. There wasn't a much worse way she could embarrass herself.

"Gabe?" she whispered, her voice strained as the knot grew larger in her throat.

She hated the pleading note to her voice. Hated that she couldn't salvage her pride when it came to this man. She was precariously close to begging, and she didn't care.

"It's over, Mia. You knew it was only a matter of time. I told you in the beginning not to fall in love with me. That I didn't want to hurt you. I should have ended it already. You're becoming too involved and that just makes it worse in the long run. Go with Jace and forget me. You deserve better."

"Bullshit," Mia spat, startling all three men with the vehemence of her rebuke. "You're a fucking coward, Gabe. *You* were the one getting in too deep, and you're a goddamn liar if you try to deny it."

"Mia," Jace said softly.

She ignored him and focused all her rage on Gabe.

"I risked *everything* for you. I put it all on the line. It's a damn shame you aren't willing to do the same for me. One day you're going to wake up and figure out that I was the best thing that ever happened to you and that you made the biggest fucking mistake of your *life*. And guess what, Gabe? It's going to be too late. I won't be there."

Jace's arm came around her, squeezing and holding her steady as he urged her away. She could barely see through her tears. She was so angry and upset that she was shaking. Jace murmured something in her ear and then Ash fell in on her other side as they guided her toward the elevator.

Halfway there she turned to see Gabe staring at her, that distant, vacant expression on his face, and it just pissed her off all the more.

She wiped at the tears trailing down her cheeks and then she lifted her chin, determined she wouldn't shed another single tear over him. She'd thought he was worth it. Her pride. Everything. She was wrong.

"If you ever wake up and see the light and decide you want me back? You're going to have to *crawl*."

This time she turned and pulled free of Jace's and Ash's grasps. She walked away by her own choice and got into the elevator, not even looking back as the doors closed behind her.

She looked down, horrified that she was clad in only the robe Ash had wrapped her in.

"Don't worry, Mia," Jace said in a soothing voice. "I'll have the car pull up to the very front. Ash and I will flank you and we'll get out to the car quickly. I'll take you to my place."

She shook her head. "I want to go *home*. To my apartment."

Ash and Jace exchanged quick, worried glances.

When the elevator opened, Jace stalked out, leaving Ash and Mia to follow at a slower pace. By the time they got to the exit, Jace was already back, and as promised, he and Ash hovered so closely around her that it was hard to see who she was or what she was wearing.

They surrounded her as she got into the car and then they quickly climbed in and shut the door behind them.

To Mia's relief, Jace supplied her address for the driver to take them to her apartment.

"How long has this been going on?" Jace demanded.

"That's none of your business," Mia said stonily.

Jace's expression grew stormy. "The hell it isn't. That son of a bitch abused you and took advantage of you."

"Oh for fuck's sake. He did not. It was a completely consensual relationship, Jace. Get off your holier-than-thou pulpit for a minute. He didn't do a damn thing that I didn't want. He was very clear as to what I was agreeing to when we started this relationship. All that bullshit you spouted was crap. I'm an adult whether you want to believe that or not. An adult who knows exactly what she wants, and I wanted *Gabe*."

"I can't believe he did this. I can't believe he'd want you to think this was normal. What about when you move on to someone else and start looking for the same kind of crap? What if you hook up with some loser who mistreats and abuses you?"

Mia rolled her eyes, irritation seizing her. "You're both such flaming hypocrites."

Ash blinked in surprise at being included in her insult.

"Do you want your women thinking it's normal to be fucking the same two guys, or that you two always want to share the same woman? What about their expectations? What happens when they move on to another relationship? Are they supposed to think it's okay for two men to want to fuck her at the same time?"

"Jesus Christ, Mia. Where the hell did you hear all of that?" Ash demanded.

She shrugged. "It's pretty common knowledge around the office. And after the night we had dinner together and the brunette's claws came out, it was pretty much confirmed."

"We aren't talking about me and Ash," Jace growled. "We're talking about you and Gabe. He's fourteen years older than you, Mia. He has every woman he's with sign a goddamn contract. Is that the kind of relationship you want? Don't you think you deserve better?"

"Damn right I deserve better," she said softly, hurt and betrayal crowding in so tight that it was suffocating. Each breath hurt. Every breath felt like she was dying. And she was on the inside. Never had she felt pain like this. It was shattering. She could feel herself breaking into tiny pieces.

She clutched the robe tighter around her body and her lips quivered as she stared at her brother and Ash.

"I *deserve* a man who will stand up and fight for me, a man who will always have my back. Gabe did none of those things. We were planning to tell you about our relationship when you got back this week. Ironic isn't it? I wonder how different things would have been if we'd been able to tell you on *our* terms instead of you bursting into his apartment like that. I guess I'll never know now."

Ash looked chagrined, and he grimaced. Jace just looked pissed.

She laughed bitterly. "I guess I'll be looking for other employment now. Too bad, because I really enjoyed my job."

"You can work for me," Jace said tightly. "It's what you should have done from the beginning."

She shook her head vehemently. "Oh hell no. I'm not setting foot into HCM. I'm not going to torture myself on a daily basis by having to see Gabe."

"What will you do then?" Ash asked gently.

Her lips thinned and bitterness crawled into her chest. "I don't know right now. I guess I have plenty of time to figure it out."

chapter thirty-nine

When Mia entered her apartment in just a robe with Ash and Jace both hovering protectively around her, Caroline hurried forward, a worried expression on her face.

"Mia? What happened? Are you all right?"

Mia hugged her friend and to her horror burst into tears, no longer able to maintain her composure.

Caroline held her fiercely and then lit into Ash and Jace, demanding to know what they'd done to her.

"Just make them go away, Caro," Mia choked out. "I'm fine now that I'm with you."

Caroline ushered her to the couch, helped her sit down, and then she stood glaring at Jace and Ash.

"You heard her. Out. I've got this now."

Jace scowled and then went to the couch where Mia sat. He stared at her a long moment and then sighed as he pulled her into his arms.

"I'm sorry, baby girl. I know this hurt you. Swear to God we didn't intend anything. We had no idea you and Gabe were together. He'd texted me and said he had something important to discuss when I got back. That's why I went by his apartment and let myself in. Ash and I both have key cards to get to his floor.

Hell, I assumed it was business. He made it sound urgent, so we went over as soon as we hit town."

Mia clung to her big brother and let her tears fall. Just as she'd done so many times growing up.

"I'm not angry at you," she whispered. "I'm furious with *him*. If he doesn't have the balls to stand up to you and Ash for me, then I don't want him. I deserve better."

Jace stroked his hand down her hair. "You do deserve better, baby girl. Gabe is—or was—my friend, but I don't make any excuses for him. He does what the hell he wants with regard to women, and it's his way or the highway."

"And you're so different?" Mia said accusingly as she pulled away.

Jace sighed and glanced back at Ash who looked just as uncomfortable.

"I don't want to get into this with you," Jace said gently. "It has no relevance to what happened tonight."

Mia rolled her eyes. Typical guy sidestepping the issue. If it had been any other woman but her that Jace and Ash had walked in on, they would have left quietly, or who knows, they may have even stayed and watched. They wouldn't have given that woman even a passing thought and would have likely patted Gabe on the back.

But it wasn't just any woman. It was her. Jace's sister and, for all practical purposes, Ash's sister as well. Which meant all the rules were changed.

"You and Ash just go," she said quietly. "Caro is here and I'll be fine."

Jace looked doubtfully between the two women. "I don't want you to be alone, Mia."

"She's not alone," Caroline said in exasperation. "Do you honestly think I'd leave her right now?"

"You have to work, though," Ash said with a frown.

Mia shook her head. "For God's sake. Do you think I'm going to slit my wrists or something? I'm pissed and upset but I'm not stupid or suicidal."

"I'm going to come by and check on you tomorrow," Jace said. "And you're spending Thanksgiving with me and Ash. Understood? You aren't going to mope around over Gabe."

Mia sighed. "Whatever. Just go. I want to cry alone and not have you two hovering over me. This is embarrassing enough. I've had enough humiliation tonight to last a lifetime."

Ash winced. "Yeah, I hear you."

Reluctantly Jace rose from the couch and started for the door. He paused and turned back around. "I'm coming by tomorrow. We'll have dinner. Ash and I will plan something for Thanksgiving and let you know."

Mia nodded wearily, just wanting them gone so she could be alone with Caroline to drown her sorrows.

As soon as they walked out, Caroline sat next to Mia on the couch and pulled her into her arms.

Damn if Mia didn't get all weepy again.

"What happened?" Caroline asked as she rocked Mia back and forth in her arms. "Should I call the girls over?"

Mia sniffed and wiped at her nose as she pulled away. Hell, she was still naked under the robe—Gabe's robe—and suddenly she wanted nothing more than to get it off.

"Let me go get a shower," she said. "Then I'll tell you all about it. I need to get some clothes on, preferably ones that aren't Gabe's."

"I'll fix us some hot chocolate," Caroline said, her face creased with pity and concern.

"That sounds great," Mia said, a wan smile on her face. "Thanks, Caro. You're the best."

Mia trudged to the bathroom and peeled off the robe. After a moment's hesitation, she stuffed it into her closet instead of trashing it. She'd probably do something pathetic like wear it around the apartment since it belonged to Gabe. She couldn't bring herself to throw it away. Not yet at least.

After a hot shower in which she boiled herself, she put on a pair of pajamas and wrapped a towel atop her hair, not caring if it got tangled.

Caroline was waiting in the living room with two cups of hot chocolate, and Mia flopped onto the couch next to her. Caroline handed her one of the mugs and Mia gratefully embraced it, wrapping her cold hands around the hot cup.

"How are things with you and Brandon?" Mia asked.

She felt terribly guilty because over the last while, she'd spent all her time with Gabe. Every minute. Every hour. She hadn't even talked to Caroline in a *week*.

Caroline smiled. "Good. We're still seeing each other. It's hard because of our schedules, but we're trying to make it work."

"I'm glad," Mia said.

"What happened, Mia?" Caroline asked softly. "It's obvious he hurt you a lot. How on earth did Jace and Ash get involved and why the hell did you come home in just a robe?"

Mia blew out her breath. "It's a long story. I wasn't completely honest with you about my relationship with Gabe. It's more complicated than that."

Caroline's eyebrows bunched together. "I'm listening."

Mia poured out the entire story, leaving nothing out. By the time she got to tonight's debacle, Caroline's eyes were wide and then they narrowed in disgust.

"Can't believe he hung you out to dry like that. You were already planning to tell Jace everything."

Mia slowly nodded. "He stood there and lied to me, Caro. I know he has feelings for me. And he stood there and gave me this bullshit about how I was getting too emotionally invested, blah-blah. I wanted to choke him."

"Chickenshit," Caroline said rudely. "You deserve better than that, Mia. You deserve someone who stands up for you and who'll risk everything just as you have."

"I agree," Mia said. "I told him if he ever wakes up and realizes what a mistake he made that he'll have to crawl to get me back."

Caroline laughed. "Atta girl. And he *should* have to grovel."

Mia raised her mug in a toast. "Damn right."

Caroline's expression sobered. "So what do you think is going to happen between Jace and Gabe? They're business partners as well as best friends. Jace seems pretty pissed."

"I don't know," Mia said honestly. "This is why I never wanted Jace to find out. Maybe I was being too naïve, or maybe I didn't expect Gabe and I to be so hot and heavy into things. I thought it would be simple to keep it from Jace. I guess I thought Gabe would want me a couple of times a week and the rest of the time I'd carry on as usual. It's also why we wanted to tell Jace about us, so we wouldn't have to hide it any longer."

Fresh anger surged into her blood until she was flushed with it.

"Damn it. Can you believe the timing? All we needed was *one more day*. If Jace had just called Gabe to let him know he was back in town, we would have told him together and everything would have been fine. Gabe was falling for me, Caro. He was falling and it scared the shit out of him. And then Jace bursting in and saying all those horrible things. I could see the guilt on Gabe's face. Especially after what happened in Paris."

Caroline's face wrinkled in sympathy. "I'm sorry, Mia. It sucks. But you deserve better than Gabe Hamilton."

"Yeah, I do," Mia said in a low voice. "I deserve more for sure. But I wanted him so much. I love him, Caro. And there's not a damn thing I can do about that."

chapter forty

Mia left La Patisserie, her heart heavy as sadness crept into every part of her soul. She should be happy. She'd gotten her old job back. Louisa and Greg had been thrilled to see her and had offered her flexible hours. The truth was that she wanted to work as much as possible so she didn't have time to think. So she didn't have to spend every minute of her day reliving every moment she'd spent with Gabe.

And La Patisserie was temporary this time. She'd made it clear to Louisa and to Greg that she was pursuing other jobs. She'd work at the café while she explored other possibilities and then she'd take that step out, stop hiding and embrace her future. A future without Gabe Hamilton.

She shivered in the damp cold. It was a gray, overcast, dreary day perfectly suited to her mood. She hadn't slept the night before—how could she? Caroline had stayed up with her until she'd started yawning and Mia had shooed her to bed. And then she'd lain in her own bed, staring up at the ceiling, remembering every minute of her relationship with Gabe.

Checking her watch, she realized she'd have to get a cab when she'd intended on walking. Jace would be at her apartment soon, and she didn't want him freaking out on her again.

Tugging her coat tighter around her, she waded through the passersby to get to the corner so she could hail a taxi.

The biggest thing she struggled with was having to return to a routine she'd once found comfortable and reassuring. She hadn't stepped out of the box before. Hadn't taken risks.

Being with Gabe had definitely taken her out of her comfort zone, and she'd begun to really live. Experience the world around her. Take on new challenges.

No, the biggest thing wouldn't be readjusting to her old routine. Her biggest challenge would be being without Gabe.

She'd come to savor every moment with him. They'd had good times. He was a damn liar if he thought he wasn't as emotionally invested as she was. She knew him better than that. Knew he was developing feelings for her. And maybe that was her biggest crime of all.

Making him fall in love with her.

If he hadn't developed stronger feelings for her, they'd probably still be together.

After three taxis passed her by, the fourth pulled over and she got in, grateful to be out of the cold. After directing the cabbie to her apartment, she sat back, staring out the window as the city rolled by.

What was Gabe doing now? Had he gone in to work today? Was he moving on as if she'd never occupied a place in his life? Or was he as miserable as she was?

She dearly hoped so. If there was any justice in this world, he'd be suffering every bit as much as she was.

When she pulled up at her apartment, she saw Jace's car out front. Ash was standing with the door open, and when Mia got out of the taxi, he waved her over.

"Jace went up to get you," Ash said. "Let me call him and tell him you're down here."

As Ash pulled out his phone, he directed her into the backseat and then shut the door behind her. A moment later, he climbed into the front seat.

"You okay, sweetheart?" Ash asked.

"I'm fine," she lied.

Jace got into the driver's seat and glanced at Mia in the rearview mirror.

"Where've you been, baby girl?"

"Finding a job."

Jace and Ash both frowned.

"I don't think it's a good idea that you go back to work so soon," Jace said. "You should take some time off. You know I'll help you out."

"I don't start until after Thanksgiving," she said.

Ash turned in his seat as Jace pulled into traffic. "Where are you working?"

"I got my old job back at La Patisserie. Louisa and Greg are good to me and I enjoy working for them."

Jace sighed. "You're cut out for more than working at a bakery, Mia."

"Careful, Jace," she said. "That kind of thinking was what made me go to work for Gabe, remember?"

Ash winced, and Jace let out a curse under his breath.

"Besides, it's only temporary," she said softly. "I'm going to pursue other job opportunities. But for now I need to be working. I need to have something to do. Greg and Louisa know when I find a different job that I'm leaving. They're cool with it."

It was on the tip of her tongue to ask about Gabe, but she bit it back, refusing to give in to that temptation. She didn't want to sound like a desperate, clingy twit, even if that's what she felt like.

Almost as if reading her mind, Ash turned again. "If it makes you feel any better, Gabe looked like shit today. He doesn't look or sound any better than you do."

It was hard not to react to Ash's words. It took all her strength to act unfazed, as if she didn't care. She wanted to yell at someone—anyone—and scream out that it didn't have to be this way. All Gabe would have had to do was speak up. Given her any sign that he wanted her. She would have never left him. She'd be with him even now if only he'd given her any indication that it was what he wanted.

Instead he'd trotted out that crap about how it was better this way. Better for whom? Because it damn sure wasn't better for her. And it didn't sound like it was so damn good for him either.

"I don't want to talk about him," she said in a low voice. "I don't want to hear his name."

Jace nodded his agreement and shot Ash a quelling stare. Ash shrugged. "I just thought she might want to know."

She did. Of course she did. But she'd never admit it. She had pride too, even if she'd sacrificed it all for Gabe.

"We're taking a trip for Thanksgiving," Jace said as he glanced up in the mirror again. "We leave Wednesday and we'll come back Sunday."

She lifted an eyebrow. "Where are we going?"

"The Caribbean. Someplace nice and warm. Lots of sunshine and beaches. It'll cheer you up."

She doubted that, but she wasn't going to be a spoilsport. Jace's eyes were hopeful. He was trying so hard to help her pick up the pieces. He'd never been able to stand her being upset about anything, and he always pulled out all the stops in his bid to make her feel better.

"And hey, you'll get to see me in a swimsuit," Ash said, a devilish grin on his face. "That should make your entire year."

She rolled her eyes, a smile toying with the corners of her mouth. But she sighed because Ash wasn't spending Thanksgiving with his family. He never did. He always spent his holidays alone or with her and Jace, or with Gabe. Her heart ached because, except for Jace, Gabe and herself, Ash was alone, and she well knew that feeling now. It sucked.

"That's better," Jace said, approval and relief gleaming in his eyes. "I want to see you smiling again, baby girl."

The smile felt frozen on her lips. It was pretty damn hard to smile when her heart was splintered and lay in pieces. Dramatic maybe, but it was appropriate.

"Do you need to go shopping for the trip?" Ash asked in a coaxing voice. "Jace and I have the rest of the week off. We could take you shopping tomorrow if you need stuff for the beach."

They were both trying so hard that she wasn't going to make it any more difficult for them. So she smiled and nodded. "That sounds like fun."

The relief in Jace's eyes told her she'd done the right thing. The last thing she wanted was to worry him—and he *was* worried.

He and Ash would keep her busy through the Thanksgiving holiday. And on Monday she'd return to her old life. Working at La Patisserie. Living with Caroline in her apartment. Trying to forget that for a brief time she'd meant the world to Gabe Hamilton. Or that he still meant the world to her.

chapter forty-one

Gabe sat brooding in his office, his head aching and dull, his heart even heavier. It was early—he was the only one in the office after the holiday—but he hadn't slept since Mia had walked out of his apartment, so much hurt and betrayal in her eyes.

He stared at the two pictures of her in his phone, one of which he'd had printed and framed. It lay in his desk drawer. Often, he pulled that drawer open just to see her smile.

The Mia in those pictures was the Mia he'd done his damnedest to destroy. He'd taken the life and joy right out her eyes, and he'd damn sure taken her smile.

He ran his finger over the image of her in the snow, holding up her hands in delight as she tried to catch snowflakes. She was so goddamn beautiful that she took his breath away.

He'd spent Thanksgiving with his parents, their happiness and growing contentment almost too much for him to bear. It was hard for him to be happy that they were on the path to reconciliation when his own life was in shambles.

And he only had himself to blame.

After leaving his parents' home, he'd returned to his apartment to find it empty and barren of life. And then he'd done something he rarely ever did. He'd gotten roaring drunk and attempted to drown his sorrows in a bottle—or three.

He'd self-medicated the entire weekend, itchy and impatient because he knew that Jace and Ash had taken Mia on holiday to the Caribbean. She was out of reach, not just physically, but emotionally as well.

He'd hurt her when he'd sworn never to do so again. He'd betrayed her trust. He'd turned his back because he'd been overwhelmed by guilt and self-loathing for how he'd treated her. Like she was some dirty secret that he was ashamed of.

Fuck that. He wanted the world to know she was his. He didn't give a damn what Jace thought. Didn't give a shit if Jace approved. All he cared about was making Mia happy. Making her smile and light up the way she did when she was with him.

But he'd thoroughly extinguished that light when he'd told her that it was over. As if he'd already grown tired of her and was ready to move on.

He'd never get over her. He knew that without hesitation or doubt.

He loved her.

As deeply as it was possible to love another person. And God, he wanted her. Every day. In his life. As much a part of him as he would be of her.

Without rules, conditions. Fuck the goddamn contract.

How many ways could a man ruin the best thing that had ever happened to him?

Mia was so right. He'd known it then, when her words had hit him right in the gut. She was the best thing that had ever happened to him. He didn't need time or space to realize that.

He should have never let her walk out of his apartment that night with Jace and Ash. When she'd knelt before him and begged him to explain to Jace, he should have spoken up then. She was right. He *hadn't* fought for her. He'd been too numb, too consumed with guilt over what he'd allowed to happen.

Fear squeezed his chest. It was an alien sensation, new and overwhelming. What if Mia wouldn't forgive him? What if she wouldn't take him back?

He had to make her understand that this wasn't a meaningless, sexual fling.

He wanted fucking *forever.*

What did he have to offer her? He'd already failed at one marriage. He was considerably older than she was. She should be having fun at her age, taking on the world, not tied to a demanding, overbearing man like himself.

There were a dozen reasons why he should leave her alone and let her move on with her life. But he wasn't a big enough person to let her go. She was the only woman who was ever going to make him happy. Make him whole. And he couldn't let her walk out of his life. Not without one hell of a fight.

He checked his watch, willing the time to pass. And then his intercom buzzed and Eleanor's soft voice filled his office.

"Mr. Hamilton, Mr. Crestwell is in."

Gabe didn't respond. He'd told Eleanor to let him know the minute Jace arrived to his office. They hadn't spoken since that night. They'd avoided each other the next day in the office. And then neither had been into the office the rest of the holiday week, and Gabe hadn't wanted that confrontation so soon after the night in his apartment. Emotions had run too high.

But he couldn't wait a minute longer. He and Jace had to air this out, and Gabe had to let Jace know that he wasn't backing down. Whether he had Jace's blessing and approval or not, he wasn't letting Mia go. If it meant the end of their friendship and of their business relationship, so be it.

Mia was worth it all.

He strode down the hall, knowing he looked like shit. He didn't care. He had to get this off his chest.

He pushed Jace's door open without knocking. Jace looked up and his face grew cold. His eyes hardened as he stared back at Gabe.

"We have to talk," Gabe said in a terse voice.

"I don't have *anything* to say to you," Jace bit out.

Gabe shut the door and locked it behind him. "That's too damn bad because I have a lot to say to you."

He planted his palms on Jace's desk, leaned over and leveled his stare at his friend.

"I'm in love with Mia," he said bluntly.

Surprise flashed in Jace's eyes and Jace sat back, staring harder at Gabe.

"You have a damn funny way of showing it," Jace said in disgust.

"I fucked up. But I'm not letting her go. You and I need to come to an understanding because I don't want her hurt any more than she already is by this situation. I want her to be happy and she can't be happy if we're at each other's throats."

"You didn't give our friendship a whole hell of a lot of consideration when you jumped into bed with my sister," Jace said icily. "You *knew* I'd be pissed. Hell, I warned you off that very first day, Gabe, and you fucking *lied* to me."

"Mia didn't want you to know," Gabe said. "She didn't want to hurt you, and she didn't want you to lose your mind. I agreed because I only wanted her, and I didn't give a shit what I had to do to have her."

"What is she to you, Gabe? Entertainment? A challenge because she's untouchable? She's way out of your league and you damn well know it."

Gabe slammed his fist down on the desk, glaring Jace down. "I want to goddamn marry her."

Jace lifted one eyebrow. "You swore you'd never marry again after Lisa."

Gabe pushed off the desk and turned, pacing a tight line in front of Jace's desk.

"I said a lot of things. And no other woman has ever made me second-guess my decisions. But Mia . . . She's different. I can't live without her, Jace. With or without your blessing, I'm going after her. I can't be happy without her. I'll never be happy without her. I want her in my life. Every goddamn day. I want to take care of her, make sure she never has to worry for anything that I can give her. Fuck me, but I'm even imagining children. At my age. All I can think of are daughters who look just like her. I picture her round with my child and it's the most mind-blowing feeling in the world. Everything that I've sworn off in my life, she has me re-evaluating. Because of her. It's *all* her. I've never felt this way about another woman. I never will."

"Whoa," Jace breathed out. "Sit down. You're making me crazy pacing around my office like that."

Gabe paused and then finally eased into the chair in front of Jace's desk, but he was going stir crazy in this confined space. He didn't want to be here. He wanted to be with Mia. Wanted to go to her and throw himself on her mercy. She'd said he had to crawl. Goddamn it, he'd crawl.

"You're serious about her," Jace said, disbelief evident in his voice. "You're in love with her. She isn't some passing entertainment you amuse yourself with and then move on."

"You're pissing me off now," Gabe growled.

Jace shook his head. "Holy shit. I never thought I'd see the day. How did this happen? Have I been a complete dumbass for not seeing this?"

"It's better we not delve into a conversation that's only going to piss you off," Gabe said. "It's not important how long. What's important is that I love her, and I hope to God she still loves me and that she can forgive me."

Jace winced. "I don't know, man. She's pretty pissed. You hurt her. A lot. You've never had to work to have a woman. They've always dumped themselves onto your lap. Mia . . . She's different. She's of the mind that she deserves a man who'll stand up for her and fight for her. You didn't do any of those things, and she's not going to so easily forget that."

"Don't you think I know all of that?" Gabe said in frustration. "Hell, I wouldn't blame her if she never wanted to speak to me again. But I have to try. I can't just let her go."

Jace cupped a hand to the back of his neck. "Jesus, man, you never like to do anything simple, do you? I'm a damn idiot for not beating the crap out of you and tossing you out of my office. I can't believe that I actually feel sorry for your ass right now."

Some of the tension knotting Gabe's chest eased. He met Jace's stare. "I'm sorry, man. I handled this all wrong. You have to know that I'd never do anything to intentionally compromise our friendship. And I damn sure wouldn't ever do anything to hurt Mia. Not again. Never again. I've hurt her too many times already. If she'll forgive me, I'll spend the rest of my life making sure she never has reason to cry again."

"That's all I want for her," Jace said softly. "I want her to be happy. If you can do that, then you and I are good."

"I'm damn sure going to try," Gabe said, determination gripping him by the neck.

"Good luck," Jace said. "Something tells me you're going to need it."

chapter forty-two

Mia tugged her coat tighter around her as she walked the last block to her apartment. It had been hard to go to work in the brisk chill after spending the last several days on a beach in the Caribbean.

Jace and Ash had worked hard to cheer her up and ensure she had a good time, and she had to admit, it had been a lot of fun. It had been a while since she and Jace had gotten to have an actual vacation together and with Ash there, things had been light-hearted and happy.

That wasn't to say that she hadn't spent a fair amount of time brooding over Gabe, but she'd managed to enjoy herself. If anyone had told her that she could have a good time so quickly after she and Gabe had split up, she wouldn't have believed them.

Still, going in to La Patisserie instead of the HCM building this morning had been hard. It had been a slap in the face and a sharp reminder of Gabe's betrayal. She liked her job with Gabe. Yeah, it had been a fluff job that had been a cover for their sexual affair, but as time had gone on, she'd taken on more responsibility and she'd made the job her own. She'd proven to herself that she could take on a challenge and nail it.

Now she was back to selling pastries and filling customers' coffee cups. And while before it had never bothered her, now she was unsettled and she wanted more. More of a challenge. It was time for her to stop being afraid and to go out there and make her future. No one else was going to do that for her. Already she was perusing her career options. Looking at job openings that would fit her level of education and experience—not that she had much.

Maybe she could talk to Jace. Not about working for him. There was no way in hell she'd go back to work at HCM and have to face Gabe on a daily basis. Or God help her, whatever woman he replaced her with. That was asking way too much of her.

But Jace might have ideas or may even know other people that she could reach out to. They owned over a dozen hotels in the U.S. alone, not to mention their resorts overseas. She could work in any one of them and never have to worry about seeing Gabe.

That would require moving, and was she ready to do that?

She was used to living in the city. Being close to Jace. But she'd never made it on her own here. Jace had supported her. He'd bought her apartment. When had she ever become independent?

Maybe it was time to move out on her own and take over her own life. Make it or not make it, but she'd do it on her own merits.

As satisfying as the idea was in theory, it made her sad to think of leaving everything behind. Caroline. Jace. Ash. Her apartment. Her life.

Hell no. She wasn't going to let Gabe drive her out of the city. She'd damn well find a better job here, and she'd move on and forget his ass.

That also sounded nice in theory, but she wasn't buying the reality.

When she reached the door of her building, she saw in the reflection of the glass Gabe getting out of a car that was parked at the curb. And he was striding in her direction.

Oh *hell* no.

Without looking back—no matter how tempting it was to

drink the sight of him in—she pushed inside and lunged for the elevator. As it opened, she got in and punched the Close Door button. As she looked up, she saw Gabe brushing by the protesting doorman and hurrying for the elevator, a determined look on his face.

Close, close, close, she silently begged.

The doors began to shut and Gabe lunged forward, but he was too late. Thank God. What the hell was he doing here anyway?

She got off the elevator and unlocked her apartment. It was silent inside, and she dropped her purse by the door. Caroline wouldn't be home for a while and then she'd likely go to Vibe to see Brandon.

She jumped when a loud knock sounded at her door. Then she sighed. She'd seen the look on Gabe's face and knew he wouldn't just walk away because she'd thwarted him at the elevator. What the hell did he want anyway?

She stalked to the door and unlocked it, throwing it open to reveal Gabe standing in the hallway. Relief shone in his eyes and he started to step forward, but she blocked him with the door.

"What do you want?" she said bluntly.

"I need to talk to you, Mia," he said.

She shook her head. "We have nothing to talk about."

"You're wrong, goddamn it. Let me in."

She stuck her head out the door so he'd see her and know she was dead serious.

"Let me put it this way then. I don't have anything to say to *you*," she said in a quiet tone. "Nothing at all. I said everything I had to say at your apartment. It was your decision to let me walk away—hell, you *pushed* me away. I deserve better than that, Gabe, and I'm sure as hell not going to settle for less."

She slammed the door and locked it again. Not wanting to hear if he knocked, she went into her bedroom and closed the door. She was exhausted and all she wanted was a hot bath to warm her from the inside out.

But what she feared was that nothing would ever warm the chill caused by Gabe's absence. Nothing except him.

The next day, Mia was serving a regular customer their favorite coffee when Gabe walked in and took a seat at the same table he'd occupied all those weeks ago. She couldn't *believe* him. How was she supposed to work when he was right there in her space?

Her jaw clenched, she walked over and stared coldly at him.

"What are you doing here?"

He let his gaze wander over her, his eyes softening as he took in her features. Did he see how tired she was? How miserable? Was she wearing a neon sign advertising how unhappy she was without him?

"I'm not sleeping either, Mia," he said softly. "I made a mistake. I fucked up. Give me a chance to make it right."

She closed her eyes and curled her fingers into tight balls at her sides.

"Don't screw this up for me, Gabe. Please. I have to have this job. Until I decide what I want to do, I have to work and I can't have you here distracting me."

He reached for one of those tightly fisted hands, and he pried her fingers loose. Then he drew her hand to his mouth and kissed her open palm.

"You have a job, Mia. It's waiting for you. It's not going anywhere."

She snatched her hand back like she'd been burned.

"Just go, Gabe. Please. I can't do this. You're going to get me fired. If you want to make it *right*, then walk away and stay away."

She was precariously close to breaking down. Her emotions

were so damn unstable. Why couldn't she be strong? Why did she have to allow him to see what a mess she was?

She turned away, uncaring of whether it looked bad that she'd been rude to a customer. She had others to attend to.

But he sat there, watching her, his gaze steady as she tended to the other people in the shop. They came and went and still he sat there until she felt hunted. Stalked.

Finally she went into the back and asked Louisa for a break. She helped Greg with the orders while Louisa worked the front. An hour later when she ventured back up front, Gabe was gone.

She didn't know whether she was relieved or disappointed. All she knew was there was a gaping hole in her heart she never had a hope of repairing.

When she trudged home that evening, she found a huge bouquet of flowers at her door. Sighing, she took the card and saw the scribbled note from Gabe.

I'm sorry. Please give me a chance to explain.

—Gabe

She had to bite back the childish urge to trash the flowers. They were beautiful, and she and Caroline would enjoy having them in the apartment. She would just pretend that someone else had given them to her.

She placed them on the counter and wondered why Gabe was making the effort. Why was he doing this? He'd been the one to say that a clean break was better. Why prolong it if he had no intention of making their relationship permanent? Like she wanted to go through this all over again down the road when he did get tired of her?

Talking with Jace and Ash openly about Gabe and his relationships had been eye-opening. She'd guessed or had a very good idea of how he went about them. But during their stay in the Caribbean, the two had opened up and given her details she hadn't known before.

Gabe always had a contract with the women he was with. She knew that. What she hadn't known was the frequency of these women and the shortness of his relationships with them.

It had made her realize that she'd been on borrowed time with him.

She was lying facedown on her bed when Caroline came into her bedroom.

"Hey, Mia, who are the flowers from?"

"Gabe," she muttered.

Caroline bounced onto the bed, her expression a mixture of *what the fuck* and irritation.

"Why is he sending you flowers, for God's sake?"

Mia rolled onto her back. "Oh that's only part of it. He was here last night. And then he showed up at La Patisserie today."

"What the hell? Why?"

"I have no idea," Mia said wearily. "To drive me crazy? Who knows? I slammed the door in his face last night. Today I just ignored him."

"Good for you," Caroline said in a savage tone. "Want me to go kick his ass?"

Mia laughed and then leaned up to hug her friend. "I love you, Caro. I'm so glad I have you."

Caroline squeezed Mia back. "That's what friends are for. And hey, if you decide to kill him, you know I'll help you hide the body."

Mia burst into laughter again, her heart lighter than just a moment before.

"Hey, what do you want to eat tonight? I was thinking about takeout, but if you wanted we could go down the street to the pub and hang out for a while."

Caroline studied Mia intently. "Are you sure? I don't mind cooking for us if you want to hang here."

Mia shook her head. "No, let's go out. I can't stay here and mope over Gabe forever."

As Mia stood up from the bed, Caroline went quiet for a moment and then she turned her serious gaze up to Mia.

"Maybe he wants you back, Mia. Have you considered that? Shouldn't you at least hear him out?"

Mia's lips turned down in scorn. "I told him that if he ever wanted me back he was going to have to crawl. He's not crawling yet and hell will freeze over before I make it easy for him."

chapter forty-three

By the week's end, Mia was at a complete loss as to what to do about Gabe. He was at La Patisserie every single day for coffee and a croissant and he never came in at the same time, so it was impossible for her to avoid him by working the back.

He was a constant presence that was fraying her nerves. And her resistance.

And if that wasn't enough, he bombarded her constantly with flowers and gifts. At work. At home.

Just yesterday a delivery person had brought in a huge arrangement of flowers to La Patisserie and embarrassed her in front of everyone by reading the note out loud.

Forgive me. I can't live without you.

—Gabe

Today another delivery person had brought in a box with a pair of fur-lined leather gloves and a note card that read:

To keep your hands warm on the walk home.

—Gabe

Louisa and Greg were amused—thank God they weren't pissed—and it had become a running joke with the regulars at La Patisserie as to what would be delivered next.

The weather had cleared up, but the cold had remained. The skies were bright blue without a cloud in sight and the wind blew gusty, a knife through her coat. She was grateful for the gloves as she navigated the sidewalks back to her apartment. Dusk was descending, each day growing shorter and shorter.

As she rounded the corner to walk the last block to her apartment, an electronic billboard atop a hotel caught her eye. How could it not?

In big, neon letters, flashing across the screen was:

I LOVE YOU, MIA. COME HOME.

GABE.

Tears pricked her eyelids. What was she supposed to do? He'd *never* said he loved her. Was it emotional manipulation for him to air his feelings to the world? And to put it on this billboard, by her apartment, where she couldn't possibly miss the meaning? Come home. Not to her apartment. But to him.

It was driving her crazy. *He* was driving her crazy. And yet he hadn't attempted to confront her directly again. Not since the last time when she'd told him to leave her alone. But he was still there. In her face. Always reminding her of his presence.

She was utterly baffled by this side of Gabe. It was a side he'd never allowed her to see—*anyone* to see.

She went into her apartment, exhausted and miserable. She was convinced she was coming down with something, but she wasn't sure if it was true illness or whether it was merely a product of too many sleepless nights and her emotional devastation.

By the next morning, she couldn't deny that she was truly ill.

She walked to work and went through the motions mechanically. By the afternoon, Louisa and Greg both were eyeing her with concern, and when she dumped an entire pot of coffee onto the floor, Louisa called her into the back.

She took Mia's arm and then put her hand to her forehead.

"Good God, Mia, you're burning up with fever. Why didn't you say anything? You can't work like this. Go home and go to bed."

Mia didn't even offer an argument. Thank God it was Friday and she wasn't scheduled to work this weekend. An entire weekend in bed sounded next to heaven. And then she wouldn't be subjected to whatever Gabe had delivered for the day. She could hide from him and the world and try to sort out this whole mess.

She couldn't take it anymore. It was a gigantic weight pressing down on her.

She had every intention of taking a cab home, unable to bear the walk in her current state. But as she checked her watch, she groaned. Getting a cab at this hour would be next to impossible. They were all going off duty.

Sighing in resignation, she began the long walk home, cold settling into her bones. She was shaking, her teeth chattering, and the sidewalk blurred in her vision.

It took her twice as long as it normally did, and when she rounded the block and saw that damn billboard, she sighed in relief because it wasn't far now.

Someone bumped into her and she lost her balance. She nearly caught herself, but then she was bumped from the other side, and she slid to her knees, tears welling. She didn't even have the strength to get up and she was so close to her apartment.

She buried her face in her hands and let the tears escape.

"Mia? What the hell? Are you all right?"

Gabe. God, it was Gabe. His arm came around her, urging her to her feet.

"Good God, baby, what's wrong?" he demanded. "Why are you crying? Did someone hurt you?"

"Sick," she croaked out amid another storm of tears.

Her head hurt, her throat was on fire, and she was so cold and tired that she couldn't bear the thought of walking another step.

Gabe cursed and then he swung her into his arms and strode rapidly toward her apartment building.

"I don't want to hear one goddamn word, you understand? You're sick and you need someone to take care of you. Jesus. What if I hadn't been here? What if you'd collapsed on the damn sidewalk and no one was around to help you?"

She didn't say anything and instead buried her head against his shoulder, inhaling his scent. His warmth seeped into her skin, soothing all her aches. God, it had been so long. She hadn't been warm since he'd left her. Or she'd left him. It didn't matter, because the end result was that she was alone.

He carried her into her apartment and into her bedroom. Then he rummaged through her drawer and pulled out a warm pair of pajamas.

"Here," he said. "Get changed and comfortable. I'm going to go make you some soup and get some medicine down you. You're burning up with fever."

It took all her strength just to manage the task of getting out of her clothes and into the pajamas. Then she sank onto the edge of the bed, spent and wanting only to snuggle underneath the covers.

A moment later, Gabe returned and he promptly did just that. Tucked her in and bunched the covers around her. He kissed her forehead and she closed her eyes, savoring that brief contact. But he didn't remain. He positioned pillows so she could sit up to eat, and then he disappeared again.

When he came back this time, he was carrying a cup of soup and two medicine bottles. He shook out the pills into his palm after setting the soup on the nightstand, and then he opened the bottle of liquid cold medicine and poured the right dosage into the small measuring cup.

After making her swallow down the liquid and the pills, he handed her the cup of soup and guided it into her hands.

"How long have you been sick?" Gabe asked grimly.

For the first time she looked at him. Really focused on him. And she was shocked by what she saw. He looked as bad as she felt. Deep shadows under his eyes. There were new lines across his forehead and at his temples. He looked . . . tired. Exhausted. Emotionally spent.

Had she done this to him?

"Since yesterday," she croaked. "I'm not sure what's wrong. I'm just so tired. This whole week. It's just been too much."

A shadow crossed his face and guilt flared in his eyes.

"Drink your broth. By then the medicine will have taken effect and then you need to rest."

"Don't go," she whispered as he got up from the bed. "Please. Not tonight. Don't go."

He turned, regret deep in his eyes. "I'm not leaving you, Mia. Not this time."

After she finished the soup, Gabe took it from her and went back to the kitchen. She dug deeper into the covers, a shiver overtaking her. Even the soup hadn't been able to warm her.

Her eyelids were heavy, and she struggled to keep them open. A moment later, the bed dipped and to her surprise, Gabe slid into bed next to her, his arms wrapping tightly around her.

"Rest now, Mia," he murmured. "I'll be here if you need anything. I just want you to feel better."

Forgetting everything else but the fact that she was back in his arms, she pushed herself as tightly against him as she could get, and then she relaxed, allowing his heat to seep into her veins.

He was better than any drug, any remedy for her illness.

With a sigh, she closed her eyes and gave in to the sweet temptation he offered.

The next morning when Mia awoke, the bed was empty and she wondered if the night before had been just a crazy dream brought on by her fever. Maybe she'd imagined it all. But when she turned on her side, nestling her cheek against the pillow Gabe had slept on, she saw a note propped on the mattress in front of his pillow.

> *Take your medicine. Jace will be by to check on you later*
> *today. Rest this weekend and feel better.*
>
> *Love, Gabe*

Beside the note were several ibuprofen pills, and on the nightstand, already poured into the dosage cup was the liquid cold-reliever medication.

She sat up, frowning. She hadn't imagined he'd leave. He'd been so . . . persistent.

A shiver overtook her and she reached for the medicine, gulping it down with the water he'd left for her. She leaned back, resting her head on the pillow where Gabe had lain.

She closed her eyes. She could still smell him. Could still feel his warmth surrounding her. God, she missed him.

Was her pride worth them both being miserable? Did he truly love her, and did he want another chance for them?

All the indicators were there, but she was afraid to trust him. Afraid to give him that chance again when he'd hurt her so badly by not fighting for her in the first place.

• • •

Gabe called Jace in the lobby of Jace's building and waited for his friend to respond. A moment later, Jace responded and Gabe didn't give him any time to question anything.

"Jace, it's me, Gabe. I need to talk to you. It's about Mia."

A few moments later, Gabe rode the elevator up to Jace's penthouse apartment. Jace was there to greet him when he got off the elevator, a slight frown marring his face.

"What's up?" Jace asked.

Gabe walked inside, not bothering to take off his coat. He wasn't staying long. There was too much he had to accomplish before the weekend was over.

"Mia is sick," he said bluntly. "I found her on the sidewalk yesterday when she was walking home from work. She was burning up with fever and some asshole had knocked her over. She didn't even have the strength to make it back to her apartment."

"What the fuck? Is she okay?"

Gabe held up his hand. "I stayed with her last night. Got some medicine down her and I left some for her to take when I left this morning. I left her a note telling her you'd be by to check in on her later."

Jace's frown deepened. "You didn't stay with her? Hell, Gabe, you've been relentless in your pursuit and you finally get a chance where she isn't kicking your ass and you left her sick in her apartment?"

Gabe sighed. "I've pushed her too hard. I'm part of the reason she's so rundown and sick. I don't want to beat her down. That's not the way I want her to come to me or for us to be together. I need to back off and give her time to get well. I want you to get your ass over there and take care of her this weekend. I need her well by Monday night, because that's when I'm going to fucking crawl for her."

Jace lifted his eyebrows in surprise. "What?"

Gabe ran a hand through his hair. "I've got a ring to buy this weekend and other arrangements to make. All you have to do is have her at Rockefeller Center Monday night by the Christmas tree. Don't fuck this up, Jace. I don't care if you have to carry her. You make damn sure she's there."

chapter forty-four

Mia spent the weekend with Jace—or rather he spent it with her. Ash was in and out, bringing takeout and generally fussing over her. The two men brought movies, and they crashed on the couch watching TV until Mia would drift off into a fever-induced sleep.

By Monday morning she was feeling better, but not well enough to tackle work, so she called in to let Louisa and Greg know she wouldn't be there.

Jace and Ash headed into the office but told her they'd be back, because they had something special planned for the evening.

Through it all, she hadn't heard a single peep from Gabe. No flowers, no gifts. Just silence. It unnerved her and had her questioning every decision she'd made with regard to him.

She didn't have the heart to tell Jace she didn't feel up to whatever he and Ash had planned. They'd both been so great over the weekend, pampering her endlessly and working so hard to cheer her up.

Whatever they had planned, she'd be prepared and she'd take it with a smile. Jace had told her to dress warmly, so she could only imagine whatever it was they were doing was outside.

Thank goodness she wasn't still running a fever, or the thought of being out in the cold would drive her right over the edge.

She showered in the afternoon and tried her best to do something with her hair and makeup so she didn't look hungover and dragged through the wringer. But even makeup had its limitations . . .

At six, Jace and Ash arrived, their eyes sparkling with mischief. She groaned inwardly because they were obviously up to no good, and since it involved her, she was going to be a victim of whatever they'd hatched between them.

Jace had a driver tonight, which was odd since he tended to tool around town in his car when it was just them. But they bundled her inside after making sure she was dosed in case her fever returned.

"Where are we going?" she asked in exasperation.

"That's for us to know and you to find out," Jace said smugly.

He and Ash both looked like kids at Christmas, and their eyes gleamed with unholy glee.

She relaxed in the seat and told herself she would enjoy whatever it was. Even if her heart still ached with emptiness. Gabe had disappeared after staying at her apartment Friday night. Not one word had she heard from him. Had he given up?

When they pulled up in front of Saks Fifth Avenue just across from Rockefeller Center, she gasped in pleasure at the enormous lighted tree towering above the skating rink. It was so beautiful, and it made her ache with all the memories of Jace taking her here when she was a child. They'd never missed a lighting. Not until this year, in fact.

"Oh Jace," she whispered as he pulled her from the car. "It's as beautiful as ever."

Jace smiled indulgently at her, and then he and Ash fell in beside her as they guided her toward the crowd gathered around the tree.

The tree loomed over them, aglow with thousands and thousands of colored lights. Christmas music filled the air. And then a melodious sound as a man began to sing "The Christmas Song."

"There's a concert?" Mia asked in excitement as she turned to Jace.

He smiled and nodded and then urged her toward the front. Surprisingly, no one protested their cutting in front of others, and in fact, a group made room for them at the very front where the aisle cut up to the stage.

"Oh this is perfect!" Mia exclaimed.

Ash and Jace chuckled and then Mia's attention turned to the singer performing Christmas carols.

Oh but it brought back so many warm memories of her and Jace. She reached over to catch Jace's hand and she squeezed it tightly, her heart overflowing with love for her brother. He'd been her rock for so long, and he still was. She'd have never made it through her breakup with Gabe if it weren't for Jace and Ash both.

"Thank you," she whispered close to his ear. "I love you."

Jace smiled. "Love you too, baby girl. I want this night to be special for you."

There was fleeting sadness in his gaze and before she could ask about his cryptic words, the song ended and the singer began talking to the crowd. It took her a moment before she realized he'd said her name.

She blinked in surprise, and then a spotlight bounced over her and remained solidly in place, illuminating her spot in the crowd. She glanced up to Jace in bewilderment, but he'd stepped back along with Ash, leaving her alone in the spotlight.

"A very merry Christmas and warm holiday wishes going out to Miss Mia Crestwell," the man said. "Gabe Hamilton wants you to know how much he loves you and how much he wants for you to spend this holiday season with him. But don't take my word for it. Here's the man himself to tell you in person."

Her mouth gaped open when Gabe appeared at the end of the carpeted aisle that led up the steps to where the man had been performing. His gaze was fixed solidly on her, and in his hands he carried a brightly wrapped box with a huge bow on top.

The crowd around her cheered as Gabe drew near, and then he went down on one knee, the box still held out in his hand.

"Merry Christmas, Mia," he said in a husky voice. "I'm sorry I was such an idiot. I should have never let you walk away from me. You're right. You deserve someone who will fight for you always and I want to be that man if you'll just give me another chance."

She had no idea what to say, how to respond. Tears welled hot in her eyes and threatened to fall.

"I love you," he said fiercely. "I love you so damn much that I ache when I'm not with you. I don't ever want to be apart from you. I want you in my life always. Do you understand that, baby? I want you to marry me. I want forever with you."

He held out the box to her and she took it with trembling fingers. They bounced erratically over the bow as she tried to pry the top off. Inside was a velvet jeweler's box. She nearly dropped it as she pulled it out.

Around her flashes went off. People with cell phones were recording the moment. There were loud cheers and yells of encouragement. But she shut everything out but the man in front of her. Nothing else mattered.

She opened the box to see a gorgeous diamond ring nestled inside. It glittered in the light and blurred in her teary vision. Then she glanced down at the man on his knees in front of her. He was begging her with his eyes.

Jesus, but he was crawling.

"Oh Gabe."

She went to her knees in front of him so they were on the same level. She threw her arms around his shoulders still holding on to the box with the ring.

"I love you," she breathed. "I love you so much. I don't want to be without you."

He grasped her shoulders and pulled her back, his eyes fierce with love and possessiveness. Then he reached into his coat and pulled out a thick document. Oh God, it was their contract.

And then he slowly and methodically tore it in two, his gaze never leaving hers.

"From now on our relationship has no rules," he said hoarsely. "It will only be what you and I make it. What we want it to be. No constraints. Nothing but our love. The only signature I want from you is on a marriage certificate."

He took the box from her hand and pulled the ring free. Then he picked up her left hand and slid the glittering diamond onto her third finger.

The crowd erupted around them, and then Gabe pulled her into his embrace, his mouth hard and fierce over hers. She clung just as fiercely to him, absorbing this moment, committing it to memory. It was one she'd never forget as long as she lived.

When she and Gabe were old and gray, she'd remember this night and play it over and over. It would be a story to tell their children, their daughters.

And then she realized she had no idea if he even wanted children.

"I want babies," she blurted out.

Then she blushed wildly as she realized how far her voice had carried in the crowd. There was laughter around them and one called out loudly, "Give them to her, man!"

Gabe smiled, his expression so tender that it melted her heart and warmed her so thoroughly that she didn't even register the cold.

"I want babies too," he said huskily. "Daughters as beautiful as you are."

She smiled so wide she thought surely her lips would split.

"I love you, Mia," he said, his voice gruff and uncertain. He looked so vulnerable there on his knees in front of her. "I'm going to love you forever. I hope that's good enough for you. I've done so much wrong since you came into my life, but I swear to you that I'm going to spend the rest of my life making it up to you. No one will ever love you more than I do."

Tears leaked down her cheeks as she stared back at the man who'd humbled himself in front of her and half of New York City.

"I love you too, Gabe. I've always loved you," she returned softly. "I've waited most of my life for you."

He slowly stood and then lowered his hand to help her to her feet. Then he pulled her into his embrace and held on tightly as the music began around them.

"I've waited just as long for you, Mia. Maybe I didn't always know what I was missing, but it was you. Always you."

He turned them so they faced Jace and Ash. She'd forgotten all about them, and then realized that they were in on this too. She realized the *enormity* of them being in on it.

Joy flooded her heart, and she launched herself at Jace, nearly toppling him over as she hugged him.

"Thank you," she whispered in his ear. "Thank you for understanding and for accepting, Jace. You can't know how much this means to me."

He hugged her back, emotion thick in his own voice. "I love you, baby girl, and I just want you to be happy. Gabe has convinced me that he's the man for the job. That's all any big brother can ask for."

She turned and threw herself into Ash's arms and kissed him on the cheek. "I love you too, you big lug. And thank you for helping me through these past weeks."

Ash grinned and kissed her cheek before releasing her back to Gabe. Then he ruffled her hair affectionately. "Anything for you, kiddo. We just want you to be happy. And well, I want to be the baby's godfather."

Jace scowled. "Oh hell no. That's my job. I'm the kid's uncle."

Mia rolled her eyes and squeezed herself into Gabe's side as Ash and Jace started arguing. Gabe chuckled and then tightened his hold around her waist. He smiled down at her, his love shining brighter than the star atop the Rockefeller tree.

"What do you say we go home and practice giving them a baby to fight over?"

Turn the page for a special preview
of the next book in Maya Banks's
Breathless trilogy

fever

Coming in April 2013 from Berkley Books

Please note:
The following is not final and
may differ from the published book.

Bethany Willis rubbed her palms down the worn legs of her pants and briefly closed her eyes, swaying as she stood in front of the basin containing all the empties she'd collected from the ballroom.

She was tired. So damn tired. And hungry. The best part of this gig—besides the fact it was cash paying—was the food. She was allowed to take leftovers, and judging by the amount of food bustling in and out of this place, there was going to be plenty.

Rich people always did things in excess. There was no way the number of people invited to this party justified the amount of food and booze being fronted. She mentally shrugged. At least she'd get a decent meal, even if the stuff was too fancy for her palate.

There'd be enough for Jack too.

A wave of sadness engulfed her, and just as quickly, guilt. She had no business feeling this way because Jack had come back around. He did that. Disappeared for months and then reappeared, usually when he needed a place to crash, a friendly face. Food, money . . . Especially money.

Her chest squeezed because she knew what he did with the money he asked for, even as he hated to ask for it. He never looked her in the eye. Instead he'd drop his gaze and he'd say, "Bethy . . .

there's this thing. I need . . ." And it was all he'd say. She gave him money because she couldn't do anything else. But she hated the way he said *Bethy*. Hated that nickname when it had once been one she adored, because it had been given to her by someone who cared for her.

Jack. The only person in the world who'd ever tried to shield her from anything. The only person who'd ever given a damn about her.

Her brother. Not by blood but in every other way it counted. He was hers just like she was his. How was she supposed to ever turn her back on him?

She couldn't. She wouldn't.

There was a sound at the side door, the one that opened to the alley where the trash was taken out. She glanced up to see Jack leaning against the frame, his head tilted back so he could glance down the alleyway. That was Jack. Always one eye on escape. He never went into any situation unwary and without his escape route planned.

"Bethy," he said in a quiet voice.

She flinched, knowing why he'd come. She didn't say anything and instead reached into her apron pocket for the wadded up bills she'd stuffed there. Half up front. Half when she went off duty for the night. Jack would get this half. The other half would have to feed her until she found another gig, and she never knew when that would be.

Hurrying to where he stood, she pressed the bills into his hand and watched uncomfortably as his gaze skated sideways, not making eye contact with her as he shoved the money into the ripped, torn jeans. His stance was uncomfortable. She knew he hated this. She hated it too.

"Thank you," he whispered. "You okay? You got somewhere to sleep tonight?"

She didn't, but she wasn't going to tell him that. So she lied instead. "Yeah."

Some of his tension eased and he nodded. "Good. I'm working on it, Bethy. I'll have a place for both of us soon."

She shook her head in denial, knowing it was what he always said, and also knowing it wasn't going to happen.

He leaned forward and kissed her forehead. For a long moment, she closed her eyes and imagined different circumstances. But that was pointless. It was what it was and wishing for it to be different was like pissing in the wind.

"I'll be checking on you," he said.

She nodded. And then as he started to melt back into the shadows of the alley, she looked up and said, "Be careful, Jack. Please?"

His smile was just as shadowy as the night. "Always, babe."

She watched him go as the knot in her throat grew bigger. Damn it. Rage built but she knew it was a useless emotion. Her fingers curled and uncurled at her sides and the itch invaded. The need, the craving. She fought it, but it was a hard battle. A victory that wasn't completely solidified. Instead it was an ongoing war of wills. One she fought every single day.

The need for oblivion. Just that short window of time where everything felt better and more manageable. When things looked up, even if for a few short hours.

She couldn't go back to that. She'd fought too hard to make it out and she'd lost everything in the process. Some might say that would be even more reason to allow herself that slow slide back into the inky past. But she had to be strong. She wasn't that person any longer.

"Your boyfriend?"

The dry question startled her and she whirled around, her heart racing as she took in the man standing across the kitchen, staring at her.

He was one of the richies. A guest at the party. More than just a guest, as Bethany had seen him close to the honorees. And God, but the man was gorgeous. Smooth. Polished. Like he'd stepped right out of a magazine solely devoted to everything beautiful and wealthy. A world she damn well didn't belong in.

He shoved his hands into those expensive slacks and continued to stare at her, his pose indolent and arrogant. His green eyes flicked over her as if judging her, almost as if he were considering whether to deem her worthy. Of what? His notice? It was a ridiculous thought.

He had blond hair—although not just plain blond. And she'd never really been attracted to blond men, but his hair wasn't simply blond. It had at least four different shades, ranging from muddy to wheat and all shades in between. He was so gorgeous that it hurt to look at him.

"You going to answer me?" he asked mildly.

Mutely she shook her head, and to her surprise he laughed.

"Is that no you're not going to answer me, or no he's not your boyfriend?"

"He's not my boyfriend," she whispered.

"Thank fuck for that," he muttered.

She blinked in complete surprise and then her eyes narrowed as he advanced toward her. Quickly she moved to the side so she wouldn't be pinned against the door. She couldn't leave, so running wasn't an option. She needed the other half of her pay too badly and she wanted that food.

But just as quickly he closed in on her again, moving into her space until her pulse leapt erratically and she began to eye the alley door, suddenly uncaring whether she'd get paid or not.

"What's your name?"

She glanced up at him. "Um, does it matter?"

He paused a moment, cocked his head to the side and then said, "Yeah. It matters."

"Why?" she whispered.

"Because we're not in the habit of fucking women we don't know the name of," he said bluntly.

Whoa. There was so much wrong with that statement she didn't even know where to begin. She put her hand up in automatic defense before he could get any closer.

"We?" she demanded. "*We*? What are you talking about? Who the hell is *we*? And I'm not fucking anyone. You. We. They. No way."

"Jace wants you."

"Who the fuck is Jace?"

"And I've decided I want you."

She barely suppressed her snarl of rage. Barely. She gritted her teeth and then went on the attack.

"I am not putting up with sexual harassment on the job. I'm filing a complaint and then I'm out of here."

To her further surprise he merely grinned and then reached out to touch her cheek.

"Cool your jets, sweetheart. I'm not harassing. I'm propositioning. Big difference."

"Maybe in your book," she pointed out.

He shrugged like he didn't particularly care if she agreed.

"Who the hell is Jace?" she repeated. "And who are you? You don't proposition a woman without giving your name. And you have problems not knowing a woman's name before going to bed with her? What is wrong with you? You didn't even introduce yourself."

He laughed again and it was a warm hum that felt so good she wanted to hang on to it forever. It was a carefree sound and she bitterly resented it. Was so jealous she wanted to burn with envy. This was a man who had no problems. Had no cares. Except who he wanted to go to bed with next.

"My name is Ash. Jace is my best friend."

Her eyes narrowed. "And you both 'want' me."

He nodded. "Yeah. Not so unusual. We share women. A lot. Threesomes. You ever had one? Because if not, I guarantee we'll make it an experience you won't forget."

Her nostrils flared. "Yeah. I have. Nothing special."

Something flickered in his eyes. She could tell she surprised him, but oh well. He should expect to have it handed back to him when he made outrageous propositions like this.

"Then maybe you're fucking the wrong men."

"Ash."

The sound was explosive in the confined area of the kitchen and Bethany jerked her head up to see another man standing in the doorway, his brooding, dark gaze scorching the flesh right off Ash's bones. Ash didn't seem overly bothered that this guy was obviously pissed.

Bethany was.

This guy was the one she'd caught watching her when she'd ventured out to bus the tables. Twice. She'd felt his gaze on her. Burning a path over her skin until she'd shivered with the intensity. Where Ash was lighter, carefree, that whole package of *wealthy and I know it* and *I don't gotta do nothing except what I wanna*, this man was . . . He was Ash's polar opposite.

Intense wasn't the right word. It didn't even come close to describing him. He looked like a complete badass, and she knew badasses. She had plenty of experience with men on the street and from the streets, and she had the sudden thought that she'd rather take her chances with the devil she knew rather than this man staring holes through her.

Dark hair. Dark eyes. Tanned skin. Not the fake tan some of the metrosexual pretty boys went for. There was a ruggedness to him even as he screamed wealth and polish, like Ash did. It was just a different kind of polish.

Where Ash wore his wealth like a skin, like he'd always known it, this other guy looked like he'd accumulated his wealth later in life and wasn't yet as comfortable with it as Ash was.

It was a ridiculous assessment, but there it was. There was something dangerous about this other man. Something that made her stand up and take notice.

"Jace," Ash returned mildly. "Meet. . ." He lifted an eyebrow in question, still waiting for her to provide her name.

"Bethany," she croaked.

Oh shit. Shit. Shit. Shit.

This was the threesome guy? Ash's best friend? A man involved in the outrageous proposition Ash had just given her?

Jace's lips tightened and he stalked forward. Bethany instinctively backed away.

"You're scaring her," Ash said, a reprimand in his tone.

To Bethany's surprise, Jace pulled up short, but he was still glaring holes in Ash. At least it wasn't her.

"I told you not to do this," Jace said in a quiet, angry voice.

"Yeah, well, I didn't listen."

Bethany was utterly confused. But then Jace turned to her and there was something in his gaze that caught her breath.

Interest.

Not just a look like a man gave a woman when he wanted to fuck her. It was something different and she couldn't put her finger on it. But then he'd watched her all night. She knew that because she'd watched him too.

"I'm sorry," Jace began.

"Does this offer come with dinner?" she blurted.

She was instantly mortified, but she also knew in that one moment when he looked at her, that she didn't want him to walk away. Not tonight. Tonight she wanted one night in the sun. Where it was warm and bad things didn't happen. She wanted one night to forget her life, Jack, and all the problems that came with both.

This man could give her that. She was absolutely positive on that count. And if he came with Ash, she'd just have to take that too.

She did not want to walk out of this kitchen into the cold and back to what awaited her.

"What?"

Jace stared at her like she'd grown two heads. His brows drew together and his gaze became even more piercing, like he was peeling her from the inside out.

She gestured toward Ash. "He said you two wanted a threesome. I'm asking if the offer comes with dinner."

"Well, yeah," Ash said, his tone suggesting he was insulted.

"Okay then," she said, before she could change her mind.

She knew it was stupid. She knew it was one of the most stupid things she'd ever done, but she wasn't going back.

"I have to finish here first," she said, while Jace just stood there, silent and brooding, his gaze never leaving her, not even once. Not to look at Ash. Not to look away. Fixed on her.

"No you don't," Ash said. "You can cut out at any time."

She shook her head. "I get the second half of my pay when I'm done. I have to finish."

"Party's about to break up. Gabe's not going to remain out on a fucking dance floor when what he really wants is Mia at home in his bed," Ash said. "I'll cover your second half."

Bethany went cold and she took a step back, ice forming over her face. Then she shook her head. "I changed my mind."

"What the fuck?" Ash demanded.

And still Jace stood there. Silent and forbidding, watching her the entire time. It was unnerving and suddenly that alley door was looking better all the time.

"I'm not for sale," she said in a low voice. "I get that I asked for dinner. I shouldn't have. You were offering sex. But I won't be paid for sex."

Pain, like a cloak, crept over her. Distant memories, not ebbing. Choices. Consequences. It all drifted together until it was a murky, impenetrable darkness surrounding her. One day. Just one day in the sun. But the sun wasn't for her. It never had been.

A low muttered curse tore from Jace's lips. The first sound he'd made in forever. Then that mouth tightened. He was pissed.

His gaze skated sideways at Ash and it was then she realized he was pissed at Ash. Really pissed.

"I told you not to do this," Jace ground out. "Fuck it, man. You should have listened to me."

This was getting worse. Evidently Ash wanted some action. Jace did not. Ash wanted to approach her. Jace did not. Could this get any more humiliating?

"I've got to get back to work," she said, hastily backing away until her escape route to the door leading back into the ballroom was secure.

And just as quickly, Jace was there, sliding over, a barrier to her and freedom. He was so close she could smell him, could feel his heat wrapping around her, and it felt so damn good that she wanted to do something really stupid and lean into him. Just so she could feel it brush over her skin.

Then his fingers slid underneath her chin, a touch so gentle she couldn't help but respond, lifting her face so that her gaze met his.

"You finish work. We'll wait. Then we have dinner. Anything in particular you like? And do you want to go out or eat in the hotel room?"

The questions were softly worded. They sounded intimate. He never looked at Ash once. His stare was solidly fixed on her and she was too mesmerized to look away. And she promptly forgot that she'd changed her mind about sleeping with them.

Jerking herself from the intensity of the moment, she glanced down, taking in her clothing. There was no going home and changing. No home. No clothes. Certainly nothing she could wear to any place these two would set foot in.

She cleared her throat. "Hotel is fine, and I don't care. If it's hot and tastes good I'll eat it. Nothing too fancy. In fact, what I really want is a burger. And fries."

She'd kill for both right now.

"And orange juice," she finished in a rush.

Amusement glimmered on Ash's lips but Jace was still utterly serious.

"Hamburger. Fries. Orange juice. I think I can handle that," Jace said. Then he checked his watch. "People will be cleared out in fifteen. How much time do you need after that to finish?"

She blinked. "Uh, not everyone will clear out in fifteen minutes. I mean even if the guests of honor leave, people always hang out afterward. Especially when there's food and drink."

He cut her off before she could say more.

"Fifteen minutes, Bethany. They'll be gone."

It was a promise. It wasn't speculation on his part.

"How much time do you need?" he asked impatiently.

"Thirty minutes maybe?" she guessed.

For the second time, he touched her, his fingers gliding over her cheek and up to her temple where he toyed with loose tendrils that had fallen from her clip.

"Then we'll see you in thirty minutes."